THE

BURYING

FIELD

ALSO BY KENNETH ABEL

COLD STEEL RAIN

BAIT

THE BLUE WALL

G. P. PUTNAM'S SONS   NEW YORK

KENNETH ABEL

THE

BURYING

FIELD

G. P. Putnam's Sons
Publishers Since 1838
a member of
Penguin Putnam Inc.
375 Hudson Street
New York, NY 10014

Library of Congress Cataloging-in-Publication Data

Abel, Kenneth.
The burying field / Kenneth Abel.
p. cm.
ISBN 0-399-14796-9
1. New Orleans (La.)—Fiction.   I. Title.
PS3551.B336 B87   2002   2001048848
813'.54—dc21

Printed in the United States of America
1   3   5   7   9   10   8   6   4   2

BOOK DESIGN BY MEIGHAN CAVANAUGH

THE

BURYING

FIELD

ONE

They came up through the trees, left their pickup truck back on the edge of the gravel road. The old man stood on his porch, watched them come, four boys, moving like shadows in the faint moonlight. Two of them were carrying long metal crowbars, the kind the state road crews used for breaking up stone.

"Call the sheriff," he told his wife. "It's them white boys again." Then he let the screen door swing shut, went down the steps and out across the field toward the cluster of old graves at the edge of the woods. The woman came to the door, pressed one hand against the screen.

"Caryl, you let the sheriff handle it," she shouted after him, but the old man ignored her. He walked stiffly, his arms swinging from the elbow, like he did when his back was hurting him. She watched him cross the yard, pausing to hitch up his jeans. Then she turned, went back into the living room, picked up the phone.

"You believe this shit?"

Randy Brewer kicked at some broken pottery that lay scattered among the old graves. "They make all that fuckin' noise about this place, tellin' everybody it's *historic,* just 'cause some slaves got buried here, then they don't even clean it up. Probably come throw their trash here, they're too lazy to ride out to the dump." He swung his crowbar up over his head, brought it down on a flat stone marker that lay embedded in the ground, cracking it. "Wake up, nigger! Time to clean this place up!"

Russ Barnes looked over, laughed. He stood a few feet away, holding a can of beer in one hand, pissing against a tree. "Man, you better watch out. That old nigger's gonna reach up, grab your foot in a second. Pull you in there with him."

"Yeah?" Brewer glanced over at him, grinned. "He tries that shit with me, I'll feed him to my dog." He tossed an empty beer can back among the graves, then put his boot against the top of an old headstone, shoved it over. He was seventeen, a starting quarterback on the Jefferson High School football team the season before, when they went all the way to the state finals up in Shreveport, and there was a lazy grace to his movements. He spent most afternoons down at the gym lifting weights, so now the muscles in his shoulders drew his shirt taut as he unzipped his jeans and pissed all over the overgrown grave.

Bobby Price stood at the edge of the trees, watching him. He was small for his age, and his face was serious. He had both hands shoved deep in the pockets of his jeans, his fingers clenched around the keys to his pickup. "C'mon, man, let's get out of here."

Brewer turned to look at him. "Hey, where's the beer?"

"Back in the truck."

"You *left* it?"

Bobby stared at him. "You're gonna sit here, drink beer in a graveyard?"

"That scare you?" Brewer grinned. "You like to watch those movies, huh? Some dead nigger with a chain saw's gonna get us 'cause I pissed on his grave." He laughed, turned to the fourth boy. "How 'bout you, Jason? You got the spooks, too?"

Jason Lowe swung the crowbar down off his shoulder, shrugged. "Only spooks here is underground." He let the tip of the crowbar fall on the edge of a headstone, flicking sparks into the darkness.

Brewer reached over, took the crowbar from Lowe and hefted it. Then he looked over at Bobby. "I guess that means you're goin' back for the beer."

Bobby glanced over at the other two boys. They were watching him, expressionless. He shook his head wearily, turned back toward the truck. When he'd almost reached the trees, he heard Brewer call out, "And bring the shovel."

FLAT stones, on a piece of rock-strewn corner land that wasn't worth the plowing. Slaves were buried at night so the work could go on. They'd nail two sticks together as a cross, or put up a wooden shingle with the dead man's name painted on it. After two winters, the name would have faded away. They laid the first stones after the war, put names to the overgrown graves as best they could remember. Nothing fancy, just a name carved on a small slab. It was all they could afford in the hard years after Lincoln signed the paper that set them free but left them working for the same masters in a land ravaged by fighting. Still, they saved up a few dollars those first years, enough to get a negro stonecutter over in Mandeville to carve the names on a piece of slag left over from a white man's gravestone. One man, who buried his wife and baby son in the first year of the war, worked twelve Sundays in a row to pay for a headstone with a tiny angel carved at the top. For years he'd come out every other Sunday to clear the weeds from their grave, polish the stone. He scattered bits of broken glass and pottery across the graves. Everybody gives something to the dead. Dreams. Rage. Sins. For a slave, or a man so poor he can't know what *free* means, a piece of broken glass shines with each rising sun. The glitter caught the old man's eye as he worked, like the dead moving quietly in their sleep, reaching out for him. After he died, the weeds grew wild.

Caryl Jackson had lived next to the burying ground all his life. When he was a boy, his father would send him to chase the cows away from the graves. He'd been scared to go into the shadows under those trees, but he'd done it, found it cool there, peaceful. Beyond the trees, the heat lay like melting wax on the empty fields. He'd switch the cows out with a pine branch, then stand there for a few minutes, wondering about the people buried around him. Most of the stones had only one name on them, but that name was scratched deep in the granite, like it was meant to last to the final call. *Jesus know my name, Lord, raise me from the ground . . .*

When he left, the cows turned, walked slowly back into the shade.

Now the full moon hung above the scrub pines like a blister against the dark sky. He could see three white boys moving among the graves, could hear their laughter and the bright crack of metal against stone. Sparks flew where the crowbars struck off the granite, and he saw one of the boys put his foot on a headstone, push it over. Then a branch snapped under Caryl's boot, and one of them looked up at him, coming toward them through the trees. For a moment, he thought he saw fear on the boy's face, then the moon drifted behind a cloud and the boy straightened up, called out, "Who's that?"

"You boys clear on outta here," Caryl called out to them, and he waved his hand toward the road, like you might scatter a pack of dogs. "You got no business here."

One of the boys lifted his crowbar onto his shoulder, like a ballplayer stepping back from plate. He pushed past his buddies, took a step toward Caryl. "What you say, old man?"

Caryl stood his ground, felt his back stiffen up until it felt like somebody'd hung his shoulders up on a metal beam. "Sheriff's comin'. You get on home, now."

"What the fuck you know about our *business,* nigger?"

The shadows lifted slightly as the moon slid out from behind the cloud, and Caryl saw the liquor shine in the boy's eyes. "These folks ain't done nothin' to you. How come you can't let 'em rest easy?"

"You own this land?"

Caryl shook his head. "Ain't nobody owns this land but the dead."

"Bullshit." The boy swung his crowbar down off his shoulder, stuck it in the ground. "You go down to the courthouse, ask them who owns this land. They got a map, shows every piece of land in the parish, and they ain't no nigger graveyard on it." He wedged the tip of the crowbar under a flat gravestone, raised it slightly, his eyes coming up to Caryl's face. "This shit's just some old rocks we got to clean away."

"It don't pay to mess with the dead, son."

The boy laughed. He raised his crowbar, pointed toward Caryl's house. "Get on home, old man."

"Sheriff's on his way."

"Yeah? Then you better go call him, save him a trip. Ain't no law says we can't come out here, clean up all this trash you people threw in the woods." He laughed again. "Hell, we just doin' our part. So you just go on home, old man, let us do what we come for."

Then he turned away, swung the crowbar up over his shoulder, brought it down hard on the flat gravestone. Caryl heard the stone crack, felt the sound like a knife in his eyes, its point stabbing deep into where all the anger lay after fifty years of working for white men, fifty years of taking it in silence, eyes squeezed tight against that anger. When he saw the boy swing that crowbar up over his shoulder again, getting set to take another shot at it, something inside him cracked. He stepped forward, wrapped his arms tightly around the boy's shoulders, just as he was getting ready to swing that crowbar down on the stone. He heard the boy cry out in surprise and rage, felt the crowbar slip from his grasp and hit the ground beside him. The boy tried to wrench his arms free. He was young and strong, spent two hours in the weight room over at the high school every day, but Caryl Jackson had put in fifty years working jobs that would have sent that boy to the hospital after one long day, and the muscles in his arms were like twisted wire. He tightened his grip, said—

"That's enough, now."

The boy struggled. "Get off me, nigger!"

"How 'bout we wait on the sheriff, see what he say." Caryl saw one of the other boys start toward him, tightened his grip until he felt the boy gasp. "Don't make me snap this boy's neck, son."

The other boy stopped, stood there with his fists clenched. "You hurt him, old man, I'll kill you."

"Nobody got to get hurt. We just take it easy."

Then Caryl saw the boy straighten up slightly, his eyes going past him. A twig snapped. Caryl glanced back, saw a white boy standing back among the trees, holding a shovel and a six-pack of beer.

"Jesus," the boy said, staring at Caryl. "Where'd he come from?"

Suddenly, Caryl felt the boy he was holding twist his shoulders violently, get one arm free. Caryl tried to tighten his grip on the boy's neck, but the boy brought his free arm down, drove his elbow into the old man's stomach. Caryl felt the breath go out of him, and the boy slipped free of his hold, then something exploded against the side of his head and he fell to his knees, his eyes going unfocused for a moment. When they cleared, he was looking down at the earth between his spread hands, bits of glass and broken pottery shining in the moonlight, like something important he was supposed to re-member.

He coughed, once. Then he got to his feet slowly. The white boys stood back, let him get up. He didn't say anything, just stood there, swaying slightly, and looked at each of them carefully. Then he turned, started back to his house.

Randy Brewer could feel that he'd pulled a muscle in his shoulder, trying to break free. He could feel the old man's arms gripping him, and the way he'd looked at them, like something nasty you find in your yard on Sunday morning, toss into the road. He watched the old man turn away, felt the anger rise within him. He bent, picked up a chunk of granite that he'd bro-ken off one of the gravestones. There was a tiny angel carved on it, wings spread like it was rising up to heaven. He hefted it once, then drew back, hearing Bobby Price yell out, *"No!"* behind him just as he threw it, hit the old man on the back of the head.

The old man stumbled, as if somebody had shoved him, then went down hard against a tree trunk. Randy heard a sickening sound, like a piece of fruit breaking open in a paper bag, as his head struck the tree.

The old man lay still.

LATER, the old woman told the sheriff's deputy how the 911 operator kept her on hold for almost six minutes, told him how the telephone cord only stretched partway across the kitchen, even when she lifted the phone off the table and set it down on the floor, so that what she saw was her husband walking stiffly away across the field, goin' out there to tell them boys to leave off their mischief and let them dead folk sleep. Then he walked out of her view, and what she saw was the pale full moon, hanging above the scrub pines like somebody tossed a coin against that dark sky. A moment later, she saw one of the boys walk back up to the truck parked on the road, open the door, and lift something off the floor of the cab. "Beer," she told the deputy, her voice shaking, now. "I could see them cans, shining. Then he went around back of the truck, reached over the tailgate, and grabbed him a shovel." She looked back at her empty house, the squad car's lights flaring across the dark windows. One hand rose to touch the base of her throat, trembled there. "They were gonna dig up them graves, maybe drink them a beer when they got thirsty. Like nobody cared 'bout them graves. Caryl, he went out there to tell 'em to get on home, this ain't their place. And look what they done to him."

The white deputy had to look away when she began to cry, one hand fluttering in front of her face, as if she were trying to wave it all away. He glanced back toward the cluster of graves, where an ambulance stood, its rear door open, emergency light leaving red scars on the moonlight. The headlights from three squad cars were shining among the graves, and several more were parked up along the road, where the sheriff was crouching on the gravel shoulder, examining the tire tracks they'd found where the pickup truck had roared away, spraying rocks across the grass.

"You get a good look at any of those boys?"

The old woman took a deep breath and wiped her eyes with the back of one trembling hand. "They stayed out in them trees. Caryl, he saw 'em."

The deputy watched the paramedics lift a gurney into the back of the ambulance, then close the doors. They'd been working on the old man for almost half an hour, not wanting to move him until they got him stabilized. He was alive, and his vital signs were strong, but there was evidence of a severe head injury, and his eyes were fixed and dilated. *Skull fracture,* the deputy figured. *Subdural hematoma. He's bleeding into his brain.* One of the paramedics got behind the wheel of the ambulance, started it up, and the deputy watched it move away slowly over the uneven ground toward the road. *Whatever that old man saw, he ain't gonna be tellin' us real soon.*

He looked back at the old woman, saw her turn and go back into the house. She came out a moment later with her purse.

"I got to get to the hospital." She stepped down off the porch, walked over to his squad car, got into the passenger seat. Just sat there, staring forward, as he went around to the driver's side, got behind the wheel.

Just like she's getting a ride over to the store, the deputy thought as he dug his keys out of his pocket, started up the car.

Like this happens every day.

TWO

Danny Chaisson stood at the window of his law office on the third floor of a run-down building on St. Charles, watching the streetcar make the slow turn off Canal. He could hear his secretary, Demitra, shuffling papers at her desk behind him, like she wanted him to think she wasn't watching him. He kept his eyes on the street, a crowd of tourists waiting on the corner to cross, go get their oyster po'boys at the Pearl Oyster Bar just down the block. After a moment, he heard Demitra sigh.

"You ain't got to give him an answer now," she said. "He just wonderin' is all."

Danny kept his eyes on the window. "You tell him I'll think about it."

Demitra shuffled her papers some more. Danny wondered what she could have on her desk that needed so much attention. It wasn't like they'd been busy lately, a couple insurance cases some guys he knew at the big firms had thrown his way and a half-dozen collection letters for a furniture-rental place on the West Bank, whose clients—mostly oil-rig workers—had a tendency to stop paying their bills in the weeks following April 15. It was barely enough to pay the rent and Demitra's salary, but Danny figured things would pick up in the fall. Just about everything slowed down in New Orleans during the summer, except homicides, and he was determined to stay away from criminal law. He'd spent enough time around cops.

After a few moments, Demitra said, quietly, "I just figured you'd be gettin' something *bigger* now, what with the baby comin' and all."

Danny turned, went back to his desk, and sat down. There were two collection letters in his in box, waiting for his signature. He left them there. "Just because we're having a baby doesn't mean I'm gonna sell my Mustang."

Demitra glanced up at him, raised her eyebrows. "What, you gonna put a baby seat in the back of that thing? What year is that car? Sixty-eight? You gonna take your little girl to school in a car that's older than her *mama?*"

"We don't know it's a girl."

Demitra shrugged. "Maybe *you* don't know. Anybody take one look at Mickie, they see she's carryin' a girl."

Danny leaned on his desk, rubbed at his face with both hands. "Don't you have some work to do?"

"You go get some clients, maybe I'd *have* some work to do."

Danny smiled. He'd hired Demitra Williams six months ago, had her desk moved into his tiny office so they could share a single phone line. The office was cramped, and most nights he went home with the back of his neck burning from her comments, but there was no question in his mind that her desk was an improvement on the battered Mosler safe that once occupied that corner, in which he'd usually kept between $150,000 and $200,000 in small bills during the three years he'd worked as a bagman for Jimmy Boudrieux, the powerful speaker of the Louisiana State House of Representatives, the man who'd put Danny through Tulane Law School, gotten him his first job in the New Orleans district attorney's office, hired him when he quit that job in disgust, and—as Danny had learned—the man who'd ordered his father's murder. Add it all up, Danny figured, and Demitra cost him a good bit less than that safe, even if she spent more time on *his* case than any of their clients'.

But that was before her little brother, Shawan, started calling up, wanting to know when he was going to sell his Mustang. Danny had been married for almost a year, just long enough to begin to feel comfortable with thinking of Mickie Vega—this woman who strapped on a .380 Pony semiautomatic pistol each morning for her job as a special agent with the New Orleans district office of the Bureau of Alcohol, Tobacco and Firearms—as his *wife*. But while he'd given up his tiny apartment on Lowerline in the Garden District, moving into her condo in a singles complex up by the Lakefront until they could find a house they both wanted to buy, he wasn't sure the deal included getting rid of his Mustang. Mickie had kept her job over at ATF, and he knew better than to suggest she should give it up. She spent her days setting up illegal gun buys, tracking the guns used in street crime back to their original sale from a legitimate gun shop over in Chalmette or Gulfport, then identifying the dealer who'd put it on the street and crashing through his door with the "dynamic entry team" to make the arrest. She lived for that rush, working the streets, and she spent several hours a week over at the bureau's gun range, keeping her eye sharp. When she'd found out she was pregnant, she'd reluctantly gone to her boss and requested a transfer to a desk job for the remainder of her pregnancy, but she made it clear to Danny that she planned to get right back out on the street as soon as she returned from maternity leave. So Danny figured if she could strap on a Kevlar vest and a gun before going to work every day, hell, he could keep driving his Mustang. The way his car ran lately, he figured it was pretty much an even trade.

Okay, so he'd caught himself glancing over at Toyota 4Runners on the street the last few days, peering into the backseat, where the baby seat would go. But all he could think as he looked them over was *Thirty-six thousand, huh?* He could remember when that kind of money could buy you a *house*.

Anyway, he figured it was just a stage, like the period a few months back when he and Mickie would go for a walk in Audubon Park every Sunday, always ending up—without really meaning to—at the toddlers' playground. They'd sit on a bench, watching the kids in stunned silence, like a skier pausing at the top of a black run to have one last look at the view. His friends who had kids told him it was no worse than falling down three flights of stairs. Mickie kept saying it couldn't be worse than dealing with two-strike felons.

But the idea of selling the Mustang, that stung. It was a '67 soft-top, pale blue, which Danny had bought five years ago at an auction at the city seizures garage. He'd watched two doctors from over at Charity Hospital bid the car up over $12,500, even though it needed some serious work, before he put in the high bid. Afterward, he'd walked over to the cashier's window, passed her a note that the garage manager had scribbled for him, and paid her the $7,900 they'd agreed upon the day before, in cash, small bills. There were moments when working for Jimmy Boudrieux had its advantages. Danny figured he'd put the same amount into repairs over the last few years, just trying to keep it on the road. But even *that* made it feel like you'd have to cut it away from him with a bone saw. If there was one thing he'd learned about himself in the last couple years, since the job with Jimmy Boudrieux came to its bloody end, it was that he didn't always run when he should, either.

So when Demitra's baby brother, who played tight end for Grambling, called about the car, he felt himself dig in his heels. "How come you so concerned for *my* baby," he asked Demitra, "you don't care 'bout your brother driving that car?"

She looked up at him, raised an eyebrow. "My brother just wants that car to get up on those girls they got at college. I figure, sooner he does that, sooner he'll get married, stop wantin' to come 'round my house for dinner every night. You know how much that boy eat?"

Danny had to smile. "He looks like he can put it away."

"Last Friday, I made a roast chicken, little new potatoes, baked an apple pie 'cause it's me and Ray's anniversary next week, I want him to know how much I *do* for him?" Demitra pursed her lips, shook her head slowly. "Ray, he went upstairs to change out of his work clothes, he came back down, Shawan's sittin' at the table, he's got half that pie on a plate in front of him. Boy needs him a *wife*, some girl can keep him *fed*."

"Last time I saw him, didn't look like he'd have trouble gettin' girls. Had three of 'em in the car with him."

"You mean them girls keep askin' him when he's gonna turn pro, buy 'em a Miata? He marry one a' them, I'm gonna have to put the *hurt* on his ass." She glanced at the photograph of Mickie on Danny's desk. "We got to get him a nice girl, like you got."

Danny smiled. "With combat training."

"Wouldn't hurt none. She keep him in line." Demitra went back to moving the papers around on her desk. "You mad I told him you might be sellin' that car?"

"What makes you think I'm angry?"

She looked up at him. "You always get that look around your eyes, like your skin's on too tight."

"Don't worry about it. It's no big deal."

"You don't like bein' told what to do, huh?" She sat back, smiled. "And here you gettin' ready to be a daddy, couple months. Have to answer to that little girl about *everything*."

"I thought that's why I had you."

She shook her head. "I'm nice to you. That girl you got comin', she be the *boss*. And you *know* she turn out just like her mama, so you better watch out."

Danny watched her go back to her papers. He wondered if he should feel worried. *Jesus, another Mickie?* The first one had changed his life beyond recognition. What more could the second one do?

Something told him it was a question better left unanswered. If he was going to fall down three flights of stairs, he wanted it to come as a surprise.

He reached over, lifted the collection letters out of his in box. It was depressing work, but it almost paid the bills, and God, at least it was better than taking criminal cases. Kids with guns and rage but no education, crack whores sweating out their painful withdrawal in an interview room, not even caring about the criminal charges against them but offering to get down under the table and blow him if he'd just sneak them in a piece of the rock, young black men so angry and scared that they slumped in their chairs, not answering him, just staring off at the walls as if they'd always known this was coming, so why bother fighting it? You want to practice criminal law in New Orleans, those were your choices. That or sit in your office and chew on your nails. Danny had done that for a while, too.

But as he read over the collection letters, all he could think about was the guy over in Westwego who'd come back from three weeks working on an oil rig out in the Gulf to find a letter waiting for him that said he still owed $1,200 on the bedroom suite and entertainment center that he'd bought, six months same as cash, last year, before his wife emptied their bank account and moved out to Taos with some guy who made pottery. They'd call Danny when they got the letters, angry, ready to come down to his office *right now* and show him exactly where to file his client's "demand for payment." But before long they got to talking, and the whole story would pour out. And there was always a story: lost jobs, lost wives, children who stole from them, houses that burst into flames two days after the insurance lapsed, and them stuck out there on that goddamned rig, pumping some other man's money out of the sea. Danny let them talk, and when they were done, he'd offer to talk it over with his client, see if they could come to some arrangement, but it would really help if they could make some good-faith gesture, like resuming the payments? About half the time, that was all it took. They just wanted somebody to listen. Danny would send a memo to the client, telling him that payments would resume in thirty days, then slide the file in a drawer, move on to the next letter. If the payments stopped later, as they often did, he'd simply refer the matter to a collections agency up in Metairie, which would arrange for three Italian guys and an off-duty cop to go out to the guy's house and repossess the furniture. He did his best not to think about that part.

Them or you, he thought, signing the letters. When he was finished, he tossed them into his out box, where Demitra would dig them out in time to catch the mail at the end of the day. He always felt a little ridiculous using the boxes. Demitra's desk was five feet away; when he'd first hired her, he would get up from his desk, walk over, and hand the work to her. But after a week of that, she'd stopped at an office-supply store on her way into work, bought two small trays labeled *In* and *Out,* and put them on a corner of Danny's desk before he got to the office. When he came in, she was on the phone; he didn't notice the trays at first, just hung his leather jacket over the back of his chair and sat down. Then he sat looking at his desk for a moment, trying to figure out what had changed. When he noticed the two trays, he glanced up at Demitra, surprised. She was looking out the window, the phone tucked against her shoulder, but Danny had the feeling that she'd been watching him. He reached over, picked up one of the trays. There was a price tag still stuck to the bottom: $2.99. He used his thumbnail to peel it off, flicked it into the garbage can next to his desk. Then he slid the tray back onto the corner of his desk, picked up some papers he'd been working on, and dropped them in the tray. When Demitra hung up the phone, he was already deep into his work, and neither of them said a word about it. But Danny always felt that the appearance of those two trays marked the moment that he'd been turned back into a lawyer, condemned to spend his days signing collection letters. It felt strangely like being married.

Now Demitra glanced up at the door. "You expectin' somebody?"

Danny listened, heard footsteps coming up the stairs across the corridor. It was a woman's footsteps, her high heels clicking on the marble stairs. The sound made Danny think of women in hats, walking their children to church on Sunday mornings. Mickie rarely wore high heels, and when she did, she'd grasp his arm to steady herself. But she had two pairs of steel-toed combat boots in their closet, and a pair of red high-top sneakers that she liked to wear on weekends. At night, her shoulder holster hung from a hook just above them.

Danny heard the footsteps reach the top of the stairs and pause for a moment, as people always did, catching their breath. The building had no elevator, and he'd grown used to hearing people stop there, then head for the water fountain across from the men's room. He'd hear the pipes shudder as the cold water ran, then most of the footsteps would move on down the corridor to Larry Byers's insurance office, or the real estate appraiser at the end of the hall. There were two other law offices on the floor, but they didn't get much traffic, either. Sometimes Danny sat in his office, listening to the footsteps move away down the corridor, and he'd picture the other two lawyers sitting behind their desks, raising their heads slightly to listen to the steps, then silently going back to their papers as they went on past.

But these steps didn't go past. They paused for a moment at the head of the stairs, then came straight across the corridor toward Danny's office. He had enough time to see Demitra glance over at him and raise her eyebrows before the door opened. And then he saw her, feeling the way he always felt at that moment, like he'd finished swimming a great distance underwater and had just broken the surface, so that he needed a second to catch his breath before he could bring himself to look up at her, smile, and say—

"Helen."

He could hear the tightness in his own voice, saw Demitra look over at him sharply, the way you'd see a car skidding toward you on a rain-slick road, the driver fighting the wheel. But he saw all of this out of the corner of his eye; his eyes were fixed on Helen Whelan, watching her close the office door behind her and take a moment to glance around at the pair of battered metal desks, the row of beat-up filing cabinets, the air conditioner dripping slowly into a bucket under the window, before she turned to smile at him, gently, and said—

"How are you, Danny?"

She had on one of those pale silk suits that she wore to the office in the summers, her blond hair pulled back into a thick braid. She carried her briefcase, which probably meant that she'd spent the morning over at the courthouse. She was a partner at Morgan, Field, and Stratton, a prestigious firm specializing in commercial litigation, with offices on three floors of One Shell Square. She'd been Jimmy Boudrieux's personal attorney for a while, and since his death, Danny had heard that she only accepted clients whose hands were cleaner than a virgin's confession. *Makes 'em sleep with a sword between them,* he'd heard the other attorneys joke. She worked ninety hours a week, kept three secretaries busy, and wore out litigation associates as fast as the law schools could churn them out.

Strange as it now seemed, she had once been Danny's wife. It always seemed puzzling to Danny how somebody he'd known so well—whose body he'd explored in such loving detail, whose dreams and fears he'd known as well as his own—could now seem like a stranger to him. But whenever he spoke to Helen in the last few years, he came away feeling that she had retreated into an ice cave in some distant arctic of her own heart's making, where the sun was a pale gleam that gave no warmth and everything she touched was silent and pure. And even worse, he knew that she blamed him for it all.

Not that she'd ever say it.

She didn't have to. Danny secretly agreed with her. He'd let it happen, too busy chasing his own sense of personal justice to pay any mind to who got caught in the cross fire. When it was over, he'd married Mickie Vega. Helen came to their wedding, kept her smile throughout the reception, and left with her pride intact. The next morning, Danny learned later, she submitted her resignation at Morgan, Field, and Stratton, told them she was moving out to San Francisco to start her life over. It took four partners to talk her out of it. In the end, she took a six-week leave of absence, which she spent traveling in western Ireland, walking that haunted coastline, letting the wind blow her hair into knots that wouldn't comb out. She rented a house near Doolin, planted a garden, took a lover. But when the six weeks were over, she went home to New Orleans, bought a small house in the Garden District, and got back to work. When he heard the story later, Danny'd felt ashamed of his happiness. Mickie only shrugged, said, "Sounds great. When do I get to go?"

Danny had to smile at the memory. *Marry Danny Chaisson and see the world. It's not just a job, it's an adventure.*

But now Helen had extended her hand, as if she'd just walked into a conference room over in the Central Business District and was getting ready to sit down with opposing counsel to negotiate a settlement. Danny got up, took her hand, then held on to it as he walked around his desk, leaned in to kiss her on the cheek. He caught a brief glimpse of Demitra settling back in her chair, arms folded across her chest, enjoying the show. Then Helen squeezed his shoulder, once, to let him know that was enough, and he stepped back, watched her turn to Demitra, hold out her hand.

"I'm Helen Whelan. You must be Danny's new assistant."

Demitra stood up, introduced herself, and Danny could see by the way she looked Helen over as they shook hands that she was drawing her own conclusions. He felt a sudden impulse to flee, maybe head out to Phoenix for a few days, stay with Mickie's family until the whole thing blew over. But Demitra would still be here when he got back, ready to tell him *exactly* what she thought.

Danny dragged a chair over to his desk, feeling a stab of embarrassment as Helen glanced over at the collection letters in the box on his desk. For a brief moment, he wanted to sweep his arm across the desk, clear it all away. But what was the point? They'd each done what was necessary to put the past behind them, washed the blood from their hands, and there was nothing they could do to change things now. So he sat down, gave her his most charming smile, and said, "What brings you down here, Helen?"

"I might have some business to pass on to you."

Danny raised his eyebrows. "Your firm has, what? Eighty-five lawyers?" He smiled. "And it's not like we're handling similar clients. So why would you need to pass work on to me?"

Helen hesitated, then leaned forward, rested one hand gently on his desk, as if she wanted to steady it. "Danny, I've got a client with a problem, and it's not something my firm is equipped to handle. He's a property developer, and we do his real estate closings, his submissions to state regulatory boards, any litigation that arises, even his taxes. But this is more . . . a *political* problem." She paused, saw Danny wince slightly at the word, but plunged on. "Jim Reynolds, my managing partner, handles most of this client's personal business. He came to me and asked me if I knew anybody who had the kind of contacts that could help resolve this problem."

"And you thought of me."

She sat back, and Danny watched her hand rise from the desk and settle in her lap. Her hands were long and thin, and now she folded them neatly together, so that Danny thought of a bird returning to its nest. "Does that bother you?"

"I guess that depends on what kind of contacts you mean."

She considered him for a moment, then glanced over at Demitra. When her eyes returned to Danny, they were guarded, as if she'd decided that she needed to step carefully here. "Maybe I could have you talk to my client."

"Can I bill him for a consultation?"

That made her smile, and Danny saw that it got as far as her eyes. "That only seems fair." She glanced at Danny's desk. "Are you busy now?"

"Nothing I can't drop."

"Feel like taking a walk?"

Danny got up, slid his worn leather jacket off the back of his chair, then hesitated. "How hot is it out there?"

"You don't need the jacket, if that's what you mean." Helen smiled. "Is that really the same one?"

"Can't beat a classic." Danny draped the jacket back over the chair, waited as she got up. "And I still eat breakfast standing up, if you're curious."

She looked at him. "I'm not surprised." She turned to Demitra, extended her hand. "It was good to meet you. I'm glad somebody's keeping him out of trouble now."

"Can't nobody do that." Demitra looked over at Danny. "Except his wife. She got his number."

Danny got the door open, shot Demitra an evil look as Helen squeezed past him out into the hall. But Demitra just raised her eyebrows, then turned back to her papers. Danny swung the door shut, turned to find Helen watching him, smiling.

"You two have lots of fun, right?"

"Try to imagine working with your mother."

"Please. There isn't enough Prozac in the whole state to make that happen."

Danny followed her down the stairs and out onto St. Charles, where the air felt as thick and heavy as wet cotton, wrapping itself around them. They walked up St. Charles to Poydras, then turned south toward the river. When they got to One Shell Square, Danny followed Helen into the lobby, and they stood in silence amid the crowd of office workers waiting for the elevators after lunch. It felt strange to be standing there next to her, the silence easy between them, almost as if the past they shared could be swept aside, like so much dust on a photograph that showed them both smiling. They'd been friends as children. In this shared silence, it was still possible to imagine that they could find that friendship growing between them again.

They rode the elevator up to the twelfth floor. When they stepped off, Danny saw a receptionist sitting behind a desk that looked like it had been cut from a single slab of Italian marble. "Jesus," he whispered to Helen. "What's the matter? They couldn't find any virgins to sacrifice?"

She shot him a look, then walked over to the desk, said, "Could you let Mr. Tournier know that Helen Whelan is here? I've got Danny Chaisson with me."

The receptionist nodded, picked up the phone. She spoke quietly into the phone for a moment, then hung up. "Mr. Tournier will be free in a moment." She gestured toward a pair of leather couches beside the windows. "Would you like to sit down, and I'll let you know when he's free?"

"Thank you." Helen led Danny over to the couches, and they sat facing each other. Danny felt a formality return between them. They were both silent, as if they couldn't think of anything safe to talk about.

"So your client's Michael Tournier?"

"You know him?"

Danny shook his head. "Met him a couple times at parties back when I was working for Jimmy, but he's just a face." He hesitated, then said, "Must be a big client."

"We do a lot of work for him, yes. He's got some important projects coming up."

"I meant that he keeps you waiting like this. Can't be cheap, the way you bill."

Helen gave a slight frown, as if the whole idea of somebody paying for her services was new to her. "He keeps us on retainer. We don't bill him for client conferences."

Danny grinned. "I give a discount if I have to break any legs."

She studied him, her face serious. "Same old Danny, I see."

"I'd hate to disappoint you."

Danny felt her eyes move past him. He turned, saw a door open next to the reception desk, and Michael Tournier came out. Danny hadn't seen him in person for years, but he was the kind of man whose picture appeared in the newspapers every few weeks, flashing his expensive smile. He was a real estate developer, who'd returned home to New Orleans in his early thirties from a successful career in Chicago when his father suddenly died. Within two years, he'd transformed his family's firm from a company that specialized in light industrial projects on the West Bank to one of the city's most progressive design teams, breaking ground on two mixed commercial and residential projects that the newspapers claimed would change the face of contemporary architecture in New Orleans. He hired architects with international reputations, then gave them the freedom to put their ideas into practice. The editors of two national architectural magazines had already flown in to inspect one project, built using the shells of three coffee warehouses along Magazine Street, and the second—a hotel, restaurant, and gallery complex going up on South Front Street—promised to extend the success of the city's redeveloped riverfront beyond the tourist zones of the French Quarter and Riverwalk. He had recently bought a beautiful old mansion along upper St. Charles, and the renovations had been featured in the *Times-Picayune*'s Sunday magazine. The social columnists had named him one of the city's most eligible bachelors, so his purchase of the house had put them into a flurry of speculation, with one columnist dropping open hints that *several* daughters of the city's most prominent families had told *only* their most trusted friends that a late-spring wedding wasn't out of the question. Even Danny couldn't help smiling when he read that one; he knew some of those girls and could imagine the scenes of rage and despair in the Garden District when they learned they weren't the only ones making such plans. Sherman's march to the sea could hardly have caused more destruction.

Now Danny saw Helen rise as Tournier came over. He could see why the wealthy daughters of the Garden District were so excited. Michael Tournier was a handsome man: his face looked like something a sculptor might have carved from marble, and his hair had that slightly tousled look that women seemed to find attractive, like they were seeing the little boy inside the man. His smile suggested grace, wealth, and confidence, and he flashed it at

Danny as he approached, extending his hand a few steps before he reached them, as if greeting an old friend. "Danny! Helen said she was going to get you down here, but I didn't believe her. You're like St. Francis in the desert lately. So we had to send a vision to tempt you down here." He grasped Danny's hand in both of his, then rewarded Helen with his smile, leaning in to give her a quick kiss on the cheek. Danny saw her stiffen slightly, then Tournier took a step back, waved a hand toward the door next to the receptionist's desk. "Come on back to my cave. I just got an espresso machine installed this morning, and I'm dying to try it out."

They followed him back through a cluster of cubicles, people bent over design boards like they were putting their whole weight into it, fighting to hold the lid on a bubbling pot. Framed architectural drawings hung on every wall. Danny wondered briefly if Tournier saw them as drawings, or as buildings spread out over a piece of ground, sunlight glinting on the glass.

Beyond the cubicles, there was an open conference area with a large table made from a single sheet of hammered copper. A bracket of red lights had been mounted on nearby walls, making the table look like it was on fire. In the center of the table, a cardboard model of an office building seemed to float on a sea of flames. Tournier paused, gestured to the model.

"You like the effect?" He flashed Danny a broad smile. "We're building this project for a law firm over in Houston, so we thought we'd make it look like Satan's beach house. Make 'em feel right at home."

"Careful," Helen warned him. "We're legion."

Tournier gave a laugh, waved them on toward a glass-enclosed office beyond the conference table. "You ever see *Blade Runner?*" he asked Danny. "Guy who runs the evil corporation has an office on top of this huge pyramid, it's got like three pieces of furniture, including a mechanical owl flying around." He opened the door, stepped back to let them pass. "That's what I want someday. Meanwhile, I work in this fish tank."

Danny glanced around the office, trying to imagine what it would feel like to come to work in a place like this every day. Two of the walls were made completely of glass. One window faced the conference area, the light reflected off the copper table making the office look like it had been splashed with red and gold. Tournier's desk was made of steel bent into a cube, and it stood in front of a row of floor-to-ceiling windows that looked out across the Central Business District toward the French Quarter.

Danny walked over, ran his hand across the desk. It felt like a block of dry ice. "You get a deal on all the sheet metal?"

Tournier laughed. "Yeah, I know. But everybody who comes in here, they remember the desk." He pressed a button, which lowered a set of blinds on the window facing out into the conference room. "You're a real estate developer, people expect you to have all the latest toys. We have to redo the whole office every year, keep up with all the trends." He came over to the desk, stood looking down at it with his hands in his pockets. For a moment, Danny felt like they were admiring a sports car. "I have to admit, though, I'll be sorry to give it up. When I was a kid, my dad took me over to a factory on the West Bank where they make the decking for offshore oil rigs. They had all this hammered sheet metal lying around, and I remember thinking how great it looked under all the fluorescent lights." He grinned. "Not that you could say that to any of the guys who worked there. It was just scrap to them. These days, they had that stuff lying around, they'd have to beat off the interior designers with a stick."

Danny smiled. "Probably enjoy it."

"Yeah, I guess they might." Tournier turned, pointed to a pair of leather sofas in the corner. "Why don't you grab a seat over there, and I'll make us some espresso."

"I'll pass," Helen said. "I just had coffee."

"Really?" Tournier looked crushed. He turned to Danny. "You'll have some, right?"

Danny smiled, shook his head. "I'd better pass, too. I drink espresso, I start talking like Marcello Mastroianni. It's pretty scary."

Tournier threw up his hands. "Okay, I tried." He moved over to one of the couches, settled into the thick leather cushions like a man who'd been stacking bricks all day.

Danny sat on the couch across from him, watched Helen join Tournier. Facing them, he suddenly felt as if he were interviewing for a job. *Take it easy,* he thought. *You aren't asking these people for anything.* He sat back, folded his arms, waited to see how they'd play it.

"I've told Danny that you had a problem that required some delicacy," Helen told Tournier. "But I thought you might want to fill him in on the details."

Tournier nodded, looked over at Danny. "You know what I do, Danny?"

"You're a property developer. Mostly commercial projects, some mixed residential." Danny shrugged. "That's what it says in the newspapers, anyway."

"That's true. But you know what that really means?"

"Lots of approvals by state agencies, probably. Which means you spread money around up at the statehouse."

Tournier smiled. "We like to fertilize the soil, it's true. But that's not really the hardest part of my job." He leaned forward. "You want to know what I spend most of my day doing? I call it community building. We got people can put up a building any place you want. That's easy. But before you can even make a hole in the ground, you got to get the people right there in the community to *see* this new building, and not just how it's going to look, but how it'll add to their lives." He sat back, spread his hands. "That's my job, Danny. I got architects to do the drawings, construction people to hammer in the nails, but none of that's worth a piss in the pond if I can't get the community behind the project."

Danny couldn't think of anything to say to that, so he just nodded, waited for Tournier to go on.

Tournier glanced over at Helen. "I don't guess Helen told you this, but we've set up a scholarship program for African-American children who can't afford to go to college. Wasn't in the papers or anything. It's just something we felt we had to do."

Danny raised his eyebrows. "To get the hole dug?"

"In a sense." Tournier smiled. "Although you could say it's to get us *out* of a hole this state's been digging for years." Then he got up, went over to his desk, picked up a rolled construction plan, and brought it back to the couch. "Actually, the reason I told you that is so you'll understand why we're in a sensitive position right now." He spread the plan out on the coffee table between them. "Helen tells me you've spent some time up in St. Tammany Parish."

"When I was a kid. My mother grew up there, and we'd go up there in the summers. Her uncle left her some property but she sold it a couple years before she died."

"But you know the area?"

"I can find my way around."

"We've got a piece of land up there, back off State Highway 21, about a mile from I-12, we're looking at developing it for high-end retail with some residential back end." He turned the drawing so Danny could see it, looked up at him. "You know what that means?"

"You're gonna build a mall, then put some houses around it."

Tournier smiled. "Yeah, that's basically it." He sat back, rubbed at his neck as if he spent too much time bending over building plans. "Used to be you couldn't mix commercial and residential properties. Nobody wanted to live around a mall. They wanted to live on a golf course, look out across the greens. They wanted to go shopping, they'd get in the car, *drive* to the mall. That's why shopping malls looked like airplane factories. Big square buildings surrounded by parking lots. Now we've got a different concept. We look at a commercial development as *part* of the community that surrounds it, even a new main street that can shape a community that doesn't even exist yet." He waved a hand at the building plan. "So we take that old airplane factory and we break it into ten pieces, run streets through it, put in parks, fountains, maybe a gazebo. We put a strict code on the exterior facades so all the buildings match, and the whole thing ends up looking like a Victorian village. Parking mostly underground, lots of sidewalks and trees where the people are. Before you know it, people *want* to live near the mall. Turns out they'll pay extra for the privilege."

Danny studied the drawing. "You know, I've never met a real estate developer who didn't sound like he was selling a piece of the true cross." He sat back, met Tournier's gaze. "You all talk like you've seen God in a gutter pipe."

Tournier grinned. "Nobody preaches like the devil, right?" He put his feet up on the table, spread his hands. "Anyway, it's a significant project. Could bring a lot of new jobs into the community, expand the tax base, put some new money into the local schools. But we've run into a little problem."

"Locals don't want it?"

"Oh, they want it all right. At least, most of 'em do. We've got the mayor and the city council on board, shouldn't be any problem with the zoning board." Tournier glanced over at Helen. "My attorney tells me, legally, we could start construction next week."

Danny smiled. "I figured it wasn't my legal expertise you wanted, with Helen around."

"No, that's true." Tournier spread his hands. "I got the best lawyer in the state. If this were the kind of problem I could hand over to Helen, I wouldn't be worried right now."

"You keep telling me what kind of problem you *don't* have." Danny looked from Tournier to Helen. "That's usually a real bad sign."

"That's 'cause this is the kind of problem that makes everybody nervous." Tournier leaned forward, and his voice became almost a whisper. "See, Danny, what we've got here is what my daddy's generation, back in the old days, would have called a *racial* problem. We can't call it that now, but that's what it is."

Danny was silent for a moment, studying his face. "You'd better explain."

Tournier hesitated. "As you probably know, Danny, we do all kinds of land surveys before we move on one of these projects. Title, environmental, geological, the whole deal. Ninety percent of the time, we know everything there is to know about a piece of land before we show our hand in the market. No surprises, that's how it's supposed to work." He looked up at Danny. "Fact is, we screwed up on this one. We missed something. And it was easy to miss, because it wasn't *there*. Not on the Parish maps, not in any of the legal papers, not in the field surveys. Nowhere. So we bought the land, got all the regulatory approvals, lined up the financing. Like I said, we're ready to break ground." He pointed to a spot near the corner of the drawing. "And now we learn we can't build because there's an old slave cemetery right where our anchor store should go."

Danny looked at the drawing, then up at Tournier. Then he stood up. "Forget it. You've got other projects, right? So don't build there."

"Sit down, Danny," Helen said quietly. "That's not why you're here."

Danny raised his eyebrows. "What else is there to talk about? He tries to build this project, he's gonna have protesters out front on the sidewalk. And you know what? They'll be *right*." He shook his head. "You want that kind of publicity, go buy a tobacco company. At least you'd still have some customers. You build a mall on top of a slave cemetery, who's gonna shop there? Stephen King?"

"The project's dead, Danny," Helen told him. "Michael made that decision already."

Danny looked at her. "So why are we talking about it?"

"Sit down, Danny." Helen waited until he'd settled back into his chair, then said, "We only learned about the cemetery because some people in the local black community sent a letter to Michael, protesting the project. He passed the letter on to my office, and we did some initial research that suggested there was some substance to these claims. Based on that, we recommended Michael put the project on hold until we could look into their claims in greater detail. After talking to his investors, that's exactly what he did. We put a notice in the local papers, and our plan was to schedule a public meeting next month to explain how we reached our decision." She opened her briefcase, slid out a newspaper clipping, handed it across the table to Danny. "Three days ago, some of the local white boys decided to have some fun. They went out there, started trying to dig up the graves. When the man who lives up the road tried to stop them, they cracked his skull with a chunk of cement. He's in the ICU unit up at St. Tammany General, still hasn't regained consciousness."

Danny looked at the newspaper clipping: *Man Attacked at Historic Cemetery.* He sat down. "Any arrests?"

"Not yet. Nobody got a good look at the boys except Caryl Jackson, the man they attacked. So the sheriff's hoping to get a statement from him when he regains consciousness." Helen paused. "But it's been three days, and they think there's been some swelling in the brain. It's not clear that he'll ever wake up."

Danny took a moment to read through the newspaper clipping. It didn't add anything to Helen's account. "And nobody put those boys up to it?"

Tournier shook his head. "We don't do business that way, Danny. As Helen told you, we'd already shut the project down."

"But you're worried about liability."

Helen closed her briefcase, set it on the floor beside her. "It's a hate crime, Danny. Michael made the right call, but he could still get strung up in the papers. But that's not even what scares me. If Caryl Jackson's family decides they can't get justice through the sheriff's office, they're going to start thinking about suing somebody."

"And you're the deep pockets."

She nodded. "Juries like to show they're good people. They get a hate crime and a big company in the same case, we could be looking at a ten-million-dollar judgment." She hesitated, glanced at Tournier, then said, "We've heard that Lee Fuller came down from Shreveport last night, talked to the family of the injured man."

Danny raised his eyebrows. "The anti-Klan guy? I thought he was only doing tobacco cases now."

Helen smiled. "He's still got some civil rights cases pending in federal court. He uses them in his fund-raising appeals, and they're useful when he gets in front of a jury, but most of his practice is class-action commercial liability, now. That's where the big money is."

Danny looked at Tournier, gave a thin smile. "Okay, so I see why you're worried. If a guy like Lee Fuller can convince a jury that your company encouraged those boys to do their little midnight run, they could seize all your assets."

"Let's call that a worst-case scenario." Tournier stood up, went over to the window. "My father built this company, Danny. When he had his first heart attack, I was up in Chicago, working in an architectural consulting firm up there. All I wanted when I was a kid was to get out of New Orleans, see someplace else. But I guess what I was really trying to do was get away from my father, show everybody I could make it on my own." He turned, looked back at Danny. "You know how that is, Danny? You run away from your father's life, and then before you know it, you're living it?"

Danny smiled. "Yeah, I know how that is."

"Well, then you can appreciate that the only way I could run this company is to make it into something my father might not recognize." He waved a hand at the cubicles beyond the glass wall. "I came down here from Chicago, this was a company that ran on contacts. My father knew all the old guys up in Baton Rouge. Hell, it turned out he had most of 'em on the payroll." He smiled. "I guess that's how he knew you, huh? When you carried money for Jimmy Boudrieux, kept everybody up at the statehouse fat and happy?"

Danny didn't answer, so Tournier came back, sat down on the couch facing him, leaning forward like he had something he really wanted Danny to understand. "See, that's the way my father built this company. And political contacts are still important, don't get me wrong. We have to get regulatory approvals, like everybody else. But I'm not going to conduct my business under the table. That's not how I feel comfortable working. When I build a project, I want to make something all kinds of people can feel proud to have in their community. We've worked hard to make people realize we're in it with them for the long haul. We don't just come in, shove something down their throats, and leave. That means we have to build *trust*. People have to know we'll do what we promise." He sat back, and his face suddenly looked exhausted. "That's why we can't afford to let some stupid white boys drag us into a hate crime. We've got great lawyers, so I'm not worried about paying judgments. I'm worried about being *judged*. Not in the courtroom, but in people's hearts."

Danny saw that Helen was listening to Tournier intently. Her expression was serious, but Danny recognized the look in her eyes. She wanted to believe this man, wanted to hear him say the right thing so badly it looked like a hunger. For a moment, Danny was surprised. Then he looked at Tournier, and it struck him that if he were a woman, he'd probably want to believe this man, too.

"So what is it you want me to do?" Danny spread his hands. "You've got great lawyers, and I don't do this kind of work, anyway. You don't want me doing your legal work, but you want *something* badly enough to send Helen over to my office to get me." He smiled. "I'm guessing it's something serious, or you might have spared Helen that unpleasantness."

Tournier looked over at Helen. "Was it that bad?"

"I found my high school yearbook last week. It's not as bad as that."

Tournier rewarded her with a smile, then turned back to Danny. "But you're right. I wouldn't have asked Helen to bring you here if it wasn't important." He paused, looked down at the construction plans on the table. "What we need is somebody who's not connected to the company to go up there and make sure this doesn't get any bigger. If it turns out these boys are just a bunch of stupid kids, had too much beer on a Saturday night, that's fine. We'll stand back, let the sheriff take care of it. But if somebody wants to drag us into it, we've got to know before it breaks."

"Why not hire an investigator? Helen's firm must have somebody they can recommend."

Tournier spread his hands. "Danny, look at my position. If I show my concern, it could give people ideas. My company gets anywhere *near* this, we're asking for trouble." He smiled. "Like you said, first thing any smart lawyer's going to ask is where the big money is here."

"Did I say that?"

"Close enough." Tournier reached out, laid a hand on Danny's knee. "What we need is somebody with a reason to go up there, talk to these people."

Danny glanced over at Helen, then back at Tournier. "What's my reason?"

Tournier sat back and stretched his arms across the back of the sofa, like he'd been waiting for Danny to ask that question and could relax now. "You're a lawyer. Got a small practice, but anybody can see you're struggling. You read about this in the paper, saw a chance to rustle up some business."

Danny stared at him. "You want me to go up there and pretend I'm an ambulance chaser?" He shook his head. "If I go talk to these people about their legal standing and I don't tell them that you've already retained me, that's against the Bar Association's code of conduct. I could get disbarred."

"We're not hiring you as a lawyer, Danny." Tournier gestured toward Helen. "I've already got lawyers. You've still got contacts up in Baton Rouge that could be valuable to me in this thing. So I'm hiring you as a *political consultant*." He grinned. "That's what you called yourself when we first met a couple years ago. What I hear, it wasn't any more true than calling yourself a lawyer now."

"We're not asking you to lie to anyone," Helen said quickly. "We just need somebody to go up there and keep an eye on things. Let us know what's happening."

"And you really think nobody's gonna connect me back to you?"

She smiled. "You've got a reputation, Danny. You were an FBI informant. It's not like you've got a big career ahead of you in corporate law."

Danny looked at her, saw something else hidden behind her smile. *Anger, maybe?* She had never forgiven him for the way their marriage had ended, the way he simply seemed to give up hope when he left his job at the New Orleans district attorney's office and went to work for Jimmy Boudrieux. And after Jimmy's death, when she learned that Danny had spent the last three years gathering information on his activities for the FBI, her anger at him seemed to grow even more intense. *How come you didn't tell me?* her eyes had demanded when she saw him at Jimmy's funeral. But she moved past him without a word, as if it was too late for explanations now. And Danny knew she was right. In his anger, he had let her fade from his life, and that was something she couldn't forgive.

"How do I get paid?" he asked Tournier, seeing them both relax slightly at the question. "If I'm not your lawyer, I can't exactly send you a bill for my time."

Tournier waved the question away, like it was too small to think about. "Just figure out what your time is worth and let me know. I'll take your word for it."

Danny stood up. "I'll take a ride up there, see what I can find out. Beyond that, I'm not making any promises."

"That's great, Danny." Tournier stood, extended his hand. "We want you to feel comfortable. That's crucial."

Danny shook hands with him, then waited while Helen collected her papers, closed her briefcase, got up. They followed Tournier out to the reception area, where he kissed Helen on the cheek and shook Danny's hand again. When the elevator door closed, Danny glanced over at Helen, who was gazing at the numbers as they lit up above the door, a weary expression in her eyes.

Like you let her down, Danny thought. *She was hoping you'd say no.*

He watched her for a moment, but she kept her eyes on the numbers until they reached the bottom.

THREE

Caryl Jackson lay in a bed on the intensive-care ward of St. Tammany General, intravenous tubes draped across both arms like bright snakes coiling against his skin. His family sat in chairs they'd pulled up close to the bed, as if warming themselves at a fire. But this was a fire that gave no light. Danny could see that from the boy's face, stiff with an anger he thought was manhood. The boy was maybe sixteen, with a square, handsome face and gentle eyes that he kept trying to hide away behind his anger. He would look over at the TV mounted up near the ceiling every few minutes, where a college basketball game flickered silently—LSU vs. Auburn, it looked like to

Danny—and for a moment, he'd forget to hold that angry look, and his eyes would go empty, so you could see how tired he really was. They had been taking turns sitting up with the old man at night, the nurses told Danny, but during the day they all came and just sat there, waiting for him to wake up. None of them must have had more than four hours' sleep since they'd brought him in three nights ago, and it was starting to show in their faces. The old man on the hospital bed looked good by comparison.

"This what you brought me up here to look at?" Jabril Saunders turned away from the window. "You want to see people watch somebody die, you don't have to drive all the way up here. Walk over to Charity, you can see this all you want. Only most of the time it's the boy on the bed, somebody shot him up."

Danny was silent, watching the boy as his eyes came back from the TV to the old man in the bed and got hard again, like he'd traded them in for a pair of hollow-point bullets. "You see the look in his eyes? They could be back for that tomorrow."

Jabril shook his head sadly. "Don't say it, man. Wears me out."

When Jabril Saunders was sixteen, growing up in the St. Thomas housing project in New Orleans, he'd started a gang called the Gangster Messengers, which sold coke from a street-corner bus stop to white kids driving in from Metairie and Slidell. By the time Jabril was twenty, they were running two storefront day cares, a clinic, and a newspaper called *The Ghetto Blaster*. After a police shoot-out, he'd beaten a murder rap, raising his fist in the courtroom when the verdict was announced, while a crowd of his supporters shouted *"Fight the Power! Fight the Power!"* Now he called himself a *Community Activist*. He mediated disputes between the young boys with semiautomatic handguns who'd taken his place on the street corners, collected "donations" from neighborhood merchants, and ran a youth center in a basement of one of the buildings in the project, where boys could shoot pool, work out on a speed bag, and watch old Bruce Lee videos under posters that said *Violence kills the soul!* and *He's your brother!*

Danny had met Jabril while working for Jimmy Boudrieux, carrying envelopes stuffed full of cash that were slipped to him in restaurants and clubs across the city back to Jimmy's elegant house in the Garden District. He had walked away from a shooting that left five people dead on the floor of a Vietnamese restaurant in a strip mall on Claiborne Avenue, and when the gun turned up in the hands of one of Jabril's boys, it looked like just one more incident in a long summer of blood that swept over the city every year. When it was over, Jimmy Boudrieux was dead, and Jabril Saunders had come to look at Danny with a cautious measure of respect. In the years since, they'd slowly become friends, and even Mickie had finally gotten used to spending Friday nights at Tug's Bar on Magazine Street, where Jabril kept a table for himself with a bottle of dark rum, a bucket of ice, and a kitchen knife with a two-inch blade stuck in the wood. They would sit at the table, listening to a blues band raising the dead in the front room, while Jabril dropped a couple ice cubes into their glasses, filled them with rum, then jerked the knife out of the tabletop and sliced into a lime. It was a long way from her grandmother's tiny house in a poor Chicano neighborhood in Phoenix, even further from the Federal Law Enforcement Training Center in Glynco, Georgia, where she'd trained to be an ATF special agent, but to Mickie, it was starting to feel strangely like home. She had begun to learn that life with Danny Chaisson meant taking things as they came. It was the way he'd been taught to live, growing up in New Orleans, and after three years in the city, she could begin to understand it. So she spent her Friday nights drinking dark rum and listening to blues with Jabril Saunders, trying not to think about how badly the NOPD wanted to punch his ticket. That was how it was in New Orleans; you didn't let the day get mixed up with the night. Cops sat on their front steps as the sun sank beyond the levee, drinking beer with guys from the neighborhood who had standing warrants, and if the lieutenant ordered them to ride over here and pick the guy up the next day, that was just the job. No big deal. After a couple glasses of Bacardi, Mickie had found, it all started to make sense.

But now even Danny caught himself wondering exactly what had made him call Jabril and ask him to ride up to St. Tammany General Hospital with him to visit a man who lay unconscious in the ICU. Neither of them had ever met Caryl Jackson, or any member of his family, but having Jabril along somehow made it feel more personal, not a job, but a gesture of sympathy. *Or else you just wanted a black guy along,* Danny thought, *so they'll talk to you.*

From the look on Jabril's face, Danny suspected that his friend was having similar thoughts, but if so, he kept them to himself.

"You gonna go talk to these people, or what?"

Danny nodded silently. It had seemed like a simple enough job when he agreed to it, just come up here to St. Tammany, ask some questions, make sure that Tournier wasn't about to get drawn into something nasty. But looking at Caryl Jackson's family through the glass window, Danny had the feeling that he was seeing something that ran deeper than lawsuit. These people were *hurting,* and Danny found it hard to imagine that suing Michael Tournier was anywhere in their minds.

Not yet, anyway, he thought. *Takes a lawyer to come in here, make 'em feel like he can make the pain go away by making somebody pay.* Danny could recognize the impulse, even respect it. Hell, if Lee Fuller could focus the anger in that boy's eyes, get him thinking about something beyond getting his hands on a gun, maybe it wasn't such a bad idea.

Danny pushed the ward door open, went in. He heard Jabril catch the door as it swung shut behind him, following him. There were three patients on the ward, but the old man's family were the only visitors. They looked up at him as he came toward them, with that empty stare that you see in hospitals, like somebody had drained most of the blood from their bodies and they figured he was coming back for the rest. He could feel their eyes move past him to Jabril, a man they felt they knew, even if they'd never met him before. But Jabril hung back slightly, watching, as if curious to see what Danny had in mind.

Danny hesitated, then went over to where they sat around the bed, watching him as he approached. He slid between the young man and the window, crouched down next to an old woman he figured was Caryl Jackson's wife.

"Mrs. Jackson? My name is Danny Chaisson. I'm sorry about what happened to your husband."

She studied his face for a moment, silently. Then she gave a slight nod, like she'd made up her mind, and her eyes wandered away. "You a lawyer, then?"

Danny smiled. "That obvious, huh?"

"You ain't no doctor." She shook her head, tiredly. "Come in here smilin' at me, you either a lawyer or you sell *in*surance. And I guess it's too late for that."

Danny shot a quick glance over at the other members of her family watching him. He let the smile fade from his face. He touched the woman gently on the arm. "I'm not selling anything, but looking at your husband, I'd say it's not too late. He looks like a strong man."

"Strong enough for this life, uh-huh. We just got to hope he's strong enough for the next one, too."

Danny patted her arm. "You'll have lots of years to build him up for that. Wait and see."

She looked down at Danny's hand on her arm, then raised her eyes to his face. "I guess you just tryin' to make an old woman feel better. But I know what I see." Her eyes moved back to Caryl Jackson stretched out on the bed. "Those white boys killed him. Just takin' him a while to realize it, is all."

Danny looked over at the man on the bed, wondered what she saw that made her so certain. He wore blue flannel pajamas, and the hospital sheets were pulled tight across his chest, like somebody was afraid he'd slip away. Except for that, he could have been sleeping. But then something made Danny look more closely at his face. His eyes didn't move.

Danny was a man who had spent many hours lying in bed, watching women sleep. He knew the faint whisper of their breath, the way they'd murmur and smile slightly in their dreams, and the slight flicker behind their eyelids that told you they were still there beside you, even as their dreams carried them far away. It was that mystery that had somehow preserved him during the long nights when his marriage to Helen was dying. Lately, he'd sometimes feel the same thing watching Mickie. She slept deeply, curled up on her left side like a small child, and even on the hottest nights, she'd pull the sheet up over one ear, tuck it under her chin. He'd asked her about it once, and she told him, "My father was a cop." When he stared at her, she smiled, explained, "See, he used to pull night shifts a couple times a month, and my mom always had trouble sleeping when he wasn't home, worrying about him. I'd hear her moving around in the kitchen, and then I'd start worrying, too. So I started pulling the sheets up over my ear, pretending I was a little bear in a cave." She shrugged. "Gets to be a habit, you know? And it got me through college, so it must work."

Lying awake beside her, Danny envied her ability to slip into that cave, where a child could sleep safely, even now. But he also knew that in a few months, when the baby was born, all that would be lost. He could picture them lying awake, side by side, listening to the baby's quiet breathing and wondering how they could ever sleep without worrying.

So during these last few weeks, he took pleasure in watching Mickie dream, following the delicate movements of her eyes the way a prisoner might watch a sunset. It felt like something too precious to be wasted.

But the old man's eyes were dead. Danny could see that now. His body was an empty shell, kept alive only by a faint candle flame of breath whispering in his throat. Nothing could survive such dreamless sleep, Danny realized—not memory, not love . . . not hope. His family sat around his bed, waiting for what they knew must come. The old woman talked about her husband as if he were already dead, but in a voice that was strangely calm, as if she'd seen too much to be afraid of death.

Danny cleared his throat, said, "Mrs. Jackson, I know this is a very difficult time for you, but . . ." He paused, feeling a hand grip his arm, hard. He glanced up, saw the teenage boy standing over him.

"She don't want to talk now," the boy said, his voice barely a whisper. "Leave her alone."

Danny glanced over at Jabril, saw him raise his eyebrows. *Uh-huh?* He straightened up, looked into the boy's eyes. They looked as if somebody had snapped a match across them, held it there as the flame caught.

Danny raised both hands, palms out. "Okay. I didn't mean to make you angry." But as he said it, he saw the old woman reach out, catch her grandson's arm with one strong hand.

"DeWayne, how 'bout you go down to the cafeteria, get me some of that coffee?"

The boy glanced over at her, and something inside him seemed to ease up. "You sure?"

"Yeah, I'm fallin' asleep here." She released his arm, reached up to brush

KENNETH ABEL

something off his sleeve. "They got some of them bread rolls, I wouldn't argue with that none, either."

DeWayne shot Danny a look, like *I'm comin' back, hear?* Then he turned, walked out of the room.

The old woman sighed, shook her head. "You got to 'scuse DeWayne," she said to Danny. "He got the fire in his head, ever since those white boys messed up on his granddaddy. We got to keep him close so he won't take out after 'em." She reached out, slid DeWayne's chair over close to her. "You gonna stay, you might as well sit down." She glanced over at Jabril. "Your friend there look like he could spit with the devil. He married?"

Danny looked over at Jabril, saw him grin. "Not exactly."

She raised her eyebrows. "Like to spread it around, huh? He got a name?"

"Jabril Saunders."

"Like the angel, gonna blow his horn." She raised one hand, waved it toward Jabril. "Shanaya, you see Mr. Saunders there?"

The young woman beside her looked up at Jabril shyly. "Uh-huh."

"Well, take a good look, 'cause *that's* a man. Not like that *boy* you run with. You find you one like that, okay?"

Danny saw Shanaya stiffen. "Hush, Grandmama."

"Hush, what? Everybody knows you lookin'."

"I'm not looking for *nothin'*."

"Well, you *should* be." The old woman sighed, shook her head. "Why don't you go see how DeWayne's doin', let this man have your chair for a while." Shanaya got up, went out into the hall quickly. The old woman raised one hand, waved Jabril over. "C'mon over here, Mr. Saunders. Sit down."

Jabril came over, slid past her to where Shanaya had been sitting. The old woman watched as he settled into the chair, then reached over, picked up his hand with both of her own, like she was weighing it. "Jabril, huh? You come to raise the dead?"

Jabril looked over at Caryl Jackson on the bed. "That ain't really my field."

"Nah, I didn't think so. You ain't got that look." She smiled, squeezed his hand gently, set it back on the arm of the chair. "So how come you here with the lawyer? You work for him?"

Jabril gave a laugh. "No, ma'am. I don't work for no lawyers."

"But I'll bet you keep some busy, huh?"

"I do my best to avoid that." Jabril looked at Danny. "He asked me to come up here with him, as a friend."

"So you his friend?"

"Uh-huh." Jabril grinned. "That hard to believe?"

She shrugged. "Maybe it's different down in the city." She let her eyes wander back to Danny's face. "You figure I'd talk to you, you brought a black man along?"

Danny hesitated, then shook his head. "I came here to listen. I figured with Jabril here, everything would stay clear."

Etta Jackson considered that, then looked over at Jabril. "What's that mean?"

Jabril glanced at Danny and smiled. "What it means is, with me here, he can't lie to you. Seems I'm his chastity belt."

Etta raised her eyebrows, then sighed, shook her head. "Can't say I understand lawyers. Fella was in here yesterday, sayin' we should sue somebody. Way he talked, it was like there was all this money just lyin' there, waitin' for us to pick it up. But I got to figure that money belongs to somebody, and they ain't gonna be happy, we start sayin' it's ours." She turned to Danny. "You want to help us sue somebody, too? That why you came up here?"

"No, ma'am." Danny glanced over at Caryl Jackson. "If your husband has long-term medical expenses, you've got a right to seek damages from the people who caused his injuries, but . . ."

"You think those *white* boys gonna pay for his hospital?" Etta Jackson shook her head. "Not in this town. Never happen."

Danny leaned forward. "So you know who the boys were?"

She shrugged. "Yeah, I know. Told the sheriff they been out there causin' trouble before. Same boys, same truck. That's why Caryl went out there to chase 'em off. Didn't think they'd take after him with no rock, though. I guess it's like dogs. Just 'cause they never did before don't mean they don't grow up and get mean."

"What did the sheriff say?" Danny asked.

"What's he gonna say? He can't go arrest them boys. Everybody know who done it, but the sheriff, he says they don't have enough *evidence*." She looked at her husband on the hospital bed. "I told him come on up here and look at Caryl's *head*. That ought to be enough evidence, right there."

Danny took out a small pad, scribbled a few quick notes. "So you gave the sheriff the boys' names?"

"Uh-huh. Then we drove up to the high school, and DeWayne, he pointed 'em out, just so he could be sure."

"Did the sheriff question them?"

She shrugged. "You have to ask him that. Said he was gonna, but he ain't talked to me since then. Got more important stuff to do, I guess."

Danny jotted a few more notes, then looked up at her. "Can you give me the names?"

"Yeah, I could give you the names." She looked at him. "But you still ain't told me how come you want 'em."

Danny laid his pad down on the arm of his chair, clipped the pen to one edge. Then he met her gaze. "Mrs. Jackson, I wish I could tell you that I came up here to help you out of the goodness of my heart, but that wouldn't be true. I've got clients who want to protect their interests. As it happens, their interests lie in identifying the boys who injured your husband." He spread his hands. "I can't promise you a big settlement, like some of the lawyers you might hear from, but I'm guessing that isn't really what you're thinking about at this moment. That could change, and if it does, there'll be plenty of attorneys who'll be happy to look after you."

Jabril gave a smile. "Long as they get their cut."

"That's how it works," Danny said. "They want to get paid like anybody else." He turned back to Etta Jackson. "But you might have to make a decision between money and justice. In a way, you're lucky. Most people don't get a choice. If you want the money, then you shouldn't talk to me. Get a lawyer who'll go after the people who can pay. Chances are it'll take a few years, but you might get a decent out-of-court settlement. If you want justice, that means going after the boys. I might be able to help you with that." He rested one hand on the arm of her chair. "But I've got to be honest with you, if you go after the boys, it might make it harder for you to get a lawyer interested in pursuing a settlement later on. You could convince a criminal court that those boys hurt your husband, or you could make an argument in a civil court that you deserve a settlement from the people who own the land, but you're unlikely to convince them both. Either it's a crime, which means we hold individuals responsible, or it's civil negligence, where you can sue a company for damages. You go after the boys, or you go for the money. That's your choice. Any good lawyer will tell you that."

She studied him for a moment, then nodded. "So I guess you here for the people who own the land, huh?"

"They were hoping you wouldn't figure that out." Danny smiled. "But I'm not gonna be the one to try and put something past you, Mrs. Jackson."

She gave a sigh. "I don't care about no money. Caryl, he had insurance from the union. He was a pipe fitter over at Avondale, thirty-five years."

"Sounds like he was a good man."

"He was a lotta things, and that was one of 'em." She glanced down at Danny's pad, resting on the arm of his chair. "So you want them names, or what?"

"You get what you came for?"

"Pretty much." Danny unlocked the Mustang, leaned across the front seat to unlock Jabril's door, then waited while he got in. "I got what I needed, anyway."

"Somebody paid you to come all the way up here to get those boys' names?"

"No, somebody paid me to make sure this matter stays in criminal court." Danny reached down to start the car. "It's just money. You're the guy with the deep pockets, you got to watch out for your investment." He put the car in gear, pulled out of the visitor parking lot, paused at the edge of the road to wait for the traffic to clear. "You know what killed me about this place when I was a kid?" He nodded to a building a few hundred feet up the road.

"They got an old-folks' home over there, one side of the hospital, and on the other side, there's a funeral home. It's like the whole place was designed by Henry Ford. Keep 'em moving on through."

Jabril smiled. "So we done here? You go home, give the names to your guy?"

Danny caught a break and pulled out, heading into town. "Just one more stop."

"Where at?"

"I thought we'd go have a talk with the sheriff."

ST. Tammany Parish sheriff James Frand knew trouble when he saw it. Like the time during his first election campaign, when his manager came up with the bright idea of printing up fifteen hundred yard signs with his picture and the slogan "I'll be *your* Frand."

"You're kidding, right?" he said when they showed him the signs. "People gonna think I can't *spell*."

Still, he had to admit that it worked. Six weeks before election day, his numbers started to rise, and they didn't stop climbing until the polls closed. But even as he watched the numbers rise, Jim Frand couldn't escape the feeling that he'd live to regret that slogan. And, sure enough, the very first week in office, he'd arrived at the scene of an FBI operation to shut down a meth lab operating out of a farm up near Folsom, local TV news vans crowded onto the shoulder of the gravel road, taping as the U.S. Attorney had the suspects led out to the waiting cars, and one of the handcuffed men, looked just like he played for the Doobie Brothers, came to a sudden stop a few feet from where he stood and yelled out, loud enough for the U.S. Attorney and all the reporters' microphones to catch it, "Hey, Jim, I thought you was gonna be my *friend*!"

Embarrassing, sure, but as it turned out, the U.S. Attorney had no sense of humor. So even though Frand had been in office only ten days, he had to spend the next nine months sweating out a federal investigation to determine if his office had colluded with drug traffickers to protect their operations. Go explain that one to the voters. If you get a bad feeling about something, it's probably gonna come back to haunt you, that's what Jim Frand had learned in six years on the job. And that's how he felt now, looking across his desk at this lawyer up from the city—wanting to hand him a sheet of papers with the names of the four boys who'd messed up old Caryl Jackson's head—an evil-looking black man slumped in the chair next to him, looking around like he was sizing up the place for the best place to start the fire. So Jim Frand did what he always did when he got that feeling: he leaned back in his chair, put his cowboy boots up on the desk, and smiled broadly.

"So, you workin' for Caryl Jackson's family?" he asked Danny. "That why you're here?"

"No, but they'll probably get a lawyer in the next few days." Danny looked at the sheet of paper he'd torn out of the notebook lying on the sheriff's desk. Frand had glanced at it when Danny handed it to him, then laid it on the desk, gently, as if it might jump up and bite him. "Michael Tournier asked me to come up here, look into this thing. He's concerned that his company not get implicated in a hate crime just because they're the property developer."

The sheriff shifted his weight, then nodded thoughtfully. "I guess that's something he'd be worried about."

Danny glanced over at Jabril, who was looking out the window at the square in front of the courthouse, where a black trustee from the parish jail on the upper floors was packing soil around some new bushes with a shovel. But Danny could tell that Jabril was listening; his jaw tightened slightly every time the sheriff gave them one of his friendly smiles. Danny looked back over at the sheriff, saw that he'd picked up a pencil and slipped it into the top of one cowboy boot, was using it to scratch at his ankle.

"Have you questioned the boys Mrs. Jackson identified?"

The sheriff gave that some careful thought. When he was finished scratching, he slid the pencil out of his boot and laid it on his desk next to the phone. "Yeah, I sure have. Called up Sam Price, he's a lawyer here in town, asked him to bring his boy down here to talk this thing over." He picked up the slip of paper, glanced at it. "The other three boys, Randy Brewer, Jason Lowe, and Russell Barnes, they all play varsity ball up at the high school, so I drove over there, talked to all three of 'em after practice." He laid the paper down, looked at Danny. "They ain't bad boys. Little wild, maybe. Got into some trouble out there once before, shooting at beer cans, which is how come Mrs. Jackson thinks it was probably them. But you ask her, all she saw was four white boys in a pickup truck. They never got close enough to the house so she could see their faces. Couldn't even tell us what *color* the truck was, 'cause they left it out by the road. When I talked to the boys, they said they were over at a party in Slidell most of the night. We're working on tracking down some of the other kids who were there, see if we can figure out what time they left. Meanwhile, I got Sam Price all up on my case, wants to know where my *evidence* is."

"You got any?"

"Physical evidence, you mean?" The sheriff shook his head. "We lifted some tire tracks out on the road, tried to match 'em to Randy Brewer's pickup truck, but we came up negative. Not that it means much. His daddy runs a body shop out on the highway, so wouldn't be hard to switch the tires with one of the other trucks in the lot."

"So did you check the other trucks?"

"Couple. Some of 'em are back on the road, so we're trying to track 'em down. They do detailing and new-car prep for two of the local dealerships also, so we want to be sure, we got to look at the trucks on their lots, too." He slid his boots off the desk, brushed a hand across the leg of his uniform trousers like he was wiping away crumbs. "Big old job, I can tell you."

"Etta Jackson said they saw the boys tossing beer cans around before Caryl went out there to chase 'em off. You lift any prints?"

The sheriff looked up at him, raised his eyebrows. "You been out there, Mr. Chaisson? Had a look at this *graveyard*?"

Danny shook his head. "Not yet. I'm planning to drive out there next."

"They tell me there's people buried out there, mostly slaves who used to work the old Granville plantation back up in there, but it ain't on any of our maps. That's how come your boy Tournier bought the land. Nobody over at the courthouse knew anything about it until the local black folks started raisin' a fuss. Hell, people been dumping their garbage out there for the last thirty years. Whole place is covered with old beer cans, broken glass. We bagged up some cans, looked like they weren't too old. But even if we get a clean print off one, how are we gonna prove it was from that night?" The sheriff shook his head. "Fact is, we ain't got enough to prosecute anyone on this thing. Only person really knows who did it is Caryl Jackson, and they tell me out at the hospital he ain't gonna be sayin' anytime soon."

Danny was silent for a moment. "So there's been some legal dispute about this piece of land?"

The sheriff shrugged. "You want to call it that. Hasn't gone to court or anything. Just some people in the local black community . . ." He glanced over at Jabril, smiled. "Sorry, I guess that's supposed to be *African-American* community now. Can't keep my terms straight." His eyes came back to meet Danny's. "Like I was saying, just some local people wanted to stop this development your boss was planning to put in there. They held some meetings, got everybody all fired up, said they were going to request that the state designate it a *site of special historical interest,* which I'm told means nobody can build on it. Some of the people in the local business community weren't too happy about that. Couple people bought land all around that project, and the way they see it, they didn't invest in no slave cemetery."

"Any chance these boys were responding to that?"

"People been talkin' about it, and two of those boys got daddies who are upset 'bout the whole thing, so I guess it's possible they decided to take matters into their own hands." He shifted in his seat uncomfortably. "But we're talkin' about teenage boys here. Stuff like this, it usually turns out to be about a couple six-packs and a bad idea. Boys that age, they don't always *know* why they do stuff. My experience, they drink a few beers, wake up the next morning with me knocking on the door, wantin' to know what made 'em think it was a good idea to go piss in the high school principal's mailbox."

Jabril took his eyes off the window, looked over at the sheriff. "There's a black man up at the hospital with his head split open. Seems to me that's a little more serious than pissing in your teacher's mailbox."

"Hey, I agree. No question about it." The sheriff spread his hands. "But that still don't mean shit if I don't have any evidence."

Danny leaned forward. "Did Michael Tournier abandon the project when the cemetery protests started?"

The sheriff studied him for a moment. "You work for him. How come you don't ask him that?"

"Let's say I want to know how people up here saw it."

The sheriff was silent for a moment, then picked up a paper clip off his desk, started twisting it between his fingers. "Depends which people you ask, I guess. Way I heard it, they tried to cut a deal. Offered to pay to have the graves relocated over to the black cemetery on the east side of town, threw in some money for a new community center up their part of town." He glanced over at Jabril. "We still live pretty separate up here. Whites over on the west side and out in the subdivisions along the highway; blacks on the east side, up north of the drainage ditch behind the lumber yard. That's just how people want it, I guess."

Jabril just looked at him but kept silent.

"When did he make that offer?" Danny asked

The sheriff shrugged. "Couple weeks back. Can't say I paid much attention to it. Wasn't nobody interested. Seems they feel it's their land from the slave days. The plantation owners used to give 'em a place to bury their dead. Usually way up in the trees, where they couldn't grow anything. So I guess they feel it's got some symbolic meaning, worth more to 'em than a community center. I figured it was just so Tournier could claim he'd made an offer before he started construction." He tossed the bent paper clip on the desk. "See, since the cemetery isn't marked on any of the state's maps, legally it doesn't exist. So there's no reason he can't go forward with the project. Couple people over in the black community tried to get the state to send somebody down here, get it surveyed, but I guess they ain't had much luck yet."

Danny scrawled a quick note. "So you think this project will eventually get built?"

"Not anymore." The sheriff smiled. "I guess those boys were angry 'bout something, but they sure as hell put the nail in that project. Maybe it was a cemetery before and maybe not. But it's a crime scene now. So your boy Tournier's got any sense, he won't go near it. Looks like everybody's gonna lose on this one."

Jabril raised his eyes to look at the sheriff. "Especially Caryl Jackson."

The sheriff considered him for a moment, then nodded slowly. "Uh-huh. I guess you're right there."

"You believe that guy?" Jabril shook his head as they crossed the courthouse lawn, headed for Danny's car. "Thought he was gonna call his deputies in any minute, have 'em arrest me on suspicion of being black."

Danny smiled. "Nice to see some things don't change."

Jabril looked over at him. "That why you brought me? See if the sheriff'd be like that?"

"Sorry. But I got to know what I'm dealing with, here."

"What you're *dealing* with? Shit, same thing as always. All this stuff you hear about the New South? This place still about money and skin. That's all it's ever been, long as you got an economy based on one man's sweat and another man's land. And this guy you workin' for, Michael Tournier, don't go thinkin' he's any different. Just got a better rap."

Danny unlocked the car, looked over at him. "You know something I should?"

"Do I *know*?" Jabril shook his head in disgust. "Shit, look around you. All the wealth in this state, where you think it comes from?"

Danny glanced up at the courthouse. "Same place as always, I guess."

"You got that right." Jabril got into the car, took his black Ray-Bans out of his shirt pocket, slid them on. "Man wants the cash, there's only one way to get it. You makin' money around here, you got to be standin' on somebody's bones."

FOUR

DeWayne Jackson watched the lawyer pull into the gravel driveway leading up to his grandmother's house, driving an old Mustang convertible, like that made it all okay. The black guy who'd been with him at the hospital, looked like Isaac Hayes, was still along for the ride, one hand draped lazily out the car's window, like he had to let the wind cool it down or he'd burn the ladies. DeWayne stood on the porch watching as the car crept over the ruts in the driveway, swung into the dirt yard in front of the house, came to a stop. Even the slowness of its approach made him angry. *Guy's all worried about his car. Doesn't want to bust a strut on the old nigger woman's driveway.*

He leaned against the porch rail, his arms folded across his chest, watched them get out of the car. They walked toward him, paused at the base of the steps.

"My grandmama's sleepin' now," he said. "You can't talk to her."

The white lawyer lifted one foot, rested it on the lowest step, like he just had to get a foot up on their property. He looked up at DeWayne, squinting slightly against the afternoon sun, and said, "Actually, I was hoping to talk to you."

"Yeah? What about?"

"We were just over at the sheriff's. He doesn't seem in much hurry to arrest anybody."

DeWayne leaned forward, spit into the dirt beyond the railing. "Tell me something I don't know."

"You help me, I might be able to light a fire under him."

DeWayne squinted at the lawyer, then over at the black guy, who wasn't saying anything, just looking around at the bean fields stretching out past the road. "How you gonna do that?"

"I'm not sure yet. I'll have to look around some, see what he's not looking at." The lawyer looked over at the trees where the graveyard lay. "I was hoping to take a look at where it happened. You got a minute to show us?"

DeWayne thought about it, then pushed up off the railing, went over to the top of the steps. "Ain't much to see. Just some graves. You wouldn't even know that's what they was, my grandpa hadn't put up some new stones last year." He stood there looking out at the trees. "And look where that got him." Then he shook his head, came down to where Danny and Jabril were standing. "But shit, you want to see it, c'mon."

He led them out across the field to where the pine trees began. As they crossed into the shade, Danny turned to look back at the broad fields stretching out toward the road. This was land that had been farmed for almost three hundred years, and you could see where the men who'd first cleared this land had laid out the road along the creek so it wouldn't use up any of the good fertile bottomland, dragged out the tree stumps using mule teams and human sweat, then sat back to watch their crops grow. It was hard to imagine the labor that it must have required to cut a plantation out of this wet, fierce land, much less to make it surrender up its annual ransom of cotton and beans. Land like this was unforgiving; it had to be tamed every year, over and over again, or it would quickly slip back to mud and weeds. The only way to grow crops here was to water them with your own blood. Or with blood other men shed for you. That must have seemed like simple economics to the men who first cleared this land. So they bought slaves, set them to work on this land, and when they refused to work, they reached for the whip, or the gun, or the brand. And when the slaves died, they buried them in stony ground that would take no crop but this, land that was of no use to anybody except the dead.

Danny turned, followed DeWayne and Jabril back through the trees. The ground rose abruptly, and the thick black soil that they'd crossed in the fields gave way to clay and broken stones. Danny could see where the rain had cut channels through the clay as it ran down the slope, carried it out into the field a few feet, like a child's model of the Mississippi Delta where it stretches out into the Gulf. They climbed about ten feet up the bank, came to a small plateau where a dozen or so gravestones lay clustered together in the dense shade of the pines. Most of the stones had been knocked down; some were cracked, and one had been broken into tiny pieces. The ground around them was littered with beer cans, bits of colored glass, and broken china. But it didn't look like a garbage dump to Danny. There were no plastic bags blowing among the pines, no paper or broken kitchen chairs like you'd see sticking up out of the mounds of garbage at most country dumps. Just the beer cans that somebody had tossed around, and the glitter of thousands of bits of glass and colorful china half buried in the ground.

Danny took a pen out of his pocket, went over to one of the beer cans, and crouched down beside it. He slid the pen into the hole, lifted the can, and looked at it closely.

"That's what them white boys was drinkin'," DeWayne told him. "Sheriff told my grandmama that he got all them cans for *evidence*, but most of 'em still lyin' around here."

Danny looked around at the scattered cans. "They drink all these in one night?"

"Nah, they been out here lots 'a times. Last couple months, they come out here every Saturday night, just about. After the football games. That's how come they knew who it was."

"You know these boys?"

DeWayne looked away, out toward the road. "Yeah, I know 'em. They out at the high school every day. Football practice."

Danny tossed the can aside, wiped the pen on his trousers, and stuck it in his pocket. "If we rode over there now, could you point 'em out to me?"

"What, you gonna go talk to 'em? Get their side?"

Danny shook his head. "I may try to talk to 'em later. Right now I just want to see who we're talking about."

DeWayne bent, picked up a rock, and tossed it deep into the trees. "Well, c'mon, then." Then he walked back toward Danny's car.

They drove out along the state highway, past the lumberyard and the Winn-Dixie, until they came to the high school, which sat back from the road behind a row of stunted pine trees. It was a low, sprawling building with no windows. To Danny, it looked more like a minimum-security prison than a school, but that made a kind of sense, given his memories of high school. He turned into the parking lot, followed DeWayne's directions as they circled around back of the school to where a set of metal bleachers, strung with state-championship banners, stood along one side of the football field. Danny could see the team working out with blocking dummies at the far end of the field, taking turns driving them back toward the goalposts, while the coach stood on the crossbar, barking at them. At midfield, a quarterback took a snap, dropped back as a pair of receivers ran a pattern, then tossed a beautiful spiral that hung lazily in the sky for a moment before dropping into one of the receivers' hands.

"That's Randy Brewer," DeWayne said, motioning toward the quarterback. "He was one of 'em."

Danny watched as the quarterback dropped back, tossed another perfect spiral. "Got a hell of an arm."

"Uh-huh. Specially when he's throwin' at some nigger's head." DeWayne shook his head. "They expectin' him to make All-State this year. Team's lookin' at a district championship. You think the sheriff's gonna *arrest* that boy?"

Danny looked over at DeWayne, saw the anger burning in his eyes. "You sure he's the one who threw the stone at your grandfather?"

"Wasn't there, was I? But Brewer, man, he walk through the halls, lets you know you better get your black ass out of his way. You don't, he'll walk right on through you, knock you down."

"Teachers know about that?" Danny felt Jabril look over at him like he'd asked a stupid question, but DeWayne just grinned, said, *"Shit."* Drawing the word out real slow, as if it wasn't worth the energy to say any more.

"What about the others?"

DeWayne nodded toward the football team. "Two of 'em out there with Brewer right now. You sit here awhile, you'll see 'em come out, get in his truck. It's that red one, over by the gym. He always park in that same spot, like he owns it."

The truck was a red half-ton, with a large toolbox bolted to the bed, right behind the cab. Danny took out his notebook, wrote down the license number.

DeWayne was still watching the football team. "The other guy's called Bobby Price," he said. "He don't play on the team. He's a little guy, works over at the Winn-Dixie baggin' groceries. But he hangs with those guys, you know?"

Danny sat in silence for a moment, watching the blocking drill come to an end, the team gathering at midfield, unsnapping their helmets and sitting on the grass while the coach read something off a clipboard. Randy Brewer threw a few more passes, lazily, then walked on over, like he knew nothing the coach said applied to him. Watching, Danny realized that many of the players on the team were black, but most of the white boys sat off to one side.

"How do the black guys on the team get along with Brewer?" he asked DeWayne.

"Bunch of 'em wanted to quit the team a couple days ago, after they heard about it, but the coach got the sheriff out here to talk to 'em. Some shit about loyalty. How the law's got to take its own course, and they got a chance to prove who they are. Like they fightin' a war or something."

"And they stayed?"

"Yeah, especially after the sheriff called 'em at *home*. Told their mamas how everybody in town was countin' on a state championship this year." DeWayne looked over at Danny. "You know what happens, the sheriff calls your mama?"

Danny smiled. "I can guess."

"So, anyway, they still playin'. They try to keep it separate, you know? On the football field, it's just a guy wears the same uniform as you. Game's over, that's something different. You come by here on a Friday night, you see they split up in the parking lot. White boys go to their parties, and we go to ours. That's how it's always been."

"You wrong there," Jabril said. "Wasn't even the same parking lot when I went to school."

"Yeah, I guess that's what we got, all that marchin' Martin and them did," DeWayne said bitterly. "Everybody get to use the same parkin' lot now."

When the coach had finished reading from the clipboard, the players got up off the grass and walked back toward the gym in small groups. Randy Brewer threw a couple more passes, then went over to talk to the coach. They stood there for a few minutes, Brewer nodding at something the coach said, then he turned, walked back across the grass, went into the gym.

"They be out pretty soon," DeWayne said. "Brewer, he don't like to shower with all them niggers. Waits till he gets home."

So they waited. Jabril reached over, turned on the radio, ran through the dial, looking for something besides country. He found Sam Cooke doing "Mean Old World" on an oldies station, but then that gave way to Lesley Gore singing "It's My Party," and he reached over, shut it off.

"Damn, that's one annoyin' woman."

DeWayne shook his head. "I ain't *never* goin' to one 'a her parties."

After a while, the door to the gym opened, and four white boys came out, walked toward the red truck. DeWayne leaned forward, said, "That's them. Brewer, he's the one with the baseball cap, got one of them rebel flags on the front. Teachers pretend they don't know what that means, but you ask any of the black kids. They get the message." He pointed toward the three boys who followed Brewer toward the truck. "That's Barnes behind him, with the blond hair, and Lowe in the bomber jacket. The little guy is Bobby Price."

Danny waited as they got into the truck, then reached down to start up the Mustang as the truck pulled out of the parking lot. He followed them out onto the highway. "You got any idea where they'll be headed?"

DeWayne shrugged. "Home, prob'ly. Except for Price. He work over at the Winn-Dixie just about every night. They probably go by there, drop him off first."

And that's what they did. Danny followed the truck into town, saw it turn into the parking lot next to Winn-Dixie and pull up right in front of the entrance. Bobby Price got out, leaned on the passenger-side window for a moment, saying something to the boys inside. Danny pulled into the lot, swung wide around them, pulled into a space a few rows away. He shut the car off, and they watched Price shake his head slowly at something Brewer told him. His face looked pale in the gathering dusk, and his eyes kept flicking around, as if he felt somebody was watching him.

"Tell me about Price," Danny said to DeWayne. "What's the story on him?"

"Ain't much to tell. Used to be okay. We got assigned to do a science project together back in eighth grade. He came over to my house and everything. But last year, sometime, he got into a thing with this black guy after school, and the brother messed him up pretty good. Wasn't no racial thing, just some stupid shit. But after that, he started hanging with Brewer and them. Talkin' all that white-pride bullshit. Like, here's this little guy, real skinny, and *he's* got somethin' to say about the black man?" He shook his head, disgusted. "What's *that* about?"

Jabril grinned. "And now he's got him a job at the Winn-Dixie."

"Uh-huh. Produce department. Wrappin' them heads of lettuce and shit. Every night."

"Moppin' the floors."

DeWayne looked over at him and gave a smile. "Stockin' that *dog* food."

Danny saw Bobby Price push away from the truck's window and stand there for a moment, rubbing his hands on his jeans like he was drying them, while Brewer leaned across the other two boys to say something through the window. Then the truck's brake lights flickered off and it pulled away, leaving Price standing there, watching it drive away. After a moment, he turned, went into the store. "He doesn't look too happy."

DeWayne sat back, looked over at Price through the window. "You want me to feel bad for him?"

"Not at all. But it might be useful." Danny started the Mustang, caught up to the pickup as it swung out onto the highway. They followed it across town, watched as Brewer dropped off Russ Barnes in front of a small frame house in a working-class neighborhood, then drove out to the country club and let Jason Lowe off in the driveway of a large brick colonial that faced the golf course.

"Man, he's giving us the whole tour," Jabril said as they followed the truck back out onto the highway. "We get to see where *all* the white folks live."

"He's probably goin' to his daddy's shop now," DeWayne told them. He rested his arms on the front seats. "They got a body shop out here. You get in a wreck, that's where they tow your car. KKK meets there every Thursday night."

Danny looked up at him in the rearview mirror, raised his eyebrows. "You know that for a fact, or you just heard a rumor?"

DeWayne shrugged. "Come by here Thursday night, you'll see. They don't try to hide it none. You can see 'em in there, sittin' around in their sheets."

Danny glanced over at Jabril but said nothing. He saw the truck turn out of traffic into a gravel lot in front of a prefab building with a large garage door in front. Brewer parked next to what looked like an office in the north corner of the building, climbed out, and went inside. Danny drove on past, made a U-turn a few hundred yards up the highway, and pulled into a 7-Eleven across the highway from the building. They sat there for a few minutes, watching. After a while, Randy Brewer came out of the building, went to work washing a new Toyota near the front of the lot.

"How'd you like to be doing that?" Danny asked DeWayne, nodding to where Brewer was hosing the car down.

"Shit, work for *them?* I don't think so."

Danny smiled. "Actually, that wasn't exactly what I had in mind." He turned in his seat slightly, looked back at DeWayne. "If you're right that they hold KKK meetings in that building, and we can connect Randy Brewer to the attack on your grandfather, then you could file a civil suit, ask the court to award your family the property as damages."

DeWayne looked at him, surprised. "What, you mean we could take the whole body shop?"

"Not much sense in asking for half." Danny smiled. "Unless you want to try sharing it with them."

"Nah, we skip that." DeWayne looked at the body shop across the highway, shook his head. "*Man,* that'd be something. Take their business? That'd put a bug up their sheets, huh?"

"Be a start." Danny started the car. "I'd better get you home before your folks start worrying."

DeWayne's eyes were still fixed on the body shop. "We could really do that? Shut 'em down, like you said?"

"It's been done." Danny pulled out onto the highway, headed back toward Etta Jackson's house. "It ain't quick, and it ain't pretty, but sometimes the law works."

From the corner of his eye, Danny saw Jabril smile, shake his head sadly.

THEY dropped DeWayne back at his grandmother's house. She was sitting on the porch when they drove up, and Danny saw her eyes follow them up the gravel road, but she didn't move. When DeWayne got out of the car, she stood up slowly, came to the edge of the porch. Danny opened his door, got out.

"You find them white boys?"

Danny nodded. "Your grandson pointed them out to me up at the high school."

"You talk to 'em yet?"

Danny smiled, glanced over at Jabril. "I thought I should do that on my own."

Etta Jackson nodded. "I got some sausage and dirty rice on. You boys want to stay?"

Jabril got out of the car, swung his door shut. "Put them keys in your pocket," he told Danny. "'Cause we stayin'."

Danny glanced at his watch. "Tell you what," he said to Etta. "You don't mind feeding my friend here, I'll go have a talk with Randy Brewer right now."

"Fine with me," she said. "There's plenty of food." Then she turned, went into the house.

Jabril turned to stare at him. "Man, tell me you're not gonna miss sausage and dirty rice to go talk to some *white* boys."

"It's gotta happen sometime. Might as well get started." Danny smiled. "And this way I don't have to drive you all the way back to the city."

"Shit, don't even think about it. I'm not going *no*where until I get me some 'a this lady's dirty rice." Jabril followed DeWayne up the porch steps, then paused with the screen door in his hand to look back at Danny. "You be careful 'round those boys, okay? Don't assume they'll talk to you just 'cause you white." He turned to go inside, then paused, stuck his head back out the screen door to call out, "And *don't* go tellin' 'em you no *lawyer!*"

DANNY saw Randy Brewer glance up at him as he pulled into the body shop's gravel lot, but by the time he got out of the car, the boy had picked up his bucket and rag and disappeared into the open garage. Danny thought about following him, but then he glanced over at the office window, saw a man come out of the back to check something on a computer screen on the counter. He was a heavyset man with red hair and a thick beard, and he wore a baseball cap with a Confederate flag stitched to the front. He looked out at Danny, then came around the counter and over to the office door, opened it, and called out—

"Can I help you with somethin'?" Then his eyes moved past Danny to the Mustang parked near the lot's entrance, and something changed in his face. He came all the way out the door, walked over to the car, looking it over as if he might pull out a knife any moment and cut him off a piece. "Man, that's a beauty. Yours?"

"Yeah. Had it about six years now."

The man leaned in the driver's window, looked at the control panel. "You keepin' it original?"

"When I can get the parts."

"Yeah, that's a bitch." He straightened up, walked all the way around the car slowly. "You could use some new trim on the doors."

"That's why I'm here," Danny said. "Guy over in Slidell said you might know where I could pick some up."

He looked over at Danny, and his eyes narrowed. "This guy got a name?"

"Boy, you got me there." Danny grinned. "Works in the Texaco out on the highway."

"Wears a little ponytail?"

"That's the guy."

The man nodded. "That's Jim. He's up here every couple weeks, lookin' for parts for his GTO. He likes to take it over to Pascagoula, race it against the locals down there. Keeps burnin' out his bearings." He stuck out his hand, said, "Denton Brewer."

"Danny Chaisson."

They shook hands, then Brewer turned, walked back toward the office. "C'mon. I'll take a look on the computer, see what we got for you."

Danny followed him inside. The office was about what he'd expected—a couple threadbare couches against one wall, a table with a stack of old *Car and Drivers* and a copy of the *Sports Illustrated* swimsuit edition. A television tuned to ESPN flickered silently above the counter, and Danny saw a calendar hanging up on one wall that showed a girl in a bathing suit trying to polish a Corvette with her thighs. The only thing that was different was on the computer, where a screen saver showed a man's muscular hand reaching out to grasp a sword, with the words *WHITE PATRIOT!* scrolling across the bottom of the screen in elaborate Gothic script. Brewer went over to the computer, punched a key, and the screen saver vanished, replaced by a parts inventory.

"Guy I know up in McComb has a junkyard, sells a lot of Mustang parts." He punched a few keys, waited, then entered a password. "Even got us an old DELCO radio for a friend of mine. Sounds like shit, but it looks sweet. Got those big old silver buttons you had to push to change the station, you remember?" Brewer grinned, shook his head. "You didn't like a song, you just reached right on over there, hit one of those buttons, it was *gone,* man!"

Danny smiled. "Lesley Gore."

"Uh-huh. Or that guy used to play the guitar through that fuckin' tube in his mouth. You remember?"

"Peter Frampton."

"Right. You reach right out, hit that big silver button, man, he's fuckin' *gone*."

A door opened behind him, and Randy Brewer stuck his head in, said, "I'm finished with the Toyota, Dad. I'm gonna take off, okay?"

Danny studied the boy's face. Broad nose, pale blue eyes. It was the face of a slightly handsome, supremely self-confident high school kid. A boy who knows that as long as he can toss a football forty yards in a tight, lovely spiral, there will be girls waiting outside the locker room door and men to shake his hand, pat him on the back, and say, "Nice game, son." It was a face that seemed immune to doubt or fear, and there was nothing in it to suggest that he'd tried to kill a man he barely knew only a few days ago.

"You sweep up?"

"Yeah, and I put some bleach on that oil stain by the door."

"Then I guess you're done."

Danny watched the door close behind him. "That your son?"

"One and only." Brewer glanced up at him. "Maybe you seen him play ball out at the high school."

Danny shook his head. "Haven't made it to a game this year. Heard he's got quite an arm, though."

"They're sayin' All-State."

"Must get pretty exciting around your house, Friday nights."

"Friday nights, hell." Brewer grinned, tapped a few more keys on his computer. "Can't keep that boy home. He was born to raise hell in the morning."

Danny dug in his pocket, pulled out his wallet, and slid a business card out of the inside pocket. He tossed the card on the counter, said, "That's why you're about to lose your business."

Brewer glanced up at him sharply, then looked down at the card lying on the counter. He reached over, picked up the card, read what was written there: *Daniel Chaisson, Attorney at Law.*

"You got a choice," Danny said. "You can keep your boy out of jail and face a civil suit. That happens, the court can award your business to the family of the man he injured. Or you can take him down to the sheriff, cut a deal to plead him guilty to felony assault, and say a prayer the old man makes it. That way you can hang on to your business, but your boy'll spend the next couple years up in Angola, making some nice new friends."

Brewer looked up at Danny, his eyes hard. Slowly, he crumpled Danny's card, tossed it into the trash.

"Get off my property."

FIVE

As Danny turned up the gravel drive toward Etta Jackson's house, he saw lights moving among the pine trees back by the graveyard. He slowed, watching them move along through the woods, like a pair of hunting dogs snuffling along a trail, then he sped up, continued on to the house. Etta Jackson was sitting on the porch, gazing out at the darkness.

"There's a plate warming in the oven for you, if you haven't eaten," she said as Danny got out of the Mustang. "Had to hide some away for you or your friend would have finished it."

"You see those lights out there in the trees?" Danny asked her, coming up the steps onto the porch.

"That's DeWayne and your friend. They went out there to set them stones back up." She got up out of her chair with a sigh, opened the screen door. "C'mon in and get you somethin' before they get back and find out I held out on 'em."

Later, as Danny drove Jabril back across the Lake Pontchartrain Causeway, the lights of Metairie coming toward them across the water, he saw Jabril reach back to rub at the back of his neck, like something had stung him there.

"You okay?"

Jabril shrugged. "Can't get that boy's face out of my head."

"Yeah, he's takin' it hard."

Jabril looked over at him. "You think?"

"We're talking about DeWayne, right?"

"Maybe *you* talkin' about DeWayne. I'm talkin' about that white boy we watched get out of the truck at the Winn-Dixie." He looked back out at the approaching lights, shook his head. "You look at him, that's a boy shouldn't be 'round this mess. Look like a regular white boy. Not a redneck, you know? But there it is."

Danny was silent for a moment. "Does that surprise you?"

"*Surprise* me?" Jabril laughed. "Man, nothing surprises me anymore. Especially about angry white people."

"He didn't look angry to me," Danny said. "He looked scared."

"What you think makes most people angry? They scared they ain't gonna get what they want, or they scared somebody's gonna take away what they got. That's why they so scared of black folks. 'Cause we ain't got shit." He smiled, shook his head. "We all standin' on a ladder, man. And somebody's always steppin' on your head. Ain't nothin' you can do about it, either, except kick the guy below you. That's how it works around here, at least."

"That's how it works everywhere."

"You got that right."

When they reached Metairie, Danny took a left on West End Boulevard, drove Jabril back where he'd left his car in the parking lot of a movie theater three blocks from Mickie's condo. Jabril always left his car there when he came to visit, had Danny come pick him up. "Your neighbors see me come drivin' up, they're gonna call the cops." Danny didn't argue. There were cops all over the city who'd be happy for an excuse to take Jabril Saunders down, toss a throwaway handgun into the gutter next to his hand. So if Jabril wanted to leave his car where it wouldn't be noticed, Danny figured he knew what he was doing.

They swung into the parking lot, and Danny pulled up next to Jabril's Lexus. Jabril got out, then leaned on the passenger door, looked in at him. "You plan on goin' back up there tomorrow?"

"I should talk to those boys."

Jabril raised his eyebrows, looked off across the parking lot toward the movie theater. A movie was just letting out, and the crowd was spilling into the parking lot. "You know what you're into here?"

"Much as I ever do."

Jabril smiled. "Can't say that makes me feel better." He ran one hand gently along the edge of the car's door. "Everybody thinks they a good driver, man. But I see some messed-up cars gettin' towed away."

"I'll take it slow, okay?"

"Slow's good. Gets you home." Jabril pushed back off the car. "But keep your eyes on the mirror, too."

MICKIE was asleep when Danny got home, and he stood in the doorway of their bedroom for a long moment, watching her. She lay on her side, her knees drawn up and her arms folded across her small breasts. He felt a sudden urge to strip off his clothes, crawl into the bed, and ease up against her back so that he could reach around to rest one hand on her belly, feeling the baby stir and kick as she slept. But he didn't want to risk waking her, so instead he went into the kitchen, found some toffee-chip ice cream in the freezer, and sat at the counter to eat it right out of the carton. He felt grateful every time he came home and found Mickie there. No man really deserves his wife, but in Danny's case, he knew it was especially true. She'd saved him, both from a killer's bullet and from his own rage. And Danny had no doubt which of those had been most dangerous. He had learned that he was a man for whom anger was a white flame that could consume him. When he felt it rise up within him, he wouldn't hesitate to plunge his hand into that fire, and only Mickie had been able to pull him away.

Danny finished off about half the carton of ice cream, then shoved it back into the freezer. He went to the door of the kitchen, then paused. Mickie hated it when he ate straight from the carton. It was a single man's habit that he'd never been able to break, especially late at night, when she was sleeping. What's the point of messing up a bowl, right? Just get a spoon from the drawer and go at it. Afterward, though, he always felt a little ashamed, like he'd let her down. Not that she'd say anything, but he could picture the way she'd tighten her lips when she woke up during the night and went for the ice cream only to find it half eaten, an unwashed spoon lying in the sink. Marriage, Danny had decided, was like trying to keep his Mustang running. You fix the big things, but the little stuff can drive you crazy.

So you toss some duct tape in the trunk and learn to improvise.

He went over to the cabinet, took a bowl down, and carried it to the sink. He ran some water over it, washed the spoon, and put them both in the dish drain to dry. Small repairs. If she got up during the night, her lips wouldn't tighten, except to smile at the stupidity of his gesture. But in a way, the gesture was enough.

Danny went into the bedroom, sat on the edge of the bed to take off his shoes. He could see the outline of Mickie's pregnant belly where she'd gotten the sheets twisted around her. He had never gotten over his surprise that she'd agreed to marry him, and now the idea of her carrying their baby struck him as somehow beyond his comprehension. When he'd met her, Mickie Vega had claimed to be a juvenile officer assigned to the public defender's office in the Orleans Parish juvenile courts, but there was something too confident about her movements for Danny to picture her as one of the overworked, underpaid women struggling to hold that demoralized office together. Her real name was Mercedes, she'd told him, pronouncing it with a slight Hispanic accent that caught him by surprise— *Mar-the-des*. She had moved to New Orleans from Phoenix and still had trouble getting used to all the trees, the way the water just fell from the sky. She was small and muscular, with fierce dark eyes and black hair cut short as a boy's. But there was a gentleness in her face when she looked at him, even when she'd believed that he spent his days carrying illegal political payoffs for Jimmy Boudrieux. Later, when he learned that she was a special agent for the ATF, he figured her interest in him was simply professional, a way to break a tough case. But a week after the case was closed, she called him, invited him out for coffee. He had hesitated, wondering if she was planning to question him further about his involvement in a suspicious fire that destroyed a gun warehouse belonging to the man who'd tried to kill him. But something in her voice suggested this was a call she'd had to work up her nerve to make, as if she had something personal at stake. He accepted, and a late-afternoon coffee at a café on Magazine Street turned into dinner at Tujaques, then beignets at the Café du Monde, and finally, with an inevitability that surprised both of them, breakfast in her Metairie kitchen. Six weeks later, he moved in.

Danny felt Mickie stir, then turn over. Her hand came out and touched his back. "You okay?" she asked.

"Fine," he told her. "How's my family?"

"Restless." Her hand went away, and she got up, went into the bathroom. After a moment, he heard the toilet flush, then the water running in the sink, and she came back to bed. "God, I can't wait until this baby can pee for itself. They make this big deal about how you're eating for two, but they don't tell you you're going to be peeing for two also."

Danny peeled off his shirt, draped it over a chair in the corner. "I guess it's nature's way of telling you not to expect any sleep for the next eight months."

"Yeah? So how come you're not up six times a night?" She lay back, looked up at him through half-closed eyes. "Maybe I should give you a shake every time I get up to pee, so you can get used to it."

Danny stood up, took off his pants, tossed them onto the chair with the shirt. "Would that make you feel better?"

"Absolutely."

"So when I'm sixty-two and my prostate's the size of a grapefruit, I can wake you up every two hours?"

"That's different. I'm not gonna be feeding your prostate every time it wakes up crying." She yawned, curled up on her side, facing him. "Might play with it sometimes, just to keep it from feeling neglected."

Danny winced. "You think we could change the subject, please? This is starting to sound painful."

Mickie gave a sleepy smile. "So tell me about your day, dear." She reached out, touched his face gently. "Make some nice new friends?"

Danny lay back, felt his exhaustion sweep over him as soon as his head hit the pillow. "Well, it's not clear that they *all* want me to choke and die."

"Must be your winning smile."

"Yeah, that's what I figured, too."

He told her about it, feeling her come awake as she listened. When he was done, she was silent for a while, then asked, "You going up there again?"

"Tomorrow. I have to see Tournier in the morning, but then I'm going back up there to talk to those boys."

Mickie got up, went over to where her briefcase lay in a chair beside her dresser, and opened it. Surprised, Danny watched her dig through it and come out with a small appointment book.

"What are you doing?"

"Checking my calendar to see what I have to cancel tomorrow," she said. "I'm coming with you."

He sat up. "Mickie, really . . ."

"There's no point in arguing with me," she said, keeping her back to him. "I know how you work. You get in people's faces until somebody gets pissed off enough to take a shot at you. And I'm not raising this baby without a father."

"If you're worried, I'll take the gun." Danny kept a .9 mm Beretta handgun in a shoe box in the top of his closet. Every couple months, Mickie made him take it down, clean it, and accompany her to the ATF range to practice.

Now she just shook her head. "I've seen you shoot, Danny. That doesn't make me feel better."

Danny rubbed at his eyes wearily. "It's no big deal, Mickie. It's not even my case. I'm just doing an errand for Michael Tournier, okay?"

"So how come I don't see Helen up there?"

"Because they can pay a guy like me to go." He got up, went over to her, and took her hand, drew her back to the bed. "Look, we're talking about some teenagers who committed a hate crime. It looks like somebody's gonna have to push the sheriff to get him to prosecute, but there's nothing to suggest it was anything more than some boys who'd had too much beer. So you know what's gonna happen tomorrow? I'm gonna go up there, ask them some simple questions, and they're gonna tell me to get fucked. Then I'll drive home, send Tournier a bill, and we'll go over to Tujaques, see if we can't eat up my paycheck." He pulled the sheet up over her shoulder, tucked it around her. "You think you can trust me on that?"

She looked up at him. "You finished?"

"Uh-huh."

"Good." She threw back the blankets, got up. "'Cause I've gotta pee again."

ETTA Jackson sat up in bed, listening to the car come up the driveway, gravel crunching under its wheels. She glanced over at the clock on her bedside table: 3:20. Who'd be comin' 'round at this hour?

And as soon as the question had fully formed itself in her tired mind, she knew the answer. "Ah, Lord," she said, then pulled the curtain back, caught a glimpse of a dark pickup pulling up in front of her porch, the passenger rolling his window down, the bare skin on his arm pale in the moonlight as he raised the gun.

"DeWayne!" Etta shouted. "Get down on the floor!"

Then a window shattered somewhere up front by the kitchen, and she heard the *pucka-pucka* of the bullets punching their way into the house's wooden frame, even before she heard the gun itself firing. She rolled off the bed, pulled her blanket after her, and swept it over her as the sound came toward her. Then the window over her bed exploded, and she felt the glass landing on the blanket, heard it bounce and scatter across the floor. Then the mirror on the wall above her dresser exploded, and some bottles of perfume Caryl gave her every year on their anniversary, which she'd never used. She could hear the gun now, sounding like a flat tire on a wet road when you're doing sixty. And, strangely, she found herself thinking about her new living room curtains, the ones she'd sewn herself from a roll of fabric she'd bought last month up at Jo-Ann's on the highway, which a white salesgirl had stretched out on a counter for her to look at, saying how it was one of her favorites, too. Spring Roses.

Then, abruptly, the gun stopped. She heard harsh laughter, then the sound of the truck's tires throwing gravel against the porch as it roared away. For a moment, everything was quiet, then DeWayne called, "Grandmama?" from out in the hallway, his voice not scared or hurt, but worried. "Grandmama? You okay?"

And the sound of his voice was like a weight lifted from her mind, as if somebody had raised the lid on a boiling pot, so that she suddenly felt the anger rise up within her . . . *Sweet Jesus, her brand-new curtains!* Certain even as she thought it that it was wrong and sinful to think such things, especially since DeWayne was out there in the hallway thinking she was dead, probably.

"Yeah, baby?" She threw the blanket off her. "I'm okay. You all right?"

She heard him get up and come into the room, picking his way through the broken glass in his bare feet to get to her. And then there he was, standing over her in his underpants and New Orleans Saints T-shirt, looking like he was still eight years old, until he reached down to help her up off the floor. Feeling the strength in his arms, she realized he was almost a man. That scared her. You make the mistake of growing up to be a black man in Louisiana, they never forgive you.

She got to her feet, wrapped her arms around him. "We okay, baby. That's all that counts."

But when she drew back, looked at his face, she could see the tightness there, like he was holding something back, trying not to let her see it. Anger. Fear. She sighed, let her arms fall from his shoulders. "Go call your mama," she told him. "And I guess we better get the sheriff out here."

"Sheriff won't do nothin', Grandmama," DeWayne said quietly.

"No, I guess not." She bent, picked up a shattered picture frame off the floor, set it back on her dresser. "But he's gonna want to come out here, count up all these holes."

DeWayne scowled. "Yeah? Well, I got a hole he can count."

She threw him a disapproving look. "I guess he's seen enough 'a those." Then her hand came up to her mouth, as if to hold something back, but the words slipped out before she could catch 'em—

"All he gotta do is look in the mirror."

SIX

Danny sat in Michael Tournier's waiting room, watching as the receptionist spread a newspaper out on the counter, then took six roses out of a florist's box, cut the stems, and arranged them in a vase. She was almost painfully beautiful, with perfect, elegant features, silky blond hair tied back in a French braid, and a simple cotton dress that was so tight Danny figured she must have bought it at Sherwin-Williams. *Leave the flowers,* Danny couldn't help thinking. *Run away with me to Paris. We'll sit in a sidewalk café and work on our ennui.*

She brought the vase over, set it in the middle of the coffee table next to Danny's chair.

"You do that every day?" he asked her.

She looked up at him, smiled. "I love fresh flowers. Makes it feel less like one of those sterile corporate offices."

"You'd love it where I work. It's never been sterilized."

She gave him a look, like the idea disgusted her slightly, and Danny decided that she could do a pretty quick job of sterilizing him if he pushed his luck. So he shut his mouth, watched as she took a moment to get the flowers just right, then went back behind her desk. After a few moments, she picked up a phone that Danny hadn't heard ring and said, "Yes?" She was silent for a moment, then said, "I'll send him in."

Danny got up, waited as she hung up the phone and turned to look at him with an expression like she was holding an ice cube carefully between her thighs, keeping it nice and safe there. "Mr. Tournier will see you now. Do you know the way?"

"I just hop in the handbasket, right?"

She frowned. "No, you follow the hall straight back."

"Right." He smiled. "Got it."

He walked back past the cubicles, feeling like a balloon with a slow leak. Then he wondered what the receptionist would do if he brought Jabril with him next time, and the thought made him smile. *Hell, he'd probably get her number.*

Michael Tournier came out of his office at the end of the corridor, raised a hand to Danny. "You got some good news for me?"

"Yeah, your reception area is no longer sterile."

Tournier grinned. "She's something, isn't she? Makes us all feel right at home." He waved Danny into his office, closed the door behind them. "You want some espresso? I'm getting pretty good with this new machine."

"Thanks. I had some coffee before I left home. My wife gave it up while she's pregnant, but she still likes making it. Stands there over the pot, smelling it."

"So you get to drink it for her, huh?"

Danny smiled. "I don't get out of the house before eight, I'm a nervous wreck."

Tournier sat down on the leather couch, waved Danny into a chair beside him. "So what's the story across the lake?"

"The sheriff's dragging his feet, but it looks like the family's focused on getting the boys prosecuted, not a personal injury suit. They might have to go with a civil action if they can't get him to move, but it doesn't look like they're after a big settlement from you. One of the boys looks like the leader, and his father's the local race warrior. He's got a body shop, holds KKK meetings there. So the family could file an action to seize that property and you'd walk away clean."

Tournier was silent for a moment, looking off toward one of the picture windows, where Danny could see the Mississippi River Bridge rising beyond the Central Business District. "How's the old man?"

"He looks like somebody cracked his skull with a rock."

Tournier nodded. "Any chance he'll come out of it?"

"His wife doesn't think so. She's the one holding the family together right now. There's a grandson who goes to school with the boys, and he looks like he's ready to take care of the whole thing himself. But his grandma's got him on a tight leash for now."

Tournier stood up, went over to the window, stood looking out. "So what's our next move?"

"That depends. If the sheriff ever gets off his ass and makes an arrest, then I'd say you should hang back, wait and see how the whole thing plays out. Ordinarily, I'd probably say that would be the wisest option from a legal standpoint. If you can stay out of a case, that's always best."

"But you're not sure I can."

"Based on what you said to me last time I was here, it sounds like you've got more pressing concerns than litigation. You've got to keep an eye on your public image, and that's a tougher game to win."

Tournier reached up, rested one hand on the window in front of him, like he wanted to stretch out his hand and touch the city before him. "You ever wonder what makes a great city, Danny?"

Danny looked up at him, surprised. "I hope this doesn't have anything to do with football, or we're screwed."

Tournier smiled. "No, nothing to do with football." He turned to look at Danny, slid his hands into his pockets. "This is the kind of stuff I have to think about, 'cause I spend my day with architects. They've got real specific ideas about how to improve this city, make it more livable without losing its charm. A lot of this stuff is crazy, but some of it makes real sense. We ever got 'em built, they'd be the kind of projects that would get people excited to live here. And people come to me with these ideas because they believe I can get things done. You see what I'm saying?"

"Yeah, I see." Danny sat back on the couch. "I guess I never thought it was buildings that made a great city."

"You're right. Buildings are containers. But they shape the people who live in them." Tournier came back to the couch, stretched his legs out, and put his feet up on the table in front of them. "Look, Danny, I'm not in this for the money. When my dad died, he left enough just in investments for me to spend the rest of my life on the beach, if that's what I want. But I've got a chance to do something exciting here. And it won't mean a thing if I can't convince people to trust me."

Danny shrugged. "Okay, I'm sold. So what's next?"

"Hey, I'm just the big-picture guy. You're my man on the ground. So what's your instinct?"

"Play it straight," Danny told him. "Don't get caught trying to cover your ass. You cut some corners when you bought the land, but you can let people see that you're doing everything you can to clean up the mess. That way you polish up your reputation, and if this goes to litigation, you can show that you've done your best to act in good faith."

"You suggesting we offer the family a settlement?"

"That's one way to go, but I'll let you talk to Helen about that, since you might run into some liability issues."

"Okay, so what are we talking about?"

"I'd get somebody from the State Historical Commission to go down there *today*, run up a complete survey on the burial site. You'll lose any chance to build on the land, but you'll make it clear that you're trying to do the right thing. Then, if you're smart, you'll find out what church Caryl Jackson attends and give them the land."

Tournier winced. "Jesus, Danny. I ain't goin' for sainthood here."

"You still planning to build there?"

"I guess not." He sighed, shook his head. "All this racial shit around it, we got no choice except to write it off now."

"So you're okay if I call somebody I know up in Baton Rouge, see if we can get an archaeologist to come down and take a look at it?"

"Don't have much choice, do I?"

"No." Danny stood up. "But in my experience, that's the only way anything good ever gets done."

"You're a cynic, Danny." Tournier got up, walked him over to the door. "Helen didn't mention that."

"Helen likes to think the best of people," Danny said. "That way she can always be disappointed."

Tournier raised his eyebrows. "I'll keep that in mind." He opened the door, then reached out as Danny started to walk away, caught his arm. "This ain't the Old South, Danny. That racial shit's what's kept us in the toilet for the last hundred years. Way I see it, it's just crumbs on the floor, and everybody's arguing about who's got the broom."

Danny nodded. "I'm glad you feel that way. 'Cause this could get expensive."

"Tell me about it." Tournier smiled. "Danny, I knew the moment I laid eyes on you that this was gonna cost me a fortune."

Then he reached out, swung the door closed.

ETTA Jackson sat on her porch, watching the sheriff gaze at the bullet holes in her front door and shake his head sadly.

"Well, Etta," he said finally. "I hope you know a good contractor."

"Caryl used to do all that."

"That right?" He rubbed at the back of his neck with one hand, lifted his hat and got it settled again. "Caryl gets out of the hospital, he's not gonna be in any shape to go fixin' your windows. I'd call Jimmy Dunn over at Reliable Glass. He'll fix you right up."

Etta looked at the bullet holes in the door frame, then followed the trail that led across the front wall of the house to her window; some kind of machine gun, she figured, like you see 'em shoot in the movies, bullets goin' everywhere. *Sounded like a Uzi*, DeWayne had said when he'd helped her up off the floor, brushed the bits of glass off her nightdress. Soundin' almost proud, the way he'd said it. Like it was something he'd tell his friends, standin' around in the parking lot over at the high school. It struck her to wonder how he'd know what an Uzi sounded like. Then she thought about the CDs he liked to play, those gangster boys talkin' about *drive-by shootings*. Wasn't that what they'd done? Drive on up the road, stop the car long enough to spray the house with bullets, then just hit the gas, drive on away. Only these weren't no gangster boys. She thought about the harsh laughter she'd heard before the pickup truck roared away. Grow up black in Louisiana, one thing you know is how a white man laughs. This one sounded like a man driving nails into sheet metal.

The sheriff shoved his hands in his pockets, walked over to say something to the deputy, who was down on his knees, digging one of the bullets out of the porch railing. He'd dug four out of there already, dropping 'em in a little plastic bag so they could take 'em back to the lab, run their tests. At least, that's what they did on the TV shows Caryl liked to watch sometimes. Etta wondered if they'd ever caught anybody that way in real life, just lookin' at bullets. She couldn't picture it, but if they had, then she could sure give 'em plenty to start on. DeWayne had counted over twenty bullets in her bedroom wall, and nine more in the kitchen, making a neat line across the back wall, just below her framed photograph of Dr. Martin Luther King. She'd swept up all the glass she could reach with her broom, but when she got down on her hands and knees, she could still see some glinting in the cracks along the floorboards, back under the stove. She'd tried to shove the broom back in there, but it wouldn't reach. So she stood up, leaned the broom against the wall, and wiped off her hands on her cleaning apron. *Be there forever,* she thought. *Caryl comes back, I can show him.* She pictured him down on his knees, shaking his head slowly in amazement: *Uh-huh, look't here. All the trouble you folks get into, I'm not here.*

Ain't no trouble, she'd tell him. *Just some white folks breakin' glass. We swept it up. Left that last bit for you so you wouldn't feel left out.*

And Caryl would get to his feet, smiling. *Ain't that sweet. Makin' it a fam-ily thing.*

But before she could return his smile, reach up to touch his cheek gently, Etta had heard a car come up the gravel drive. She stood up, went over to the door to see the sheriff getting out of his cruiser, takin' a moment to get his cowboy hat on just right before he came up the porch steps, had a look at those bullet holes. She went out to meet him, took a seat on the bench while he looked it over, shook his head, then told her where to get her glass fixed.

She wondered what Caryl would say to *that*.

The deputy dug out another bullet, dropped it in his plastic bag. He had half a dozen in there now, but he kept right on digging. Probably wanting to check and see that they all came from the same gun, Etta thought. Make sure we don't sit around shooting up our own house, Saturday nights.

The sheriff brought out a handkerchief, wiped the sweat off his face, then ran it over the back of his neck, tucked it back in his pocket. "Etta, I know you're upset, but I gotta ask you some questions. You feel up to that?"

She shrugged. "I been sittin' here waitin' for you to ask 'em."

He nodded, then turned, looked out at the road. "How much you know about your grandson's friends?"

She looked at him, expressionless. "What you mean?"

"He made any new friends lately? Somebody drives an expensive car? Wears fancy clothes?"

She glanced over at the deputy, still working those bullets out of the wood with the tip of a screwdriver. "They just some boys from over at the school. How come you ask?"

He waved a hand at the line of bullets stretching across the front of the house. "This kind of thing, it looks like what you see in gang shootings."

"Uh-huh," she said. "I was just thinkin' that. But DeWayne ain't in no gang."

The sheriff sighed, shook his head. "I wish it was that simple, Etta. Where you could just know that. But these kids, they got their own world. Gangs, drugs. All that stuff. They see it on TV, so they want it. And guns? Etta, I wish you could see some 'a the guns we've taken off these kids.

Machine guns, street sweepers. Even a couple grenades. I mean, you could fight a war with this stuff."

Etta gave him a hard look. "So what you sayin' is this is *nigger* business. Ain't no white boys gonna drive by here, shoot up my house."

He raised both hands quickly. "Now, hang on a second, Etta. That ain't what I'm sayin' at all. I know you and Caryl had that trouble with those white boys, and I'm sure gonna look into where they were last night. You got my word on that. I'm just sayin' that ain't the *only* thing I'm gonna have to look at. You want me to find the people done this, right?"

Etta looked off toward the road, said nothing.

The sheriff came over, sat down next to her. "C'mon, Etta. You and me, we've known each other for a long time. You ever known me to be like that?"

"You wasn't the sheriff then."

"It ain't the uniform, Etta. It's the man."

She looked over at him, met his gaze with eyes that looked as angry as two coals getting ready to flame up. "Then how come them white boys ain't in jail?"

DANNY stopped at his office, where Demitra glanced up from her typing as he came in, picked up a pink message slip off her desk, handed it to him. "Etta Jackson up in Jefferson called about a half hour ago, lookin' for you."

Danny glanced at the number on the paper. "She say what it's about?"

"Sounds like somebody shot up her house last night."

Danny stared at her, then went over, picked up the phone on his desk, dialed the number on the paper. As he waited for the phone to ring, Demitra saw that his eyes had gone hard, and his jaw was tight with anger.

DeWayne answered.

"This is Danny Chaisson," Danny told him. "The lawyer who was up there yesterday. Is your grandmother around?"

"She's over at the hospital, visiting my granddaddy." DeWayne was silent for a moment, then asked, "She call you before?"

"She left a message with my secretary. Somebody shot up her house?"

"Uh-huh. I was right here, sleepin'. Sounded like a Uzi, you know? They just lit the place up. Got bullet holes *everywhere*."

"Anybody hurt?"

"Nah, we got down on the floor, like in the movies. You could hear glass breakin' all around. I still got some in my hair."

"You call the sheriff?"

"*Shit.*" DeWayne gave a laugh. "He come out here this morning, dug a whole bag 'a bullets outta the front door. You know what he told my grandma before he left? We should *call* him, these guys come back. You believe that guy?"

"I'm not surprised. I've met him." Danny rubbed at his eyes. "Listen, tell your grandmother that I'll be up there later today. We can talk then. But I wanted you to know that I'm gonna call the State Historical Commission in Baton Rouge and ask them to send somebody down to have a look at the graves. They'll knock on your door first, so you'll know it's them, but I thought I should warn you they're coming."

"All right," DeWayne said. "Just tell 'em to leave their Uzis at home."

Danny hung up, got Demitra to place a call up to Baton Rouge while he went through the stack of collection letters she'd left in his in box, scribbling his signature at the bottom of each one. When she got hold of the guy he knew at the State Historical Commission, Dave Terry, Danny got on the phone, spent a few minutes explaining the situation.

"Well, it sounds like our kind of thing," Terry said. He was silent for a moment, and Danny heard some papers rustling. "We could probably get somebody down there to look at it in October."

"How about today?"

"That's funny, Danny. You hear me laughing?"

"The property belongs to Michael Tournier."

Terry gave a deep sigh, rustled his papers some more. "Three weeks. Really, that's the best I can do. And that's only if I pull one of my people off another site."

"Dave, you remember how you got this job?"

There was a long silence. No papers rustling this time. Then Terry said, "That was a long time ago."

"I got a long memory. So does the U.S. Attorney."

"Danny, are you *threatening* me?"

"I prefer to think of it as calling in an old favor."

Danny heard Terry's chair squeak as he sat back, giving it some real careful thought now.

"And that's all you want? Have a site surveyed?"

"That's all I want," Danny told him. "I just need it now, before somebody else gets hurt."

More rustling papers. "Okay, I got somebody working on a site over by Mandeville. She'll give you a quick site survey, nothing fancy."

"That's great, Dave. Thanks."

"One more thing, Danny?"

"Yeah?"

"Don't ever call me again, okay?"

Danny smiled. "C'mon. Now you're makin' me feel bad." He reached over, hung up the phone before Terry could hang up on him. "Don't ever work for the state," he told Demitra. "Ruins your attitude."

She raised her eyebrows. "After workin' for you? Not much chance of that."

Danny lifted the phone again, put in a call to Mickie, but she wasn't in her office.

"She's over at the gun range," the receptionist told him. "Wants to get that baby qualified even before it's born."

Danny hung up, grabbed his leather jacket off the back of his chair, told Demitra, "I'll be up on the North Shore, anybody's looking for me."

"Uh-huh." She didn't look up from her typing. "I'll be holdin' my breath."

SEVEN

It was late afternoon when Danny pulled into the parking lot at the Winn-Dixie on the highway near Jefferson. He sat in his car for a moment, watching the heat making still, black pools on the asphalt. Something made him hesitate, like a man standing at the top of a cliff, measuring the distance to the water below. He could feel a tightness in his hands, as if they were anxious to grasp on to something, hold it tightly against his chest.

He got out of the car, went into the store, walked up and down the aisles until he saw Bobby Price stocking shelves among the canned vegetables. He wore his school clothes and a green vest with a name tag pinned to it that said *Hello! I'm Bobby*. Danny stood at one end of the aisle, took a can of diced tomatoes off the shelf, and pretended to examine the ingredients while he watched Price out of the corner of his eye. He had a razor knife and a plastic pricing gun, and as Danny watched, he sliced the top off a carton of canned baby peas, adjusted the numbers on the pricing gun, then slapped the price stickers on the top of all the cans, *pop, pop, pop*, like he was shooting ducks in an arcade. Then he set the pricing gun down on the edge of a shelf, started taking the cans out of the carton and stacking them on a display bin. He looked like any high school kid working an after-school job, making the time go past while he dreamed about growing up, leaving home, driving out to California in a convertible to cruise along the beaches, waving at the girls.

Danny almost hated to ruin it.

Then he thought about Caryl Jackson lying over in the hospital, tubes coming out of his arms, and he put the can of tomatoes down, walked over to the kid. "Excuse me."

Price looked up, a can of peas in his hand. "Can I help you?"

"Hope so. You Bobby Price?"

The boy's eyes narrowed slightly. "Yeah. Do I know you?"

"Not yet. But you will." Danny dug out one of his cards, handed it to him. He watched the boy look down at it, his face going very still as the words sank in. "I wondered if we might have a talk about Caryl Jackson."

Bobby Price looked up at him, confused. "Who?"

"He's the man you put in the hospital."

Bobby's face gave no sign that he knew what Danny was talking about. He looked at the card in his hand, turned it over to look at the back, then shook his head, handed it back to Danny.

"I've got no idea what you're talking about, man."

"Really?" Danny raised his eyebrows. "The sheriff seems to think you're up to your neck in it." He frowned, looked down at his own card as if the answer might be concealed there, then tapped it lightly against his hand a few times, like a man coming to an important decision.

Playing all the easy cards. After all, this was just a kid working in a grocery store. Danny almost felt bad for him.

"Listen," Danny told him, "maybe there's been a mistake. It happens sometimes, they go after the wrong guy. Could be that's what we got here."

He looked up at the boy, watched him nod. *Uh-huh, you bet.* Starting to hope. "But see," Danny went on, "the problem is the sheriff got your name from one of those *other* three boys, so he's gotta take that seriously."

He saw Price stiffen, then start to shake his head. "No way, that ain't possible."

"What? That they could put it on you?" Danny smiled. "They're your friends, huh? Wouldn't do that to you?"

Now Price looked confused, like he wanted to agree but realized that wasn't a good idea. Then his eyes suddenly got hard as he realized the trick.

"Hey, who the fuck *are* you?" He looked down, saw he still had a can of peas in his hand, set it down on the shelf angrily. "Let me tell you something, I want a lawyer, I'll fucking *call* one. You think I'm gonna hire some guy comes up to me in the grocery store?"

Danny shook his head. "Sorry, I should have explained. I've already got a client, so you can't hire me." He gave a smile. "Even if you fucking wanted to."

"Who's your client? This Caryl Jackson guy?"

"No, his family's waiting for the sheriff to arrest you. That's how the criminal-justice system works. Since Jackson's the victim of a crime, the district attorney represents his interests by prosecuting you." He paused, looked at Price closely. "You're what, seventeen?" Price didn't answer, but then Danny didn't expect him to. "See, that means they can charge you as an adult. So Jackson's family gets their satisfaction when the D.A. sends you up to Angola, seven to ten on assault." He spread his hands. "And that's if the old man doesn't die. That happens, you're looking at murder two. And that's a mandatory twenty. Even for white boys."

Price turned away, reached into the carton, and started stacking cans.

Danny sighed and laid his card on the carton beside Price. "You think hard about which side of this thing you want to be on. 'Cause that old man dies, this is what your whole life is gonna be about. Some lawyer's gonna put you on the stand, make sure everybody in this town understands what you boys did. And people don't forget. But that's not even your real problem. What's worse is that *you* won't forget. Won't be a day, for the rest of your life, you don't think about it. You leave here, it'll follow you. You'll take it to your grave. So I hope those boys are *real* good friends of yours, 'cause you'll be stuck with 'em for the rest of your life. That how you planned your life to be?"

Price kept stacking the cans, but Danny saw his hand begin to slow. Then the boy shot a glance over at the card lying on the carton, and Danny could tell he was thinking about what he'd heard, feeling it all like a weight on his shoulders that somebody was offering to lift away. Danny thought he was about to say something, but then he kept right on stacking the cans, as if that was all he could think to do, stacking up those sweet peas for the weekly special so they'd be ready when all the women came rushing in, looking for that three cans for a dollar.

Danny gestured toward the card. "Couple moments in your life where you get to choose. After that, it's out of your hands. So you hang on to that, give me a call when you make up your mind."

Danny was almost out of the store when he heard a voice behind him call out, "Hey!" He turned, saw Bobby Price coming toward him, the card in his hand. He waited, hearing the store's automatic door opening and closing behind him, people coming in out of the late-afternoon heat, bringing it in with them. Bobby Price walked toward him stiffly. Danny let nothing show in his face, simply stood there, waiting.

Price stopped a few feet away, said, "Look . . ." He hesitated, glanced down at the card in his hand; then he looked up at Danny's face, studying his eyes. He seemed to make up his mind, and he started to say something, but just then something behind Danny caught his eye. He stopped, looked past Danny, out through the glass door toward the parking lot. What he saw made him stop short.

Danny turned, followed his gaze. Randy Brewer was getting out of his pickup truck, walking over toward the store. He walked like every ballplayer Danny had ever known, as if somebody had taken the muscles of his legs and tied them in knots and he'd only just gotten them straightened out.

Bobby Price glanced down at the card in his hands, then shook his head. "Here," he said, shoving the card into Danny's hands. "You left that. I don't want it."

And then he walked quickly back into the store, like he was anxious to get back to stocking shelves. Danny heard the door open behind him, and Randy Brewer pushed past him.

"You mind?" He threw Danny a disgusted glance, shook his head. "Go stand someplace else, okay?"

Danny raised his eyebrows. "Was I in your way?"

"You got it."

Danny smiled. "Just wait." Then he turned, walked out of the store.

As Danny drove up the gravel road to Etta Jackson's house, he saw a mud-splattered Subaru wagon parked among the trees near the graveyard. He pulled in beside it, got out, and walked up through the trees. A white woman with long black hair pulled into a ponytail stood among the graves, taking notes on a pad. She had laid out several of the broken pieces of headstones, and as Danny approached, she tucked her pen into the pocket of her jeans, dug a camera out of the backpack at her feet, and bent over to photograph the broken headstones. DeWayne Jackson sat on a rock a short distance away, watching her.

She glanced up at Danny as he came toward her. "Watch where you're walking. I've got a grid laid."

Danny paused, looked down at his feet. She'd driven a series of small stakes around the perimeter of the cemetery, strung white string between them to divide the area into a dozen large squares, each a few yards across.

"Should I stay out?"

"No. Just don't mess up my grid."

He stepped carefully over the strings, nodded to DeWayne, and went over to stand next to the woman. "You must be the archaeologist Dave Terry sent down."

"That's right." She took one more photograph, then lowered her camera, wiped her hand on the leg of her jeans, and offered it to Danny. "I'm Anna Graf. Actually, I was working on a site over near Mandeville already, so it wasn't much of a trip."

"I'm Danny Chaisson. Thanks for coming."

She turned, looked out across the graves. "Well, I wasn't happy when I got the call. But this was worth the trip." She waved a hand toward the cluster of headstones. "Some of it's clearly recent, but the site's remarkably intact. Usually, I only get called in when somebody's putting up a shopping mall and the bulldozer digs up some bones. Means I have to do my job with a whole construction crew standing around, waiting to get back to work."

"That's not far from the story here."

She nodded. "I spoke to the family. Sounds like they've had a rough time." She glanced over at DeWayne, lowered her voice. "I think he's watching to make sure I don't finish the job those boys started."

"You blame him?"

She stepped over the white string in front of them, crouched down in front of one of the broken headstones. "I've seen these old burying fields scattered across the state. Most of 'em don't have any markers, except these bits of broken glass, old plates, pots. Looks like garbage to some people, but that's all the slaves had to mark their graves." She waved a hand toward the broken glass scattered across the ground. "What you see here is a promise that the dead won't be forgotten. In some cases, when we can't excavate the graves, we can try to date this surface evidence. Sometimes you find five or six generations of mourners have visited these graves, and every one has left something behind. It's like a gesture of communal memory." She looked up at Danny, and he saw that there was a smudge of dirt on the right side of her forehead, like she'd reached up to wipe away the sweat with the back of her wrist and left a streak of dirt there, as he'd seen Mickie do when she was potting plants on their deck. "There's a theory that it's an extension of traditional African burying practices. When somebody important in the village died, you broke something and scattered it across the grave to signify that your own life was broken now. But I don't buy that." She nodded at the bits of glass sparkling in the sunlight that filtered through the trees. "You come out here on a summer morning, you'd see this whole area would look like somebody'd seeded it with jewels. The sun hits those bits of colored glass just right, these trees would look like a cathedral." She stood up, rested a hand on her lower back for a moment. "You ask me, it's a celebration. Like singing for the dead."

Danny bent, picked up a crumpled beer can lying next to his feet. "Looks like we ain't all singing the same song now."

Anna was silent for a moment. She turned, looked over at the broken gravestones. "One of my professors in graduate school wrote a book on grave desecrations in Eastern Europe. It's Jewish graves there, but you see the same thing." She shook her head sadly. "It's like we can't let the dead sleep."

Danny dropped the beer can back in the dirt. "Sheriff told me he'd picked these all up for fingerprinting."

"Well, I usually end up with a sack of 'em," Anna told him. "If you want, I can send 'em over to his office."

DANNY drove on up the gravel road, parked in front of Etta Jackson's house. He got out, looked at the sheets of plywood nailed across two of the windows, bullet holes stitched across the front porch like somebody had flicked a paintbrush at it, then dipped and flicked it again. The front door had been removed and left leaning against the wall a few feet away. He could see Etta Jackson moving around the kitchen through the screen door, which somebody had patched by putting a few strips of duct tape over the bullet holes.

He walked over, knocked on the door frame. "Mrs. Jackson? It's Danny Chaisson."

She came over, wiping her hands on a dish towel. "I saw you drive up. You been out there where they working?"

"Yeah." He smiled. "DeWayne's keeping an eye on things."

She reached over, unlatched the screen door, held it open for him. "She gonna have to dig them dead folks up?"

"That depends." Danny leaned against one of the counters, watched her go back to washing dishes. She had a stack of them from a shelf she'd cleared off, where a bullet had punched through the cabinet, scattered bits of wood chip across her plates. "It would help if she could establish a date for those graves, so we can get the site listed as a protected area. She'll try digging around them first. If she can find enough evidence that way, she'll leave the graves alone." He reached over to run his finger across the splintered notch left by a bullet that had hit the front of the counter. "I'm sorry for all the trouble we've caused you, Etta."

"You ain't caused me any trouble." She picked up another dish, dipped it into the soapy water in her sink. "I appreciate you tryin' to help."

Danny was silent. He watched her swirl the soapy water across the plate, then rinse it under the tap, place it in the drying rack. He'd always believed you couldn't be afraid to stir up trouble if you wanted justice. But looking down at the bullet holes in her counter, he couldn't help wondering if it was his visit to Denton Brewer's body shop that had pushed Etta Jackson and her grandson into the line of fire.

"This could get rough," Danny said to her now, "if these people start thinking they can scare you off."

She shrugged. "Looks like it got rough already. Caryl, he ain't lyin' up in that hospital 'cause he like the food." She put the last dish in the drying rack, turned to look at Danny, wiping her hands on the dish towel. "And they can't scare me. Shootin' at my house, that ain't nothing. They put some holes in my walls, broke some windows. But I'm still here, and I still got my boy. That's all that matters."

Danny decided that he wouldn't like to be in Denton Brewer's shoes. He glanced at his watch and eased up off the counter.

"I should get going," he told her, and she nodded, hung her dish towel across the edge of the counter to dry. "You mind if I ask somebody to come stay with you, make sure nobody tries to shoot this place up again?"

"Like your good-lookin' friend, came out here to dinner last time?"

"Sure, if you don't think he'd eat too much."

"I like a man can eat. Means he's got some soul."

Danny smiled. "Then Jabril's your man."

"Uh-huh. He *somebody's* man, that's for sure!"

Danny heard a car coming up the gravel road toward the house. He glanced over at Etta, saw her turn to look out the window over the sink.

"Sheriff's back," she said. "Lookin' to dig some more holes in my porch, prob'ly."

Danny went over to the screen door, watched the sheriff's patrol car pull up behind his Mustang. The sheriff got out, took a moment to adjust his cowboy hat, then came up toward the porch.

"Thought I might find you out here," he called up to Danny. "How 'bout takin' a ride with me? There's somebody wants to talk to you."

Danny glanced back at Etta, but she'd dug out a cleaning rag and some spray, was using it to wipe down the counters. He pushed open the screen door, went out on the porch.

The sheriff propped one foot on the lowest step, waved his hand at the bullet holes lazily. "You come out here to see this?"

"Among other things." Danny came down the steps. Anna Graf was lifting a heavy bag of tools out of the back of her station wagon. DeWayne came out of the shadow of the trees, helped her carry them back toward the graves.

"Friend of yours?" the sheriff asked.

"State Historical Society sent her down. She's doing a preliminary site survey."

The sheriff raised his eyebrows. "Didn't waste much time, did they?" He pushed his cowboy hat back slightly, rubbed at the line it left on his forehead. "You do that?"

Danny looked out across the fields, said nothing.

"Got some connections up there in Baton Rouge, huh?" He grinned. "Hell, remind me to talk to you about my taxes." He hitched up his uniform trousers, waved Danny toward his cruiser. "C'mon. You can leave your car here. Etta won't mind."

Danny got into the front of the cruiser, and they rode back into town. The sheriff drove in silence until they reached the outskirts of town. As they pulled up at a stoplight, he raised his hand to somebody in the next car, then nodded toward the row of discount stores and fast-food restaurants along the edge of the road.

"See all those stores?"

Danny followed his gaze.

"That's the last wave of commercial development we had in this town. Got us a McDonald's, Wal-Mart, and a new drugstore in that one block. Couple months after that, they put up the movie theater. Ten screens. Gives the teenagers something to do on a Friday night. Shoot, when I was a kid, we just rode around all night raisin' hell."

Danny looked over at him. "Sounds like you got a few still do that."

"Always will. Small town like this, that's what they get up to."

Danny said nothing. The light changed, and they drove on, turning up the main street, then into the parking lot behind the courthouse. They got out, and Danny followed the sheriff in through the glass door that led to his office.

The sheriff paused at his receptionist's desk, sorted through some phone messages quickly, then asked her, "Sam here?"

She nodded. "Got here about ten minutes ago. I sent him on in."

He tossed the messages back on the counter, waved Danny back toward his office. "You'll like Sam. He's a lawyer, just like you."

Danny smiled. "I hope not."

The sheriff paused, his hand already resting on his office door, looked Danny over. "Okay, maybe not. But he's a lawyer." He swung the door open, went in.

Danny followed, saw a man in a pale summer-weight suit sitting in one of the battered wooden chairs next to the sheriff's desk, reading over some papers in his briefcase.

"Hey, Sam." The sheriff went behind his desk, sat down. He nodded toward Danny. "This is Danny Chaisson, the lawyer I was tellin' you about."

The man closed his briefcase, set it carefully on the floor, then stood up to offer Danny his hand. "Hi, Danny. Sam Price. Looks like we're in the same line of work."

Danny shook hands with him, studying his face closely. "Sam Price. You got a boy who works over at the Winn-Dixie?"

Price smiled. "That's right. I guess you've already met my son." He sat down, shot a quick glance over at the sheriff.

The sheriff held up both hands. "Hey, I didn't say a word."

Danny took the empty chair. "Is that why we're here? Talk about your son?"

"You can understand my concern, right?" He leaned forward. "They're just *boys*, Mr. Chaisson. My son, he plays trumpet in the band. You know what he worries about? He's got a math test next Friday. There's a girl he likes, but he's scared to talk to her. When's he gonna have enough saved to get a car. Couple years, he'll go away to college, probably mail his laundry home to his mother. You see what I'm saying?"

"Maybe you should tell all that to Caryl Jackson's family."

Price sat back, shook his head. "Look, I understand what they're going through, and if I could fix that old man's head, I would. But I got to look out for my boy. He's got some friends I don't approve of, but that don't make him a bad kid. You remember what it's like, that age? Hell, I had friends like that, and we got into some scrapes. I guess we all did. Teenage boys got wild blood. That's just how it is."

Danny looked over at the sheriff, who had swiveled his chair so he could gaze out the window. "I'm curious, why isn't he talking to you?"

The sheriff turned to look at him, shrugged. "Sam's an old friend. It's not like I don't know what he's feelin'."

Danny started to respond, then thought better of it. He turned back to Price. "You're talkin' to the wrong guy. I'm just an observer here."

"You talked to my boy."

"I'll talk to all of 'em if they'll let me. I want to hear their side of the story."

Price's eyes narrowed. "But you're just an observer."

"That's right."

"Mind if I ask who you're observing for?"

"No." Danny smiled. "But I won't tell you."

"Turns out Mr. Chaisson's got some interesting connections." The sheriff picked up a paper clip off his desk, started twisting it. "Got somebody down from Baton Rouge already to look at them graves."

Price kept his eyes on Danny's face. "There's not a jury in this parish will convict those boys," he said. "Not unless they stack it with niggers."

The sheriff sighed. "Now, Sam. That's no way to talk."

Price shook his head slowly. But his eyes never left Danny's face. "I won't let anybody ruin my boy's future over this thing. You understand?"

Danny nodded. "Yeah, you've made yourself real clear." He looked over at the sheriff. "We done here?"

The sheriff sat forward, tossed the paper clip into a garbage can next to his desk. Then he sat back wearily. "Yeah, I guess we're done."

. . .

A deputy drove Danny back to his car. From the moment he led Danny out to the patrol car, he never said a word, just kept his eyes fixed on the traffic ahead of them. Danny had the feeling the man was enjoying the silence. He squeezed a small rubber ball with one hand while he drove. When they stopped at a traffic light, he switched hands.

"Looks like you got a system there," Danny said, nodding at the ball.

The deputy looked over at him, then glanced down at the ball in his hand. He smiled, squeezed it until it vanished completely in his palm, the knuckles on his right hand bulging like they might burst through the skin any second. Danny looked up at his face, saw the muscles in his jaw tighten.

Danny grinned, raised both hands. "Okay, go easy on it. I get the point."

The deputy slowly relaxed his grip. When the light changed, he switched the ball back to the other hand, drove on.

As they turned up the gravel road to Etta Jackson's place, Danny saw a red Jeep Cherokee parked under the first row of pines just beyond the house. "Shit."

The deputy glanced over at him. "You got a problem?"

"My wife's here."

The deputy grinned. "Yeah, I guess that's a problem."

Danny got out in front of Etta's house, walked up the steps. He could hear laughter from inside the kitchen, and as he came up to the screen door, he saw Mickie sitting at the kitchen table, pouring a cup of coffee from a silver pot, while Etta Jackson got up to get more sugar from the cabinet.

"You sure got your hands full, girl." Etta laughed, shook her head. "It's like my mama always said, God gave us men so we could practice for children."

Danny knocked on the door, saw them both look up. He could tell by their expressions that they'd heard him come up the steps.

Mickie smiled. "Hey, Danny. We were just talking about you."

"Yeah, I heard." He pushed the screen door open, went on in. "What are you doing here? I thought you had meetings all afternoon."

Mickie swung a hand toward the row of bullet holes that ran across the cabinets opposite the door. "I got a message from Demitra. She said there was some trouble up here last night. Thought I should come up here, keep an eye on you."

Terrific, Danny thought. *All these women, deciding they need to take care of me.*

He pulled out a chair, sat down. Etta reached him down a coffee cup, laid a spoon on the table in front of him. "I figured I'd call Jabril," Danny told Mickie. "Ask him to come up here."

Mickie raised her eyebrows. "You really think that's a good idea?"

"Sure. Why not?"

"Danny, Jabril's got enough problems with the police down in New Orleans. You're gonna bring him up here, get some country sheriff after him also?"

"You got a better idea?"

Mickie picked up her coffee cup. "I've got a couple vacation days coming."

Danny glanced up at Etta. She smiled, shook her head sadly. "Don't look like you gonna get much choice about it."

"You noticed that, huh?"

"She got you outnumbered. Better get used to livin' in a house full of tough-minded women."

Danny looked over at Mickie. "You know something I don't?"

She shook her head. "Far as I know, it's just a baby."

"Listen to you." Etta gave a laugh. "You so busy tryin' not to know, you missin' the whole show."

Danny raised his eyebrows. Mickie shrugged. "Maybe you better tell us," she said.

"Nothin' to tell. You wearin' red, honey."

Danny looked at Mickie's clothes. Dark blue skirt, gray jacket, pale blue shirt. Her fed clothes. He could see where the leather strap of her shoulder holster had made a crease across the shoulder of her silk blouse. He saw her glance down at herself, thinking the same thing he was. *Wearing red?*

"Not *there,* girl." Etta reached out, pressed her finger against Mickie's cheek. When she lifted it away, Danny saw the mark her finger left on Mickie's light brown skin, like a blush.

"That's where you wearin' it," Etta told her. "Right there in your face." She leaned forward, whispered, "She gonna look like you, too. Have that pretty brown skin."

Something in Danny's chest tightened. He'd seen lots of pictures of Mickie when she was a little girl, her mother sitting him down on the couch in their house out in Phoenix, pulling out the photo albums while Mickie groaned, "Mama, *please.*" There were lots of pictures of her brothers to get through first, playing football, dressed up for some Mexican church carnival, and her mother would turn the pages slowly, shaking her head in amazement. "Look at Miguelito! I forgot we had that picture."

But Danny would wait patiently until they reached the pages where little Mercedes appeared, just a wad of blankets at first, then a tiny naked girl fleeing away down a hallway with her left hand reaching out to brush the walls, and then, quickly, a girl of five or six, hair cut straight across her forehead, squirming miserably in a flouncy party dress.

Mickie, looking over his shoulder, could only groan and say, "There's a girl who really needs a couple hours at the gun range." When they got to junior high school, Mickie always fled the room, but Danny could only grin and shake his head. *Jesus, she'd been so young!*

Now he looked over at Mickie, and all he could see was a small girl who looked just like her, their *daughter,* so beautiful with her dark hair and eyes that it broke his heart.

Then Etta looked over at him, shook her head, and grinned. "You gonna have your hands full, son. Hope you ready."

Danny met Mickie's eyes, and he smiled. "I guess I'm in trouble, huh?"

"Yeah," she said. "I guess you are."

EIGHT

"You sure you won't come with us?"

Etta Jackson shook her head. "I got to go up to the hospital, see Caryl. DeWayne's gonna ride me up there. Then I got to stop by the church later. But you have a good time, hear?"

Danny nodded. He went out onto the porch, where Mickie was sitting on the top step, talking to Anna Graf in the soft twilight.

"Looks like it's just us," he told them. "Etta wants to spend some time at the hospital."

Anna stood up. "What about DeWayne?"

"Sounds like he's driving her."

They went down the steps, and Danny started toward the Mustang, then realized that Mickie had taken Anna's arm and steered her over toward the Jeep.

"We'll take my car," she said. "You won't stick to the seats."

Danny had no choice except to follow. He climbed into the back behind Mickie, had to shove her Kevlar vest aside to find the seat belt.

"This looks new," Anna commented, looking around. "I thought they discontinued this model."

"They did," Mickie told her. "I got one of the last ones. But I'm gonna sell it when the baby comes, get something bigger."

Humvee, Danny thought, smiling. *Or one of those Volvo baby wagons. Like driving a tank.*

They drove into town, Danny listening to the two women talk about Mickie's pregnancy, car seats, nursing. Like they'd known each other for years. He leaned forward, rested an arm on each of the two front seats, said, "Anna, you find anything I should know about?"

She turned to look at him. "Nothing you wouldn't expect. It's a slave cemetery, obviously. The oldest graves probably date from the first couple decades of the nineteenth century. But I haven't started to do any serious digging yet, so those dates might change. I'm just looking at the surface stuff. Pottery, carvings on the old stone fragments."

"What are the chances we'll get the site protected?"

She shrugged. "That's not my call. I just make a report. But based on what I'm seeing, I'd say it's the kind of site my office usually acts on."

"Thanks." He sat back. "DeWayne still keeping his eye on you?"

She smiled. "I think he's getting interested. He started asking questions after you left. Burial practices, how we can work out the dates without digging up the bodies, all that stuff."

"History comes alive." Danny grinned. "He's probably wondering where you keep your hat and whip."

"Yeah, no doubt." Anna sighed, shook her head. "You can't get a degree in archaeology these days without somebody sending you that stuff. Everybody thinks they're the first person to think of it."

Danny looked out the window at the passing trees. "I'm glad you've got

DeWayne involved. Might be a good idea to keep him busy until that fire in his eyes goes out."

She nodded. "I'll see if he wants to help me dig tomorrow."

Mickie turned into the gravel lot of a seafood restaurant built to look like an old tin-roof Cajun shack. Etta had told Danny they had all-you-can-eat catfish, Thursday nights, with jalapeño hush puppies and cold Dixie beer on tap.

"Lots 'a families go in there," Etta had said. "They take good care of y'all."

"We'll tell 'em you sent us."

Etta looked at him. "Well, you can, but it won't mean nothin' if you do. I ain't never been there. Can't eat catfish. We used to have it five times a week when I was livin' with my mama. She cooked at a roadhouse, and that was all they'd let her bring home." She smiled. "You won't catch me eatin' that stuff now. Can't even take the smell. But people say it's real good."

They waited while Mickie locked up the Jeep, set the alarm. Then they walked up the wooden ramp to the door. Fishing gear hung in the entryway, and the tables had sheets of red plastic draped over them, a thick wad of paper napkins stacked in a holder, and several bottles of Tabasco, in case everybody reached for it at once. They sat down, and Danny watched a waitress bring out a large tray stacked with plates of fried catfish, stopping at several tables to set them down.

"Must be easy to keep the orders straight, Thursday nights."

Mickie looked at Anna, smiled. "Danny always brings me to these places. We first got together, I thought he only ate in places where they spread newspaper out on the tables."

Anna nodded. "But I guess it's pretty obvious why Etta and DeWayne decided not to come. There's not a black person in the place."

Surprised, Danny glanced around. The restaurant was packed with families, two hundred people, easily; but she was right, there wasn't a single black face. "C'mon," he said. "You really think they wouldn't serve Etta? This isn't 1962. You try that kind of shit now, you'll end up on the wrong end of a lawsuit."

"There's laws," Mickie said, "and there's custom. You don't have to refuse to serve somebody. There's lots of ways to let 'em know they're not welcome. Tell 'em they'll have to wait for a table, 'cause all the empty ones are reserved. Then you leave 'em sitting up front for an hour. After a while, they get the message. People don't go where they aren't comfortable." She shrugged. "That's how it worked in Phoenix, anyway. They figure if you're Mexican, you don't mind waiting. Take a little siesta."

Danny looked at her. "You're telling me this happened to you?"

She laughed. "Danny, I hate to tell you this, but you married a spic. Wait'll the baby's born. You got that dark hair. One day you're going to walk into a restaurant with your Mexican wife and a child who's half Mexican, and they'll decide we're all a bunch of greasers. Then you'll get a real good taste of how it works."

"So why do you think Etta would send us here?"

Mickie shrugged. "She probably figured we'd get a good meal."

They looked at each other silently. Then Danny sighed, stood up. "You're not supposed to eat fried food, anyway."

"Hey, you noticed. I wasn't going to say anything." Mickie got up, tossed her napkin on the table. "C'mon, there's a Hunan place up the block."

Anna got up. "Spicy food's okay for you?"

"Wakes the baby up, but that's okay." Mickie touched her belly, smiled. "Just think what we'll save on dance lessons."

THEY split three dishes, and while they waited for the food to come, Anna told them about some other cases of grave desecration she'd seen in slave cemeteries over the last few years.

"You get a couple cases every year," she told them, "most of it small stuff. Spray paint, gravestones kicked over. That's what you might call mischief vandalism. Teenagers, mostly. Trying to prove how brave they are, messing around in a graveyard. But sometimes you get cases where it reflects a larger dispute. Property rights are the big issue lately. Back when these graveyards were built, the land was basically worthless. You're running a plantation, you don't bury slaves on the crop land. You go find some worthless piece of ground, where it's too steep to plow, or there are too many rocks to make it worth clearing the land. That's where we find these graves. They're almost never marked on any maps, but if you look closely at the old records for these plantations, you can find 'em." She paused as the waitress brought their food, set it down on the table. Danny passed her the rice bowl, and she spooned some onto her plate, handed it to Mickie. "Now that land turns out to be valuable for exactly the same reasons it was only good for burying slaves when the plantations were the major source of wealth. It's elevated, so you don't get as much flooding, and all the rocks that made it bad for farming give you a solid foundation for construction. We see lots of towns trying to seize these sites by eminent domain, mostly for utilities. Pumping stations, generators, that kind of thing. You get these little towns starting to expand, and suddenly all that agricultural land is going residential or commercial. Everybody wants a Wal-Mart, and all those little grocery stores on the edge of town decide they have to build superstores out by the highway or they won't survive."

"Must put a lot of pressure on your office," Danny said.

Anna shrugged. "It's hard to argue for the past, if that's what you mean. But I talk to the people who work over in environmental protection, they feel the same pressure. It's just as hard to argue for the future. We all get focused on right now. That's what people really mean by progress. Not what's going to happen twenty years from now, but can you get your building permit next month." She took another dish, spooned some vegetables onto her plate, passed it on. "What happened here looks like a combination of mischief vandalism and a property-rights dispute. On the one hand, you've got teenagers out drinking beer on a Friday night, they decide it would be fun to knock over some gravestones, but from what Mrs. Jackson was telling me, it sounds like there's a land-use dispute somewhere behind it."

"Except in this case the developer isn't pushing to build. He's ready to back away from the whole project, based on your findings." Danny saw Mickie glance over at him, smile. "What?"

"Danny's working for the developer," Mickie told Anna. "He likes to think he's on the right side."

"I can understand that." Anna looked over at Danny. "Anyway, you called us, so I suspect you won't try to obstruct my work."

Danny smiled. "You haven't spent much time around lawyers, have you?"

When they finished, it was after ten. The house was dark when they pulled up beside Anna's car, so they figured Etta and DeWayne were still at the hospital.

"You really have to drive back to Baton Rouge tonight?" Mickie asked Anna. "I'm sure Danny's client can afford to spring for a hotel."

"Thanks, but I've got a cat who needs feeding. If I don't come home, he'll start on the furniture." She got out, looked up at the unlit gravel road. "Maybe somebody could help me find my way back to the highway?"

Danny got into the Mustang and led her as far as the interstate, then swung around, headed back to the house. The night was clear, and there was a pale moon hanging just above the trees. The kind of night, when he was a teenager, he'd dream about just pointing the car west, driving until he hit the ocean. Desert, mountains, bright summer moon. But when he thought about Mickie sitting in the dark on Etta's porch, her gun resting on her lap in case somebody showed up to finish what they'd started the night before, that thought vanished, and he picked up his speed. Mickie could take care of herself; she had a Kevlar vest in the back of her Jeep and a .380 Pony she carried in the holster under her arm. But a couple guys riding by in a pickup truck wouldn't know that, and Danny figured it was better to avoid her teaching them any painful lessons.

When he turned up the gravel road, still half a mile from the house, his eye caught movement among the pines. Red light, moving lazily through the dark woods, like the spray from a water sprinkler on a ball field after a night game in late summer. Danny felt something hard form in his throat, and he punched the gas, the Mustang sliding on the gravel road as he raced the last two hundred yards up to the house.

A sheriff's cruiser sat in front of the porch, its emergency lights knifing out across the dark fields. Danny swung the Mustang across the grass, hit the brakes, and had his door open before he saw Mickie standing calmly on the unlit porch, talking to the same deputy who'd dropped him off earlier that afternoon. There were no bodies lying in the front yard, no burning wreckage of a pickup truck piled up against the nearby trees. And, as far as Danny could see, no new damage had been done to the house.

He got out of the car, walked over to them. The deputy stood at the base of the porch steps, one foot planted on the lowest step, as if claiming territory. He had his hands on his hips and was gazing up at Mickie like he was working up his courage to ask her to dance. She had her arms folded across her chest, and her face was expressionless.

"No shit?" Danny heard him say. "You really with ATF?"

"That's right."

"Were you at Waco?"

She shook her head patiently. First question everybody asked. "That was before my time."

"But I'll bet you know people who were there, huh?"

"Yes, I do."

The deputy grinned. "Hey, you ever get to ride in one of those black helicopters they talk about?"

She didn't answer, just looked over at Danny, watched him come up the steps to stand beside her.

"What's going on?" he asked

"Sheriff's got an arrest warrant out on DeWayne." She nodded at the deputy. "He came out here to pick him up. They sent a couple deputies over to the hospital, too."

Danny stared at the deputy. "Why? What's the charge?"

"Well, we got a boy beat to death with a tire iron up on Twenty-first Street. So it's the district attorney's call, but I'd guess it'll be murder one."

"And you suspect DeWayne Jackson?"

The deputy shrugged. "Me, I don't suspect nobody. I'm just doin' like I'm told. The sheriff sent me out here to pick up the Jackson boy. You want to know why, you better ask him."

Danny looked over at Mickie. "You be all right here until Etta gets back?"

"Yeah. I guess somebody better stay." She glanced at the deputy. "In case DeWayne turns up."

The deputy bent, picked something up off the ground, and looked at it.

Brass gleamed in the moonlight. A shell casing. He tossed it into the trees. "Y'all do what you like. I gotta stay here until the boy gets back or somebody calls me."

Danny met Mickie's eyes, and she gave a slight nod. He got back in the Mustang and drove over to the hospital, where a nurse in the ICU told him that Etta Jackson had left about an hour ago, stopping first at the nurses' station to thank them for looking after Caryl, as she did every night. The nurse glanced over at a sheriff's deputy sitting in the waiting room. "You're not the only person looking for her, either."

"Did you happen to notice if her grandson was in there with her tonight?"

The nurse waved a hand back toward the nurses' station. "I've got two people out tonight. It's all I can do to keep up with the patients."

Danny thanked her, went back out to the Mustang, and drove the six blocks over to the sheriff's office behind the courthouse. A female deputy sat behind the reception desk, reading *USA Today*. She glanced up at Danny as he approached the desk. "Help you?"

"Is the sheriff around?"

She shook her head. "He's out working a crime scene."

"Over on Twenty-first Street, right?" Danny glanced at his watch. "He said I should meet him over there if he wasn't back yet."

"You know where it is?"

"Remind me."

"Up past the ditch." The deputy picked up her newspaper, turned to the sports section.

Up past the ditch, Danny thought as he walked out to his car. You grow up in one of these little Louisiana towns, you know exactly what that means. Ask one of the old boys sitting in the coffee shop across from the courthouse, they'd still call it *Niggertown*.

He followed the deputy's directions, heading north out of town until he crossed a shallow drainage ditch and the row of tire stores and auto-parts dealers abruptly gave way to small run-down houses, corner liquor stores with boarded-up windows and metal security grates across the front door, bars with names like Junior's Hot Spot, and tiny storefront churches where you could hear the faint sound of singing, even late on a Thursday night.

Danny saw the sheriff's lights from three blocks away, three patrol cars and an ambulance, their emergency lights flaring through the darkness from the edge of a vacant lot at the northeast corner of Twenty-first Street. A crowd of people from the neighborhood stood on the sidewalk, just beyond the yellow crime-scene tape, watching. The emergency lights slid across their faces, moved away into the trees, then came slowly back, no hurry now.

Danny pulled up behind the ambulance, got out, and walked over to the tape. He could see the sheriff talking to one of his deputies near a tall clump of weeds. A body lay on the ground a few feet away, covered by a sheet. Danny could see one white sneaker sticking out from under the sheet. It lay on its side, the laces untied and trailing in the mud. For some reason, that image struck Danny as faintly obscene. Like somebody had just tossed the sheet across the dead boy, left him there while attending to something more important. He lay at the center of the scene, forgotten.

Danny saw the sheriff was finished talking to the deputy. He glanced over, and Danny raised a hand. The sheriff frowned, turned to say something to the deputy, then walked over to the yellow tape.

"Well, you do get around. I'll give you that much."

"One of your deputies told me you had a warrant out for DeWayne Jackson on a homicide."

"Uh-huh. Picked him up about five minutes ago. Couple of my deputies stopped him out on the highway, driving his grandma home from church. They're bringin' him in right now."

Danny glanced over toward the body on the ground. "You think he did that?"

"I got some questions for him, let's put it that way." The sheriff studied him for a moment. "Funny thing, I was just gettin' ready to send one of my boys after you, too."

"After *me?*"

"Uh-huh." The sheriff reached into the top pocket of his uniform, slid out a crumpled business card, handed it to Danny. "That's Sam Price's boy lyin' on the ground over there. And I found this on the body."

Danny glanced at the card. *Daniel Chaisson, Attorney at Law.* He turned it over, glanced at the back. Nothing.

He looked up at the sheriff. "He had this in his pocket?"

"Uh-huh." The sheriff reached down, lifted the yellow tape. "Come on over here. I want you to see what happens, you go messin' around in something you don't understand."

Danny hesitated, then ducked under the tape. They walked over to where the boy lay on the ground, and the sheriff nodded to one of the deputies, who squatted down, raised the edge of the sheet for Danny to look.

Bobby Price lay on his back, one arm bent under him, his eyes open and staring. His face was covered with blood, and Danny could see that his scalp had been split open just above the hairline.

"Jesus," Danny whispered. "Is that what killed him?"

"Looks like it." The sheriff nodded, and the deputy let the sheet drop. "Have to wait for the autopsy to know for sure, but I'd say somebody cracked his skull open." He shook his head sadly. "Now I gotta go tell Sam Price his boy's dead."

Danny held up the business card. "Sheriff, he didn't get this from me."

"I heard you were over at the store yesterday, talkin' to him."

"Sure, I went to see him. But when I tried to give him a card, he wouldn't take it." Danny turned the card so that he was holding it carefully by the edges, passed it back to the sheriff. "If I were you, I'd see if I could lift some prints off that thing before too many people handle it."

The sheriff looked at the card, raised his eyebrows. "You hand out a lot of these things, last few days?"

"One to you, one to Etta Jackson, and one to the guy over in the body shop, Brewer."

"Etta Jackson, huh?" The sheriff smiled. "Well, I guess we know where this one come from." He slid the card back into his shirt pocket.

"You don't really think DeWayne Jackson killed that boy?"

"We got a witness saw them talking in the parking lot, right after the Winn-Dixie closed. Said they were arguing."

"That doesn't mean DeWayne killed him."

"No, but it puts them together just before he died, and the Jackson boy's been runnin' around town sayin' how he's gonna make them white boys pay for what they done to his granddaddy, so we know he's got motive."

"This witness who saw them together, he got a name?"

"Uh-huh. It was Randy Brewer. Denton Brewer's boy."

Danny stared at the sheriff. "You're not serious."

"Matter of fact, I am." He shrugged. "Not that it matters, really. We got a murder weapon. Tire iron." He turned, pointed toward some bushes about twenty yards away, close to the tree line. "One of my deputies found it right over there, blood all over it. It's over at my office now, getting dusted for prints. We get any, that should clarify things a bit. Meantime, I plan to get the Jackson boy in and ask him a few questions." He looked over at Danny. "We'll get around to talkin' about that card later."

Danny started to say something, then decided against it. He just nodded, walked back to the yellow tape, slipped under it, and got into his car. He sat there for a moment, thinking, then started the car, drove back to the sheriff's office. As he pulled into the lot, he saw the deputy who'd been at Etta Jackson's house getting out of his car.

"Well, sounds like they got him," he called out to Danny. "Stopped him on the highway going home. Had his grandma in the car with him and everything."

"So he's inside?"

"Probably upstairs in the jail by now. Unless they put him in somebody's office for questioning." The deputy glanced at his watch. "Any luck, I might still get home before midnight."

Danny followed him inside, saw Etta Jackson sitting on one of the hard plastic chairs near the reception desk, her bag on her lap, like she was waiting for a bus. Her eyes were tired, and she looked like she'd been crying.

Danny went over, sat down beside her. "Etta?"

She looked up at him, and Danny saw that it took her a moment to recognize him. She reached out, laid a hand on his arm, relief in her eyes. "Lord, I thought you was one 'a them, come out here to ask me some more questions."

"What's happening, Etta? Is DeWayne inside?"

"Uh-huh. They say he killed some white boy. Over on Twenty-first Street. I ask 'em, what's a white boy doin' on Twenty-first Street? That's the wrong side of the ditch. He go over there, he just lookin' for trouble. But my DeWayne, he ain't done nothin'."

"Wasn't DeWayne with you at the hospital?"

She shook her head. "He dropped me off. Said he had to go home, get some things at his mama's house. She's working nights over in Slidell, but he's got a key. He was gonna pick up some clean clothes, then come back and sleep at my house tonight. So I stayed up at the hospital with Caryl until he came back. Then he drove me over to church. We was there about an hour. Police stopped us on the way home." Her eyes began to fill. "I ain't had the heart to call his mama yet."

"You want me to?"

She shook her head. "Nah, I got to do it." She opened her bag, took out a neatly folded cotton handkerchief, wiped her mouth with it, like even the thought of making that call made her feel like she was chewing on hot coals.

"Etta, how long was DeWayne gone?"

"Couldn't 'a been more than an hour. He came back right when he said he was, had all them clean shirts in the backseat, too. But they wouldn't listen to me when I tried to tell 'em that. They must 'a been lookin' for his car, 'cause they stopped us a couple blocks from the church. Had their guns out. They made DeWayne get down with his face in the dirt so they could handcuff him. I tried to tell 'em, but they wouldn't listen." She looked Danny in the eye. "DeWayne wouldn't kill no white boy, Mr. Chaisson. And he don't know *nobody* over on Twenty-first Street."

Danny nodded, reached up to squeeze her hand. "Etta, listen to me. The first thing that's got to happen here is to get a lawyer in there with him, before they get him to say something he'll regret. You know any lawyers in town?"

She shook her head. "Just the ones been callin' me up since Caryl got hurt, askin' me do I want to sue somebody." She wiped at her eyes, looked up at Danny. "And you."

"I'm not a criminal lawyer, Etta. You need somebody in there who can look out for DeWayne." He glanced at his watch. "Let me make a couple calls. I know some criminal lawyers down in New Orleans. I'll see if I can get you a name."

He got up, went out to his car, and got his cell phone out of the Mustang's glove compartment. Then he took out his wallet and dug through it until he found a business card with several phone numbers scribbled on the back. He tried the first number, got an answering machine, hung up and tried the second. No answer. Wednesday night, getting up on eleven o'clock, there'd be a blues band warming up at Tug's Bar on Magazine Street, the crowd packed tight against the bar to open up a small dance floor in front of the low stage in the front room. But there would be one empty table that everybody knew better than to take, with a bottle of dark rum, a bowl of ice, a dish of limes, and a knife resting in the center. Sometime before midnight, Jabril Saunders would come in and stop to greet his cousin, who worked behind the bar, then walk back to his table. The crowd around it would draw back one step farther, waiting to see if that knife was for the limes, or was there gonna be trouble. Danny had sat at that table with Jabril many times in the last few years, watched him slice up those limes, drop a wedge into each glass of rum, and he knew there were men in that room who couldn't take their eyes off that knife, like rats hypnotized by a snake's slow swaying. But Jabril would simply slice up the limes with a few quick motions, drop them in the glasses before him, then stick the knife blade back into the table, sit back and listen to the band. This was Jabril's place, Danny had learned, and not simply by habit. He'd bought it almost ten years ago, although his name wasn't on any deed, and his cousin took home most of the profits. For Jabril, it was simply a place to drink a glass of rum, nod to the ladies, and listen to some fat and nasty New Orleans blues. And if he wanted to stick that knife in the tabletop when he was done with it, wasn't nobody's business but his.

Still early, Danny thought, glancing at his watch again. *But it's worth a try.*

He dialed the number, let the phone ring for a long time, until finally Tug got around to picking up. Danny could hear the music thumping in the background, people talking loud, like they'd been waiting a long time to feel this free.

"Jabril around?"

"Who wants to know?"

"Danny Chaisson."

Tug put the phone down on the bar, and Danny did his best not to think about all the drinks that had been spilled on that bar, what it would feel like to pick that phone up, put it against your ear. After a moment, he heard somebody pick it up, and there was a muffled scraping sound as the receiver was wiped off, then Jabril said, "What's up?"

"It's Danny. I'm lookin' for Greg Nowles. You know where I could find him, fast?"

Jabril gave a laugh. "Man, you spooky. He's right here. We was just talkin' about you, too."

"Could you put him on? I need the name of a good criminal lawyer up here on the North Shore."

"You in trouble, man?"

"No, but they just arrested DeWayne Jackson on a murder charge."

"That's the grandson?"

"Yeah, they found one of the white boys beaten to death in a black neighborhood. Sheriff seems to think DeWayne might have gone after him."

"Can't say I'm surprised. That boy had the fire behind his eyes."

"Sounds like he didn't do it."

"Yeah? Well, that wouldn't surprise me none, either."

Danny heard laughter in the background, then it ended abruptly. He could picture Jabril turning to glare at the people at the bar next to him, silencing them with a look.

"Hang on," Jabril said now. "I'll get my man Nowles, see what he can tell you."

Jabril set the phone down, and Danny heard the nearby conversations slowly resume. *Must have gone back to his table.* A moment later, somebody picked up the phone, and Danny heard Greg Nowles say, "I hear you lookin' for a *real* lawyer."

Gregory Nowles worked in the juvenile courts division of the New Orleans public defender's office, twelve lawyers working out of an office the size of a storage closet with one long counter, a single computer, and an endless supply of sullen, hopeless children who needed somebody to stand beside them when they faced the judge on charges that could get them sent up to the state penitentiary at Angola for twenty years to life. For most of the lawyers in the office, three years of this work could squeeze the hope out of your heart, send you running for private practice, but Greg Nowles had been doing it for almost twenty years. His hair and beard were flecked with gray, and on a bad day, his skin would slowly turn the color of ash, like a rock dropped in a fire. But he'd found that many of the boys he defended had come out of tough projects like Desire or St. Thomas never having *seen* a black man who carried a briefcase to work, so he stuck it out, doing his best in a hopeless job, like a man trying to hold back a rising tide.

Nowles listened as Danny explained the situation. When he'd finished, Nowles gave a sigh, said, "Yeah, you got a problem all right. This boy smart enough not to open his mouth till he talks to a lawyer?"

"Much as anyone, probably."

"That ain't much. He's innocent, like you say, he's gonna start tryin' to convince 'em they got the wrong guy, end up sayin' something they can use to put his ass away."

"That's why I called you. You know anybody up here would be able to help?"

"You someplace where I can call you back?"

"On my cell phone." Danny gave him the number. "The sheriff's still out at the crime scene, and he's the kind of guy gives the impression he's gonna want to be in the room when they start the interrogation."

"So we got a few minutes."

"If we're lucky."

Nowles gave a sour laugh. "You had any luck, my man, you wouldn't be callin' me now."

He hung up, and Danny looked out across the parking lot at the bugs beating against a streetlight. Somebody had kicked over a trash can behind the restaurant across the street, and a dog came by, stopped to sniff at the balls of crumpled aluminum foil before turning up his nose and trotting away. Danny made a mental note never to eat there. But then he'd learned that any place you could grab a meal around a courthouse was *always* bad, which only made sense, given that there was something unappetizing about what went on in such buildings.

He stood up, slipped the cell phone into his pocket, then locked the Mustang and went back into the sheriff's office. Etta was on a pay phone just inside the door, and he heard her say, "I don't *know* why they think he done it, baby. Don't look like they need no reason to me."

Jesus, Danny thought. *How do you tell your daughter that her baby's been arrested for murder?*

He'd grown up believing that some families have tragedy burning in their blood, like a ghost that haunts the birth room, waiting to brush his thumb across each child's forehead, leaving his mark. But maybe you have to grow up in a big house in the Garden District to believe in something as abstract as fate. If you're born poor and black in Louisiana, you don't need a fancy word to describe what's waiting for you up at the crossroads. Fate is what's written on your skin.

Danny sat down in one of the plastic chairs, leaned his head back against the wall, and closed his eyes. His mind drifted, and he found himself thinking about a small girl whose face was Mickie's, holding his hand as they waited for a school bus to come and take her away. *Daddy,* she was asking him, *what's a lawyer do?*

His phone rang. He took it out, pressed the button, said, "Yes?"

"That you, Danny?" Nowles had found a quieter place from which to call. *Probably went back in the storeroom,* Danny thought, *like Jabril does when he wants to make a private call.* The heavy wooden door pulled shut, cork on the walls so you could hear while the band was playing. Cases of whiskey and beer stacked up on the floor, the only place to sit. Danny could see it, could almost smell it.

"Yeah, what you got for me?"

"This boy who's been arrested, he's related to the man who got attacked in the cemetery up there, right?"

"Grandson. They'll probably use that to suggest motive. Why?"

"I made a couple calls to some people I know up there, but nobody wants to touch this case. They heard what I was talking about, they all backed off real quick. Like something's got 'em spooked."

Danny sat back slowly. Behind the reception desk, the deputy turned a page in her newspaper, folded it back. "They give you any idea what?"

"Could be local politics, they don't want to make any enemies up at the courthouse. But most of these guys have handled tough cases in the past, so I'm guessing it's professional."

"What's that mean?"

"Could be they invested in the project. Developers go into a town like that, they like to line up local support. One of the first things they might do is toss a few shares to the local professionals, let 'em feel they got a stake in the deal going forward." Nowles hesitated, then said, "I also heard Lee Fuller's interested in the case. That could have something to do with it."

"You mean they're *scared* of him?"

"He leaves some pretty big footprints. There's a couple lawyers around the state who'd tell you the guy won't hesitate to steal a client if he thinks it'll get him on TV. I guess it's no fun doing all the pretrial work only to have Lee Fuller show up a few days before the case goes to trial and talk your client into changing counsel."

Danny rubbed at his eyes. "Jesus, that's great. So this kid's gotta sit up here in an interrogation cell without counsel just because Lee Fuller's come down here and pissed on all the trees?"

"Have you tried calling him?"

"Lee Fuller's a fraud. That whole Klan Watch is just a fund-raising operation with a couple lawyers attached for credibility. You subscribe to *Mother Jones*, he'll send you an appeal for emergency funds every couple weeks. They got the highest overhead of any organization I've seen, something like eighty cents on the dollar, just to do more fund-raising. It's nothing but a pyramid scheme for liberals."

"He was a good lawyer once."

"That won't help DeWayne Jackson. He needs somebody who'll put on a defense, not a news conference."

Nowles sighed. "I'm just saying you might not have a choice here, Danny."

"That seem right to you?"

He laughed. "Man, you talkin' to the wrong guy. I've seen *way* too much to be surprised by this shit. Try spending a couple days in juvenile court. I've seen defense lawyers sleeping through trials. Tell me those kids wouldn't be happy to have Lee Fuller givin' a news conference out on the courthouse steps. I been doin' this almost twenty years now, and I got no problem with Lee Fuller. He wants to put on a show, raise some money, that gets people to pay attention. Took us a hundred years to get the Voting Rights Act. Maybe a guy like Fuller can help us get a hate-crimes law sometime before the end of the century."

"It doesn't bother you that he's a white guy making money off this?"

"Hell, no. White people figure out they can make money helpin' blacks, we *might* get some justice."

Danny couldn't help smiling. "Sounds like you got this all worked out."

"You damn right. I'm gonna sell stock, hold an IPO. Wouldn't want you folks to miss out on an opportunity."

Danny dug out a pen and one of his business cards. "You got a number where I could reach Fuller this time of night?"

"I talked to him a couple minutes ago. He's already on his way." There was a silence. "You disagree?"

"Might help to talk to the family first."

"They're not buying a car, Danny. They need a lawyer tonight, and Fuller's ready to go. I see this guy on *Larry King,* man. He's got a busy schedule. But he's on his way down there. You really gonna tell these people to say no?"

Danny thought about the apprehension in Helen's face when she mentioned Fuller's interest in the case. Then he looked over at Etta Jackson on the pay phone, trying to explain to her daughter how her son was being held on murder charges. "You got any idea when he might get here?"

"He's driving down from Baton Rouge. Figure two hours."

"All right," Danny said. "I'll let 'em know he's coming."

He hung up, went over to Etta, and touched her arm gently. She looked up at him, said, "Hang on," and put her hand over the phone's mouthpiece.

"Lee Fuller's coming down from Baton Rouge to talk to DeWayne. He's the lawyer who came to see you a couple days ago about a civil suit."

"I know who he is," Etta said. "Can he get my grandson out of jail?"

"I hope so. But the main thing right now is to let the sheriff know you've retained an attorney. Since he's a minor, that constitutes a request for counsel, so they can't question him until his lawyer's present."

Etta nodded, turned back to the phone. "We got a lawyer, baby. You get on over here. We'll make sure they treat him right."

She hung up, and Danny led her over to the deputy behind the reception desk. She looked up at them. "Yeah?"

"Mrs. Jackson has retained a lawyer for her grandson."

"Okay." She went back to her newspaper.

Danny reached out, pushed the paper down. "We're requesting presence of counsel during any questioning. You don't take that seriously, we'll slap you with a civil rights lawsuit, and any charges you try to file against the boy are gonna end in a mistrial. So I suggest you let your people know that nobody better try to question him until his lawyer arrives. You understand?"

The deputy jerked her paper away from Danny. "You his lawyer?"

"No. He's on his way."

"I don't care if he's flying in from Washington. You're not the boy's lawyer, then back off."

Danny started to say something, but he felt Etta take his arm, pull him away. "You told them 'bout the lawyer," she said. "Now, don't make 'em angry."

"I'm just trying to protect DeWayne's rights."

She nodded. "I understand, but that's my grandson they got in there. And one thing I learned, sixty-four years livin' 'round here, you don't go tellin' the sheriff 'bout your *rights*, he's got some poor black boy in his cells. We got a lawyer comin'. They know that. So now there's nothin' we can do but sit down and wait for him to get here."

Danny looked at her, then nodded. "You're right. I'm sorry. It's not even my case."

"Don't be sorry. I appreciate what you tryin' to do." She sat down on one of the hard plastic chairs, patted the chair beside her. "Not really sure *why* you doin' it, since you ain't gettin' paid, but I guess that's your business, huh?"

He sat down, leaned his head back against the wall behind them, the tired-ness hitting him now. "I'm getting paid," he told her. "Just not for this." And the thought of Helen trying to explain to Michael Tournier how Lee Fuller ended up representing DeWayne Jackson made him wince slightly. Is that why he'd been so reluctant to get Fuller involved, not wanting to face Helen's anger? Or had he begun to think of it as *his* case and Etta's family as his clients? Either way, it seemed clear to him that he should back away now that Fuller was coming onto the scene. If the case ended up in civil court, as Helen feared, then Fuller might have good reason to question Danny's mo-tives for getting this involved. Good intentions, Danny knew, were a tough sell in a courtroom. Better to walk away, let Fuller handle it, and hope none of this came back to haunt him.

Etta reached over, tapped the cell phone still in his hand. "Your wife got one of those?"

"Yeah, in her car."

"Why don't you give her a call. Tell her there's a key on a nail by the back porch, she wants to wait in the house."

He nodded, stood up, and went out into the parking lot. The bugs were still throwing themselves against the streetlight, and the moon was a cold, dead rock hanging in the sky. He leaned against the hood of the Mustang, di-aled Mickie's cell phone. She picked up on the first ring, said—

"Vega."

"I love that. Your cop voice."

"You gonna make me arrest you again?"

"Nah, you make the cuffs too tight. Took me three days to get the feeling back in my hands."

There was a pause, and he heard her shut the door of her Jeep. It was a habit she'd picked up on stakeout. People don't realize how their voices travel when they talk on their cell phones, so get in your car, close the door, roll up your windows. Play the radio if you want to drown out your words. When she'd called him at his office with the results of her pregnancy test, he'd heard Stevie Ray Vaughan in the background, doing "Little Wing."

"So what's up," she asked now.

"They've picked up DeWayne. The boy who's dead was Bobby Price, one of the four teenagers they suspect in the attack on Caryl Jackson."

"That's bad."

"He had one of my business cards in his pocket."

"*Jesus*, Danny! Did you know him?"

"I talked to him this afternoon, over at the grocery store where he worked."

"So are they calling you a suspect?"

"No, it looks like the sheriff's got his heart set on DeWayne. Apparently, they've got some kids from up at the high school who say he's made threats against those boys."

"And they think this boy got killed tonight?"

"Couple hours ago."

"So that rules out DeWayne. He was with Etta up at the hospital tonight, right?"

"He dropped her off, went home to get some clothes."

"Shit." Mickie was silent for a moment. "You don't think he did it, do you?"

"No, I don't. That card they found on the boy? I tried to give him one, but he wouldn't take it. Somebody else left it on him."

"You tell the sheriff that?"

"I tried. He wasn't interested. I'm guessing he sees arresting DeWayne as the answer to his problems on this case."

"Why? Because he's black?"

Danny hesitated. "I'm not sure it's that simple. I mean, on one level, yeah, it's because he's black. But talking to this guy, I get the impression he's always thinking about his next election. He didn't want to arrest those white boys because they come from prominent families. Who's Caryl Jackson compared to some white lawyer who could destroy his chances for reelection? Now he's got a case his voters can get behind. You've got an angry black kid and a dead white boy. That's the kind of case that he can run on."

"Jesus," Mickie said, disgusted. "So you lock up enough black men, you don't have to think about what you've done to them."

Danny said nothing.

"They get a lawyer?"

"Lee Fuller's coming," Danny said. "Should be here in a couple hours."

Mickie gave a low whistle. "You set that up?"

"I called Greg Nowles, and Nowles called him. Wouldn't be my first choice, if that's what you mean. But Nowles was okay with it, and he's a better judge of this stuff than I am."

"Might make your situation tougher."

"Only if I get between him and a TV camera." Danny glanced at his watch. "You've been out there awhile. You doing okay?"

"It's just like working a stakeout, only I don't have to listen to some guy talk about his vacation plans." She gave a laugh. "I've been making lists of baby names."

"Come up with anything?"

"That you'd like?"

"I'm not that tough."

"Yeah, right. Tell me one name you've liked."

Danny thought for a moment. "Sophie. We both liked that."

"And for a boy?"

She had him there. Danny had decided there *were* no good boy's names, at least not in America. They all either made him think of insurance salesmen or reminded him of boys he'd known in high school with acne and gym bags that smelled like three-month-old socks. And you couldn't get fancy with a boy's name, give him some lovely foreign name, or he'd end up getting beat up every day at recess. Danny wanted his child to have a name you could imagine on a book cover, not below a mug shot, but he didn't want to condemn the poor kid to a life of abuse from the other boys by naming him something that could be followed only by *and I'll be your waiter today.*

"How about Napoleon?"

"He'd have to marry a girl named Brandi."

"You're right," Danny said. "I'm not sure I could live with that on my conscience."

"And don't just say Spike, like last time. I'm waiting for a serious contribution from you."

"I like Spike. A kid named Spike is never gonna get picked last for basketball."

"That's your standard for a good boy's name?"

"Damn right. And if we name the boy Spike, then his little sister will have somebody to protect her when we call her Arugula."

She laughed. "This is a Greek tragedy in the making."

"Shoot high. That's what I always say."

"Uh-huh. That's why you never hit anything."

They were silent for a moment, then Danny said, "There's not much point in your sitting there all night. The sheriff's probably gonna have some of his people out there with a search warrant in the next couple hours. Why don't you go on home, get some sleep?"

"Nice try," she said. "But I'm staying right here with you until this thing's settled."

"Lee Fuller gets into it, we could be looking at next year before this thing comes to trial. He's big on motions to delay. Lets him give more news conferences."

"You really think it'll go to court?"

"Depends what the sheriff comes up with. But Fuller will go after a civil suit. That's his specialty." Danny leaned forward, rubbed at a spot on the Mustang's hood. "I guess I'll have to call Tournier tomorrow, let him know what to expect." He saw headlights coming toward him, watched a patrol car turn into the parking lot. "Looks like the sheriff's here."

"You gotta go?"

"Yeah, I want to let him know that DeWayne's got a lawyer before they start asking him questions." He stood up, walked back toward the door. "Why don't you get us a room. I'll meet you at the motel."

"Sounds romantic."

"Wish it could be, but I better hang out here until Fuller shows up. You get some rest."

"I'm fine. I've just been sitting here looking at the stars. I can see why people like it out here."

"Well, don't get too attached. I'm a city boy."

She laughed. "Tell me about it. I'll see you out at the motel, city boy."

He hung up, watched the sheriff get out of his patrol car and walk over toward the entrance. When he saw Danny, he sighed, shook his head. "Don't you ever sleep, son?"

"DeWayne Jackson's family have retained Lee Fuller to represent him, Sheriff. Since he's a juvenile, they've requested that his attorney be present during any questioning."

"They have, huh? I guess you been busy."

"You know who Lee Fuller is, Sheriff?"

"I've heard the name."

"Then you know he's gonna be watching to make sure you do this by the book. And he's got good connections in the media. Any mistakes, you could end up looking like Jim Clark."

The sheriff frowned. "Who?"

"Jim Clark. He's in all the history books."

"Well, it's been a while since I had time to read any history books. Maybe you better fill me in."

"He was sheriff in Selma in 1965. The guy who went after Martin Luther King with bullwhips and attack dogs."

The sheriff stared at him. "Boy, you don't let it rest, do you?" He pushed past Danny toward the door. Then he turned, his hand resting on the door handle, looked back at Danny. "You figure this whole thing's just a bunch 'a crackers pickin' on the black folks, don't you?"

"I think you moved pretty fast when it came to arresting DeWayne Jackson, but I've been here three days and I haven't seen you make any arrests for the attack on his grandfather."

"Like I told you, I don't have enough evidence." The sheriff smiled. "But if you think your boy DeWayne's just a victim in this thing, you *might* want to know that I got a call from my crime-scene people just a couple minutes ago tellin' me they lifted his prints off that tire iron we found up at the murder scene. Nice clear set. And we got a blood-type match to Bobby Price. Couple weeks, we can probably get a DNA match, which means we got the weapon in that boy's hand and Bobby Price's blood all over it. So you go tell Lee Fuller he can come on down here and defend that boy if he wants, but

I ain't seen a jury yet wouldn't convict him on that kind of evidence. That ain't racism, Mr. Chaisson. It's justice."

He swung the door open, left Danny standing there. Behind him, he could hear the faint crackle as one of the bugs got itself caught in the street-lamp, dying in all that light.

NINE

"Well, looks like we got a nice mess here, don't we?" Lee Fuller flipped through the file on DeWayne Jackson's arrest, then tossed it on the table. "And for a guy who doesn't represent any of the central parties, you've managed to leave your fingerprints all over everything."

Fuller was a slim man in a neatly tailored Italian silk suit and loafers. He wore his gray hair pulled back into a tight ponytail as if in a last small gesture toward his days as a student radical. Danny found the effect disconcerting. Seen from behind, he looked like an ex-hippie, but when he came at you head-on, he could have been any corporate litigator, his eyes alert for any sign that he might cut you from the herd. Talking to him was like flipping a coin. You never knew which side might come up.

"My client wanted to make sure Caryl Jackson and his family were treated fairly," Danny told him. "He's never met them, and he had nothing to do with the dispute over the land—except to withdraw his plans to build when he learned about the burial site—but he felt it was important to demonstrate his sympathy with the concerns of the local black community."

Fuller raised his eyebrows, amused. "Well, that was white of him." He waved a hand toward the file. "I suppose it's got nothing to do with the fact that he's the deep pockets in this case."

Danny shrugged. "He's aware that he might get drawn into a lawsuit, sure. And if Caryl Jackson's family decides to go that way, he knows that he's the obvious place for them to look for a settlement. We're confident we could win that case in court, given his actions before the attack on Caryl Jackson, but that's not the reason he sent me up here." He spread his hands, met Fuller's gaze. "Look, we both know that doing the right thing never kept anyone from getting sued. He just wants to be able to face himself in the mirror without feeling that he's the kind of person who'd look the other way in a situation like this to save a few dollars."

You're talking in paragraphs, he caught himself thinking. *That's always a bad sign. Makes you sound like a lawyer.*

Through the window, Danny could see Mickie drinking her morning tea in a lawn chair next to the motel pool. She'd given up coffee when she learned she was pregnant, switched over to herbal tea, which she carried around in her bag. The morning air was still cool, and he could see steam rising from her cup as she raised it to her mouth. She had a newspaper spread out across the table. When a breeze came up, she'd lean forward to rest her elbows on the page, hunching her shoulders so she could keep reading an article that had caught her eye, the whole thing unconscious, just a problem solved. If he left the room now and went around through the passage with the vending machines, he could sneak up on her through the grass, surprise her with a light kiss on the back of her bare neck, just brush his lips across the skin there so it sent a shiver up her back. She'd only be pretending to be surprised, of course, as she would pretend not to see where their child was hiding in a few years. If Danny watched closely as he crept up on her, he might see the moment when she heard him coming, her shoulders stiffening slightly, then relaxing as she identified the sound, no threat, only her husband coming to surprise her with a kiss.

But Fuller was saying something now, giving Danny that look he recognized, like he'd been holding back for the last two hours but couldn't keep himself from asking the question any longer—

"You used to work for Jimmy Boudrieux, right?"

Danny looked over at him. "That a problem for you?"

Fuller shrugged. "I liked Jimmy well enough. He was corrupt, but then most politicians in this state would have trouble standing up to an FBI investigation, especially the ones who've been around for a while."

Danny said nothing. He figured if Fuller was fishing for something, he'd get around to saying it before too long.

And, sure enough, a moment later, Fuller got up, went over to his jacket hanging on a chair, dug around in the pocket like he was looking for something. "Lucy, you remember where I put that fax?"

His assistant, a young black woman with a law degree from Duke and a father who'd recently been appointed to the federal bench in Georgia, got up from where she was working on her laptop, went over to the closet, and got a paper out of Fuller's garment bag. She smiled at Danny as she handed it to him, then went back to her laptop.

"I asked some people I know about you," Fuller told him, coming back to his chair with the paper in his hand. "Got all kinds of funny answers."

"I'm not surprised."

Fuller raised his eyebrows. "Guy I know over at the U.S. Attorney's office called you a hero. You a hero, Danny?"

"I look like a hero to you?"

"I'm still making up my mind about that." Fuller smiled. "But just to give you the range of opinion, I talked to a guy up the statehouse, said he wouldn't scrape you off his shoes."

Danny had to laugh. "That's great. I have to remember to tell my wife that one. She'll love it."

Fuller considered him for a moment, then slowly crumpled up the paper, leaned forward, and tossed it into the trash can next to the desk.

Two points, Danny thought, *no rim.*

"I get strong feelings about people." Fuller sat back, slipped his shoes off, and rubbed his feet across the carpet a few times. "Sometimes I regret them."

"If it makes you feel any better, I've got my doubts about you, too."

Fuller smiled. "That's probably wise. I'm a lawyer." He reached over, picked up the file on DeWayne Jackson again, opened it. "Well, now that we've established a firm sense of mutual distrust, let's think about what we can do to help this kid."

"You talk to the sheriff yet?"

"Last night. Looks like the cat that caught the mouse."

"He tell you they have DeWayne's fingerprints on the murder weapon?"

Fuller smiled. "What they've *got* is a bloody tire iron with some prints on it. You ever watch somebody try to fingerprint a tire iron? It's too small a surface to lift a complete print. Turns out they got one partial, seven points. The rest are smeared." He glanced up at Danny. "You were with the D.A.'s office in New Orleans, right? Before you got into politics?"

Danny nodded. "Three years."

"So you've done some criminal work."

"Yeah, but it's been a while."

"You ever come across a fingerprint technician who'd feel comfortable going into court with a seven-point match?"

"Depends on how unusual the points are, I guess."

"Have to be pretty damn unusual or it wouldn't come up as a match on the FBI computers. Hell, there are countries where the law says you need a twenty-four-point match or you can't use the print."

Danny shrugged. "All they have to do is convince a jury. Most jurors don't understand all that stuff anyway. You get the right people in the box, they'll believe whatever the prosecutor tells 'em. That's my experience, anyway."

"Then you were up against idiots." Fuller shook his head. "You get a decent lawyer on cross, you can make those fingerprints look like something a kid drew on his math book to piss off the teacher."

"So you're saying they don't have anything on DeWayne?"

"Oh, they got plenty, if they know how to use it. Sheriff impounded the car and they found a jack in the trunk, but no handle. You put that with the print on the tire iron and his anger about his grandfather, starts to look like you've got motive and means." He flipped through the papers. "Also, they got a witness saw him talking to the victim a couple hours before he turned up dead."

"Randy Brewer."

Fuller looked up at Danny. "That important?"

"He's one of the boys involved in the attack. His father runs the body shop out on the highway. DeWayne told me the local Klan meets out there."

Fuller made a note in the file. "Interesting. So we can bury their witness if it ever gets to court."

"You put in a request to look at the car?"

"Not yet." He glanced at his watch. "I doubt I'll get to it today. I'm supposed to talk to the Jackson kid in forty minutes, then I've got to get back up to Baton Rouge for a hearing."

"You mind if I go take a look?"

Fuller shook his head. "Just let me know if you touch anything. I'm planning to have it dusted for prints." He scribbled another note in the file.

"I'd like to talk to DeWayne, too."

Fuller looked up at Danny. "You planning to try this case, or you gonna let me carry some of it?"

"Just want to make sure he's all right."

Fuller considered him for a moment. "He's my client, Danny."

"That's right, but I can't help feeling responsible for his being up there in the jail now. I'm the guy who came in here and got everybody stirred up."

"Careful, that's how I got started." Fuller laid his pad on the table, tossed his pen on top of it, and stood up. He went over to the desk, lifted his jacket off the back of the chair, and slipped it on, taking a moment in front of the mirror to make sure it was lying right. "Okay, c'mon. You can talk to him when I'm done."

DEWAYNE sat in a tiny interview room two floors above the sheriff's office, wearing a pair of orange jail overalls a couple sizes too big for him. He slumped in his chair, arms tight to his body, like he was afraid somebody might come at him any moment. Danny had seen that look before. Young men got it their first night in jail.

"You okay?" Danny asked him, pulling out a chair. "They treating you okay?"

DeWayne kept his eyes fixed on the table in front of him. "It's a jail. People shouting all night. But they feedin' me, so my mama's happy."

Danny sat down, waited until DeWayne looked up at him, met his gaze. "I wouldn't say she's *happy*. Her son's been arrested for murder. She's worried."

"You know what I mean, man. First thing she asked me, were they feeding me. Shit, I only been here a couple hours." He reached out, ran one finger along a deep scratch in the table. "I told her she could stop worrying, 'cause I heard they gave you pancakes for breakfast up at Angola."

Danny looked around the room. Green plaster walls and a one-way mirror next to the door so the deputies could stand in the hallway, keep an eye on the prisoner while he talked with his lawyer. There was an intercom also, though they weren't supposed to listen. Courts took the attorney-client privilege *very* seriously. But Fuller had made a point of checking the intercom before he went into the room, as if he'd run into police departments that had trouble remembering this little detail.

"What'd you think about your lawyer? You guys have a good talk?"

DeWayne shrugged. "He's okay. And that woman he brought in here with him is too fine."

"She's one of the lawyers who work with him. Her father's a federal judge."

"I don't care who she is. She's still too fine."

Danny leaned forward, rested his arms on the table. "They tell you about the tire iron?"

"I don't know nothing 'bout that shit." DeWayne flicked one finger against the scratch on the table, like he was brushing something away. "I didn't kill nobody."

Funny, Danny thought, *how just putting somebody in this room makes them sound guilty. Even when you want to believe them.*

"They got a witness who saw you talking to Bobby Price yesterday."

DeWayne shrugged. "So what? Sure, I went over there to the store and talked to him. Tried to, anyway. I known Bobby since we was kids. He wasn't like those other guys. So I wanted him to look me in the eyes, tell me he wasn't there when my granddaddy got hurt." He looked up at Danny, his eyes angry. "He couldn't do it. Kept walkin' away from me, like *he* was all mad at *me*. But I didn't do *nothin'* to him. Just left him standin' there, stampin' that tuna fish with that fuckin' little gun of his." He shook his head. "Shit, if I was gonna go after one 'a those boys, it'd be Brewer. He's the one always talkin' that white-power trash in the hall at school."

"Can you see how a jury might have trouble seeing the distinction there?"

DeWayne settled back in his chair, let his eyes wander away. "Don't matter anyway. I'm here 'cause it's *easy,* you know what I mean?"

Danny shook his head. "How's it easy?"

"Easy to say I'm goin' after those boys. Easy to send a black man up to Angola." He rubbed at the table some more, like something he felt there was bothering him and it was important to smooth it out. "Jury'll probably see it that way, too. Then it don't matter *what* I say, I'm gone." He said it calmly, like it wasn't his problem. Something his lawyer would have to worry about or he'd lose his case.

"How did Bobby Price look when you talked to him? He seem scared?"

DeWayne shrugged. "Yeah, sure. He first saw me, I thought he was gonna take off running."

"So you figure he was scared of you."

"Hey, I'd be lyin' if I said I didn't *want* him to be scared. Shit, let him know what it's like."

Danny nodded. "You wanted him to know how your grandfather felt."

"Nah, man. My granddaddy, he wasn't scared of *nothin'*. Why you think he went out there?" DeWayne looked up at Danny. "But I been scared. I ain't afraid to say it. Drive through this town on a Friday night, all them white boys are out, lookin' to pick a fight. They see you, they'll come after you. Jump in their cars and follow you home sometimes. Catch up to you out there in your driveway, ask you how come your mama so ugly. Shit like that." He shook his head angrily. "You can walk in your house, but then you a pussy, and they come after you at school. And you can't stand up, 'cause it ain't never just one of 'em. So you just stay scared. That's how I wanted Bobby to feel, man."

Danny was silent for a moment. "And what happened when you talked to him?"

"He still looked scared, but it wasn't like he thought I was gonna jump on him. He kept lookin' around, you know? Like he's out with some real ugly girl and he's all worried that his friends are gonna see."

"You think that's what he was scared of? That somebody would see him talking to you?"

"Just tellin' you how it felt."

Danny caught a slight movement out of the corner of his eye, glanced over at the mirror. DeWayne grinned.

"You saw it too, huh? They think you can't see 'em out there, but there's like a shadow when they go past. Your boy Fuller kept jumping up every time it happened, runnin' out there to make sure they weren't listening."

Danny pushed back his chair, stood up. "I'm going out to your grand-mother's house this afternoon. Anything you want me to tell her?"

Something seemed to give way in DeWayne, and he slumped back in his chair. "Tell her I'm okay," he said quietly. "Tell her she don't need to worry."

Danny looked at him, but DeWayne wouldn't meet his eyes. "I'll tell her," Danny said. "Hang in there. We'll do everything we can to get you out of here."

DeWayne kept his eyes on the floor. "Yeah. No problem."

Danny waited for him to say something more, but his eyes became dis-tant, as if his mind had wandered off to some island where the sun gleamed on a bright sea. Danny turned, left the room.

"I'm done," he told the sheriff's deputy waiting outside the door. The deputy just smiled.

Danny went downstairs, waited outside the sheriff's office until a meet-ing broke up, and caught him in the hallway on his way to the men's room. "I want to take a look at DeWayne Jackson's car."

The sheriff looked at him blankly; then, without a word, he pushed open the door to the men's room, went inside. Danny stood in the hall, waiting. When the sheriff came out, he raised one hand to stop Danny before he could say a word.

"Go talk to my secretary. She'll set it up."

Then he pushed past Danny, disappeared back into his office.

Like he doesn't have time for this shit, Danny thought, staring after him. *He's got more important things to worry about.*

TEN

As he turned onto the gravel driveway, Danny caught a glimpse of Anna Graf's beat-up Subaru parked in the trees a short distance from Etta Jackson's house. He could see her moving among the graves, like a woman planting flowers in a garden. As he drove past, she straightened, watched him go by. He raised a hand to her, continued up the gravel driveway to the house. But when he got out of the Mustang, he saw her coming toward him, wiping her hands on a rag that she dug out of the back pocket of her jeans.

"How's DeWayne," she called when she got close enough for him to hear. He started to answer, then glanced up at the house and thought better of it. Instead, he walked down the gravel driveway to meet her at the edge of the pasture.

"They're planning to charge him with murder," he told her. "He's trying not to act scared, but you can see it in his eyes."

She looked away, back toward the trees. "Do they have a case?"

"I don't think he did it, if that's what you mean."

She nodded. "You got a minute? There's something I think you should see."

He followed her back into the trees, where she'd begun to dig along one edge of the cemetery. She had dug a shallow trench along an outer edge of the grid, like she was dipping a toe into the water. The trench ended abruptly in a small circle of stakes, a plastic sheet on the ground beside it with some tools spread out on it.

"You've made progress," Danny said.

She shook her head. "I was still doing the preliminary survey. Finding the edge of the burial site so I could take samples from different sections of the grid."

He looked over at her. "You sound like you've changed your mind."

"I found something I wasn't expecting."

She led him around to the other side of the grid, next to the shallow trench. Danny could see now that it was about six inches deep. A small gardening spade lay at the edge of the weeds. He figured that was what she'd used, taking her time, working carefully in case she hit something.

She went over to the small circle of stakes, crouched down, and pointed to something in the dirt where the trench ended. "I thought I'd just misjudged the edge of the site. We're outside the main burial area here. But I've come across some bone fragments."

Danny went over, looked down at where she was pointing. At first he didn't see anything except dirt. Then he saw that there was something different about the texture in one spot, realized that he was looking at a piece of dirty canvas with something white sticking out of one end. He felt something rise in his throat, swallowed it back.

"Is that a bone?"

She nodded. "I hit it with the spade. You can see where I cut through the canvas." She looked up at her grid. "I should've started out by the rocks."

"Can't you just cover it back up, dig around it?"

She looked up at him, squinting slightly against the afternoon sun. "No, you don't understand. That's not the problem." She took a pencil from her pocket, reached down, and used it to lift the edge of the canvas back slightly. Danny saw that the bone was part of a lower arm, covered with a bit of rotting fabric. Then, as Anna moved to her left to keep from blocking the sun, he saw something glint in the dirt. With her left hand, she reached over, picked up her spade, and used the tip to clear some of the dirt away carefully.

Danny saw that it was a cheap wristwatch wrapped loosely around the skeleton's wrist. Anna straightened up, tossed her shovel to one side, and wiped the sweat from her forehead with the back of her wrist. Then she looked over at him.

"This body's not as old as the others."

"WELL, I gotta hand it to you, boy. You sure got a way of keepin' me busy."

The sheriff crouched down, used the tip of a cheap plastic pen to lift the bit of rotting canvas, looked at the watch on the skeleton's wrist. Then he straightened up, rubbed at the back of his neck slowly for a minute.

"Okay, I guess I better go call Judge Walcott, get an exhumation order." He looked over at Danny, smiled. "Looks like we're gonna have to dig this place up after all."

"What do you mean?"

The sheriff waved a hand toward the rest of the graves. "Might have more bodies buried out here. Only way to tell is to dig 'em all up."

Danny saw Anna look over at him, alarmed. "Is that really necessary?"

The sheriff shrugged. "This is a crime scene now. We're not talkin' about history anymore."

Danny felt a wave of anger sweep over him. "It was a crime scene before, Sheriff. But I haven't seen you take any action on that case."

"Yeah, I figured you'd say that." The sheriff took off his hat, pulled a handkerchief out of his pocket, and wiped at his brow. "I guess you don't like how I've handled this case, and you ain't the only one. But the thing you people keep forgetting is I got to play by the rules. I want a search warrant, I gotta go before a judge, show him there's a reasonable expectation that a search is gonna turn up evidence. I want to make an arrest, I better be able to show there was something behind it." He folded the handkerchief carefully, shoved it back into his pocket. "Now, I know you think I been draggin' my heels on that other case, but the fact is, I just don't have the evidence." He nodded toward the trench. "This here's a different situation. All we know for sure is we got some bone fragments and a wristwatch, but that's enough to convince a judge. Beyond that, I don't *know* what I got until I start diggin'. So dig's what I'm gonna do." He looked up at Anna. "And if that messes up all your nice work, I'm sorry, but that's the way it's gonna have to be." Then he grinned. "Hell, we find anything that looks like history, we sure will let you know."

THREE hours later, Danny stood with Anna on the porch of Etta Jackson's house, watching as two sheriff's deputies unloaded a backhoe from a trailer. After a moment, Anna turned away.

"I can't watch," she said. "Tell me when it's over."

Danny felt the same way. One of the deputies looked over and waved, like a neighbor getting ready to go work in his field.

Then a thought struck Danny. He turned to Anna. "Is there somebody up at your office who can look at the bodies when they've finished digging them up?"

"Sure. We've got a couple of forensic anthropologists." She smiled thinly. "I was figuring I had a few days before we'd need to get one of them down here."

"Might be a good idea to make that call. It could make it easier for us to argue that they should be reinterred, once the sheriff finishes his investigation."

Anna nodded. "I'll go see who's available." She went over to the door, knocked, and spoke quietly to Etta, who pushed the screen door open, stood back to let her pass. Danny stood watching the deputies for a few more minutes, then went over to the door, tapped on it.

Etta came out of the darkness, said, "You folks thirsty? I got some lem-onade."

Danny smiled, shook his head. "Thanks. It's not bad out here." He waited until Etta pushed the door open, then said, "Has anybody been interested in that piece of land before?"

"What? The burying ground?" Etta looked out at the sheriff's deputies, shook her head. "Not 'less you count comin' out here to kick them gravestones over. We get that every couple years. Whenever the white folks feel like they got somethin' to be mad about."

"So people around here have known about the graves for a while?"

"When they get to thinkin' about it, sure." Etta smiled. "Seems like they forget sometimes, and there's other times they remember. White folks can be like that."

Anna came out of the back, said, "Okay, they're going to send somebody down tomorrow afternoon." She looked over at Danny. "We might need a court order to get a look at the remains, if the sheriff tries to get them all classified as crime-scene evidence."

He nodded. "I'll ask Fuller if he wants to make an application. He might not want to let this get mixed up with DeWayne's case. If that's how he feels, I can always file it on behalf of the landowner."

Anna met his eyes. "And your client will be okay with that?"

"From what he says, he wants to handle things as cleanly as possible, so nobody can accuse him of bad faith. I'll have to check it with him, of course, but I'm guessing he'll authorize it."

Anna looked out at where the deputies were unloading the backhoe. They'd gotten it off the trailer, and as she watched, one of them started it up and drove it slowly up into the trees.

"Might be a good time to make that call," she said. "They start digging away with that thing, they're gonna have a nice pile of dirt and bones inside an hour."

It took a few calls, but Danny finally caught Helen as she came out of a meeting, got her to set up a conference call with Tournier. He listened as

Danny explained the situation, then said, "Helen, you got any objection to this?"

"What's your sense of our exposure on a civil suit?" she asked Danny.

"Hard to say," he told her. "The whole thing's gotten all tangled up in a couple possible criminal cases. The sheriff still hasn't filed any charge for the assault on Caryl Jackson, but he claims he's still investigating. Then there's DeWayne's case. And now they got another body up there, which could lead to a whole separate investigation. We could be looking at a couple years before they get all the criminal charges sorted out."

There was a pause, then Tournier said, "Any chance they're connected?"

"No way to know until they identify this new body." Danny hesitated. "Your company bought the land, what? Five years ago?"

"Not quite. Be five years in October."

"Well, based on what I saw, I'd guess this body's been in the ground a lot longer than five years."

"So it's like when those shrimpers drug up a body out in the bayou last year," Tournier said. "Ruined their nets, and I guess they lost most of a day answering questions down at the sheriff's office, but that was as far as it went."

"Yeah, except it's still your land," Danny told him. "Look, in a way, you're lucky. If you hadn't stopped construction on this project last month, it might've been one of your bulldozers that dug up this body. Then you'd really have a mess on your hands."

"Only then we would've hit all the other graves, too." Tournier gave a dry laugh. "You want to imagine what I'd be payin' in construction delays right now?"

Danny didn't answer. After a moment, Helen said, "Go ahead and put the papers through, Danny. All we're asking is that the State Historical Commission get a chance to examine the bodies. That seems like a reasonable request, given that our interest lies in clarifying the legal status of this land."

"Can I make another suggestion?"

"Go ahead."

"I'd consider unloading the land, quickly. Things are getting messy here. I'd give it to the local black community, set up a trust through one of the churches. Then release a statement saying you're simply recognizing their historical claim to the property."

"We'll give that some thought," Helen said. "There are some legal issues that still need to be resolved."

Danny hung up, stood looking at a photograph that hung on the wall above the phone: Etta and Caryl Jackson with their grandchildren. They'd had it taken a few years ago, when DeWayne was just a ten-year-old kid in a Chicago Bulls jersey, grinning at the camera like he'd just hit a three-pointer on the buzzer to win the game. Caryl had his arm draped across DeWayne's shoulders, was gazing down at the boy affectionately.

"Looks like they had a special relationship," Danny said to Etta as she made her way toward him down the hall.

She stopped, looked at the photograph. "Caryl and DeWayne?" She sighed, shook her head. "Like havin' *two* kids in the house, you get 'em together. They was always up to some kind 'a mischief."

Danny followed her out into the kitchen. Anna was sitting at the table, a cup of coffee in front of her. In the distance, Danny could hear the backhoe's engine, straining as the bucket dug into the ground.

"They're all out there now," Anna told him. "Looks like most of the sheriff's people, plus a couple guys from the parish medical examiner's office."

Danny went over to the screen door, looked out. "What's the flatbed for?"

"I don't want to think about it." Anna shook her head. "They've stretched plastic sheets across it. I'm afraid that's where they're planning to sort out the remains."

"Jesus." Danny turned away from the door. "They might as well toss 'em all in a bag, shake it out when they get back to the office."

"I've seen that. Last year I got called down to Plaquemines Parish, they had a bag of bones lying on a guy's desk. He hands it to me, says, 'Thought you might want to take a look at these.'"

"What did you say?"

"I asked him to call me *before* he dug them up next time."

Danny went over to the table, sat down opposite her. "Didn't do much good this time."

"No, but we tried." She raised her coffee cup to sip at it, then set it down and said, "I don't usually spend this much time dealing with the local sheriff. Most of the time, all they want to know is are the bones over fifty years old. They must have a rule somewhere. Fifty years ago is history. Anything under that is a crime."

He nodded. "Be nice if it was always that clear."

BY the end of the day, Danny learned later, they had dug up twenty-two bodies, laid them out on the flatbed, and rolled them in heavy sheets of plastic for the trip back to the morgue. Bones wrapped in rotten canvas.

"Feed sacks," Anna told him. "That's all they had to bury their dead in."

Only one body appeared to be recent, based on the remains of the clothing and some recent dental work. When pressed by the sheriff, the local coroner estimated that the woman had been in the ground for fifteen or twenty years, but as he admitted to Danny in the days to come, it wasn't the condition of the body that led him to that conclusion but the clothes. Nylon shirt, imitation-leather skirt. Cheap wristwatch. Big shoes.

"Looked like the kind of thing girls wore to a disco in the late seventies." The coroner glanced over at the bones laid out on his autopsy table. "Otherwise, you could have looked at her, figured she'd been out there since the slave days. There's a lot of groundwater around here. Takes the flesh off the bones pretty quick. They hadn't buried her in her clothes, we'd be stuck."

That evening the sheriff pulled some old missing-persons files, went through them looking for young girls who had vanished wearing clothes that matched those they'd found on the body. But as Danny learned, it didn't take the black community long to get word of what had been dug up, and they didn't have to go through any files to come up with a name.

"I heard they found Shonya out there," an old woman who called during dinner said to Etta Jackson. "Dug her up in the shirt her mama bought her."

"I guess you know more than I do, then," Etta told her. "All I know is they was out here diggin'."

"Yeah, I heard it was Shonya. Girl got herself killed, messin' with them white boys."

"What did she mean by that?" Danny asked when Etta told him what the woman had said. "We're talking twenty years ago, right?"

Etta looked at him. "Twenty years ain't long when you my age. We had white boys twenty years ago, same as now." She smiled, turned away. "They just a little bigger now is all."

"SHE didn't tell you nothin' about this Shonya?" Jabril sat in a deck chair next to the motel pool, watching as Mickie took a seat on the diving board, trailed one foot through the cool water. "She just some black girl who disappeared?"

"I got the impression this was something people got used to staying quiet about."

"Nah, they talk about it. Just not to white folks."

"That's what I figured."

Jabril smiled. "You want me to go ask around, see what I can find out?"

"Couldn't hurt."

"Yeah, it could. Could hurt a lot. But somebody got to do it."

Danny was silent for a moment. "You think they'll talk to you?"

"I guess I'll see." Jabril stood up, brushed the front of his jacket to get it to lie straight. "But they'll talk to me a damn sight quicker than they'll talk to you."

He walked away, but paused as Anna Graf came out of the motel restaurant carrying four paper cups in a cardboard tray. Danny watched Jabril exchange a few words with her, then he reached out, took one of the cups from the tray, and carried it away with him toward the parking lot.

Anna came over, set the tray down on the table.

"He likes you," Danny told her.

She looked up at him, surprised. "Who? Jabril?"

"Uh-huh."

"I just met him a few minutes ago." She gestured back toward the parking lot. "And then I gave him some coffee, that's all."

"What did he say when you gave it to him?"

"He said, 'Thanks. Looks great.' That's it."

"And he took the coffee out to his car."

"Yeah."

Danny smiled. "Jabril *never* allows any food or drinks in his car. It's like an operating room in there."

"I guess he changed his mind." She took a cup out, offered it to Danny. "Black with sugar?"

"That's me." Danny took the cup from her, peeled the lid off it to let it cool a little. "If Jabril wanted coffee, he would have stayed here to drink it. He was letting you know he appreciated your going for it."

She raised her eyebrows. "No big deal." She took another cup out of the tray, took it over to Mickie. "I'm afraid the only herb tea they had was chamomile. I hope that's okay."

"Perfect." Mickie took the cup, removed the lid, and set it on the diving board next to her. "Danny's right. He likes you."

"Okay, stop it. Both of you." Anna laughed, shook her head. She came back to the table, took her coffee, and sat down. "Now I won't be able to look the man in the eye."

"There's other places to look." Mickie smiled. "That's what I hear, anyway."

Anna looked over at Danny. "Sounds like you'd better keep an eye on her."

"Keep her on that herb tea, I got nothing to worry about." Danny smiled. "But if she catches a whiff of this coffee, we're both gonna be in trouble."

Mickie shot him a look. "I can smell it from here."

In the afternoon, Danny drove out to the tiny Baptist church that Etta Jackson and her family had attended for almost twenty years. It was a small woodframe building set back slightly off the state highway, a mile up the road from Etta Jackson's house, with a gravel parking lot and a sign out front that said:

Salvation Baptist Church.
God's knocking on your door.
When will you answer?

Danny spent half an hour talking to the minister, a heavyset black man with mournful eyes who confirmed that Etta and DeWayne had stopped by for an hour the night of Bobby Price's murder. He had prayed with Etta while DeWayne sat in the back row with his eyes closed, like he was sleeping.

"Anything strike you as unusual about his behavior?" Danny asked him.

"You mean did he seem like a boy who'd just killed somebody?" The minister shook his head slowly. "He looked like he wished he was someplace else. But that's how all these boys act. Like they're scared you'll catch 'em carin' about something."

Danny considered asking the minister how he'd feel about his church taking on the gravesite as a trust if Tournier made the decision to return it to the community, then decided he'd better wait until he spoke to Helen, found out if she saw any liability issues around such a move. So he simply thanked the minister for his time and assured him that they were doing their best to get DeWayne Jackson home to his family.

The minister nodded, shook Danny's hand. "Jail ain't no place for a boy. Bad enough that family's got Caryl lyin' up in the hospital. We're prayin' they'll all get home real soon."

Danny drove over to the jail, looked in on DeWayne. Fuller had stopped by in the morning, then rushed off again to Baton Rouge for a press conference on a hate-crimes bill that had just been killed by the state legislature. DeWayne looked tired, and when he spoke, his voice was barely more than a whisper. He kept his eyes fixed on the table, answered most of Danny's questions with a shrug.

Like he's given up, Danny thought. *Just wants to lay his head down on the table, go to sleep.*

When their forty minutes were up, Danny watched the guard lead DeWayne away, then got up from the table slowly and walked out through the crowded hall to the parking lot. Jabril was sitting on the hood of Danny's Mustang, waiting for him.

"You feel like takin' a ride?"

"Where?"

Jabril got down off the car. "Talk to Shonya Carter's parents."

Danny paused next to the car, ran his hand across the hood. Not a ripple. "That's the girl who went missing?"

"You want to call it that, yeah. Sounds like there's a little more to the story, you talk to the people who knew her."

Danny unlocked the Mustang, tossed his briefcase onto the floor of the backseat, then stripped off his jacket, threw it in after. "Okay, let's go."

They took Jabril's Lexus, drove north out of town until they hit the drainage ditch, crossed over. For a moment Danny thought they were headed for the corner where they'd found Bobby Price's body. But Jabril made a quick right, headed down a street of small wood-frame houses, slowing as he glanced at the numbers next to the doors. Then he sped up again. "Next block," he said. They drove on, past an empty elementary school with plywood nailed across the windows, and then Jabril pulled over onto the gravel shoulder in front of a house that looked to Danny like it hadn't been painted in forty years.

"All these houses are on rental subsidy," Jabril told him, waving an arm toward the other houses along the street. "I heard the guy who owns 'em is a cousin of the sheriff."

Danny had seen a lot of poor neighborhoods—crime-ridden housing projects in New Orleans, farmworkers up in the Delta who still lived in old sharecropper's shacks—but this one looked like something out of a Walker Evans photograph from the Great Depression. A sagging porch ran across the front of the house. A beat-up sofa missing its cushions stood beside the door; next to it was a refrigerator lying on its side, which somebody had turned into a workbench.

"The old man's on disability," Jabril said. "Used to work on the city's road-maintenance crew before he retired. His wife worked in the cafeteria over at the elementary school until they closed it."

Danny nodded. He got out, followed Jabril up the gravel driveway to where three concrete blocks had been laid on end to make steps up to the porch. A cat slept in the shade next to the refrigerator. He raised his head, then stood up and walked carefully away, disappearing around the edge of the house.

Jabril climbed the steps and knocked on the screen door. There was movement somewhere back in the darkness of the house, and then an old woman in a housedress emerged out of the shadows. Danny guessed that she was in her seventies; at first glance, she looked small and frail. Then you saw her eyes. She peered at Jabril, then past him at Danny. "What you want?"

Jabril gave her his easiest smile. "It's Jabril Saunders, Mrs. Carter. We talked on the phone before?"

She studied him for a moment, then her eyes flicked back to Danny. "You didn't say you was bringin' no friend."

"No, you're right. I didn't say nothing about that." Jabril turned, took Danny's arm, and drew him forward until he was right up close to the door. "This is Danny Chaisson. He's been out at Etta Jackson's house the last couple days, lookin' out for her since Caryl's in the hospital." He let go of Danny's arm, spread his hands. "You want, go call her. She tell you."

The woman seemed to consider this briefly. Then she shrugged, said, "I heard his name." She reached out, flipped the latch on the screen door. "C'mon in, if you want. I got some iced tea on the windowsill, might cool you down some."

Then she turned, vanished into the darkness. Jabril glanced back at Danny, then opened the door, went inside.

They sat at the kitchen table, drinking sweet iced tea from plastic glasses. She had set the pitcher in the middle of the table, and a bowl of sugar cubes. Then she poured four glasses, dropped a cube of sugar in each. She handed one to Danny, slid one across the table to Jabril, then turned and called back through the house, "Ervin, there's tea here, you want some."

A man came shuffling out of the hallway, carrying a screwdriver and what looked to Danny like a blade off a lawn mower. He nodded at them, then laid his tools down on the counter, paused at the sink to wash his hands, and came over to the table.

"You're the lawyer," he said to Danny. "Been out by Etta's house."

Danny nodded. "I appreciate your taking the time to talk to me."

Ervin Carter sipped at his tea, then reached across the table, took another sugar cube from the bowl, dropped it into his glass. "You here about Shonya?"

"Yes, sir. If you feel up to talking about her."

The old man shrugged. "Been a lot of years now. Talkin' ain't gonna bring her back, but it don't hurt me none anymore."

His wife went over to the counter, tore some paper towels off a roll, and brought them back to the table. She folded each into a neat square, handed them around. Danny hesitated, watched Ervin slip it under his glass to soak up the ring of water where the glass was sweating. He lifted his glass, slid it under.

"It true they found her?" Ervin looked off toward the sunlight beyond the screen door. "Man called me up from the newspaper this morning, asked me did I know they dug up a body out at the old burying field. Said it could be Shonya." His eyes came back, settled on Danny's face. "Asked how I *felt* about them diggin' up my daughter. I told him she's buried there, they should leave her alone. Can't do nothin' for her now, and at least she's with her own people." Then he looked down at the table, shook his head. "I don't know if that's Shonya they found up there. All I know is I ain't seen my little girl since those white boys started messin' around up here twenty years ago."

Danny leaned forward. "Can you tell me what happened, Mr. Carter?"

Ervin had a piece of the paper towel between his fingers, folding and unfolding it. His eyes stayed fixed on that process, like it was important that he get it just right. "She went to a dance, up here at the community center on Twenty-first Street. Never came home."

"And you reported it to the police?"

"Called the sheriff." Ervin looked up at Danny. "Not this one, but the sheriff before him."

"What did he do?"

He shrugged. "Told me she prob'ly run off with her boyfriend. Said she'd show up in a couple months after he run off, left her with a baby. I tried to tell him Shonya, she wasn't like that. Sang in the choir over at Glory Tabernacle. Wanted to be a teacher, that girl."

"Did he take a report?"

"He wrote it all down, if that's what you mean. But he said there wasn't no point in doin' nothin' until she'd been gone a couple weeks."

Danny took his small spiral pad out of his pocket and made a note. "Did you go back?"

"Uh-huh. Twice. He asked us if we heard from her."

Danny looked up at him. "So you stopped going."

"Yeah. Couple years ago, we tried to get her picture on a milk carton, like you see on TV? But they said she'd been missing too long."

"She'd be all grown up now," the old woman said. "Thirty-seven this year. We'd have grandchildren now."

"So the sheriff didn't even investigate?"

Ervin shook his head. "Sent some of his deputies out to the high school, talk to some of the girls she knew. Mostly they just asked if she had any boyfriends. Did she like to go into the city. Questions like that."

"Nothing about the night she disappeared?"

Ervin crumpled up his napkin, tossed it on the table, then shoved his glass away angrily. "Nah, they didn't ask *none* 'a that. I had to go talk to them girls myself."

Danny looked at him. "What girls?"

"She went with a couple other girls. They saw her leave." He was silent, his eyes wandering away toward the screen door, then continued, "It was only four blocks. She walked it every day." Then his throat seemed to tighten, and Danny saw that his eyes were suddenly full of tears. "And that's when them white boys got her."

"What white boys, Mr. Carter? Do you know their names?"

But the old man shook his head, and Danny saw that he was crying now. His wife stood up, came around the table, and laid a hand on her husband's forehead, like she was trying to wipe something away.

"You want to hear about it, go talk to Rhonda Pritchett," she said to Jabril. Her eyes avoided Danny's. "She was there. Lives up two blocks, next to the gas station."

Then she leaned down, pressed her cheek against the top of her husband's head.

"Go ask Rhonda," she whispered. "She knows."

RHONDA Pritchett lived in a one-bedroom apartment on the first floor of an unpainted concrete building on Twenty-first Street. The front door was closed, and an air conditioner dripped steadily from a window next to the door. Jabril knocked, motioned for Danny to keep back, so she wouldn't feel them both pressing in close to the door like a couple of guys trying to bring her to Jesus.

A woman opened the door—late thirties, Danny figured—and looked out at Jabril through the screen, a baby perched on her hip. "Yeah? What you want?"

Jabril gave her his lazy smile. "Mama, you should know better than to ask a man that, he come knockin' on your door."

Okay, Danny thought, *so she won't think we'll be bringin' her to Jesus.*

She studied Jabril, then looked beyond him to where Danny stood beside the car. Then her eyes came back to Jabril, and she said, "You boys gonna tell me what you sellin', or I gotta guess?"

Jabril grinned. "Ain't sellin' a thing right now. But if I was, I'd sure come see you first."

She shifted the baby from one hip to the other and leaned against the door, her free hand coming up to rest on it, like she was getting ready to swing it shut in his face. And then Danny saw her give a smile. "Damn, you got the moves, huh?"

Jabril laughed, spread his hands wide. "Yeah, you right. I got *all* the moves. And you ain't seen but my *outside* moves yet."

"That don't mean I'm gonna let you come in."

"I ain't heard nobody ask you."

"Look like you fixin' to."

"Yeah." Jabril grinned. "I guess that could happen. One 'a these days, anyway." He turned, waved a hand toward Danny. "My friend, he's a lawyer. Been out at Etta Jackson's house, tryin' to help them out. We just been over talkin' to Shonya Carter's folks. They said maybe you could tell us what happened to her, night she disappeared." He looked up at her, rubbed at his jaw. "That right?"

"It true they found her?"

"Can't say yet. They found somebody. Could be Shonya."

Rhonda glanced over at Danny. "You cops?"

Jabril gave a laugh. "Nah, we ain't cops. Like I said, he's a lawyer. I'm just helpin' out."

"So how come you doin' all the talkin'?"

"'Cause I'm the one got somethin' to say."

She looked off toward the trees beyond the road. "Can't nobody help Shonya now. All you gonna do by askin' about it is stir up trouble."

He nodded to the baby on her hip. "That's a pretty child. Yours?"

She shook her head. "This my daughter's boy. She's workin'."

Jabril looked surprised. "Wait, that's your *grand*baby?"

"Uh-huh."

"Fine-lookin' woman like you got a *grand*child?"

She laughed. "Yeah, I see you got them inside moves, too."

"Damn right." He reached out, touched the screen gently, and Danny saw the baby smile. "Sure is a sweet-lookin' child." Then his eyes came up to Rhonda's face. "Carters, they got a picture of Shonya on their wall from when *she* was a baby."

The smile faded from Rhonda's face. "You ain't got to tell me that. I known Shonya since we was kids."

Jabril nodded. "Then I guess you know how they feel, somebody dug up their baby girl."

For a moment Rhonda was silent, and Danny half expected her to reach up, shut the door in Jabril's face. But instead she shifted the baby to her other hip, flipped the latch on the screen door, and said—

"I guess y'all better come on in."

THEY sat on her sofa, watching her give the baby a juice bottle. Danny saw that the kid kept looking over at Jabril, both hands wrapped around that bottle, like he had a question he wanted to ask if he ever got a free moment.

"I wasn't really friends with Shonya," Rhonda Pritchett was telling Jabril. "I just saw her at school, you know?"

Jabril nodded, then his eyes drifted back to the baby, got real wide for a moment, and Danny heard the baby giggle, watched him let go of the bottle with one hand, wave it frantically in Jabril's direction.

"Shonya, she was a *good* girl," Rhonda went on, then smiled. "Not like me. Sunday morning, you'd see her walkin' to church. And after school she'd walk on home, didn't hang out like the rest of us. Always had her homework, you know? We'd all ask her could we copy it, every morning."

"She have a boyfriend?"

Rhonda looked over at Danny. "That's what the sheriffs kept askin'. Only thing they wanted to know 'bout." She shook her head. "Shonya, she wasn't like that. She'd get real *quiet* when the boys come 'round. And she filled out real nice that year. Lots 'a them boys comin' 'round."

"But she wasn't interested?"

Rhonda smiled. "That girl had all the equipment, but she didn't know what to do with it. Like her head didn't have no idea what her body was sellin'."

Danny took out his pad and made a note. "You told the sheriff that?"

"Uh-huh. Didn't seem like they believed a black girl could be like that. Innocent, you know? They figure we all got babies by fifteen up here." She bounced the baby on her lap. "My daughter, she's twenty-two, works over at H&R Block doing taxes."

Danny nodded. Jabril was rocking back and forth slowly, watching the baby's eyes follow him.

"Tell me about the night she disappeared," Danny said.

Rhonda lifted the baby up, sniffed at his diaper, then settled him back on her lap. "Ain't much to tell. They was havin' a dance over at the community center Friday night. Bunch of us girls went out to the parking lot behind the gym to smoke, talk about boys, like we always did."

"Was Shonya part of that group?"

She shook her head. "Nah. She was still inside. Didn't even dance much. Just sat over on the side, by the wall, watchin'."

"So what happened?"

"Some white boys in a pickup truck started drivin' by, yellin' things at us."

Danny made a note. "Was that unusual?"

"Nah, used to happen all the time. Like them white boys, they just couldn't make up they minds. One minute it's 'C'mon over here, baby,' and then the next it's 'Get your nigger ass back to Africa.'" She shrugged. "That's how it was that night, only these boys, they kept on comin' round, like they wasn't gonna be satisfied just yellin' stuff."

"But Shonya wasn't out there."

"Shonya didn't go out in no parkin' lot. That was just for girls were fixed on messin' up their lives, like me." She shifted the baby on her lap. "Shonya didn't even know them boys was around, or she wouldn't never walked home. They came 'round again, after she set off, only there was some boys out there with us then, had some liquor in 'em, and I guess them white boys knew better than to mess with us. So they drove on down the road, same way Shonya set off."

"And you told the sheriff all this?"

"Yeah, but they say it didn't mean nothin'. Like I told you, they didn't want to hear nothin' 'bout no white boys. Just kept askin' did she have a *boyfriend*. Like all they wanted to know was how she got wild, run off somewhere."

Danny was silent for a moment, then he leaned forward, said quietly, "These white boys who kept coming 'round, you know their names?"

She ran one finger gently across the back of the baby's hand where he gripped the bottle. "They still around town, that's what you mean." She looked up at Danny. "Only they ain't boys no more."

And that was all she would say. As they got up to leave, she glanced over at Jabril, still making faces at the baby, said, "I know where you can get you one 'a these."

He smiled at her. "That right? Maybe I'll come by one night, let you show me where that is."

"I'll be here."

When they got out to the car, Danny looked over at Jabril, said, "How do you *do* that?"

"Do what?"

"You know what I'm talkin' about."

Jabril smiled, reached down to start the car. "Ain't just a bear knows where to find honey."

ELEVEN

Denton Brewer sat in his pickup truck outside Bahama Joe's, across from the beach in Bay St. Louis, Mississippi, watching as a silver BMW turned off the highway, slowing to a crawl as it pulled into the gravel parking lot. Ninety miles from New Orleans, most of it red clay and scrub pine, and this guy shows up in a car that looks like it's just been washed, got one of those little headsets hooked up to his car phone so he can keep on cutting deals while he drives out here. Brewer watched the BMW swing past him, taking its sweet time, then pull into a spot, Jesus, way off by the restaurant's sign, like he's scared some guy in a Bronco is gonna come along, chip his paint when he opens his door.

Brewer got out of his truck, walked over to the BMW. Michael Tournier sat behind the wheel, his eyes fixed on the bright glitter of the gulf across the highway. His hands rested on the steering wheel, the headset dangling from the rearview mirror now, like he'd glanced out there as he got ready to climb out of the car and gotten lost in all that sunlight. Brewer rapped on the window with one knuckle, laughed when Tournier jumped, looked up at him like he was afraid somebody was about to steal his pretty car.

"Wake up!" Brewer grinned. "Time for school!"

Tournier gave a sigh, got out. "You been waiting long?"

"Couple minutes. Saw you drive in."

Tournier glanced over at the water one last time, then said, "All right. Let's get this over with."

Brewer followed him across the parking lot into the restaurant. Tournier paused in the entrance, looking around the empty restaurant, then led Brewer over to a table by the window, away from the crowd of senior citizens working their way through the late-lunch special. Tournier sat down, picked up the napkin on the table, then tossed it aside. "Coffee," he told the waitress when she came by. He looked at Brewer. "You want anything?"

"You buyin'?" Brewer reached over and slid the menu out of the waitress's hands. "Give me a couple minutes, okay?"

Tournier waited until the waitress walked away, then leaned across the table, grabbed the menu out of Brewer's hands, dropped it onto the table. "We're not here to have lunch."

"Hey, I'm hungry."

"Eat on your own time." Tournier looked out the window toward the water. "You talk to Sam?"

Brewer picked up the menu. "I left a couple messages. Hasn't called me back yet."

"He been to his office?"

"Nah, just sits up in his house with the shades drawn. Like if he sits there long enough, his boy'll come on home."

Tournier nodded. "Be a good idea to talk to him before he gets to thinkin' on it too deeply."

"His kid's dead. I guess he's gonna think about it."

Just like that, Tournier thought, watching Brewer look down at the menu. *His kid's dead. Like it's just something that happened.*

Brewer tossed the menu aside. "Think I'll have the fried-shrimp special. They can't fuck that up too bad." He raised a hand to wave the waitress over, and Tournier saw that he had flecks of dark blue paint under his fingernails.

Body work, Tournier thought. *You run into something, he'll straighten it out for you, cover it all up.*

The waitress came over, and Brewer said, "Honey, I gotta ask you something. What the hell is popcorn shrimp?"

"It's fried shrimp."

"But you also got fried shrimp." He opened the menu. "Says so right here. 'Lunch Special, Fried Shrimp, $6.99.'"

"That's right."

He looked up at her, raised his eyebrows. "So what's the difference?"

"Popcorn shrimp are smaller. They're the baby shrimp."

"Fuck that." Brewer thrust the menu at her. "Bring me them big ones." He grinned at Tournier. "Who says size don't matter?"

Tournier leaned forward. "Listen to me. This is important. You've got to talk to Sam or this whole thing could come down around us."

Brewer shrugged. "I've tried. He doesn't want to talk. Maybe after the funeral."

"Try harder. You know how Sam gets."

Brewer shot him a look. "Better than you, I guess."

"Then you don't need me to tell you how this could end up."

"Nah, I don't need you tellin' me. I'm there. I'm on the ground, where it's hot. Where're you? Sitting up in your expensive office, trying to cover your ass."

"I'm just doing what I have to do, same as you."

"That include sendin' that lawyer up there, go around getting the niggers all fired up?"

Tournier was silent, looking out at the ocean. Then he said quietly, "You start talking like that, I'm leaving."

Brewer sat back, grinned at him. "That's right. You don't like that kind 'a talk. Never did, as I recall."

"I'm not like you." Tournier leaned back, let his eyes return to Brewer's face. "I had any choice in the matter, I wouldn't be here now."

Brewer gave a laugh. "Hell, you had any choice in the matter, you'd ship my ass up to Angola on a charge of being a white man." He rested his elbows on the table. "Only I'd take you with me. Shit, I can fix it so we'd be cell mates. Bet you'd like that a whole bunch, huh?"

Tournier said nothing, looked away.

Brewer shrugged, reached back to rub at his neck lazily. "There's no statute of limitations on murder, boy. That's how they play the game."

"It was an accident."

"Tell that to a nigger jury. They went after Byron de la Beckwith, they're gonna love comin' after us. Won't matter to nobody how that girl got there. Only thing they'll care about is puttin' somebody's ass in prison. And you can cry all you want about how you love the niggers, all they're gonna see is a couple white boys." Brewer smiled. "And I'll be sittin' there right next to you the whole time. So they know what good buddies we always been."

It was something that Michael Tournier still couldn't explain. For six months, near the end of his senior year in high school, he'd become friends with Denton Brewer. They had hung out together, drunk their share of beer, gone riding in Brewer's pickup truck when they got bored—out past the fast-food restaurants on the highway, over to the old ski-boat landing back in the trees along the river, and up into the colored section of town when they needed a place to buy beer. Some nights they'd make the long drive into New Orleans, go to the bars in Fat City, where the secretaries and college girls might let them buy a round of drinks, pretending for a few minutes not to notice just how young these boys really were. They shot pool at a strip club at the corner of Causeway Boulevard and Veterans Highway, watched the middle-aged strippers go through the motions, and felt older somehow when it didn't excite them.

Most nights Sam Price had come along, and another boy named Kenny Doyle, who had joined the navy and died in a helicopter crash a year later. Just four guys out looking for trouble because they figured that's what it would take to make them men. For Sam Price and Michael Tournier, it was easy to think of these months as a kind of Indian summer, the shattered edge of childhood, which they couldn't help running a finger along to see how deep it could cut. Both knew they were leaving in a few months for college, out of this town, out of this life. They avoided each other's eyes, as if that knowledge were somehow shameful. They knew better than to mention it around Brewer. His laughter had a bitter sound, like a finger bent back, the bone snapping. It made them feel like tourists, made them want to say something hard and mean, as if that could turn the laughter's edge away. Brewer drove. He kept the radio under his tight control, punching up Charlie Daniels, Lynyrd Skynyrd, .38 Special, anything that sounded like heat on a highway and white boys burning gas. They went where he took them, drank the beer he bought with his fake I.D., followed him into redneck bars where the band played behind chicken wire and fights broke out over the pool tables every night. Sometimes there were girls, but mostly it was just the four of them, leaving rubber on the road.

And then one night it all changed. They had spent the night sitting in the back of Brewer's truck out on the river landing, drinking beer and shooting at the empties with a .22 Ruger revolver that Brewer kept under the seat. When they ran out of beer, they drove out to a Quick Stop on the highway, but the old man behind the counter took one look at Brewer's I.D. and laughed.

"Nice try." He tossed the card back across the counter. "You actually pay somebody for that?"

Tournier could see that Brewer was angry when he came back to the truck, climbed behind the wheel, jammed the key into the ignition. "Man, I fucking hate that guy. You see the way he threw it back at me?" He shook his head in disgust. "Now we gotta go up to Niggertown."

They drove up to Twenty-first Street in silence. When they crossed the bridge, Brewer reached over, rolled up his window. Tournier glanced over at him, surprised.

"You ever notice the smell up here?" Brewer looked over at him, made a face. "It's like they don't pick up the garbage."

That's 'cause they don't, Tournier thought. Legally, the land north of the bridge was an unincorporated township, which received no city services. Private garbage collection, private water and electric. But if you worked in town, they still collected your taxes. He had learned that when his father was negotiating to build a sewage-treatment plant and had trouble convincing the parish council that they couldn't just put it up on Twenty-first Street without annexing the property and extending city services to the surrounding neighborhoods. He'd come home every evening and complain to his wife over dinner about the council's foot dragging. When they finally acted, it was to relocate the project to a site near the river, preferring to negotiate with the EPA than to take on the expense of so many new citizens.

Tournier didn't say any of this to Brewer, just watched as he rolled up his window, reached down to flip through the radio again. "Fuckers always play the same stupid songs. I ever get rich, I'm gonna buy me a radio station, play nothing but Marshall Tucker Band all night long."

They pulled into the gravel lot in front of a market. Brewer pulled out his wallet and slid out the I.D., tossed it over to Tournier. "You go buy it. I hate goin' in these places."

Tournier looked at the photograph on the I.D. "They're not gonna sell it to me. I don't look anything like you."

"C'mon. When was the last time you saw anybody check an I.D., this part of town. Why you think we come up here? Just flash it at 'em when you put the money on the counter. That's all they care about."

Reluctantly, Tournier got out of the car, went into the store. He nodded to the old black man behind the counter, got two eight-packs of Miller ponies out of the cooler, and carried them up front. He laid the I.D. and a twenty-dollar bill on the counter, then went over to the snack-food display, grabbed a bag of Doritos, and brought it up to the counter, like he'd just thought of it. The old man looked at the beer on the counter, the money and I.D. lying next to it, then out at Brewer's pickup truck in the parking lot.

"Tell you what," he said, in a voice that sounded to Tournier like a chain saw biting into hardwood, "I'm not even gonna look at that I.D. you laid down, 'cause I *know* you ain't no eighteen." He turned his eyes toward the pickup truck beyond the front window. "And you can tell your friend in the truck that he don't have to keep comin' 'round here. I don't need his business."

Tournier stared at him for a moment, then picked up the money and the

I.D. and walked out. When he got in the truck, Brewer said, "He wouldn't sell it to you?"

"No." Tournier handed him the I.D. "And he told me to tell you not to come back. He doesn't want you in his store."

"Wait, he doesn't want *me*?"

"That's what he said."

Brewer looked up at the front window of the store, the old man watching them from behind the counter. "Son of a *bitch*!" He reached down, started to open his door.

Tournier reached out, caught his arm. "C'mon, man. It's not worth it. We'll go someplace else."

Brewer shook off his hand, pushed the door open, and started to get out. Inside, the old man reached under the counter, took out a sawed-off shotgun, and laid it on the counter. Then he smiled.

Brewer stopped, one hand still resting on the door. He stood there for a long moment, staring at the old man, then slowly got back in the truck. "I guess we ain't shoppin' here."

Six months later, the store burned to the ground during the night, but by that time Tournier was away at school, and if he thought of Brewer when he heard the news, he quickly drove the thought from his mind: that night contained other horrors for him, scenes he'd done his best to forget, and Denton Brewer's grinning face rose up before him from that darkness, lit by a more terrible kind of fire.

They had driven back toward town, none of them saying anything. Brewer even reached down to shut off the radio, so all they heard was the sound of the wind blowing in through the open windows. Tournier started thinking about calling it a night, getting Brewer to drop him back at his house, where his dad would be working late in his study, the radio playing quietly on a classical music station, and his mom would be upstairs reading in bed. Nothing special, nothing he hadn't seen a thousand times, but there it was, waiting for him, and suddenly all he wanted was to walk in the kitchen door, steal a mint from the cabinet over the stove to cover the beer on his breath, and head upstairs to bed.

But Brewer was smiling, turning the truck into a gas station and swinging through the parking lot so that they were headed back up Twenty-first Street.

Tournier looked over at him. "What's up?"

"I just remembered someplace where we can have some fun."

They drove back up Twenty-first, crossed the bridge, then made a right on one of the smaller streets. Up ahead, Tournier saw a bunch of cars parked along the edge of the road, some black kids hanging around, talking.

"They havin' a dance up here at the community center," Brewer said, slowing the truck down. "Doin' that jungle boogie."

Tournier got a sinking feeling in his stomach, caught Sam Price glancing over at him. "You know what?" he told Brewer. "I'm gettin' tired. And this shit ain't my scene."

Brewer shot him a look. "This ain't your *scene?*" Then he shook his head. "Man, that's the saddest thing I ever heard. That old man made you look like a fool. I thought you might want some payback. But that ain't your *scene.*" He glanced over at Doyle, grinned. "Hell, I like a little pussy as much as the next guy. Just not in my truck."

"Look, I don't want to go messin' with these kids for no reason."

"Uh-huh, I got it. That ain't your scene." He grinned at Doyle again. "Must be some kind 'a *special* scene, 'cause he ain't never showed it to us, huh?"

Doyle shrugged. "He just wants to go home. Had enough fun for one night."

Brewer raised his eyebrows at Tournier. "That right? You want to go home? That where you got your special *scene?*"

"That's not what I'm saying."

"I *know* what you're sayin'." Brewer gave him a cold look. "I'm all the scene you got. You wouldn't have no damn scene, wasn't for me."

Tournier gave up, looked out the window. Brewer gave the truck a little gas, and they cruised past the line of parked cars, a couple black girls glancing up at them as they went past. Tournier avoided their eyes, but Brewer leaned across him, called out the open window—

"Hey, girls! Who wants to come for a ride?"

The girls stiffened like they'd caught sight of something disgusting.

Then they moved back off the road, getting the row of parked cars between them and the truck. Brewer laughed, sped up, and took a right at the corner. Tournier thought maybe he'd had enough, just making those girls draw back like that, fear in their eyes. But at the end of the block, Brewer made another quick right, and Tournier realized he was going around the block to take another run at them.

That's when I should have gotten out of the truck. No, before that. Back when he first turned around. Tournier had thought this many times in the years that followed, a sudden knowledge that came on him like a pain in the heart, causing him to wince slightly in the middle of a business meeting or a dinner party, so that everybody stopped talking for a moment, wondering if it was something they'd said. Memory like a knife blade, which could make him double over in pain if it came on him in the shower. *You were scared. That's why you didn't get out of the truck. Scared to be a white boy on Twenty-first Street at night, scared to be what Brewer was making those girls.* He'd convinced himself it was only that, a fear of being lost in a strange part of town, not some more profound weakness, a fear that even if he got home safely, this part of his life would be over and he would be faced with the future he'd spent so long waiting to see. In a couple months, he'd leave this town. Hanging out with a guy like Denton Brewer was just a way to shut the door behind him.

Just get out of the truck. That's all it would have taken and he could have walked away clean, spent his life worrying about business or love, like everybody else. But he was afraid, so he let the truck carry him forward as it swung around the block, came back to where the black girls were still standing a few yards from the road, like they'd moved just enough to show they weren't scared of no stupid white boys in a dirty pickup truck, yellin' stuff at them but don't have the guts to stop and get out here on Twenty-first Street.

Brewer slowed, leaned across Tournier again to yell out the window, "I got somethin' real tasty here. Who wants it?"

This time the girls turned to stare at them, their eyes angry. "I wanted something *that* small," one of them yelled, "I'd go out back, dig me up some worms."

"You boys better get on outta here," another called out. "Before somebody find out what you dreamin' 'bout."

Brewer laughed. "You want to know what I'm dreamin' 'bout, c'mon over here."

"Let's go," Tournier said quietly. "This is stupid."

Brewer ignored him, called out, "I bet y'all got some good drugs, huh?"

"That what you boys come up here for?"

Brewer grinned at Doyle. "One of them girls got a mouth on her, huh?" Then he leaned back toward the window, yelled out, "Sure. We're cops. C'mon over here, so I can search you."

"You don't look like no cop."

"That's what makes me so good. I'm undercover." Brewer raised a hand, waved her over lazily. "C'mon over here. I'll show you what an undercover man does."

"Boy, you ain't gonna show me *nothin'*."

Brewer looked the girls over, then laughed. "Yeah, I guess that's right. I bet you girls done seen it all already."

A group of boys came around the corner of the community center, walking like they'd just finished off a bottle. One of them gave a yell and pointed at the truck. They all looked, then several of them started over at a run. Brewer put the truck in gear, eased off the brake, and let it roll forward slowly.

"Last chance," he called out to the girls. "We got to hit the road."

One girl looked back at the crowd of boys headed toward them, gave a laugh. "Nah, stick around. Party's just gettin' started."

Brewer made his hand into a pistol, pointed it at her, and jerked his thumb like he'd squeezed off a shot. "I'll see you again, girl." Then he hit the gas, laid some rubber down on the road as he sped away. When he reached the corner, he made a right, glanced over at Tournier, grinned. "Now there's a girl I can *talk* to."

"Glad to see you made a friend."

"Hey, I make friends wherever I go. I got a great personality." Brewer suddenly spun the wheel, made another quick right at the end of the block. "Watch them boys jump, we come back around."

Jump in their cars, Tournier thought. *Chase our asses all the way back to town.*

But Brewer had spotted something that made him change his mind. Up ahead, a young black girl was walking quickly along the edge of the road, like she was in a big hurry to get home, change out of that silk shirt and tight pants before her daddy got a good look at what she was wearing.

"Well, looks like one got cut from the herd." Brewer slowed way down, pulled up beside her. "Hey, girl. Looks like you in a big hurry. You want a lift?"

She jumped slightly when he spoke to her. Tournier saw her face freeze when she got a look at the four of them, packed tight in the truck's cab. She didn't say a word, just turned and walked away as fast as she could, wobbling slightly in her high heels.

"What'd I say?" Brewer gave the truck some gas, came up alongside her again. "Hey, you hear me talkin' to you?"

The girl didn't look at them this time. She kept walking, her eyes fixed on the gravel shoulder a few feet ahead of her. Brewer let up on the gas so the truck fell a few feet behind her.

"Check this shit out." He swung the wheel to the right, gave the truck a little gas, and it nudged her gently from behind, made her stumble. He hit the brake, and she caught her balance, looked back at them with eyes full of fear. They sat gazing out at the girl through the truck's windshield, noticing how their headlights made her skin look the color of a bright penny. Then she bent, took off her shoes, straightened up with one in each hand. She stood there barefoot, looking at them, and for a moment Tournier wondered if she was going to throw her shoes at them. But instead, she took a cautious step back, then hesitated, not wanting to turn her back on them until she saw what they would do.

Brewer gunned the engine.

And with that, the girl took off, running wildly across the gravel parking lot to their left, vanishing into an alley between two warehouses.

Brewer laughed, put the truck in gear, and went after her.

"C'mon, man. That's enough." Price's voice sounded scared. "Let her be."

"Let her be what?" Brewer spun the wheel so the truck slid across the gravel; then he hit the gas, brought them back out onto the road. "We ain't gonna hurt her. We just gonna scare her a little." He made a left at the corner, accelerated down to the end of the block, then cut across a parking lot to come up on the alley from the opposite end. "Check out the look on her face when we block the alley." He swung the truck in tight against a warehouse loading dock and cut his lights as he came up on the end of the alley.

Later, Tournier would remember only a flicker of movement among the shadows, no warning, and then the jerk as Brewer hit the brakes, hard. Then, suddenly, the girl's face, up close to the windshield, her eyes wide with surprise as she went over the truck's hood, landed in a heap in the deserted street.

For a moment, nobody moved. They sat there in silence, looking at the dark alley as if expecting to see her appear there any moment, running, her party shoes still in her hands. Then Brewer opened his door, got out, and went over to where the girl lay, stood there looking down at her. She lay with one leg bent back under her at a strange angle.

"Shit," Price whispered. "Where'd she come from?"

Tournier got out, went over, and crouched down next to her. Her eyes were closed, and she was moaning softly. He reached out, then hesitated, unable to bring himself to touch her.

"Jesus," Brewer said. "Ain't this some shit."

Tournier heard the sound of somebody being sick behind the truck, then Price came toward them, stopped a few feet away. "Oh man, I can't believe this."

"We have to get an ambulance," Tournier said, the words heavy as stones in his mouth.

"Put her in the truck," Doyle said. "We could take her up to the hospital. That'd be quicker than waiting on an ambulance."

"She ain't goin' to no hospital."

They all turned to stare at Brewer. His face was like the shattered end of a bone. "I ain't goin' to jail for no nigger."

Then, as they watched in silence, he crouched down beside her, put his hand on her throat, and pressed, hard.

"What the fuck are you doing?" Doyle said.

Brewer didn't answer. His eyes were fixed on the gravel next to the girl's face, like he was looking for something important that he'd lost. Tournier saw one of her hands move slightly, like she was trying to flick away a bug. Then she stopped moving. Brewer kept his hand on her throat, looking away. Then he stood up, wiped his hand on his pants.

"Hospital won't do her no fuckin' good now." He looked over at them. "You guys just gonna stand there, or you gonna help me get her in the truck?"

They lifted the girl's body into the back of the truck, and then Brewer climbed in, dug a tarp out of the toolbox bolted to the truck bed, tossed it over her. He weighted the edges with a couple cinder blocks Doyle found next to one of the loading docks. Then Brewer climbed down out of the truck bed, said, "Get in. We gotta go find someplace to bury her."

Tournier and Doyle got into the truck, but Price just stood there, staring at them. "You guys are crazy," he said. "You can't just go bury her."

"You got a better idea?"

Price took a step back. "Fuck this. I'm leaving." But he didn't move.

Brewer turned, looked back at Tournier in exasperation. "Can you help him get his head out his ass? We ain't got all night, here."

Tournier got out of the truck, but before he could say a word, Price shook his head, said, "This ain't right. I ain't gonna do this." And he turned, walked away into the night.

Brewer looked over at Tournier. "You better go after him, make sure he doesn't tell somebody. Me and Doyle will take care of the girl."

ALL *you had to do was get out of the truck,* Tournier thought. *And you wouldn't be here now.*

The waitress brought Tournier's coffee, told Brewer that his shrimp would be a couple minutes, and did he want anything while he waited? He ordered a Dixie, told her not to bother with the glass. "I drink 'em the way God made 'em," he told her. "Knock the horns off it and run it in here."

Simple as that. Just get out of the truck.

As it was, he'd ended up walking down Twenty-first Street after all, searching for Price, while Brewer and Doyle drove south out of town, look-ing for a place to bury the body. He'd found Price sitting on a curb outside a feed store three blocks south of the bridge that marked the border between the white and black sections of town, his head buried in his hands. He raised his head when Tournier came toward him. His eyes were scared.

"He *killed* that girl, man!" Price shook his head in disbelief. "Just put his hand on her throat and choked her."

Tournier looked back up the deserted road, then sat down next to him.

"We're so completely fucked, man," Price went on. "You know that, right? We just killed a girl."

"It was an accident," Tournier said quietly.

"Fuck that, man! Brewer, he just fuckin' murdered her! You saw it!"

"Yeah, I saw it," Tournier agreed. "But you think some judge is gonna believe us, we try to tell him we had nothing to do with it?" He reached out, grabbed Price's arm. "Listen to me, man. Nobody wanted this to happen. I'm goin' to college in a couple months. You think I want to end up at Angola 'cause of a guy like Brewer?"

Price looked out across the road toward the thick stand of pine trees beyond. "Jesus. Why did I come tonight?"

"Look, nobody saw it happen. Brewer and Doyle, they're gonna find a place to bury the girl, she'll never be found. Far as anybody knows, she ran off somewhere. All we gotta do is stay cool and keep our mouths shut." Tournier stood up, grabbed Price's arm, and pulled him to his feet. "C'mon. We can't stay here."

They walked home in silence, ducking off the road into the trees whenever they saw a car's lights. The next day, when Tournier saw Price at school, they avoided each other's eyes. But Brewer caught up with him outside the gym at lunch. "Everything okay?" he asked.

"Yeah, no problem. What about you?"

"Problem solved. You want to know?"

Tournier shook his head. "Just tell me you did it right."

Brewer laughed. "Gabriel's gonna have to blow that horn, they find this girl."

Tournier nodded, turned to walk away. Brewer called after him, "Hey, you want to get a beer later?"

Tournier kept on walking. For the next two months, he stayed away from the others. He kept waiting for the sheriff to show up one day, pull them all in for questioning, but it never happened. It was like the girl had simply vanished, and nobody cared. He felt the black kids at school stare at him in the hallways, learning from their silence that nothing's ever really a secret, that there's a big difference between what people know and what the law can prove. Okay, so nobody had seen them chasing that black girl down, or loading her body into the back of Brewer's truck. If somebody had, they'd be in jail by now. But they knew that there had been a truck full of white boys out riding around on Twenty-first Street the night she disappeared, and it didn't take 'em long to put names to the faces those girls had seen out by the parking lot. They knew Brewer by reputation, recognized his truck as the one that cruised their neighborhood many nights, the driver slowing to shout words that burned the ear, then hitting the gas, throwing up a cloud of gravel and dust as he sped off toward town. The other three boys were a surprise, faces they hadn't expected to see staring out at them from Brewer's truck. But if you live up on Twenty-first Street, you get used to learning that the worst is true, so you shake your head and watch with empty, guarded eyes that say *Yeah, okay. But there's no going back.*

It was that look that made Tournier want to get out of town, to get away as fast as possible to someplace where nobody looked at him like that. Doyle must have felt the same way, because he dropped out of school six weeks before graduation to join the navy. One day he was there, and the next he wasn't. Tournier envied him.

But his turn came. Three weeks after graduation, Tournier packed up his car and left for Chicago, where his uncle gave him a summer job in his real estate office. That September he started school at Northwestern, and within a few weeks, the memory of what had happened began to fade, became little more than a sudden stiffness in his walk as the image of the girl going over the hood of Brewer's truck would hit him without warning while he was crossing campus. *That's not you,* he'd tell himself. *It's somebody else, who lived long ago.*

His parents came up to visit him in Chicago for Christmas. From the moment he saw her, Tournier knew that his mother had something on her mind. Finally, on the last day, they took him out for dinner, and over dessert she told him, "We have some news. Your father and I are moving into the city. We've found a lovely house, a block off St. Charles, so he'll be able to take the streetcar in to his office on nice days. Most of his projects are there now, and it makes sense." Then she paused, looked over at him sadly. "We know you'll miss the house in Jefferson, all your friends, but it only makes sense. Your father's spending all his time in the car."

Tournier raised a hand to stop her. "Hey, it's okay. I always wanted to live in New Orleans."

His mother looked relieved. His father looked away across the restaurant, probably adding up all the tables, figuring out the night's take. Tournier went back to his crème brûlée.

That spring, his parents moved into New Orleans. Tournier never again went home to Jefferson, tried to avoid going home to Louisiana at all. He got summer internships, visited friends on holidays, and when he graduated, he took a job working for a brokerage house in Chicago. He watched from a distance as his father finally broke into the big money doing commercial development along the riverfront. Tournier was happy for him, but he never thought about going home to join the family business. When his father died, Tournier was in his late twenties, starting to taste his own success, and beginning to get bored with a business he'd learned was like running the tables when you've fixed the game. Ten years had passed since he'd left Louisiana, and while the memory of that night still woke him in a cold sweat every couple of months, the girl going over the truck's hood as they hit her had gradually faded to a quick, bright blur and a wave of regret. She might have been a deer, or some neighbor's dog darting out into the road ahead of his car. She might have been alive somewhere, walking with a painful limp, not buried in a shallow grave, the flesh rotting from her bones.

And so he went home. He took over his father's real estate development business, found to his surprise that he was good at it, enjoyed the challenge of turning an architect's preliminary sketch into a building of glass and steel, a place where people could go in search of their dreams. Everything went well for the first few years; a couple of his casino projects over on the Gulf Coast made news, and in 1998 he took the company public, which gave them the capital to expand into new markets throughout the region. He was riding high, and then one day he came back from lunch up in Baton Rouge to find a pile of pink telephone-message slips on his desk. Buried among them, he found a message from an old high school buddy: Denton Brewer.

He stood there looking at the message slip for a long time, then abruptly shoved it into a drawer. For three days he went about his business, doing his best not to think about it. But the thought of it lying in his drawer haunted him. Was it better to ignore a guy like Brewer, or could that be dangerous? And how could Brewer hurt him now without destroying himself also? Finally, he couldn't take it any longer. One evening, when his secretary had gone home, he dug the message slip out of the drawer, dialed the number she'd scribbled on it.

"North Shore Auto Body."

Jesus, Tournier thought. *He works in a* body *shop.* The thought of that made him slightly nauseous.

"Denton Brewer around?"

"Hang on, I'll get him."

There was a clunk as the phone was set down on a counter, and he heard the high-pitched whine of a power drill starting up; then the man who'd answered the phone called out, "Brewer! You got a phone call!"

The sound of the drill faded, and Tournier heard footsteps and the phone being picked up. Denton Brewer's voice said, "Yeah? Who's this?"

"It's Michael Tournier. I got a message that you called me."

"Hey, I was startin' to think you blew me off."

"I just got back from a business trip," Tournier lied. "I've got a stack of messages here."

Brewer laughed. "Yeah, I guess an important guy like you gets a lot of calls."

"What's on your mind, Denton?"

Money. What else? Tournier should have guessed it when he first saw the message. A guy like Denton Brewer didn't play complicated games. He saw Tournier's name in the newspaper, connected to a casino development in Gulfport, and he heard his dreams calling out to him. His own body shop, he told Tournier, over on the highway near Jefferson. All it would take was eighty thousand in capital, and he knew a couple guys on the highway patrol, some local sheriff's deputies, could send him all the business he'd need. Tournier listened, feeling something heavy settle in his chest.

"I'm in real estate," he told Brewer. "I don't know anything about body shops."

"Shit, I been working here five years. Ain't a thing I don't know 'bout runnin' a body shop." Then he gave a laugh. "You remember how good I am takin' care of bodies, right?"

Tournier wrote the check out of his personal account, cashed in some securities he'd been holding since Chicago to cover it.

"I'm havin' my lawyer write up some papers," Brewer told him on the phone the day after the check arrived. "We'll be partners."

"Why don't we keep this between us," Tournier suggested. "You can pay me back when you get the business on its feet."

"You sure? Wouldn't want you to feel like I'm takin' advantage of an old buddy."

Tournier closed his eyes, felt a headache coming on. "I appreciate that, but I've got stockholders to think about. They might worry about me getting involved in a small business start-up."

"Yeah? Well, I guess you got to know 'bout all that shit. Me, I just knock the dents outta cars."

Now, sitting across from Brewer, watching him work his way through a plate of fried shrimp, Tournier wondered how he ever could have believed that Brewer would let it go at that. It took eight months before the next message slip showed up on Tournier's desk.

"Tow trucks," Brewer told him on the phone. "There's a guy over in Corpus who's getting out of the business, he's selling off his whole fleet. If I get four, I can bid on the city towing contract." Then he laughed. "Anyway, you know how it is. People get in accidents all the time. Lots 'a money in accidents."

Eighteen months later, it was custom auto detailing. "This guy who's selling out," Brewer told him, "between you and me, he don't know nothing about business. Don't get me wrong, he's a friend of mine, but he's got a gold mine there, and he can't make it go. He'll sell the whole operation to me for forty cents on the dollar."

"Aren't you worried about expanding too quickly?"

Brewer laughed. "Me? I'm building a franchise. And I just read in the papers how you've got these new projects going up in Memphis. How come you're not worried about that?"

"We're an established company. We ran the numbers on those projects three years ago."

Brewer was silent for a moment. "So what're you saying? I should focus on my core business?"

"That's what I'm saying."

A year went by, and Tournier began to wonder if Brewer had gotten the message this time. Then, one night in early July, he got a call at home, heard Brewer's laugh as soon as he picked up the phone. "Hey, Mike. Thought you'd heard the last of me, huh?"

This time it was real estate. His family owned some old farmland out near the highway. "Hasn't nobody wanted to live on it for about twenty years," he told Tournier. "So it just sits there. Mostly coloreds live out there now."

But now one of the neighboring farms was up for sale, and Brewer figured they could pick up some of the other property along that stretch of road cheap. "Lots of white families in town still own land out there, lookin' for somebody to take it off their hands. You got the interstate right there, plus the state highway. Could be a nice piece of commercial property."

Tournier tried to picture the land he was talking about. "You're talking about north of the highway, right?"

"You got it."

"Isn't that mostly bottomland? You get some serious flooding up in there every spring."

"Nah, that's back by the river. I'm talkin' about the land up by the highway."

"I don't think you realize how much land you'd need for a serious commercial development. You've got to consider parking, access road, utilities. It's like building a small city."

"Uh-huh. I'm talkin' about a lot of land. Some of it might be bottomland, but there's plenty that don't flood. Come on up here and take a look, you don't believe me."

Tournier glanced at his watch. It was after ten. "Look, I'll tell you straight. We try to avoid projects brought to us by local landowners. Word gets out that we're buying up land for a project, everybody jacks up the price. Turns into a pile-on."

"Hey, you don't want your name on it, I understand that. So you get a local guy to front for you, buy the land up one or two pieces at a time, nobody realizes it's your project until you got the property nailed down."

Tournier smiled. "And you're the local guy, right?" He could figure about fifteen ways that Brewer could line his pocket on this one. Probably cut separate deals with the landowners to inflate the selling price, then split the profits. Tournier tried to imagine what his board of directors would say about that idea.

But then Brewer said, "Nah, I'm not the guy for this deal. I was thinkin' 'bout Sam. You remember Sam Price? He's a lawyer in town now. My boy plays JV ball with his kid. He's done a couple real estate deals, small stuff mostly. Nobody would think twice, he started buying up land."

Jesus. Tournier closed his eyes. *Sam Price.*

"You sure it's a good idea to get Sam involved in this?"

"Sure. He can keep his mouth shut. Hell, you remember."

Tournier was silent for a moment. "I think it's better if I stay away from Jefferson. The risks are just too great."

"What risk? Hell, the people that own the land up in there, they *run* this town. You give 'em a chance to make some money on that property, you got nothing to worry 'bout." Brewer laughed. "You prob'ly riskin' more if you *don't* make 'em happy. That's when somebody might go runnin' off his mouth."

Tournier winced. "Look, I'll run the idea past my financial people. No promises, okay? If they think it looks promising, we'll get back to you."

"You're not just sayin' that, right? To get me off your ass?"

"All depends on if the numbers work out. I leave that to my people."

"You want me to go ahead and have a talk with Sam, see if he's interested?"

"Why don't we wait and see what the money people say, okay?"

"Right." Brewer's voice sounded excited now, like a kid who'd gotten his parents as far as *maybe* and knew it was only a matter of time until they came around. "Give me a call when you're ready to talk land."

Tournier's head was throbbing when he got off the phone. He poured some single-malt whiskey in a glass, carried it into his study, sat down at his computer, and sent an e-mail to his financial planning department, asking them to run some preliminary numbers on the property. Then he put on some Etta James, went and stood at the window, looking out into the darkness.

You shouldn't have come back. The past never goes away.

Four weeks later, he was surprised to find a report on his desk from his strategic planning group recommending that they proceed with the Jefferson project, provided that the land could be acquired at current market price. Tournier felt strangely betrayed, and he considered tossing the report into the garbage and forgetting about it. But there was a file on the project now, and the report had been forwarded to people in two other departments. If he tried to walk away from it without even questioning the report's conclusions, it would look like he'd thrown away an opportunity for no reason, something he'd have to explain to his stockholders. So he passed it on to his architects, who came up with some basic plans and promptly doubled their size when the second set of financial numbers came back strong. Over the next year, Tournier got used to seeing the project binder show up on his desk every six weeks, each time thicker. Everybody figured it was his pet project, he realized, since he'd set the whole thing in motion with his memo. So now the whole company was anxious to get behind it, show the boss how quickly they could get it up and running.

Funny, Tournier thought, sending it on to acquisitions. *Like you can't escape it.*

They started buying land, using one of the partners in Helen Whelan's law firm to front for them. Tournier made sure Brewer and Price got a small piece of the action, and they both made some money off it, but he didn't reveal the scale of the project to them until his legal people had locked up the real estate. He received a couple of phone messages from Denton Brewer after the project plans were released to the public, but he didn't call back. The guy had made money on the deal, right? What did he think, they were going to make him a partner?

Tournier tried to keep his distance, but his publicity people insisted that he make a trip up to Jefferson, have his picture taken shaking hands with the mayor. He agreed reluctantly, brought some paperwork to read in the back of the car, trying hard not to glance up at the window as they drove through town. The mayor said a few words about a local boy bringing economic opportunity back to the town that had given him his start, and then Tournier read a brief statement written by his publicity people, saying he was glad to be back home in Jefferson and he'd always be a small-town boy at heart. Then he got back in his car, told his driver to take him back to New Orleans, and turned the whole project over to his design and construction team. When the protests over the cemetery began a few weeks later, he spent an hour on the phone with Helen and found himself secretly relieved when she advised him to put the project on hold. He'd figured that was the end of it, and he took some quiet pleasure in the irony that it was the anger of Jefferson's black community that had given him the excuse he needed to bail out on the project. He tried to imagine Brewer's fury when he'd heard the news. Like turning your face into a hot wind.

Tournier gave his secretary instructions to screen his calls more carefully over the next few days, not because he really hoped that would stop Brewer from getting through, but to make it clear that there was nothing personal in a deal like this. Just a company cutting its losses.

Great idea, Tournier thought, watching Brewer finish off the last of his shrimp. *Worked terrific.*

Brewer pushed his plate aside. "Hell, that wasn't half bad." He took a deep drink from his beer, emptying the bottle, then raised the bottle at the waitress so she'd know to bring him another. "Most of the time I won't eat in these places. They spend all their money gettin' an ocean view, then they bring out the food and it's the same old frozen fish you get in the fuckin' airport." He saw the waitress nod, so he set the empty bottle on the edge of the table, and a busboy picked it up as he went past.

Brewer sat back, tossed his napkin on the table, and grinned at Tournier. "Boy, you sure got your flap caught in the zipper, huh?"

Tournier looked out the window toward the distant horizon, where the Gulf burned with sunlight. "Why didn't you tell me where you buried the girl?"

"Hell, I tried. Must have left you ten messages as soon as I found out where you was buyin' land." He shook his head. "I could 'a told you not to go buyin' no nigger graveyard, but I guess you know better."

Tournier looked away. They'd tried to get clever, expanding the project and cutting Brewer out of the picture. By the time they'd finished buying up land, they owned a couple hundred acres of farmland and woods stretching from the highway back to the river. Enough to accommodate their plans for an ambitious retail shopping complex, parking, utilities, and access roads, plus surrounding land in anticipation of the build-out that always followed a successful development—gas stations, chain restaurants, discount stores. Buy up the land cheap, then sell it back to 'em at a profit when the news breaks. Pays for the development costs if you manage it right.

If they'd known about the cemetery, they could have designed around it, set that land aside, donated it to one of the local black churches, as Danny had suggested, to get a publicity jump on the building permits. They had bought out as far as Caryl Jackson's farm but hadn't planned to use that land for the main development until one of the architects pointed out that they could save some money on utilities hookups if they sited it farther out by the highway, a section of land on the outer edge of the plans where they could get some decent elevation, keep the electric plant up out of any flood risk. Tournier had agreed, told them to resubmit the revised plans to the town's planning commission, then forgot about it. The protests started a week later, and Tournier could only rage at his design team for failing to do a more careful site inspection. And then, four days later, before they could get the situation under control, Caryl Jackson had been attacked by four white boys out kicking over gravestones.

Tournier heard Brewer give a laugh. "Kind 'a funny, you gotta admit. You owning the land where they dug up that girl? Like she just been waitin' on you all these years."

Tournier rubbed his eyes, looked over at him. "Let me ask you something. Did you tell your boy to go out there, kick over those graves?"

"Nah, they just had a couple beers, got a little hotheaded." Brewer grinned. "You know how things can happen, boys get to messin' around."

"How worried should we be?"

Brewer shrugged. "Hell, now they dug up those graves, you got *nothing* to worry 'bout. You can start construction anytime you want."

"What about the sheriff? He's got an investigation going, right?"

"Don't worry about Jim. His family's got some land up along the access road, he's been tryin' to unload it for a couple years now. This project goes forward, he's gonna make some nice money. What's he care about some nigger, died twenty years ago? You start building, he'll bury the whole thing." Brewer leaned forward, spoke quietly. "But you got to get that lawyer outta there. He's the one's got things all stirred up. Sam tried talkin' to him before his kid got killed, but the guy doesn't listen."

"I can't just call him off. I sent him up there when I thought we were talking about the old man who got hurt in the cemetery."

"How come you didn't call me?"

Tournier shook his head. "You're the *last* guy I could call. Your name's all over this thing. Somebody asks me about my problem, I could show 'em your picture."

"I ain't your problem now." The waitress brought Brewer another beer, and he picked it up, took a sip. "Sam's your problem. He's sittin' up there in that big house of his, thinkin' about his kid lyin' in that field up on Twenty-first Street, his head cracked open. You know Sam. Just a matter of time before he starts talkin' to somebody about how it's all his fault that his kid's dead 'cause we buried that girl up there."

"I thought his kid got killed before they dug up the girl."

"Hey, tell that to Sam. He'll be down at Saint Peter's confessing his sins by Thursday, you watch. Then we're all fucked."

"That's why you've got to talk to him."

"He don't want to hear from me. He probably figures I got him into this mess."

Tournier stared at him. "Didn't you?"

"Me?" Brewer laughed. "Shit, I guess. Seems like I'm always the guy behind the wheel."

"That's probably why we've ended up here."

"Hey, somebody's got to drive." Brewer rested both hands on the table, waiting until Tournier met his gaze. "Look, I hear what you're sayin'. You want me to take care of it. So I'll take care of it. That what you wanted to hear me to say?"

Tournier didn't answer for a moment, then his eyes drifted away. "Like you said, somebody's got to be behind the wheel."

TWELVE

"So what you gonna do now?"

Danny looked over at Jabril. He drove with one hand draped across the car's steering wheel lazily, like he figured it knew the way already.

"Get some sleep, probably."

"Mickie still out at the house?"

Danny nodded. "She'll probably stay out there tonight, keep an eye on things."

"You want me to drop you out there?"

"Swing by the sheriff's office. I need to pick up my car." Danny watched the town change abruptly from black to white as they crossed the bridge on Twenty-first Street. Rhonda Pritchett's story had left him feeling exhausted, like a man wading through a vast swamp, feeling the mud suck at his feet with each labored step.

Jabril glanced over at him. "You learn anything, talkin' to these people?"

"Learned nothing changes."

"You just learnin' that now?"

Danny smiled wearily. "Takes me a while, but I get there."

"Yeah, I noticed that." Jabril turned into the gravel parking lot behind the courthouse, swung around, and pulled up behind Danny's Mustang. "You want me to hang around?"

"Not much point. Looks like we're just going to have to wait, see what the sheriff comes up with." Danny shrugged. "I'll talk to Lee Fuller, see if we can't put together some court filings, get a judge to order the bodies they exhumed reinterred. Not much more we can do until they file charges against DeWayne."

"They ain't done that yet?"

"Fuller's comin' up tomorrow morning. They'll probably bring him before a judge then."

"Might as well take him out, beat his head against a rock. They send that boy up to Angola, he'll get eaten alive." Jabril looked over at Danny. "You ever been up there?"

"Angola?" Danny shook his head. "My dad went up for the rodeo with Jimmy a couple times. I asked him to take me, but he wouldn't."

"I went up there a couple weeks back, see one 'a my boys. They got him doin' twenty years 'cause he sold some rock to a couple white boys from up at Tulane. Those white boys prob'ly in law school now." He glanced over at Danny, smiled. "Make their living shuffling papers, just like you."

"Not if they're smart."

"Well, they ain't gonna be pickin' no cotton up in Angola, that's for sure." Jabril looked over at the courthouse, shook his head. "That's what you see, you ride up there. Bunch 'a black men, pickin' cotton. I asked a guard, 'Where's Miss Scarlett?' He look at me like he's got a uniform waitin', just my size."

"It used to be a plantation, back before the Civil War. Louisiana never had a penitentiary until after the slaves were freed."

Jabril laughed. "Didn't need one. Whole place was a prison."

"Well, they figured they needed one once they had all those freed slaves on their hands. The guy who owned the old plantation up there was struggling to keep the place running after the Union army had come through, set his slaves free. So he cut a deal with the state. Told 'em he'd clear all the prisoners out of the parish jails, pay for their food and board, keep 'em up there on his place as long as the state wanted, no charge. Only thing he wanted was their labor. He put up some barracks, set the prisoners to work in his fields, and paid off his war debts."

"So what you're saying, prison's just another way to keep the black man workin' in the fields."

Danny shrugged. "That's how it started, anyway."

"They send any *white* prisoners up there?"

"A few."

Jabril grinned. "Got to have a few, keep all them niggers in line." He looked over at Danny. "What's that you were sayin' 'bout how nothin' changes? Set the slaves free, they build prisons. Same deal, just got the law behind it."

"I got nothing against prisons," Danny said. "I'd just like to make sure the right people are in them."

"Listen to you." Jabril gave a laugh. "I keep forgettin' you used to be in politics." He nodded at Danny's Mustang. "How long you gonna keep drivin' that old car, man?"

"Long as it runs."

"You provin' a point, huh?"

"I just like the car."

"So what makes you think these people 'round here any different?" Jabril asked. "You know why they do things the way they do 'round here? 'Cause that's how they always done 'em. Simple as that. You can ride on up Twenty-first Street, ask the folks why they get dressed up nice, go to church on Sunday morning. You ask 'em that, they gonna look at you like you crazy. Might as well go ask a cow why it stand in a field. You get what I'm sayin'?"

"I'm workin' on it."

"You act like you figure people gotta have a *reason* to do all the stuff they do. Like they think it through, figure out all the angles." Jabril shook his head. "Maybe that's how you live, but most people, they do what they do 'cause that's what they do. Drive an old car 'cause they like it. Beat up niggers 'cause they can. Don't ask 'em why, 'cause it makes 'em mad. Guy like you gets into politics, he forgets all that. Tries to make people like each other or give up their guns. That's how come we keep gettin' them country-club Republicans, like to talk about God, crime, and taxes, runnin' things up in Baton Rouge. 'Cause guys like you think you can change people's hearts. Makes the white folks mad, so them good ole boys come in, kick your butts 'round the block every time. They got it figured out. Quickest way to get a poor white man's vote ain't to promise him a job, or a hospital, or a school. Hell, they *hated* school. Made 'em feel stupid. No, you want that old boy's vote, you got to make him *mad*. Tell him the niggers comin' to steal his job or rape his daughter. Tell him all them black folks up on Twenty-first Street is livin' off his taxes, spendin' their welfare checks on Cadillacs. That's a good one, 'cause then you can tell him how you'll cut his taxes and he won't ask you 'bout the school that don't get built, or the factory up the street that closes down, or how much all your country-club buddies made on the deal. Just so them niggers don't get their hands on his money."

Danny smiled. "I'm not in politics anymore."

"Hell you ain't. What you doin' up here, anyway? This rich guy really payin' you to watch out for Etta Jackson's family? Or you doin' that 'cause you got a big old hole in your heart, lets everything come leakin' out?"

Danny opened the car door, got out. "I've got to go see how Mickie's doing."

"It ain't Mickie I'm worried about, my man."

"Yeah? Well, she's not your wife."

Jabril grinned. "Still can't figure that one out." He leaned across the front seat, pulled Danny's door shut, then put the car in gear and drove away.

Danny stood there, watched the taillights vanish up the road. Then he shook his head, walked over to the Mustang, got behind the wheel. The car always gave him a feeling like he used to get when he was a kid and his dad would steal a couple days away from the office up at the statehouse, drive the family down to Pensacola, windows open, hot summer air blowing Danny's mother's long dark hair around. When they got close to the beach, you could smell the salt on the warm air, and Danny would finger the elastic strap on his swimming goggles, anxious to get free of the car and run across the beach into the water. He liked to scare his mother by swimming way out beyond the breakers to a spot where the current flowing beneath the surface suddenly turned cold and insistent; he'd hang there, feeling its dark pull, before he turned his head toward shore, let the waves carry him home. She'd be on her feet at the water's edge, one hand shielding her eyes against the sun, when he came staggering out of the surf. Her eyes when she looked at him were the color of wet sand and filled with sadness. It was a look that, as a boy, he couldn't understand, but something about it made him want to plunge back into the water and swim out even farther, out to where the sunlight glittered on the water like beaten gold.

Danny drove slowly out along the highway, wondering what had brought this memory to him, until he came to Etta Jackson's house. He turned up the gravel drive, saw Mickie's Jeep parked under some trees. There was a light on in the kitchen, and some of it spilled out through the screen door, lay across the front porch like ice melting in the late-afternoon shadows. As he climbed the front steps, he could see Mickie standing beside a counter, watching Etta chop up some vegetables and herbs, then slide them off the cutting board into a large pot.

"C'mon in," Etta called out to him. "We just makin' some dinner."

Danny opened the screen door, felt the heat from the stove rise up at him as he stepped into the kitchen. "Cooking lesson?"

Mickie shot him a look, but Etta smiled, said, "I'm showin' her how to make growin' stew. Best thing for feedin' a baby when it's still up inside you. And when the baby's born, you give it to the mama so her milk will come." She glanced over at Danny. "Come on over here, I'll show you, too. Then you can make it for her, she got an armful of child."

Danny went and stood beside Mickie, and they watched Etta chop up every kind of vegetable, adding each to the steaming pot, then go out into her herb garden, returning with a handful of leaves Danny couldn't identify.

"This one we call Early Bird," she said, "and this one here is Fool Rabbit." She chopped them up on her board, releasing a smell that made Danny think of skinned knees and burning cane. "They got other names," Etta told them. "You go up the road twenty miles, they call 'em somethin' else. But we ain't never called them that. They grow all 'round here, back up in the woods. I'll show you later. You can pick you some, plant it in your backyard, have you some whenever you want."

Danny caught Mickie's eye. Their condo in Metairie had a tiny patio and a strip of grass the size of a bathtub. He tried to imagine what their neighbors would say when they laid in a conjure woman's herb garden. Then he saw Etta look up at them and smile.

"You can also buy it, you willin' to go shoppin' in them stores down on Rampart Street."

When the herb broth was ready, she chopped up a chicken, dumped it in the pot, then threw in some hot boudin for flavor.

"That boudin, it also help the baby know when to come," she told Mickie. "Wakes 'em right up, and they say, 'Shoot, they got food like that out there, I'm ready, me.'"

Then she filled her palm with rock salt from a box on the counter, tossed it into the pot, added some cayenne, and set the lid on the pot. "That's all it take. She cook like that for a couple hour, till them chicken comin' off the bone. Put 'em on some rice, eat 'em up."

They all sat on the porch until dinner was ready, then Etta served them each up a bowl of rice, ladled the thick stew over it.

"Me and Caryl, we eat on the porch when it's hot." She opened a cabinet, took out some paper napkins. "We could sit at the table, the heat don't bother you."

"Porch sounds good to me." Mickie took the napkins from Etta, carried them out onto the porch. Danny got some glasses down from a shelf over the sink, waited while Etta took a pitcher of iced tea out of the refrigerator.

They sat on the steps, looking out across the fields as they ate. "It's so beautiful here in the evening," Mickie said. "Like something in a painting."

"We like it." Etta raised her eyes toward the field off to their right, where the weeds had begun to come up along the rows of bean plants. "Don't know how I'm gonna keep it up, Caryl's not here. Been thinkin' I'll have to move into town, go live with my daughter. I guess she'll have room, they put DeWayne in prison." She glanced over at Danny, then quickly away.

For a moment, nobody said anything. Then Danny cleared his throat, said, "He's got a good lawyer, Mrs. Jackson. We'll do our best to see he's treated fairly."

She set her bowl down on the porch beside her, put one hand on her lower back and stretched, like it was giving her trouble. "Yeah, I guess I know that. You been doin' everything you can. But you put that boy in front of a judge, what you think he gonna look like? Judges we got 'round here, all they gonna see is a nigger. Won't *say* it, maybe, but they be thinkin' it."

"He's got a right to a jury trial. Lee Fuller's known for being good at choosing juries. If he gets that right, it might not matter what the judge thinks."

Etta shrugged, said nothing. They sat in silence for a while, then she turned to Mickie and asked, "You folks got room for that baby to run around?"

"We've got a pretty small backyard. We're thinking we'll have to move soon."

"Child needs room to run or they grow up wild."

Mickie looked over at Danny. "You hear that?"

"What's wrong with letting them grow up wild? That way nothing surprises you when they turn fourteen." Danny saw Mickie give him a dirty look, decided it was a good time to finish his stew.

"We've talked about looking up here on the North Shore, either in Slidell or Mandeville. But Danny doesn't want to move out of the city."

Etta nodded. "Ain't no place got everything a child needs. Some got too much. My daughter, she was livin' down in the city when she got DeWayne, moved back up here so he could grow up safe. Away from all them gangs." She looked over at Danny. "But tell me them white boys ain't a gang. Run around bustin' people's heads, and everybody scared to say a word. But you turn on the TV, they talkin' 'bout *gangs*, it's always colored boys. How come that is?"

Danny shook his head. "Depends on who runs the TV stations. Nobody makes money telling people things are complicated."

Etta thought about that for a while, then silently picked up her bowl, ate some more stew.

"That's why I want to stay in New Orleans," Danny went on, talking to Mickie now. "It's not easy."

"Tourist board might argue with you."

Danny smiled. "Try telling tourists your city's a rich cultural mosaic. They'll pack their bags, head straight for Orlando. All that Big Easy stuff, it's true in a way. People in New Orleans are different. If they take it easy, that's mostly because it's the only way to get by in a city that's busy having a nervous breakdown every day."

Mickie sighed, shook her head. "The truth is, he loves it there," she told Etta. "I'll never get him to move."

"Don't sound like it."

"You know why I love it? *Because* it's a mess." Danny stood up, set his bowl down on the upper step. "You mix up some gumbo, all you makin' is a big mess. Or your growing stew. Get those flavors all mixed up. When you're done, nothing tastes like it started out. That's New Orleans. Just a big pot with the heat turned up high. You got to learn to live with people who don't live like you. Hell, you don't watch out, you might start liking 'em."

Mickie laughed. "We got him started now."

"He get like this often?"

"Mostly when we talk about moving."

Danny slid his hands into his pockets, stood looking out at the gray evening settling across the fields.

Mickie rested a hand on her belly. "Baby's restless."

Etta smiled. "Gettin' ready to push on out. You just in her way now."

"Don't remind me. I'm trying not to think about that part." Mickie shifted in her chair. "They tell you it hurts, so you think you're ready. But when you've had that baby inside you for nine months, it's hard to imagine how it's gonna get out."

"I won't lie to you, girl," Etta told her. "Hurt like smokin' hell."

Danny rested a hand on Mickie's shoulder, then stepped down off the porch and walked across the gravel driveway out into the field on the other side. Breathing, prenatal exercise, baby care. They'd done all the classes, but the edge in Mickie's voice when anybody talked about childbirth still surprised him. It wasn't *pain* that she feared. Danny had never known anybody with less concern for physical pain. She had limped her way through the close-combat course at the training center with a knee swelling around the tightly wrapped bandage, refusing to let anyone know that she was injured for fear of washing out. Later, as a field agent, she'd faced down heavily armed suspects without hesitation, entered buildings so dark that the gunfire flashing inside looked like heat lightning bursting in the branches of pine trees on a hot summer night. No, she'd confronted the fear that pain can inspire, and Danny knew that didn't scare her. What put the tightness in her voice when she talked about giving birth, he figured, was the same thought that terrified him—holding a newborn infant, aware that whatever they'd been or done in their lives up to this point could not prepare them for what lay ahead. In recent weeks, Danny had found himself waking up in the middle of the night, listening for a baby's cry from the next room. After a moment, he'd realize that it was his anxiety that had woken him, and he'd turn over to go back to sleep. One night he found Mickie lying beside him, her eyes open, staring up into the darkness.

"You worried?" he asked.

She looked over at him, and in the moonlight coming through the window, he saw that she was crying. "What if we're not good parents?"

He reached out, took her hand, raised it to his lips. "Were your parents good?"

"Yeah, they were. Four kids and not one junkie. We all went to college. Nobody in jail. I'd say they did pretty well."

Danny nodded. "See, and mine always *seemed* like good parents, until I got old enough to figure out what was really going on."

"That's supposed to make me feel better?"

"I'm saying being a good parent isn't some mystery. Most of the bad mistakes are pretty obvious. Don't beat on 'em. Don't lie to 'em. Don't do stupid stuff and then expect them to know better." He squeezed her hand gently. "They'll still think we're crazy when they grow up, but that's just natural."

"You keep saying *they*. You got plans I don't know about?"

He smiled. "I promise, you'll be the first to know. Now, go to sleep."

And she'd curled up with her head on his shoulder, closed her eyes, and slipped back into sleep. That was six weeks ago, and Danny had found himself waking up even more, several times a night as the time passed, wondering if he really believed what he'd told her. Was it really enough to avoid the obvious mistakes? He could imagine those words coming back to haunt him.

"You think Denton Brewer's kid thinks his dad did a good job raising him?" he asked now. He turned, looked back at Mickie and Etta sitting on the porch steps. "You think they got a happy family?"

Etta frowned, looked off across the fields. "Boy with that much violence in him got some kind 'a snake crawlin' 'round in his boots." She looked over at Danny. "Who you figure put it there?"

Danny thought about that, then squatted down, picked up some rocks off the gravel driveway, hefted them in his palm. "What if he set out to teach him violence? Wants his boy to be tough so people don't push him around."

"Big difference between standin' up for yourself and bustin' an old man's skull."

Danny straightened, dropped the rocks on the ground. "I should go call Fuller, let him know what's happening."

"I thought I'd spend the night out here," Mickie told him. "Keep Etta company."

"Wish I had room for the both of you," Etta said. "But the couch is broken, and there's just that one bed in DeWayne's room. He don't even hardly fit in it no more."

"Anna head back to Baton Rouge?"

Mickie shook her head. "She's over at the motel. She said her cat needs to work out his abandonment issues, so she's gonna try going back every other night, spend the rest down here."

Danny smiled. "I should talk to her, find out what her plans are." He looked over at Mickie. "You'll be all right out here on your own?"

"Sure. We'll probably stay up late talking."

"And you got everything you'll need?"

She laughed. "You mean do I have my gun? Yeah, I'm all set. We got a couple more hours of light, maybe I'll give Etta a couple lessons."

Etta looked up at her, surprised. "What? Shootin' lessons?" She shook her head sadly. "I'm gonna let you keep that stuff, it's all right with you."

"You sure? It's not hard once you get the feel for it."

"Uh-huh, and that's what I don't want to get. Book say don't kill, turn the other cheek. Don't say *sometimes*."

Mickie considered her for a long moment. "You feel that way even after what's happened?"

Etta shrugged. "Way I see it, times like this is what the Book was talkin' 'bout. God don't need no easy promises." She glanced over at Danny. "That's what I told DeWayne, anyway."

Mickie met Danny's eyes. He could see that she wanted to say something to him, but then she seemed to draw back, looked off toward the shadows getting thick among the trees. "Try to get some sleep," she told Danny.

He nodded, walked back to his Mustang, and got behind the wheel. When he drove away, he saw the two women sitting in silence, watching the sun sink out beyond the hill where the graves lay open in the fading light.

"WANT some company?"

Anna Graf looked up from her newspaper, smiled. "You think I only talk to the dead?" She was sitting in a booth next to the window of the hotel restaurant, a copy of the local newspaper spread out in front of her.

Danny slid into the booth. "Anything about us in there?"

She shook her head. "DeWayne's arrest is on the front page, but that's it. I guess they had to go to press before the rest of the story broke."

"Maybe."

Anna closed her newspaper, folded it up, and laid it on the seat beside her. "I talked to my office. Looks like I'll be headed back to Baton Rouge in the morning."

"I'm sorry to hear that. I was hoping we could convince you to stick around a few more days, help us establish the historical value of the site."

"What site? There's nothing left out there but some holes in the ground."

"We're filing a motion to have the bodies reinterred as soon as the sheriff's done with them."

"That's good. I'm glad to hear it. But that doesn't change my situation. I'm afraid there's not much left worth preserving as an archaeological site."

Danny was silent, then said, "Is that its only value? As an archaeological site?"

"Well, no. It's still got historical value, especially if you can establish some connection to an existing community. Then they've got a claim to it as a heritage site."

"How hard would that be to establish?"

"Not that hard. It's just a different process. Gather some family histories, spend a few hours in the archives establishing that their accounts conform to the original property records. If we could get an accurate date on any of the stuff we dug up at the burial site, that would help."

Danny met her gaze. "Look, I realize you've got more work than you can handle, and this situation must be pretty frustrating for you."

She laughed. "You try digging up broken pottery for a living. We get pretty used to the idea that things don't always work out."

"I guess I'd make a pretty lousy archaeologist, then. I don't have the patience." He let his hands rest on the edge of the table, as if he were afraid it might get away from him. "These people have a real claim to that land, don't they?"

"Yeah, they do."

"I can't see giving up on that just because the sheriff's found an excuse to dig up all those graves."

Anna gave a smile. "I always figured I'd make a lousy lawyer." She lifted her hands, held them out for Danny to see. "You get enough dirt under your fingernails, you start thinking a little slower than most people. Ten years starts to look like a few ticks on the clock, and history gets to be the only way to think about the kinds of arguments people have about land, or property rights, or any of those claims people think they should take to a lawyer. You know how I know who owned a piece of land? I dig up the bones they buried there or the garbage they left behind. That's the kind of historical reality I deal with."

"I understand all that. But it doesn't help Etta Jackson."

Anna held up a hand to stop him. "Let me finish, okay? That's what I've learned digging in the dirt. But working up in Baton Rouge, that teaches you a couple things, too." She lowered her voice slightly. "You may not *need* me to give an opinion, Danny. When the sheriff dug those bodies up, he established the facts better than I could by writing up a report. You might have to go to court to get them reinterred on that site, but they're evidence in a criminal case now. You can request copies of the forensics exams, use that to establish their age, then use the sheriff's records to establish where they were dug up." She spread her hands. "The sheriff's already done my job. He wrote up their history when he got the court order to dig that place up."

The waitress chose that moment to bring Anna's spinach salad, and for a moment, she thought that the couple at the table must be in love, the way they were smiling at each other. But then the man began to laugh, and she decided that it didn't have the sound of a man who was getting ready to reach across the table, take the woman's hand. No, this was closer to the laugh you hear when the fat guy in a movie slips in the mud and goes down on his ass. Not cruel, exactly, but with an edge. The kind of laugh where you can only shake your head, be glad it isn't you sitting there in the mud, that surprised look on your face.

She went away, and Anna whispered. "We've gotten her hopes up. People who laugh a lot leave big tips."

"You learn that by experience?"

"I carried a few plates in grad school."

Danny nodded at the salad. "Go ahead and start. I had some stew out at Etta's place."

She took a couple bites, saw him gaze off across the restaurant. Now that the laughter had passed, she saw that he was very tired. "You should get some sleep."

He looked at her, surprised. "Sorry. I guess I'm not much company tonight."

"I wasn't complaining. Just looks like you had a long day."

"We may have identified the girl you dug up." Danny told her what they'd learned about Shonya Carter. Anna laid her fork down on the edge of her plate, sat listening until he'd finished.

"You really think this is the girl we found?"

Danny shrugged. "No way to know until they finish the forensics, pull the dental records. Could be some hooker from down in New Orleans who got in the wrong car, the guy didn't mind driving a couple hours to get rid of the body."

"Whoever buried her there knew about that gravesite. They knew that years can pass without anybody going out there, so they could bury her up there without having to worry about somebody finding a fresh grave."

"So maybe the killer's local. Or it's some guy who used to come up here to hunt, spent some time walking around in the woods. That doesn't mean it's Shonya Carter buried there."

Anna picked up her fork, then put it down again. "Say you wanted to get rid of a body. There's all this empty woods around here, why not just dig a grave under a bush somewhere, bury it there? Etta told me she and Caryl have lived in that house for thirty years, so whoever buried the girl there took a risk that they'd be seen. Why do that unless you've got a reason for wanting to bury her up there?"

Danny studied her face. "You're saying this is more than just some guy dumping a body. They wanted to make a statement."

"I'm no expert, but that's how it looks to me." She took a few more bites of her salad.

"How is that?"

She looked at the plate in front of her. "About what you'd expect." Then she shrugged. "I spend a lot of time eating in bad restaurants. It's part of the job."

"And you're still here?"

"Spinach salads." She gave a laugh. "One of my professors in college had a theory that salad is one of the signs of advanced culture. You get people eating raw vegetables early on, then they discover cooking, and for the next couple thousand years, they start throwing everything they can find in a pot.

Which makes sense from an evolutionary standpoint, simply because it's the only way to kill all the bacteria until you've got modern plumbing. That's when you start to see salad coming back onto people's plates. Around the time they could be sure of getting all the animal dung washed off the lettuce."

Danny made a face. "I wish you hadn't told me that."

She laughed again. "Sorry. I tend to forget that most people don't find this stuff as interesting as I do." She took a bite of her salad, then smiled. "It's only a theory, anyway. For all I know, people were eating salad all along."

"How can you know what people ate?"

"Actually, that's pretty easy. Especially in dry climates. Out in New Mexico, they've dug up fifteen-hundred-year-old dung heaps, which are so well preserved that they can identify individual seeds—"

Danny held up a hand to stop her. "Okay, I get the point." He shook his head. "Sounds to me like you'd make a great lawyer. God knows, you've got all the skills."

LATER that night, Danny woke in his motel room and lay there motionless, staring up into the darkness. A strange yellow light moved on the wall above his bed. He got up, went over to the window, and looked out through the curtain.

Outside, in the parking lot, flames rose from under his Mustang, crawling up the sides like a bright red vine.

"Shit!" Danny grabbed his pants off the chair next to his bed, pulled them on, then started out the door toward the parking lot. He'd taken only a few steps when he felt something sting his cheek. He winced, raised a hand to slap at it, but even as he did, he heard the sharp crack of a rifle drift toward him across the humid night air, and then, behind him, a duller sound—*chunck!*—as a piece of wood splintered off the edge of the door. Without thinking, he dropped to his knees, heard a second shot hit the brick wall above him.

Across the highway, Danny thought. *Over in those trees.* He crawled to his left, got behind the Mustang, then caught a clear glimpse of a muzzle flash from across the highway as another shot shattered the car's near side window.

The door to the next room opened, and a man stuck his head out angrily. "What the hell's going on out here?"

"Get back inside!" Danny yelled to him. "Somebody's shooting!"

A bullet struck the light mounted on the wall next to his door. The man looked startled, ducked back inside, and slammed the door behind him.

The Mustang was burning fiercely now. Danny could smell scorched rubber, then the thought struck him that he was crouching behind a burning car with a full tank of gasoline. He waited, heard a bullet bounce off the concrete sidewalk to his left, then scrambled back into his room, swung the door shut behind him. A shot broke the window above him. Then he heard an engine start, tires throwing up gravel as the driver punched the gas. Danny raised his head to the window, swung the curtain back, and caught a brief glimpse of a dark pickup truck cutting through the parking lot of the steak house across the highway, laying down some rubber as it hit the pavement, heading north toward town.

Later, he would barely remember getting on the phone to call the sheriff, or the fire truck that arrived a few minutes later to bury his Mustang in a blanket of white foam. A pair of deputies arrived to take his story, spent a few minutes drawing chalk circles around the bullet scars on the outside wall of the building, then walked across the highway to look for shell casings among the trees, their flashlights moving slowly through the darkness like the gentle falling of leaves. When the sheriff arrived, he gave Danny a weary look.

"Have I mentioned how much I'm enjoyin' this time we're spendin' together?" he said.

Then he walked down to the motel's office, talked to the desk clerk, and set a second pair of deputies to knocking on doors, questioning any guests who weren't already standing around in the parking lot, watching the firefighters pack up their gear. By the time they were done, a pale light was coming up in the sky. The two deputies searching in the trees across the highway made one more pass, then came back shaking their heads. The sheriff spent a few minutes talking to them, then walked over to where Danny was standing beside the ruins of his car.

"Looks like your shooter picked up his brass." The sheriff glanced over at the bullet scars on Danny's door. "Pretty surprising, somebody shoots that bad."

"What about tire tracks?"

The sheriff sighed. "Won't get nothing. He was sitting on gravel."

"So you're telling me you've got no way to identify this guy?"

"Just a dark pickup." The sheriff gave a slight smile. "That's what you saw, right?"

Danny turned away. He could feel the anger burning in his face. He walked a few steps back toward his room, then stopped, turned to look back at the sheriff. "What about my car?"

"Have to impound it as evidence." The sheriff contemplated the remains of the Mustang. The paint had blistered off the metal, the windows had burst out, and there was nothing left of the interior. All four tires had burned away, so the car rested on its charred metal rims. "Don't look like you're gonna be drivin' it anywhere. I guess we'll have to get a flatbed out here, haul it away."

Danny looked over at his car, then quickly away. He walked down to Anna's room, knocked on her door. She came to the door, a pair of mud-caked work boots dangling from one hand. She set them down, took Danny by the arm, and drew him into the room. "Are you okay?"

He nodded. "They did a job on my car, but I'm still in one piece."

She reached up, touched his cheek, and he winced. "You're bleeding here."

He raised a hand, felt the cut just below his eye. "Jesus, I forgot all about it."

"Hang on, I've got a first-aid kit in the bathroom." She went away, came back with a small backpack, which she dug through until she found some antibiotic cream and a Band-Aid. "You can always spot an archaeologist. They're the ones with a Band-Aid on every knuckle." She nodded to the bed. "Sit down. I'll fix you up."

He sat on the edge of the bed, waited while she dabbed on some cream, then gently spread the Band-Aid across the cut.

"Have you told Mickie yet?"

"I figured I'd let her wake up first." He smiled. "Actually, I'm just putting it off. She's gonna give me hell for this."

"For what? Getting shot at?"

"She'll say I should have figured out they were gonna take a shot at me when I saw the car burning. It's all that ATF training."

Anna stepped back, and he raised a hand, felt the Band-Aid carefully. She picked up her boots, went over to a chair, and sat down to start putting them on.

"Looks like you've put some mileage on those boots."

She smiled. "You're looking at years of digging in the dirt."

"Does this mean you're staying?"

She laced the left boot up quickly, jerked it tight. "I spend most of my time digging through things other people have broken. Turns out we don't leave much behind, and most of it's the stuff we try to throw away." She stood up, picked up her tool bag. "I guess it won't hurt to go dig around in that hole they left out there. You never know what might turn up."

DANNY caught a ride with the flatbed driver who showed up to haul his Mustang out to the sheriff's impound lot behind Brewer's Auto Body. The gate was locked when they pulled up outside the chain-link fence, so the driver got out, walked over to the office.

Beyond the fence, Danny could see the battered Toyota that DeWayne Jackson had been driving when the sheriff's deputies stopped him out on the highway, got him out of the car at gunpoint, and put him facedown on the ground to handcuff him while his grandmother looked on helplessly.

The driver came out, got behind the wheel, started the flatbed up. But he left it in neutral, leaned forward to take a pack of Marlboros out of the glove box. He shook one out, then tossed the pack back in the glove box and slammed it shut.

"We goin' somewhere else?" Danny asked him.

"Just waitin' on the man."

Denton Brewer came around the back of the body shop to unlock the gate and swung it back so the flatbed could pass through. He locked the gate behind them, then strolled over to where the driver was unloading Danny's Mustang. He stood with his hands in his pockets, shaking his head at the car's burnt wreckage. Then he looked at Danny, grinning.

"I guess you won't be needing that trim now, huh?"

Danny walked off down the line of wrecked cars. Near the gate sat a dark blue pickup with a rifle rack in the back window, a single hunting rifle mounted on it. He glanced through the open window. An open box of shells lay on the passenger seat. On the floor lay an empty can of charcoal starter.

Brewer was standing next to the Mustang, watching Danny, his face curious. "Nice truck, huh?" He walked over, ran a finger across the paint. "Guy over in Abita Springs brought it down here. He was out shining white-tailed deer, and he drove into a ditch, messed up his front end. Had to repaint the whole truck, but it looks pretty nice, huh? Midnight blue." He laughed. "Deer'll never see him comin'."

Danny nodded toward the Toyota. "Is that DeWayne Jackson's car?"

"You mean the nigger they picked up for busting that white boy's head?" Brewer walked over to the Toyota. "Yeah, that's his car. Got it impounded as evidence." He rested a hand on the car's hood, shook his head. "You ever heard of a nigger drivin' a Toyota before? I see 'em on the road, they're all drivin' busted-up Cadillacs. Or those little Samurai things all the gang-bangers ride 'round in down in New Orleans. Stick their guns out the window, they want to pop some guy standin' on the corner."

Danny went around to the back of the car. The trunk was slightly open. "Somebody been in here?"

"Just the sheriff's boys. They come out here yesterday, got to diggin' 'round."

"And they left the trunk open?"

Brewer shrugged. "Looks that way." He reached over, pushed it shut.

Danny stared at him. "Why'd you do that?"

"What? You just said they left the trunk open."

"That's evidence. You leave it the way you found it."

"Oh, for Christ's sake." Brewer walked over to a pickup truck parked beside the entrance, unlocked a large toolbox welded to the truck bed just behind the cab, just like the one Danny had seen on his boy's pickup, and took out a long, slim tool with a hook on one end. He walked back to the Toyota, slid it into the narrow crack under the trunk's hood, popped the latch open.

"Anything else?"

Danny shook his head. Brewer walked back to the pickup, tossed the tool back into the box, slammed it shut. "Take your time," he told Danny. "I ain't got nothin' better to do."

He disappeared into the office. Danny waited a moment to make sure he wasn't watching from the window, then pulled the tail of his T-shirt out of his jeans, used it to open the trunk a few inches.

The deputies had clearly gone through it in a hurry. Tools lay scattered about, and a spare tire had been lifted out of its hub and slashed open. Danny saw a jack but no handle. No surprise there. Even if the deputies had found one, they would have seized it as evidence.

He ran one finger along the edge of the trunk where Brewer had slid the tool in to pop the lock. The paint was scraped away, and a few flakes of blue paint had fallen onto the rubber mat below the latch. No rust on the metal, so the paint had probably been scraped off only a couple days ago, when Brewer opened the trunk for the deputies to search it.

Danny started to turn away, but something caught his eye, made him squat down to take a closer look at the narrow rim of metal beside the trunk's latch. When Brewer had popped the lock open, he'd slid his tool in a few inches to the right of the latch, then worked it back toward the lock until it caught. But now Danny saw that there was a second set of scratches on the left side of the latch, as if somebody had gone at it from the other direction.

He straightened up, walked over to the office. Brewer was behind the counter, running a computer search on some parts. He glanced up as Danny came in, then went back to tapping at the keyboard, his face empty.

"When the deputies searched that car, did you open the trunk for them?" Danny asked.

"Uh-huh. You got a problem with that, too?"

"Anybody else open that trunk?"

"What for? They got all the evidence they need against that boy right now." Then he reached under the counter, took out a business card, and tossed it to Danny. He caught it, turned it over, and looked at it. *North Shore Car Rentals*, it said. *Your friend in need!*

"I was you," Brewer said, "I'd start thinkin' about where I could put my hands on a car. Don't look like you're goin' anywhere in yours real soon."

ANNA Graf secretly liked to think of herself as a gardener. Years of digging in the dirt had left her hands tough as old leather, and she was used to the bright roses of pain that began to spread through her lower back every afternoon, vines winding their way up her spine. She dug up teeth, bits of bone, rotted scraps of the sacking used to wrap the dead. Bits of colored glass, broken pottery, a rusted knife blade. She'd learned that history could be measured in pain. Pain was the soil it grew in, and it always came slowly out of that bitter earth.

So she was surprised when she came across a bone protruding from the dirt wall of the hole that the backhoe had left when the sheriff exhumed the bodies. Graves were dug shallow in this country, even on hillsides. People laid a few feet of soil over the dead for respect, but if they dug too far down, the graves began to fill with muddy water, and the walls fell in on both the living and the dead. But this bone had been buried deep, as if someone had been anxious to lay it far beyond sight or memory. She crouched down, used a small trowel to dig around it carefully, then brushed the loose dirt away. Now she could see that there were burn marks on the bone, and when she went to lift it out of the dirt, a small piece of metal dropped out, landed at her feet. She bent, picked it up. It was an old musket ball. She laid the bone on the sheet of plastic she'd spread out across the bottom of the hole, set the musket ball next to it. As she straightened, her eye came to rest on another fragment of charred bone sticking out of the mud.

And suddenly, she realized that there were bits of bone scattered through the dirt all around her. She knelt on the plastic sheet, looked closely at the dirt walls, running her fingers across the bits of shattered bone, and it struck her that this rock-strewn hill she'd been excavating so carefully wasn't really a hill at all. It was a mass grave, a place to hide the violence that lay thick as smoke on this land. Later, they'd buried slaves here. And nobody except the few black farmers who lived out here among the pines had remembered what lay hidden beneath this rocky mound.

She stood up, wiped her forehead with the back of her wrist, feeling for a moment that it was all too thick, too written in blood, for her to make sense of it with these delicate tools. All she could do was scrape away the dirt, bring something into the light. Then it was up to the local community to decide how to face their past.

She had just bent to pick up her trowel when she heard the roar of heavy equipment coming up the road. The ground shook. She climbed out of the hole, saw a long column of trucks loaded with construction equipment turning off the road, spreading out across the neighboring field. Men began clambering down from flatbeds, unloading bulldozers and front-end loaders.

Anna turned, ran toward Etta's house to find a telephone.

DANNY didn't care what the guy at the rental-car place told him, there was no way you could call what they'd rented him a Mustang. Air-conditioning, power windows. You might as well be driving a Volvo. What the hell ever happened to cranking the windows down, he wondered, letting the wind mess up your hair?

Still, it didn't rattle when he went to pass, and if he wanted to, he could put the top down, take it to the lakefront, let the sunlight off the water fill his eyes. And, he had to admit, they'd made some progress on radios in the last thirty years.

He drove out to the high school, parked in a visitor's spot close to the entrance, then walked back to where the students' cars were parked out behind the gym, and found Randy Brewer's truck parked in the same place he'd seen it when DeWayne had pointed the boys out to him a few days ago. He dug his notebook out of his shirt pocket and double-checked the license plate, but he recognized the large toolbox bolted to the truck bed, just like Randy's daddy had. Randy Brewer was a boy who took some things for granted. Like tossing a football forty yards downfield in a tight, perfect spiral, or the way other boys quietly stepped out of his path as he walked through the school's halls. Nobody would be stupid enough to mess with his truck while it sat in the school parking lot. So he left it unlocked, left the windows down to keep the heat from building up inside it, even left a Randy Travis CD lying on the front seat, where anybody could reach in and grab it. And he left the padlock hanging on the toolbox's hasp open, like he was daring some kid to reach on in there, grab something.

Danny glanced around, then reached over the side of the truck, lifted the padlock carefully out of its hasp, and opened the toolbox. A slim metal tool, identical to the one that Denton Brewer had used to open the Toyota's trunk, lay right on top, as if somebody had used it and tossed it back into the toolbox in a hurry. Danny picked it up, looked at it closely. There were flecks of blue paint along one edge, the same color as DeWayne Jackson's car. Danny dropped it back in the toolbox, closed the lid, and hung the padlock in the hasp. Then he walked back over to his rental car and sat on the hood, thinking about the events of the last few days until he heard a bell ring somewhere inside the school. The gym door opened, and a crowd of boys dressed in T-shirts and gym shorts headed out past the parking lot to the football field. A few of them glanced over at Danny as they passed, then quickly looked away. Randy Brewer was one of the last to appear, strolling out of the gym with a group of the other football players. They were big white boys, with skin as pale as a baby's and necks so padded with muscle that they looked like they'd all tried to swallow something that was too wide for their throats. They were laughing when they came out of the gym, but Brewer fell silent when he saw Danny, and the others picked up on it, glaring as they went past. Danny didn't say a word, just followed Brewer with his eyes until they'd passed through the chain-link fence surrounding the football field. Danny heard Brewer say something he couldn't make out, and they all burst out laughing again.

Danny got up off the car, went over to lean on the fence, watching the coach get the boys organized into different groups, running laps, speed drills off the forty-yard line, a few heading over to the bleachers, where they began pounding their way up and down the stairs. Watching it, Danny had to smile. *You get the football coach for your gym teacher, you're truly screwed. Probably has 'em in the gym, hurling basketballs at each other's heads on rainy days.*

Brewer and the other football players clearly had their own deal. They ignored the rest of the boys and went off to the far end of the field, where they started running football drills. Danny watched Brewer take the snap a couple times, then drop back to toss the ball thirty yards upfield to hit one of the boys running a crossing pattern. He had a nice, easy action that reminded Danny of Steve Young or Ken Stabler, taking that extra step to plant his left foot, drop his right shoulder, and fire the ball left-handed. Danny watched him run a few plays, then went back and sat down on the hood of his car.

Denton Brewer had opened the trunk of DeWayne Jackson's car from the right, leaning on the car with his left hand while he worked that tool around behind the lock. Must have left a nice set of prints on the hood. But even if his boy had done the same thing, Danny doubted that the sheriff had bothered trying to lift any prints off the hood. And even if they got somebody out to print it now, the car had been sitting in Brewer's lot, deputies digging through the trunk. All Randy had to say was that he'd leaned on the hood, watching the deputies. No way they could prove he'd broken into the car's trunk *before* Bobby Price was killed, unless they got a warrant to search his truck, found the flecks of blue paint on his locksmith's tool, and matched it to DeWayne's car. And even if they got it, probably all Lee Fuller could do with it would be to cast doubt on the state's case against DeWayne.

Danny went back to the fence, stood there watching Brewer toss his long, perfect spirals.

You can't just let him walk, he thought. *There's two people dead, and he's out here tossing a ball around.*

The bell rang, and the boys started walking back toward the gym. Danny waited by the fence, feeling their eyes on him as they passed. Brewer was among the last to leave, tossing the football a few last times before heading for the showers. When he finally walked toward the gate, he locked eyes with Danny, held his gaze until he was right up on him. Danny was aware of the other football players, but he ignored them, just kept his eyes on Brewer until he saw the anger rise up in the boy's face like heat.

Brewer stopped at the gate, stood facing Danny, his hands on his hips. "You got something to say to me?"

Danny dug in his pocket, came out with a quarter. He tossed it to Brewer, watched as the kid reached out, caught it with his left hand. Brewer looked down at it, surprised.

"What the fuck is this?"

"It's for the phone," Danny told him. "Call me when you're ready to talk about what really happened to Bobby Price."

Then he walked away. As he got close to the rental car, he heard something whip past his ear, and the coin clattered off the front of the car. He looked back at Brewer, standing there among his football buddies with a look on his face like the glitter on a knife blade.

"Your daddy already tried that," Danny called to him. "And if you're gonna throw, you better not miss." He nodded toward the ballplayers standing around Brewer. "Your receivers might start getting nervous."

DANNY drove to the motel and parked the rental car around back, as far as possible from the burnt spot his Mustang had left on the pavement. He walked through the lobby, his mind on what he was going to say to Mickie when he got her on the phone. Jesus, his throat tightening up at just the *thought* of telling her how somebody had burned his car, taken three shots at him, while his gun sat in a shoe box on the top shelf of their bedroom closet, next to a pile of ties she'd bought him on sale at Maison Blanche last Christmas.

"Mr. Chaisson?"

Danny looked up, surprised. The desk clerk held up a pink message slip.

"Your wife's been trying to reach you. Apparently, she's left several messages on your phone." He nodded toward the coffee shop. "And there's somebody waiting to see you. I told him I didn't know when you'd get back, but he decided to wait."

Danny took the message slip. "He been there long?"

"About half an hour."

Danny went into the coffee shop. It smelled like eggs, coffee, and cigarettes. A pair of tired-looking waitresses were clearing tables after the late breakfast crowd, stacking the dishes on bus trays and wiping down the glass-covered tables. Danny suddenly realized he hadn't eaten anything, but the smell made him feel slightly nauseous.

Then he saw Sam Price sitting at one of the tables back by the window. He was staring out the window, a coffee cup cradled between his hands. His face looked like the pale sand at the bottom of a river as the current sweeps past.

Danny walked over, stood looking down at him. "You wanted to see me?"

Price turned his head very slowly to look up at him. Danny could see the exhaustion that had settled in the man's eyes, like weeds growing in good soil.

"Do you believe in sin, Mr. Chaisson?"

Danny pulled out a chair and sat down. "I heard about it from the Jesuits. But I guess there's some fires you got to let burn, so I try not to judge a man for what the flesh commands."

Price shook his head. "No, I mean do you believe we'll all be called to pay for our sins."

"The past never goes away, if that's what you mean."

Price let his eyes wander back to the window. "My son is dead. They say that black boy they got up in the jail killed him."

Danny started to say something, but Price raised a hand to stop him. "I don't blame him. Not in my heart. Because I know that my boy died for my sins."

Danny sat back slowly. For the next twenty minutes, he kept his mouth shut, his eyes fixed on a spot in the middle of the table, listening as Price told him the whole story. He winced slightly when Price came to Michael Tournier, but Price was too caught up in his story to notice, telling him everything—what had happened to Shonya Carter, how he'd eventually learned to live with it, even go a whole week sometimes without remembering that night, until his boy had turned sixteen and started hanging out with Denton Brewer's son, getting into trouble.

"Can you imagine how I felt, Mr. Chaisson? Like God has a sense of humor. For a while I thought about pulling my boy out of school, sending him to one of those military academies up in Virginia. My wife was against it. She said he wasn't cut out for military school, that he'd hate us for sending him there." He looked up at Danny, his face pained. "I didn't want my boy to hate me. God forgive me, but I wanted his love, and now he's dead." His eyes filled with tears.

"You couldn't know that," Danny said gently.

Price wiped his eyes with the back of one hand, shook his head. "Nobody knows better than me what kind of trouble a teenage boy can get into. What happened to that girl, it's haunted me every day of my life. I thought that was my punishment, having to think about what we did, knowing she was buried out in the woods someplace. Seeing her face when she went over the hood, that look of surprise in her eyes, like we'd done something she hadn't expected." He swallowed hard, looked out the window toward the highway again. "We had Bobby's funeral yesterday morning. I come home from burying my boy, and Denton Brewer calls me to say they found that girl's body." He looked at Danny, and his eyes were suddenly hard and bright. "It was me killed my boy. As sure as if I'd done it myself."

Danny felt a wave of impatience surge over him. He shook his head angrily. "I sympathize with your loss, Mr. Price. But your grief won't help the boy they got up there in the jail."

Price stared at him. "My grief's all I've got left, Mr. Chaisson. If that boy killed my son, you can't expect me to—"

"DeWayne Jackson didn't kill your boy. Randy Brewer killed your boy to keep him from talking. They took that tire iron from DeWayne's trunk, used it to set him up so that it would look like he killed your boy. The tool they used to break into his trunk is lying in the tool chest on Randy Brewer's truck. If the sheriff ever gets his thumb out of his ass, he can get his crime-lab boys to lift paint flecks off it that match DeWayne's car." Danny spread his hands. "'Course, maybe you're just interested in your own guilt, don't have time to worry about stuff like that."

The blood rose in Price's face. He worked his jaw silently, like he was chewing on something hard, trying to break it into small enough pieces to swallow it down. When he finally spoke, his voice sounded like gravel under a truck's wheels.

"What do you want me to do?"

THIRTEEN

Sam Price sat behind the wheel of his car, staring at the courthouse. Danny could see his hands trembling.

"You having second thoughts?"

Price looked down at his hands. "Just give me a minute, okay? I've been living with this a long time."

Danny leaned his head back against the seat and closed his eyes. Twenty years eating at your soul. Going to sleep every night with that dead girl's face haunting you, waking up in the night with a jerk as Brewer suddenly hits the brakes, throwing you all forward, and the girl tumbles over the truck's hood, her face startled. It's a suffering that can deserve no sympathy, the kind that can make a man grow angry and cruel, make him turn his eyes away from the light, until they glitter with some bright inner fire.

Danny knew that bitter music. He'd lived in his own room full of smoke, felt the weight of his anger almost bury him alive. He knew how the night could whisper in a man's ear, could tell him that nothing he's done is his fault, just a trick the world has played on him, laughing behind his back. So he sat and waited for the trembling in Price's hands to pass, like rain falling on a riverbank, a sudden wind shaking the leaves.

"I never told my wife."

Danny opened his eyes, looked over at Price. "You want to go talk to her first?"

Price shook his head. "Sheriff's easier. Worst he'll do is throw me in jail."

"You didn't kill your son, Sam." Danny reached over, took the keys out of the ignition, dropped them in Price's lap. "If your story's true, you can't even be held responsible for the girl's death. Not legally, anyway. You weren't driving the truck, and you didn't hide the body. Worst they could charge you with is obstruction, maybe conspiracy. I'm not even sure they could make an accessory charge stick, since there was no intent to do harm."

Price shook his head. "Don't try to shine me up, Danny. I'm a lawyer. I've been thinking about this for fifteen years. We ran that girl down in a pickup truck. Even if we didn't mean to hurt her, we *chased* her. Any prosecutor worth his leather would go after us on that, get the jury believing we meant to run that girl down." He glanced at Danny. "Hell, I'd see it that way. You got a guy like Brewer behind the wheel? That's a hate crime right there. You line us up in a courtroom, all that jury's gonna see is Brewer and his Klan buddies. Won't matter what I've done since then, what kind of life I've tried to lead. All that's gonna matter is we put that girl in the ground."

Danny just looked out the window and waited.

"I've spent my life trying to pretend that night never happened. Now I've got to live with the knowledge that what I did got my son killed." Price looked over at Danny, and his voice suddenly took on an edge, as if he'd come to a decision. "That's worse than anything a jury could do to me."

He picked up the keys in his lap, considered them for a moment. Then he opened the car door, glanced over at Danny.

"You comin'?"

THE woman behind the counter wore a deputy's uniform, but she looked to Danny like she'd just come in from plowing the back forty with a mule. Her thick gray hair was tucked back into a bun like somebody's grandma, but her uniform could barely contain the muscles that bulged in her shoulders, and her face was as empty of emotion as a sun-cracked highway.

As Danny came in, she made a face like she'd rather be scrubbing toilets. Then her eyes moved past him to Price, and something in her manner stiffened.

"Sheriff in?"

Her eyes came back to study him. "He went out to the construction site."

"Which construction site is that?"

"Where they dug up all them bodies." She smiled. "They're breaking ground on that shopping plaza this afternoon, and the sheriff wanted to make sure nobody gave 'em any trouble."

Danny felt Sam Price's eyes on him. "They can't start building out there. That's a crime scene."

She shrugged. "Just tellin' you what they told me."

Danny turned to meet Price's gaze. "I have to get out there. You better go on home, wait for me there."

Price looked at Danny, his eyes thoughtful. "Sounds like your client's looking after his own interests."

JESUS, Woodstock. Danny had seen the pictures same as anyone, cars lined up for miles along the side of the road, people walking across the fields. Only all these people were black, and they didn't look like they'd come prepared for three days of peace and music. Mostly they looked like they'd stopped off here on their way home from work. Danny spotted some

boys he'd seen up at the high school as he drove through the narrow lane between cars parked on each shoulder, slowing to a crawl as he made his way
through the crowd streaming up the gravel road toward Etta Jackson's
house.

Picnic, he thought, for no reason. *Family reunion.*

But nobody was carrying food or picnic blankets. The men weren't carrying heavy coolers full of iced beer between them, making jokes about how
much longer those arms would be by the time their wives picked out a good
spot under a tree, spread the blankets out, and pointed one finger to a spot
where they thought the cooler should go. Their faces were stiff with anger,
their eyes bright and hard as broken glass. Danny saw them glance over at
him as he drove slowly past, and for a moment, it struck him that he might
have reason to be afraid. But nobody tried to stop him, and when he turned
into the gravel driveway leading up to Etta's house, he saw that they had
something more pressing on their minds.

A row of flatbed trucks had pulled into the field near the graveyard, and
some white men had gotten the heavy equipment unloaded. But that was as
far as they'd gotten. A long row of black families stood between them and
the trees, facing them, holding hands. More people were arriving every
minute to take their place at the end of the line, which stretched around the
back edge of the graveyard and left the construction equipment no way to
get through the trees. Danny saw Mickie, Etta, and Anna Graf at the center
of the crowd. Mickie, with her ATF I.D. pinned to her shirt, had left the line
and was standing a few paces away, talking with the sheriff. Then Danny
saw that the black man standing beside them was Jabril, and it all began to
make sense. Jabril had spent years perfecting the art of street protest, and if
Mickie had been unable to track Danny down when the construction crew
showed up, her next thought would have been to call up Jabril, see if he
might know where her husband had gotten to. Jabril would have heard the
urgency in her voice, and after she'd explained what was happening, he
would have told her, "Get on the phone and get some people out there.
Don't let 'em do this without somebody watchin'."

Well, she'd brought them out. Had Etta get on the phone, probably, start
calling the neighbors. Danny guessed that there were over two hundred

people surrounding the site already, with more on their way up the road. The sheriff looked angry, but he was clearly hesitating about taking action with a federal officer present. Danny saw him glance nervously over toward Etta's house. He followed the sheriff's gaze, saw a local TV news crew setting up.

Danny grinned, shook his head. *You tell Mickie to get some people out here, she don't mess around.*

He pulled the rental car up on some grass behind the construction gear, got out, and walked over to where Mickie was arguing with the sheriff.

"Let me see if I can make you understand this," he was saying to her, as though trying to explain the workings of some complicated piece of machinery to a very young child. "These boys got a construction permit. That means they got a right to start work, and anybody tries to stop 'em is trespassing on private land and subject to arrest."

Mickie stood with her hands on her hips, gazing down at the ground. Watching her, Danny had to laugh. As much as he disliked the sheriff, he felt a sudden urge to do the poor guy a favor, tell him not to waste his breath. One look at the way Mickie was standing, and Danny could have told him that it would have been easier to get one of those earthmovers in here, level what remained of that rock-strewn hill where they'd dug up the bodies, than to change her mind.

She motioned at the line of people behind her. "You really going to arrest all these people?"

"Yes, ma'am. If I have to."

"That would be a real bad idea."

The sheriff shifted uncomfortably in his boots. "Look, lady, I gotta face the voters next year. I'm not happy about any of this. But I don't make the laws, I just—"

She raised a hand to stop him. "Save it. You should try enforcing gun laws sometime." She gestured to the hill behind her. "Yesterday you told my husband that was a crime scene, but today you're out here protecting the builder's right to start construction. Looks to me like you're making it up as you go along."

He took a moment to raise his cowboy hat, get it settled just right on his head. "Lady, I been doin' my best to extend you every courtesy, seein' as how you're a fellow law officer, but if you continue to block this site, I'm goin' to have you removed like all the rest of 'em. You understand me, or am I gonna have to say it in *español?*"

Mickie's eyes went hard. She started to say something, then thought better of it and turned away. Danny saw her look up at him coming toward her, and her face suddenly looked like a sky blown clear of rain. "Oh, thank God. Where the hell have you been?"

"I had some car trouble." Danny glanced at the sheriff. "I was over at your office with Sam Price. He's got a story might interest you."

The sheriff shrugged. "He knows where to find me." Then he turned, called out to the heavy-equipment operators, "Start 'em up. We're gonna clear the site."

The TV crew picked up their cameras, and the line of protesters began to sit down, locking arms to make it harder for the deputies to carry them away.

Mickie looked at Danny. "You got something up your sleeve, now's the time."

"Got your cell phone with you?"

She slipped the phone off her belt, handed it to him. "I tried Lee Fuller already. He's in court."

Danny smiled. "Lawyers, guns, and money." He dialed a number. "Sometimes you got to dig up the past."

The sheriff started giving instructions to his deputies, and the men looked over at the line of protesters warily. On the other end of the phone line, a secretary picked up, said, "U.S. District Court."

"Judge La Rocca, please."

"I'm sorry, he's in a hearing. Can I take a message?"

"Can you slip him a note? He'll want to take this call."

She hesitated. "Who should I say is calling?"

"Tell him it's Eldon Duplantier."

The secretary put Danny on hold. Mickie gave him a funny look. "Who the hell is Eldon Duplantier?"

"Just a guy I used to know."

A guy who lay buried in the mud of a bayou outside Abbeville, a harmless guy who'd run a sports book in the Irish Channel and knew a little too much about an ambitious young prosecutor named Joseph La Rocca. Since he'd been five figures in the hole with a mob guy who sold video poker machines up in Metairie, he figured that his knowledge might be worth a few bucks. But La Rocca had some good friends who saw his rising career as a valuable asset. So Eldon Duplantier disappeared into the bayou, and Joseph La Rocca became a judge. There were rumors, of course, but nothing that could derail the career of a man like La Rocca, who had lots of friends, including a few in the U.S. Senate. Then one day, a small-time button man named Vinnie Falzi made a couple stupid mistakes and got himself picked up in a bust of some methadone labs over in St. Bernard Parish. It was his third fall, and he knew he was looking at some serious time, so he offered the detectives who were questioning him a deal—cut him loose on the drug charges and he'd give up some of his old mob associates. Curious, they agreed, and Vinnie began to talk. He talked for almost six hours. They had to change the tape three times. One of the things he talked about was a sorry-ass little bookie named Eldon Duplantier who knew a few things about a judge and got himself planted in a bayou outside of Abbeville. Vinnie swore he hadn't pulled the trigger, but when they pressed him, he admitted that he'd helped bury the guy.

"Fuckin' hole kept fillin' up with water, too," he told them. "Should 'a put him in higher ground."

They were interested, he could take 'em out there, show them where to dig.

By this point, the cops were starting to get nervous. You don't build a career by filing murder charges against a federal judge. Danny was working for Jimmy Boudrieux at the time, and one of the cops knew him from his days as an assistant D.A. They figured he'd understand their problem, seeing as how he'd been a prosecutor once but quit to carry envelopes of cash for a guy who had half of the statehouse in his pocket. A change like that gives a guy perspective, they decided. Helps him see the complexities in a situation.

Danny had met them in a bar on Toulouse Street, listened as they explained their situation.

"You charge Falzi yet?" he asked them when they'd finished.

"Yeah. We thought about cutting him loose, but the paper on the meth-lab bust already went through. Any deal would have to come from the D.A.'s office now."

Danny nodded. "What about losing the tapes?"

One of the detectives shook his head. "This guy's got a mouth on him. Now he's started talking, he's just looking for an audience."

"So if he tells somebody else, it's their problem."

"Not if he mentions how he told us first."

Danny sat back, thought about it. "Let me talk to Jimmy. He's got some friends on the state police. Maybe we get them to take the guy off your hands, say he's tied up in one of their operations."

"Just make him go away, okay?" the detective pleaded. "This guy, he won't shut up."

And so the tapes ended up in a safe-deposit box that Jimmy had over at Hibernia Savings, where he kept a portion of the cash Danny collected and the odd piece of evidence he'd picked up that could be used to sway a legislator's vote on a crucial issue. The box was registered in Danny's name, in case the feds ever got to sniffing around it, and they both kept a key. When Jimmy died, Danny put the key in a drawer and waited. A few months earlier, Joseph La Rocca had been appointed to the federal bench, after an undistinguished career as a state superior court judge. With the support of several crucial senators assured, his confirmation hearings were uneventful. For a few days, Danny considered mailing the tapes to a reporter he knew on the *Times-Picayune*, but something made him hesitate. Maybe it was Jimmy's theory of politics, which he'd enjoyed announcing to his opponents over beer and oysters: *Way I see it, you never play your best cards early in the game. Guy knows you always got an ace up your sleeve, he'll think twice about getting in the game.*

Danny must have heard him say it a hundred times over the years, mostly followed by a long, hard look to let the guy know that the cards he held were beyond imagining. Pretty soon you'd see the guy start to sweat, and before long he'd be talking about cutting a deal. It never failed. In the end, Danny took Jimmy's advice. He told the feds only a small portion of what he knew about the state's politicians, most of it stuff they already knew but couldn't prove. He got used to people looking at him strangely around New Orleans in the months that followed, as the men he'd visited to make his collections, or who had come to Jimmy with their delicate problems, began to realize that the subpoena they'd been expecting every day wasn't coming. New Orleans was a small town, and it didn't take long before they began to hear rumors about Danny's testimony from somebody's cousin who worked as a file clerk or typist over at the federal building. Slowly, the looks Danny got started to change. There were still plenty of people who wouldn't speak to him, or stared at him with silent hatred in their eyes when he walked into restaurants, but every now and then somebody would catch his eye and give a brief nod, as if to acknowledge that they knew he'd cut them some slack. Danny kept his distance, went about trying to build his law practice. But in the back of his mind, he always knew there were still cards he could play.

He heard somebody pick up the phone, and a man's voice said angrily, "What is this, some kind of joke?"

"It's Danny Chaisson, Judge La Rocca. I used to work for Jimmy Boudrieux."

La Rocca was silent for a moment, then he said, "What do you want? I'm in the middle of a hearing."

"I need you to issue a restraining order to block a developer from beginning construction on a historical site."

"Then get your ass over here and file a request for a hearing, like everybody else."

Danny glanced over at the construction equipment warming up, the sheriff giving orders to his deputies. "There's no time for that, sir. Believe me, I wouldn't have called you like this if it wasn't urgent. I'm standing at the site right now, looking at a bulldozer that's about to plow up the whole area. We'd need you to issue a restraining order just to give us time to apply for a hearing."

"You got any cause?"

Danny explained the situation to him briefly. "We'd also like an order requiring the return of the bodies that were exhumed for reburial, once they've been examined by a forensic specialist to determine that they predate the death of Shonya Carter."

"Sounds like you got a nice little mess on your hands up there, boy."

"I could have a hearing request with more details on your desk by later today."

"You better include the archaeologist's affidavit."

"No problem." Danny nodded at Mickie. "Should I give you a fax number?"

"Give it to my secretary. But put the sheriff on first. I'll let him know it's coming."

Danny walked over to where the sheriff was talking to his deputies, tapped him on the shoulder. When he turned, Danny handed him the phone. The sheriff looked at him, mystified.

"What the hell is this?"

"It's a federal judge. He wants to talk to you."

The sheriff's mouth tightened. He raised the phone to his ear, said, "This here's Sheriff Frand. Can I help you, sir?" He listened, his eyes fixed on the ground, then he said, "Okay, Judge. I'll make sure they hold off until you can hear from both sides." He passed the phone back to Danny, his eyes cold. "He wants to talk to you again." Then he raised a hand to catch the construction foreman's eye, drew a finger across his throat. "Shut 'em down," he called out. "We're done here for today."

Danny raised the phone to his ear, heard a cheer go up from the demonstrators behind him. "Thank you, Judge."

"You'll get those papers to me this afternoon?"

"I'll have my secretary send them right over."

"Right. And Mr. Chaisson?"

"Yes, Judge?"

"I ever hear from Eldon Duplantier again, I'm gonna tell him to crawl back in his hole. You understand me, boy?"

"I hear you."

"Good."

Danny spent a few minutes talking to La Rocca's secretary, then handed the phone back to Mickie. She had a curious look in her eyes.

"What just happened here?"

"Ghost story." Danny walked over to where Etta Jackson sat on a rock at the center of the line of protesters. They'd begun to relax, stretching out on the grass, laughing and talking. It was almost starting to look like a picnic now. The sheriff had gathered his deputies together in a tight circle back by his squad car, was talking to them quietly. When he finished, they all nodded, then the sheriff got into his car and drove away, his tires throwing up twin plumes of gravel dust as he headed toward the highway.

"My man Danny!" Jabril laughed. "Looks like somebody lit a fire under that man's ass."

Danny crouched down beside Etta, told her, "I got a federal judge to issue a court order. That should stop them trying to build out here, but I'm afraid it won't help Caryl or DeWayne."

She looked off toward where the sheriff's car had disappeared among the trees, nodded slowly. "Can't nothin' help Caryl now. He's just waitin' on his time. But he'd be glad to know you stopped 'em building." She smiled at him. "Always said he wanted to be buried out here with his people. Maybe that's what he's waitin' on."

"I'm sure he's got a lot of years before he has to think about that."

She gave him a long look, then shook her head slowly. "You nice to say that, but you just get them folks they dug up back where they belong, and Caryl be all set."

Danny was silent for a moment, looking away. "I've asked the judge to order the bodies reinterred."

She rested her hand on his arm. "That's fine. Can't nobody ask you to do no more." She stood up, using his arm to pull herself up, then rubbed at her lower back. "Didn't think I was gonna be able to sit there much longer. Look pretty stupid, we're all protesting and I fall off my rock."

"Probably be the best thing could happen." Danny smiled. "All those deputies would come rushing over here to help you, forget about arresting everybody."

She looked at him sadly. "I guess you ain't spent much time around here, huh?" Then she let go of his arm, walked slowly back toward her house.

Behind him, Danny heard a piece of heavy equipment start up as the construction crew began loading things back onto the flatbeds. The deputies were standing around now, thumbs hooked in their gun belts, watching. Danny went back to where Mickie was standing, told her, "I should call Demitra, get some filings dictated."

She nodded, passed him her cell phone again. "You lose your phone?"

"It was in my car."

She gave him a puzzled look but didn't say anything as he walked away a few steps, used her speed dial to call his office.

"Law office of Daniel Chaisson." Demitra sounded tired, like she'd spent the whole morning grinding up rocks with her teeth.

"It's Danny. Anything happening?"

"You jokin', right? Want me to tell you 'bout all the calls you got, you been out runnin' 'round?"

Danny sighed. "All right, listen. I need to dictate a pleading to be filed in federal court. Judge La Rocca."

"I'm listening."

Danny walked off into the pine trees, spent about twenty minutes dictating a request for a hearing and an accompanying request for a stay that would stop any further construction at the site. When he was done, he had Demitra read it back to him, made a few changes, then told her to sign his name on it and fax it over to Judge La Rocca's chambers at the federal courts.

"You really helpin' those people up there?" Demitra asked him when they'd finished.

"Looks like it."

"Man you workin' for ain't gonna like it."

"No, I guess not." Danny rubbed his eyes. "I guess we better do a letter to him, too. Let him know I'm no longer working for him."

"You not just resigning. You switchin' sides. Ask me, they could disbar you for that."

"Not if I can show misrepresentation."

"What's that mean?"

"That he retained me under deceptive circumstances with the intention of committing illegal acts. U.S. Attorney could make a case for obstruction of justice at least."

He heard Demitra give a sigh, start shifting papers around on her desk. "So you're sayin' I'm still gonna have a job, all this is over?"

"That'd be my guess, yeah."

"Your *guess*? Honey, I got to pay my bills. You expect me to sit 'round here, waitin' to see if your *guess* is right?"

Danny laughed. "Demitra, with your skills, you'll never be out of a job."

"What skills is that? Puttin' up with you?"

"You can put it on your résumé." Danny disconnected, walked back over to Mickie.

"You get your papers filed with the court?"

"Demitra's sending them over in a few minutes. Let's hope La Rocca doesn't change his mind."

"You should call Marty Seagraves," Mickie told him. "If you're going to claim federal civil rights violations, that means getting the FBI into it."

Danny nodded. "I guess you're right." He'd been avoiding this moment in his mind. Marty Seagraves was a good guy, and he never missed an opportunity to remind Danny how much the bureau owed him for helping to bring Jimmy Boudrieux down. *Three years,* Danny always thought. *That's what they owe me.* That was how long he'd spent carrying money for Jimmy, gathering evidence on widespread corruption in the state legislature for federal prosecutors. Seagraves had missed his chance to prosecute when Jimmy put a gun to his head, but he'd brought down some of the state's biggest political operators, and six months later he'd been promoted to head the bureau's district office. Still, Danny hated the idea of calling him, as if those three years of his life were simply part of an exchange of favors, no different really from the elaborate system of payoffs and political barter over which Jimmy Boudrieux had presided.

Let it go, he told himself now. *That's not what this is about. You're just calling him to let him know what's going on up here so he can decide whether it sounds like a civil rights case.*

"You want me to talk to him?" Mickie asked. "I know the federal case law."

Danny shook his head. "Let's give him a chance to do the right thing before we start hitting him with case law. I'd rather have him send his people up here on his own, so he feels like it's his case, not ATF's."

She shrugged. "He's gonna know I'm out of my jurisdiction. But if you think that's gonna bother him, I'll keep out of the way."

He smiled at her. "Not too far, okay?"

"Anything you say, boss."

He caught Marty Seagraves at home, eating dinner. That surprised him. He glanced at his watch, saw that it was after seven. The late-summer sky was still full of light, but the sun had sunk low over the horizon.

"How's it hangin', Danny?" Seagraves always sounded like he was expecting Danny's call, even now. Like he kept expecting him to come back with more information, something he'd kept hidden during the original investigation. It made Danny feel slightly uncomfortable, as if somebody were reading over his shoulder. "You still shacked up with ATF?"

"What can I say? You never send me flowers."

"This a business call, or are we just gonna talk about whose bitch you are?"

Danny smiled. "I got a civil rights case for you."

"Shit. You're out to make me *real* popular in this state, huh? How 'bout we go shoot some pelicans this weekend, maybe dump some toxic waste in Tiger Stadium?"

"You want to hear about it, or do I have to call the papers?"

Seagraves sighed. "I guess you're gonna tell me about it whether I like it or not, huh?"

"Damn right."

Seagraves listened in silence as Danny told him the whole story, interrupting only to say, "They burned your *car?* Man, you must have *really* pissed those people off. That car was beautiful."

Danny ignored him, went on. When he was done, Seagraves was silent for a while, then he said, "Where are you staying if I need to reach you?"

Danny gave him the name of the motel. "I may have to move, though. The manager seemed pretty upset after the shooting."

"Cell phone?"

"It was in the car. But you can reach me on Mickie's." He gave Seagraves the number. "Does this mean you're gonna send somebody up here?"

"I'll have to run it past the U.S. Attorney, but my guess is he'll tell us to take a look at it."

"Are we talking days or weeks?"

"I should have a better idea by tomorrow morning."

Danny disconnected, walked over to where the protesters were sprawled on the grass. "You seen Anna?" he asked Mickie.

"I think she went to get her stuff."

He found Anna near the crest of the hill, packing up her tools. She straightened as he came toward her.

"You leaving?" he asked.

"I'll be back in the morning. Why?"

"You think you'd mind telling the FBI about what you found up here?"

She looked at him. "Does that mean they're coming?"

"Sounds like it."

"I hope they're going to do more than the local cops."

"If they come, it'll be because the U.S. Attorney believes there's been a violation of federal civil rights laws."

Danny helped her carry her tools down the hill, and they tossed them in the back of the Subaru. Several of the men in the crowd had their car stereos going, rap music booming across the field. Mickie came over, gestured toward them. "Somebody should tell those guys that if they've got weapons in those cars, they could be looking at ten years in a federal prison."

Anna smiled. "I don't think there's much we can tell those men that they don't already know." Then she touched Mickie's arm gently. "Don't worry, okay? There's been enough violence here. None of these men are anxious to see more. You go get some sleep."

FOURTEEN

"So you gonna tell me what happened to your car, or is it a secret?"

"I thought you hated my car."

"I don't *hate* it. I just think it isn't the right car for a family." Mickie was next to her Jeep, looking over at his rental. "Not that this one's much of an improvement."

"All right. You win. I'll buy a new car."

She looked at him, and her eyes narrowed. "What happened?"

"I ran into some trouble."

"How bad?"

"Totaled."

Her eyes widened. "Jesus, are you okay?"

"I'm fine. I wasn't even in the car." *Shit*. The moment he said it, he realized he'd made a mistake.

She came over to stand in front of him, blocking any escape. "Tell me."

He told her. She stood with her hands on her hips and her gaze on the ground while he went through the events of that morning. When he was done, she shook her head, walked back to the Jeep, and got behind the wheel, then just sat there, staring out through the windshield. He went over, leaned in the passenger window, waited for her to speak.

"I can't believe you weren't going to tell me."

"I didn't want to upset you."

"Why? 'Cause somebody tried to *shoot* you?" She looked over at him. "Don't you think I have a right to know that? I'm carrying our child."

"That's the reason I didn't tell you."

She shook her head. "The fact that I'm going to have a child doesn't give you the right to treat me like one."

He had to smile. "I wasn't treating you like a child. I was afraid you'd go after them."

"What? Like payback? I'm an ATF agent. We don't do that stuff."

Now it was his turn to look at the ground. An ant was crawling along the tip of his shoe. He watched it make its way to the edge, then drop off into the grass.

"I'm tired," Mickie said, still staring out the windshield. "It sounds like I'm angry at you, but I just need a night's sleep. Can we go back to the motel and talk about this in the morning?"

He nodded. "I'll ask for a room facing the pool. You can't see those from the street."

"Good. I don't feel like having a gunfight tonight."

"THAT's them."

Randy Brewer leaned forward, peered out through the windshield of the pickup truck, watching as the Jeep turned onto the highway, followed by Danny's rental car. "Guy must really like Mustangs. Went right out and got himself another one."

Russ Barnes laughed, shook his head. "Man's got to have him a horse to ride."

"Ain't that sad?" Brewer reached down, started the pickup, and pulled out onto the highway, following at a distance. "That's what happens, you get old."

They rode three across the truck's broad bench seat, Jason Lowe having to slide his leg over out of the way every time Brewer went for fifth gear. Barnes had his elbow out the window, easy-like, but Brewer could feel the tension coming off both of them, like they wished he'd let it go, drop them home, let their daddies take care of it as usual. *Fuck that,* he thought. *You want to be a man, you got to clean up your own shit.* He didn't need nobody's daddy to tell him that one.

"Wife's not bad-lookin'," Lowe said quietly.

"You like bean eaters."

"Hey, you think it's true what they say about Mexican girls?" Barnes looked over at them, grinned.

"What's that?"

"That they eat the worm."

Brewer laughed. "Yeah, but they put hot sauce all over it first. And you *know* that hurts."

"Damn, man." Barnes winced. "You one sick puppy."

"Rub a little jalapeño all over it, give it some flavor . . ."

"All right. I got it." Barnes nodded toward the taillights up ahead of them. "They're turning."

"Uh-huh. I see 'em. Takin' a shortcut." Brewer gave the truck some more gas, closing the distance. "Nice dark stretch up there before they hit the highway."

Lowe glanced over at him. "You sure about this, man? That lady's got a baby."

"You sayin' we should go easy on her 'cause she's a breeder?" Brewer shook his head. "Just means more Mexicans."

Lowe tried to think of something to say to that, but he couldn't, so he grabbed his seat belt and pulled it around him.

Brewer looked over at him, grinned. "What's the matter? You gettin' nervous? Don't like the way I'm driving?"

Barnes glanced over at the speedometer. They were doing over eighty now, coming up on the taillights fast now, and Barnes felt his legs tighten up, one hand coming up to rest against the dashboard.

"I should get me one of those bumper stickers," Brewer said, laughing. "You know, the one says 'Don't like my driving? Dial 1-800-EAT-SHIT.' Put it on the back of my truck, where all the niggers can see it when I go past 'em."

Eighty-five now. Outside the window, the trees looked like the spokes on a kid's bike wheel, he's pedaling hard downhill.

"Take it easy, man," Lowe said. "There's a curve up there."

"Easy ain't in my language. I don't do easy." Brewer reached down, switched off his headlights. Then he sat back, gripped the steering wheel lightly with both hands, smiled. "Now how much you gonna bet me I can get 'em both on the first pass?"

DANNY was working his way up the radio dial, hitting the scan button, letting it search out something that didn't have steel guitars or power chords. He'd spent days getting the stations set on his old radio, locking in all the jazz and blues in South Louisiana so he could just slide his finger along the row of chrome buttons, find something to fit his mood. Whoever had rented this car last, he'd decided, had a thing for wailing guitars. Like leaving cigarette butts in the ashtray, only worse.

When he looked up at the rearview, the road behind him was dark. He'd seen something back there only a moment ago, coming up fast, but it must have turned off. Ahead, Mickie was taking it easy, driving slower these days, like she'd begun to feel the extra burden she was carrying. He'd seen her out on the training track over the last couple years, practicing her evasive maneuvers, and the sight of her whipping the black ATF Explorer through those controlled skids had made him feel like he'd caught a brief glimpse of the teenage girl she'd once been, racing the boys across the desert outside Phoenix in her father's Dodge. Somewhere in the back of her closet she had an old T-shirt that a boy had given her with a picture of a car throwing up dust and the words *Built for Speed!* scrawled across the front. But that was the kind of thing a girl had to live with when she grew up with a name like Mercedes Vega; every boy in town wanted to find out how she handled.

It wasn't that the baby had slowed her down, exactly. Danny doubted anything could do that. But he could see her watching the road carefully when she drove, as if she could hold it all there in the bright safety of her gaze.

He caught movement in his rearview, glanced up at it. No lights, but he thought he saw a flash of moonlight on glass. Then it was gone. Ahead, Mickie's brake lights flickered briefly as she went into a curve, and Danny lifted his foot off the gas, brought it over to rest on the brake for a moment. But just as he did, he felt something coming up behind him, fast. He shot a look at the mirror, caught a glimpse of a pickup truck only a few inches behind him, no headlights. His first thought was that the driver must be drunk, that he'd staggered out of a bar, climbed into his truck, and forgot to switch on the headlights. Danny let up on the gas, let the car slow way down so the guy would pass him. But the truck stayed where it was, slowing down to match his speed. Danny sped up, and the truck did the same. It hung back there, a few feet off his rear bumper, as if the guy had decided he'd follow Danny home, find his driveway by the dull glow of the Mustang's taillights.

Danny saw Mickie's Jeep vanish around a curve, so he gave the Mustang some gas, caught up with her. The pickup truck fell back at first, then slowly came up on him again, took its place a few feet off his bumper.

That ain't no drunk, Danny thought, watching the truck in the rearview. *This guy wants you to know he could take you, anytime he wants.* He tapped his brake pedal gently, and in the red glow, he saw Randy Brewer behind the wheel, two other boys along for the ride.

Suddenly, the truck swung out as if to pass, sped up until its front hood was almost even with Danny's back window. For a moment, it stayed there, like Brewer couldn't find that last bit of power to pull past him, then Danny saw the truck swerve slightly, felt it slam into his left rear fender. The Mustang started to slide, fishtailing violently, and Danny saw the truck roar past him, closing in on Mickie's Jeep.

Danny cut the wheel hard against the skid, felt his wheels hit the gravel at the edge of the road, and for a moment he thought he'd lost it. Then he felt one of the tires grab pavement; he spun the wheel back, but he could feel that it was too late, the car had spun too far. He felt it whip around twice on the narrow road, the world beyond his windshield suddenly a blur of trees, road, and dark fields in which he helplessly spun. It felt strangely slow, almost peaceful. The only light was the red flare of brake lights up the road, which streaked across his windshield like rainwater before vanishing in the darkness. Then the car found the gravel shoulder. Danny felt one side lift slightly as one set of wheels hit the ditch, and the next thing he knew, the car was in the air, tumbling wildly. It lasted only seconds, but it seemed to Danny that it was happening very slowly, slow enough for him to look out at the ground as it spun past his windshield, to tighten his grip on the steering wheel, even though he knew that wouldn't help, and for one thought to flash through his mind before the ground came rushing up at him—

Okay, this is gonna hurt.

MICKIE saw Danny's headlights flash once in her rearview, then they were gone. Surprised, she looked back, saw that the road was completely dark behind her. *Now what's he doing,* she wondered. *Taking a shortcut?* She tried to remember where they'd last passed a road, but the only one she could picture was a couple miles back. Then it dawned on her. *Car trouble.* He'd probably pulled over on the shoulder, had his hood up already.

Unbelievable, she thought, and had to smile. *That car broke down, he's never gonna let you forget it. All these months you've been telling him how he's got to get rid of that old Mustang, get himself a new car. Now he's got one, it breaks down the first day.*

She started looking for a good place to turn around, but the road had a ditch along both sides. *Bad place to run into trouble,* she thought. *Somebody comes along while you're pulled over, they'd better be awake or you could both end up in the ditch.*

She checked her rearview one last time, making sure the road behind her was empty before slowing down to turn the Jeep around in the middle of the road. No lights, but as she was starting to step on the brake, something caught her eye. Moonlight on glass, maybe. Or just a slight change in the darkness that you learn to see when somebody's moving through the bushes. Later, she couldn't say exactly what she'd seen. All she knew was that there was something big back there, coming up fast.

She took her foot off the brake, shoved it down on the gas, felt the Jeep shudder slightly as it started picking up speed. She had learned some nice moves on her tactical vehicle interception course at the academy, but they all required power. *You got your foot on the brake,* her instructor used to say, *there's not a damn thing you can do but park it and run.*

Now she could hear the roar of an engine behind her, the driver working the clutch to get his speed right as he came up on her so he didn't have to hit the brakes. *He's gonna try to PIT you,* she realized. It was a technique they taught highway patrol officers for ending a pursuit. At the academy, they'd called it precision immobilization technique, but the patrol guys she'd met all called it tactical ramming. Wait until you get a clear stretch of road, then use your cruiser to give the guy's car a shove. Do it right and the suspect's car spins out, end of chase. Only now the TV networks were using it as family entertainment—make some popcorn, round up the kids on Friday night to watch *World's Scariest Police Chases*—and she had heard they'd caught teenagers trying it, the way she and her friends had raced their cars in the desert.

Suddenly, she remembered how she'd seen Danny's headlights flash once and abruptly go out, as if he'd suddenly turned off the road. The thought made her mouth go dry, and she felt a brief impulse to whip the wheel around, put the Jeep into a tight slide that would leave her facing back down the road, toward the spot where she'd last seen Danny's lights. But the road was narrow, and the pickup truck had pulled up close behind her now, close enough that she could see three teenage boys in the cab by the red glow of her taillights. The driver said something and grinned. The boy in the middle reached out one hand to brace himself against the dashboard.

Vehicle interdiction is like any form of combat, she heard her instructor say as she watched the pickup truck ease into place behind her and to the left. *Anticipation is the key. Know the road, know your opponent, know your own vehicle's capabilities. You'll only have a split second to react when it starts.*

She checked her speed, took a quick glance up at the road ahead, and in that brief second, she saw something that the boy in the pickup—running without lights to sneak up on her—had missed. Just ahead, the road took a sharp right turn. Mickie glanced in the rearview. The kid in the pickup hadn't seen it. He had a satisfied look on his face, like he was about to pull off a really funny joke, break up the whole class.

"Okay, boy," Mickie whispered. "You want to play games, we'll play."

Then she stomped down on the brake, swung the steering wheel hard to the left.

DANNY woke to the feeling of a gentle rain falling on his cheek. He reached up to brush it away but felt something sharp bite into his fingers. He opened his eyes, looked at his hand, saw that what he'd taken for raindrops were bits of shattered safety glass falling out of the windshield's frame. The car lay on one side in a strange silence, like the moment after a terrible noise. An air bag slowly deflated around Danny, and its hissing was all the sound there was. Then a chunk of glass fell, hit the hood, and broke into a thousand tiny pieces that scattered everywhere. Danny found it beautiful. Like the icicles he'd watched dropping off the edge of his grandmother's roof up in Shreveport one February when he was a small boy. Sunlight and ice and violence. Something magical in that.

And then Danny remembered Mickie, the pickup truck speeding past him as he'd started to lose control, going after her, and that brief flare of brake lights he'd glimpsed as his car began to spin. He tried to move, felt something painful pressing on his ribs, then realized that it was the edge of his shoulder belt where it had caught him short, held him in place while the car went through its short, violent return to earth. Now it felt like he was caught in a crowded elevator, some woman's briefcase pressing into his side. He reached back to unsnap the belt, cried out at the pain that shot through his shoulder. Like somebody had gone to the extra trouble of heating the knife in an open flame until the blade glowed red before they'd shoved it in there.

But the silence around him was worse than any pain. It seemed to hint at a world without Mickie's voice, her sudden laughter. And that thought felt like drowning.

He shut his eyes, took a deep breath, and ground his teeth together as he reached back, fumbled with the seat belt. Twice he almost got it, but then the pain in his shoulder became too much to bear, and he had to draw his hand back. Frustrated, he used his fist to beat the air bag down, then shoved it out of his way. Now he could twist slightly, get a couple inches more. His fingers found the latch, unsnapped it. The belt slid back, and he felt the pain in his ribs ease slightly.

The right passenger window was directly above him now. Looking up at it, he could see the night sky, the stars very bright where the glass had once been. Danny twisted around, groaning when he tried to support his weight on his right arm. Something was wrong in that shoulder, and he could feel his neck begin to stiffen up. But he managed to get his feet under him, stand up, and grab the window frame. He braced one foot on the steering column, got the other one up on the side of the driver's seat, and carefully pulled himself up until he could shift his footing, use the passenger's-seat headrest to climb up and sit on the car's door, where he rested a moment.

Beneath him, the rented Mustang looked like a beach towel that somebody had grabbed in both hands, wrung the water out. The front end was twisted so badly that he couldn't see the car's hood from where he sat; a wheel rim stuck out where the hood ornament had once been.

Jesus, he thought. *You are one lucky son of a bitch.*

But even as that thought passed, an image of Mickie's Jeep lying upside down in a ditch came to him, and he felt something rise in his throat.

He climbed down, looked back toward the road. It was empty, no lights as far as he could see. And then, without thinking about it, he was running back across the field, down through the ditch that ran along the edge of the road, then scrambling back up the other side to stand on the gravel shoulder, hands on his knees, catching his breath for a moment, and listening.

Dead silence. Like nothing had ever happened.

He started running again, up the road in the direction that the brake lights had disappeared. He'd gone only a few hundred yards when he passed a large chunk of metal lying in the road, as if somebody had just thrown it out their car window. A piece of a bumper, he guessed, by the look of it. But he didn't stop to take a closer look, just kept running, the pain in his shoulder constant now, a steady fire that burned deep inside the joint like coals in a grill, you're starting to think it's time to put the food on.

He came to a sharp curve in the road, followed it into the shadow of some pine trees that grew along the road. That's where he found the pickup truck. The driver had lost control on the curve, leaving a neat pair of tire tracks on the road from the point where he'd tried to hit the brakes to the spot where the truck had jumped the ditch, brought down several of the young pines before plowing into an older tree with roots that ran deep into the earth. That tree had stopped it, although it had clearly taken a while for the truck's headlights to get the message; they'd kept going after the rest of the truck had come to a stop, so that now they faced each other on the far side of the tree's thick trunk, almost touching. There wasn't much left of the truck's cab. It looked like the engine block had suddenly decided that it belonged back in the cargo bed, and the quickest way for it to get there was to follow the steering column out the back window. Danny couldn't bring himself to look into the cab. Whatever had once been in there would now be beyond recognition.

And now Danny saw the Jeep. It had come to a stop a few hundred yards up the road, its front end tipped down slightly into the ditch. A long, slewing trail of skid marks led away from the spot where the truck had left the road, as if Mickie had fought to regain control, losing it only in the last few seconds when she'd blown a tire, leaving chunks of rubber strewn across the road.

Danny stood there, frozen, staring at the Jeep as if waiting for the driver's door to open, Mickie to get out, shaking her head angrily at the stupidity of the truck's driver, trying to swing past her on a blind curve. But it didn't happen. The Jeep sat there motionless, and he saw no movement behind its windows.

He could feel himself running, saw the Jeep slowly drawing closer, but the whole thing was strange and dreamlike, stairs that climbed forever, halls that grew longer with every hurried step. *This isn't happening,* he told himself as he ran. *You'll wake up in a moment, find Mickie sleeping quietly beside you.* But even as the thought came to him, he knew it wasn't true, and it gave him no comfort.

As he got closer, he saw that the Jeep's left rear fender was badly crumpled, and most of the paint had been scraped away along that side. *They went after her,* he thought. *Tried to run her off the road the same way they did me.* Only she'd spent months training to handle this exact situation, learning to control a car when somebody shot out its tires or tried to ram it in heavy traffic, and now the pickup lay wrapped around an old-growth pine with its passenger cab crumpled to the size of a coffin. She'd taken the guy out, just the way she'd been trained. Danny only hoped that it had been enough to save her life.

He thought he saw movement, but it was too dark to be sure. The driver's door hung out over the ditch beyond his reach, so he scrambled around to the passenger side. The door was locked. He could see Mickie behind the wheel. She was hunched over, holding her belly, and he could see by the expression on her face that she was in pain. He peeled off his T-shirt, wrapped it around his hand. He took a step back, planted his feet, and punched the window as hard as he could. It shattered, glass flying everywhere. Mickie glanced up at him, her eyes clouded with pain.

"Your face," she whispered. Then she winced, doubled over in pain again. "Something's wrong," she gasped. "I think I'm bleeding."

"Hang on," Danny told her. "I'm gonna get you help." He reached in through the broken window, felt around for the door latch. He got it open, found her bag lying on the floor in front of the passenger seat, dug through it frantically until he found her cell phone. It took him several minutes to get through to 911, and when he finally got an operator, he realized that he didn't know the name of the road they were on.

"It's south of the interstate," he told her. "Back by the river."

"You'll have to give me more than that, sir."

Danny cast his mind about frantically, trying to think of some way to describe their location. "You handle calls for the sheriff?"

"Yes, sir. Why?"

"We're a couple miles from where they were guarding a construction site this afternoon. Heading back toward the highway."

She told him to hold on, went away long enough for him to start getting nervous, then came back on the line to ask, "This road you're on, you see any houses, or is it pretty empty?"

"Empty. There's a hard right turn in the road and lots of pine trees."

"Sounds like Baker Road. I'll get somebody right out there, but it might take 'em a while to find you."

"Tell 'em to hurry, please. My wife's pregnant, and she's been injured in the accident." Danny hesitated, looked back up the road toward the pickup. "There were some boys also. I don't know if they're alive, but their truck hit a tree, and it looks pretty bad."

"They're on their way."

Danny dropped the cell phone on the floor of the Jeep and crawled in to loosen Mickie's seat belt. "There's an ambulance coming," he whispered to her. "Try to hang on."

She nodded, but he could see the pain on her face. "What happened to the truck?"

He didn't answer, simply reached out, took her hand. "You're going to be fine. We just have to wait for the ambulance."

She looked up at him. "Are they dead?"

He hesitated, then said, "I didn't look. They went into a tree. It looks pretty bad."

She reached up, touched his face gently. "You're bleeding. Are you okay?"

"I cut myself on some broken glass. It's nothing serious."

"I didn't even see it happen. One minute your lights were there behind me, and then I looked again and they were gone."

"They hit me from behind. The car's in a field about a half mile back."

"They were trying to kill you."

"Or scare me, maybe." He looked back at the wrecked pickup among the trees. "It doesn't matter now."

The ambulance took fifteen minutes. When it found them, Danny was using his shirt to wipe the sweat off Mickie's face. One of the EMTs went over to look in the truck, came back shaking his head.

"No hurry there."

They helped Mickie out of the Jeep, got her into the ambulance. By then one of the sheriff's deputies had pulled up. He went over to look in the truck also, came back tight-faced.

"How'd it happen?" he asked Danny.

"They came up behind us with no headlights on, tried to run us off the road." Danny pointed down the road. "My car's back in that field. But when they came after my wife, they missed the turn, went into those trees."

The deputy frowned, turned to look back up the road. "You sayin' those boys were trying to kill you?"

"I'm telling you what happened. You want to talk about *why*, it'll have to wait until I get my wife to the hospital." Danny turned, climbed into the ambulance. "There's skid marks all back down the road. Shouldn't be too hard to work out."

The EMT swung the door closed. Danny sat down on the bunk next to where Mickie lay, reached out to take her hand.

"You're gonna be fine," he whispered.

THREE *broken ribs, internal bleeding. And they're concerned about the baby.* Danny nodded, listening to the emergency room doctor.

"Hold still," the nurse said. She was seated on a stool beside him, carefully picking bits of glass out of his face with a pair of tweezers. She dropped them into a metal tray, *clink*. He tried not to glance down at them as the doctor spoke to him, but his eyes kept drifting there, fascinated by its strange, bloody glitter. He was having trouble following what the doctor was telling him—*Evidence of serious trauma. Some possibility of miscarriage.*

"Where is she now?" Danny asked him.

"We've got her up in the ICU where we can keep a close eye on her tonight. If she remains stable, we could consider moving her in the morning."

"I want to see her."

The doctor looked down at the bloody tray on the bed next to Danny, then up at his face. "Let's get you cleaned up first, okay?" He reached out, probed Danny's shoulder gently. "How's this arm feeling?"

"Better," Danny lied. They'd run some X rays, then given him a shot that went deep into the shoulder, but in the hours since then it had stiffened up until he could barely move it.

The doctor lifted the arm a few inches, saw the pain flicker in Danny's face. "Getting a little stiff?" Danny shrugged, and that made him wince. The doctor let his arm down. "Your wife seems to think you're not entirely honest with doctors."

"She said that?"

The doctor smiled. "She told me I should have an orderly strap you to a bed. I gather you don't like hospitals."

"You know anybody who does?"

"Actually, I have a couple patients who like to come here for lunch. I think they're waiting for George Clooney to walk by." He picked up Danny's chart, then scribbled a note at the bottom. "I'm not going to push you. If that shoulder needs more attention, it'll let you know." He laid the chart on the bed. "But I wouldn't let it go too long. Shoulder pain is the kind of thing that can stay with you."

Later, Danny sat by Mickie's bed, watching her sleep. At one point, she opened her eyes, looked up at him blearily. Then she raised a hand, touched his face gently, smiled. "Look at you. You're a mess."

"Just my face. Nothing important."

She looked around at the monitoring equipment, the white hospital curtains pulled around her bed, then closed her eyes wearily. "I guess I screwed up."

"You did fine."

She shook her head. "The whole point of all my training was to keep you from ending up in the hospital."

"I thought it was to keep you out of the morgue."

She looked up at him. "Those boys in the truck . . ."

"Get some sleep. We'll talk about it in the morning."

She closed her eyes again, and after a few minutes, her breathing become steady and he knew she was asleep. He sat there watching her, then went out to the nurses' station, got a cup of coffee. He poured a lot of milk into it to cool the coffee down, drank it standing in the hallway outside the ICU. It was late, and the place was empty except for a few nurses making their rounds.

And then it struck Danny what was making him feel uneasy. *No cops.* He'd spent over two hours in the emergency room, a couple more up here in ICU, and nobody from the sheriff's office had shown up to question him about the crash. Didn't they do accident investigations? And if it really had been Randy Brewer behind the wheel, why weren't the homicide boys crawling all over it?

He drained his coffee cup, tossed it into a garbage can. He went back into the ICU, stood next to Mickie's bed, looking down at her as she slept.

"There just ain't never enough trouble around to keep you happy, huh?"

Danny turned, saw Jabril standing in the gap between the curtains. "I keep running, but it keeps finding me."

"It's all that blues you listen to. Etta Jackson says you met the devil at the crossroads and he called your name."

Danny smiled. "Yeah? I always figured that didn't happen to white boys."

"Does if they ugly. Devil likes an ugly white man almost as much as if he black." Jabril pulled a chair over, sat down. "'Specially if he's broke. So I guess you right up there." He nodded toward Mickie. "How she doin'?"

"Got banged around some. Doctor said there was some internal bleeding, and they're worried about the baby."

"Heard she took them white boys out, though."

Danny nodded.

"I guess the devil called them, too." Jabril looked over at Mickie, grinned. "She somethin', man. Seven months gone, and she took 'em *out.*"

"How'd you find out?"

"Sheriff's deputies came 'round askin' questions. Who saw you leave, shit like that."

Danny looked over at him. "You get the sense they were working out what happened, or they have something else in mind?"

Jabril shrugged. "Hard to say. Those boys always look pissed off, they're talkin' to black people. Like they don't want you to see they scared."

Danny was silent, running over it all in his mind.

"You got something you ain't sayin'."

"Nobody's been down here to talk to us," Danny told him. "You ever hear of a fatal accident, they don't go to the hospital to take a statement from the survivors?"

"Maybe they figured out it wasn't no accident."

"Then it's a crime scene. Even more reason they should get a statement."

Jabril spread his hands. "We talkin' 'bout the *law*, here. You askin' the wrong guy. I'm just the nigger they scare the poor white folks with, get 'em to vote for all that stuff won't help 'em none."

Danny couldn't help smiling. "But you love your work."

"Hey, I'm down with it." Jabril grinned. "Got that whole divide-and-conquer thing happenin'. I keep waitin' for my invitation to the White House. Must 'a got lost in the mail."

Danny rubbed at his eyes.

"You should get some sleep, man. I'll sit here, keep an eye on things."

Danny shook his head. "I want to be here when the sheriff shows up."

"You think he's gonna try to blame y'all for those dead white boys?"

"Wouldn't surprise me."

Jabril laughed. "Damn, man! Y'all been hangin' out with black folks too long. These people look at you, they ain't seein' white no more."

A nurse came in, checked Mickie's pulse and blood pressure, then left.

"Must be a lousy hospital," Jabril said. "They didn't wake her up."

They sat there not saying anything, and Danny felt his eyes begin to close. He forced them open, looked over at Jabril.

"Go ahead," Jabril told him. "I'll wake you up, sheriff comes 'round."

Danny nodded, closed his eyes, and immediately slipped into a dream in which he was driving his old Mustang through a grove of pine trees, his headlights giving him brief, uncertain glimpses of somebody moving quickly through the shadows ahead of him. There was no road, only an endless maze of trees, and he'd long ago lost his way. Now he was just following the ghostly figure that darted between the trees ahead of him, never glancing back or showing his face. There was a question Danny needed to ask this man, something urgent that weighed on his mind, but he knew it would have to wait until they'd made their way through this forest, came out onto the empty highway, where Danny could catch up to him. For now all he could think about was getting through the narrow gaps between the trees without scratching the paint on his Mustang.

"Don't worry," he heard himself say in a soothing voice. "We're almost there now." And it was only as he said it that Danny realized that there was somebody else in the car, a little girl strapped into a child's car seat directly behind him. He glanced up at her in the rearview, smiled. She had dark hair and eyes, like Mickie, and Danny saw that she was holding a beat-up Raggedy Ann doll with a stitched-on smile and one missing eye.

"Trees!" she said, pointing to the window.

"Yes." Danny nodded. "Big trees."

Ahead, the man they were following vanished into the darkness. Danny watched for him, saw him reappear in the next group of trees, hurrying away. There was something familiar about him, as if Danny should have recognized him simply from the way he scurried past the trees, from the way he seemed to exist at the edge of his lights, never quite in focus, always just within sight.

"I'm hungry," the little girl in the backseat announced. Then she held up her doll. "Annie's hungry, too."

"Just a few more minutes," Danny told her. "We're almost there."

But he knew even as he said it that it was a lie. He had no idea where they were, or where they were going. He glanced around, wondering if there was something in the car that he could give her. But there was nothing. He reached over, opened the glove compartment. Inside, bathed in the yellow glow of the courtesy light, was a silver semiautomatic pistol.

"A gun!" the little girl cried out gleefully. "Is that Uncle Jimmy's?"

"Yes," Danny told her. "It's Uncle Jimmy's." He shut the glove box. "We're bringing it to him."

And now he knew why the figure hurrying through the trees ahead of them had looked so familiar. It was Jimmy Boudrieux, and Danny's job was to catch up to him, give him this gun. Then Jimmy would get behind the wheel of his Cadillac, put the gun in his mouth, and shoot himself in the head.

When that was done, they could go and eat.

Danny opened his eyes, saw Jabril watching him. "What time is it?"

Jabril glanced at his watch. "Almost four." He looked up at Danny. "Looked like you was havin' a bad one."

Danny rubbed at his face. "Wasn't pretty."

"Comes with the territory." Jabril smiled. "When my son was born, I kept having this dream, I was wrestlin' with a lion on the floor of my kitchen. I'd wake up all covered in sweat, then lie there tryin' to figure out how a lion got all up in my house, how come one 'a those boys hang out down on the corner didn't shoot its ass when it walked by."

Danny looked over at Mickie, the IV tube taped to her arm. "Maybe it's them you were protecting your kid against."

"Yeah, that's what I figured. Street's a jungle, all that shit." Jabril shook his head. "I'm tellin' you, ain't nothin' the same after you have a kid. World don't look like a place to go play in no more. All you see is the sharp edges."

Danny stood up, went over to the window, looked out at the darkness beyond the glass. "Can I ask you something?"

"Go 'head. Can't promise I'll have an answer."

"Let's say you're a big real estate developer . . ."

Jabril gave a laugh. "Damn! You must 'a been dreamin'."

"I'm serious."

Jabril raised both hands. "Okay, fine. I'm a real estate developer. What you want to know?"

Danny reached up, rested a hand on the window. It felt cool under his fingers, and slightly moist. "Why would you hire a lawyer who does insurance claims, used to talk to the FBI?"

"I thought he told you why he hired you." Jabril smiled. "'Cause you got all them friends up in Baton Rouge."

Danny said nothing. He could see Mickie on the bed, reflected in the dark window. She lay on her back, motionless. "Jimmy always used to say that in politics, a friend is the guy who knows the stuff that can send you to prison."

"Well, I guess you proved him right, huh?"

Danny went back to his chair. "I'm supposed to meet Seagraves this morning."

"FBI guy?"

Danny nodded. "He wants me to go talk to the sheriff, wear a wire."

Jabril raised his eyebrows. "You gonna do it?"

Danny shrugged. "We won't get anything. This guy's smarter than he looks. He never says anything straight out, just talks about how he can't do anything until he gets more evidence."

"Those three dead boys in the pickup, that ain't evidence enough?"

"Only if he charges me." Danny gave a tired smile. "That'd solve his whole problem. The boys who attacked Caryl Jackson are dead, he's got DeWayne up on murder charges, and they run me in on a vehicular homicide charge, claim I ran 'em off the road."

"Was Mickie ran those boys into the ditch," Jabril said. He looked over at her. "Tough to make a homicide case against a pregnant lady. Take a lot to convince a jury that she's a killer, even in this town."

"So he charges me."

Jabril shook his head. "Man's got a wife carrying a baby, he's gonna protect her. Mickie gets up on the stand, tell the jury how those boys came after her, tried to run her down, they'll give you a medal."

Danny looked at him. "My wife's lying here with a tube stuck in her arm, and they're worried she might lose our baby. Nobody's gonna give me a medal."

"Sometimes gettin' through it's all that matters. Go ask Etta Jackson. She tell you that."

"I want to see him."

"Denton, trust me. You don't want to see him." The sheriff took Denton Brewer's arm, tried to steer him away from the door of the morgue at the rear of the hospital. "Better you should remember him the way he was."

Brewer shook the sheriff's hand off his arm, pushed the door open. Cold air hit him, like falling into a lake, and the hard white light made his stomach rise. There were five metal tables, each with a plastic sheet draped over it. A man in a white medical jacket stood next to one of the tables, making notes on a clipboard. He looked up at Brewer, surprised.

"I'm sorry, but this area is restricted," the man said, squinting slightly, like a mole caught in the light. "You'll have to leave."

"I'm here to see my boy," Brewer told him. His voice sounded like he'd swallowed some stones, got them caught in his throat. "They brought him in last night."

He saw the man glance at the shape under the plastic sheet on the metal table next to him, then down at his clipboard. "Name?"

"Brewer. Randy Brewer."

The man lifted a page on the clipboard, then moved over to one of the other tables, lifted the plastic sheet. Brewer caught a glimpse of a bloody foot lying on its side on the metal table. There was a white tag tied to the big toe.

He felt a hand on his arm. "You don't have to do this," the sheriff told him. "I already identified the bodies."

"The hell I don't! That's my boy!" Brewer stepped forward, grabbed the plastic sheet, and ripped it off the table.

What he saw froze his heart. Behind him, he heard somebody whisper, "Oh, Jesus!"

Brewer let the sheet fall to the floor. He stood there for a long moment, looking. Then he turned, went out into the hall. He rested one hand against the wall, felt its coldness against the skin of his palm. The sheriff came up behind him, said, "I'm sorry, Denton. I tried to warn you."

Brewer swallowed. "That ain't my boy."

"We took their prints. It's him."

"Then you wrong. My boy was beautiful. You seen him play ball. Couldn't nobody throw like him. Even that nigger coach said so."

The sheriff was silent, looked away.

Brewer raised a hand, pointed toward the morgue. "That thing on the table, that ain't my boy. I know he's dead. But that ain't him." A tremor went through his body, like he'd laid his hand on a high-voltage cable. "That ain't him."

"You want me to drive you home?"

Brewer looked at the sheriff. "What for? Ain't nothing there but more like this." Then he let his hand fall from the wall, looked off toward the glass doors at the end of the hall, daylight streaming through, people walking around out there like nothing had happened. "What happened to the lawyer?"

"Look, Denton . . ."

He shot the sheriff a brutal look. "What *happened* to the lawyer?"

The sheriff hesitated, then said, "He walked away. His wife's upstairs. They're worried she might lose her baby."

Brewer raised his head, like he'd noticed something on the ceiling. "They're worried she *might* lose her baby?" Then he shook his head. "Jesus, that's sad, huh? Nice lady like that, she might lose her child?"

The sheriff's eyes narrowed. "Stay away from them, Denton. I don't want to have to lock you up."

Brewer looked at him. "You think that'd be worse? Shit, I'll tell you what, I get five minutes with the people who done that to my boy, you can lock my ass away. Won't be no hurt to me. You'll hear me up there in that cell laughin'."

He looked back at the door to the morgue for a moment, then straightened his shoulders, walked away down the hall.

DANNY must have dozed off again. He woke up to find a pair of nurses gingerly helping Mickie out of bed and into a wheelchair.

"What's going on?" he asked.

Mickie looked over at him, gave a pained smile. "They're taking me down for an ultrasound. I was hoping you could get some more sleep."

"Jabril here?"

"I sent him out to check on Etta. She'll make sure he gets a decent breakfast."

Danny went over to her. "How do you feel?"

"Better. The doctor came in a few minutes ago. He said the bleeding's stopped." She took his hand. "I'm okay, Danny. My ribs feel bruised, and my shoulder hurts, but I don't feel like the bottom's dropping out anymore."

Danny glanced at his watch. It was almost nine-thirty. "I'm supposed to meet Seagraves."

"Go ahead. I'll be fine. They're just going to take some pictures."

Danny walked down the hall with her, waited while they got her ready for the ultrasound.

"Go," she told him finally, pushing him toward the door. "Say hello to the FBI for me. Tell them not to screw it up or I'll have to come down there and kick their feeble butts."

Danny smiled. "I thought that was last year's word."

"The feebles?" She shook her head. "Those guys always find a way to live up to it."

Danny had one of the nurses call him a cab, waited in the hospital's lobby for it to show up. Standing there, he had to smile, imagining Mickie storming into the FBI's regional office, seven months pregnant, to kick some ass.

When the cab pulled up, he went outside, climbed into the backseat, and told the driver to take him back to the motel. The driver glanced up at him in the rearview, then took a long second look.

"Rough night?"

"Yeah, why?"

"You look like you just went nine rounds with a telephone pole."

Danny sat forward, looked at himself in the rearview. He had a bandage across one side of his forehead, where the flying glass had cut him, and there was a faint trail of dried blood along one side of his jaw. He caught the driver watching him in the mirror. "You should see the other guy," Danny said.

Marty Seagraves sat at a table near the back window of the motel coffee shop, watching some kids splash around in the pool. He looked up as Danny came toward him, then glanced down at his watch angrily.

"Where the hell have you been? You know how long I've been sitting here?" He stopped, looking closely at Danny's face for the first time. "Jesus, what happened to you?"

"Ran into some trouble." Danny pulled out a chair, sat down. "Those white boys who attacked Caryl Jackson tried to run us off the road last night. Mickie's up at the hospital. They want to keep an eye on her, make sure there's no trouble with the baby."

Danny saw Seagraves's eyes darken. "Is she all right?"

"Too soon to tell. They're doing an ultrasound to check the baby."

"What happened to the boys?"

Danny looked away.

"Dead?"

Danny nodded. "They went off the road and hit a tree."

"Terrific." Seagraves sat back, rubbed at his face with both hands. "I wish you'd called me sooner."

"With what? Some boys threw a rock at an old man. You think the FBI would have let you come up here for that?" Danny shook his head. "I called you as soon as I had something that looked like a federal case."

Seagraves glanced around the restaurant. A few people were lingering over coffee at nearby tables. He stood up, tossed some money on the table. "C'mon, we'll go take a ride and you can tell me where things stand."

Danny got up. "Okay, but I need to stop at a phone." He took out his wallet, tossed a couple bucks on the table. "I have to call my rental-car company, let 'em know where they can go pick up the pieces."

FIFTEEN

"Thought I might see you in here today." The sheriff leaned back in his chair, considered Danny's bandaged face. "Seen you lookin' better, though. How's the wife?"

Danny felt something hot and red rise behind his eyes. He took a step forward, felt Seagraves's hand tighten on his arm, holding him back. The sheriff's eyebrows lifted slightly, and he smiled, glanced at Seagraves.

"So who's this guy? Another lawyer?"

"Worse." Seagraves took out his FBI identification, tossed it on the desk. "I'm the guy who can put you in front of a federal grand jury."

The sheriff frowned, reached out slowly to pick up the identification. He studied it for a moment, then laid it carefully back on his desk.

"Seems we got a little misunderstanding here." He gestured toward the chairs in front of his desk. "Why don't you gentlemen take a seat, and we'll talk this thing over."

"So you figure this is a federal case, huh?" The sheriff shoved his file drawer closed, tossed the case file on his desk.

"That's what I'm here to determine." Seagraves picked up the file. "This the whole case file?"

"That's it." The sheriff went back behind his desk, slumped into his chair. "'Course we got a couple *different* cases goin' on up here. Got the assault case on the old colored gentleman . . ." He nodded toward the file in Seagraves's hands. "That's that file. But we also got homicide files on Sam Price's boy and the girl they dug up. Those are different files." He glanced at Danny. "And I guess we better make up a file on that deal of yours last night. Not sure *what* to call that one yet."

"You can call it attempted murder," Danny told him. "Three counts, you include my child."

The sheriff raised his eyebrows. "I got three dead boys. Don't look that simple to me."

Seagraves leaned forward. "Did the truck belong to Randy Brewer?"

"Nah, belonged to some guy over in Madisonville. He brought it in to Brewer's Auto Body for some paint work a couple days ago. Looks like the boy took it out for a ride." He took a piece of paper out of his in box, tossed it across the desk. "His daddy actually called it in stolen about an hour before the accident."

"It wasn't an accident," Danny said quietly. "They were trying to kill us."

The sheriff spread his hands wide. "Got to look at the evidence before I draw any conclusions. That's my job."

"Your job."

"That's right, boy. My *job*." The sheriff pointed a finger at Danny angrily. "I've lived in this town all my life. Been doin' this job for almost seven years now. You know who I answer to? The people in this town. They elected me, and they got a right to expect me to protect their interests. I got three families lost their sons this morning. You expect me to go tell 'em their boys are criminals just 'cause *you* say they tried to run you off the road?" He shook his head. "I ain't that stupid. Them boys are dead, and as far as anybody in this office is concerned, they're singin' in the sweet heavenly choir right now. Case closed."

Seagraves opened the file in his lap, paged through it. "We take this case federal, you wouldn't have to worry about what the voters think. Anybody asks, you can say it's another case of the federal government intruding on a local matter."

The sheriff studied him. "You tryin' to play me like a fish." Then he grinned. "But hell, you want to take this thing off my hands, that's fine. Can't say as I'm sorry. Whole thing's a mess, and I lose votes no matter what I do."

Seagraves held up the case file. "Then I guess you won't mind if I make a copy of this."

"I'm guessin' you'll get hold of it even if I say no. That right?"

"Yes, but I'd have to get the U.S. Attorney's office involved. That's not pleasant for anybody."

The sheriff waved it away. "I'll get my girl to run you a copy."

"I'd prefer to do it myself. I can use your machine if you don't want the file to leave this office." Seagraves stood up. "I'll also need the files on the related cases. Including any police reports on the crash last night."

The sheriff got up, went over to his file cabinet, pulled out several files, and tossed them onto the desk. "There you go. Knock yourself out."

Danny picked up the slim file on Shonya Carter. The label read *Jane Doe*. "Does this include Sam Price's statement?"

"Which statement's that?"

"He came in to make a statement on the death of Shonya Carter."

The sheriff shook his head. "I ain't heard anything about Sam making a statement."

"You were out at the construction site when I brought him in." Danny stood up. "I'll tell him he should make his statement to the FBI now."

"Well, you can tell him, but I don't think he'll hear you."

Danny looked at the sheriff. "What do you mean?"

The sheriff took another sheet of paper out of his in box, tossed it across his desk. "Sam Price shot himself at six this morning."

"I see what you mean about that guy."

"Like juggling snakes." Danny stood in the courthouse parking lot with Seagraves, looking out across the narrow street toward a cheap coffee shop, the kind where lawyers take their clients after posting bail, talk over a plea bargain that would have them out in two, maybe three years. "He lets you know he's jerkin' your chain, then backs off before you can get him on anything illegal."

"Files should be interesting." Seagraves looked down at the stack of photocopies in his hands. "How many different ways you think a guy can say 'Not enough evidence'?"

Danny glanced at the files. "When can you get your people up here, let them have a look at the evidence?"

"Tomorrow, if we're lucky. I'll have to pull some people off long-term assignments." He looked at Danny. "You staying around here until then?"

Danny nodded. "Have to see what they say up at the hospital. If Mickie can travel, I'll take her home, but I suspect they'll want to keep an eye on her for a day or two."

"Be careful, okay?"

"Hey, you know me."

Seagraves only looked at him and shook his head.

DANNY went back into the courthouse, found a pay phone with a Yellow Pages, and looked up taxicabs. *Just let somebody else do the driving*, he thought. *Save everybody a lot of trouble.* There were only two companies in town. The first was the one they'd called for him at the hospital; the other one was located way up on Twenty-first Street. *Up past the ditch.*

Two companies—one white, one black. Ask a white nurse up at the hospital to call you a cab, she probably doesn't even think about it, just calls the company she uses. And if he'd asked a black nurse, she probably would have taken a look at his face and called the same place, figuring that's what he'd want.

He dug out a coin, called the place on Twenty-first Street. A woman answered, and he gave her the address.

"That's the courthouse, right?"

"That's right."

"Where you goin', honey?"

He gave her Etta Jackson's address, and she told him the cab would be there in twenty minutes. As he hung up, it struck him that she'd probably heard lots of men call from these pay phones, just downstairs from the parish jail, looking for a ride back up past the ditch. *Two separate worlds,* he thought. *And what flows between them don't smell good.*

When the cab pulled up and Danny got in, the driver glanced at him briefly in the mirror, then listened in silence to the address. Then he put the car in gear, swung out of the parking lot. They'd gone four blocks when the driver said—

"You that lawyer helpin' Etta Jackson's family?"

Danny glanced up at him. He was a young black man, his hair braided like Latrell Sprewell's. Danny could feel the rage pouring off him like sweat.

"Yeah, that's me."

The driver waited until they caught a red light, then twisted around in his seat to get a good look at Danny. "You figure you're some kind 'a hero 'cause you up here helpin' the black folks?"

Danny stared at him. "What do you mean?"

"This whole thing's about you, huh? How you such a *nice* guy, even though you white?"

For a moment, Danny said nothing. Then he nodded toward the windshield, said, "The light's green."

The driver shook his head, turned back to his driving. They went a few more blocks, and finally Danny couldn't take it anymore.

"What you want me to do, walk away?"

"Nah, man. The lady needs help. I'm just sick of white people comin' in here, tellin' us how they gonna make it all better." He flicked his eyes up to the mirror, caught Danny watching him. "Social workers, man. Cops, lawyers. White people seem like they all got ideas how black folks should live. And you a black *man,* it's up in the jail, mostly."

"Look," Danny told him, "the people who hired me didn't send me up here to help Etta Jackson. They hired me to watch out for their interests. I'm just trying to do the right thing."

The driver rolled his shoulders slightly, like he was trying to loosen a knot in the back of his neck. He was wearing a sleeveless T-shirt, and had the words *One Love* tattooed on his upper arm. "You think anything's gonna be different 'cause you come up here, man? You gonna go on home, tell yourself what a good guy you are 'cause you helped out some poor black lady. But we can't quit bein' black. We're gonna be stuck here, man, livin' it every day."

"I can't change that."

The driver shot him a look in the mirror. "Ain't nobody *asked* you to. I don't need your help, okay?"

"All I did was call a cab."

And without warning, the driver laughed. "Shit, I guess even you got a right to do that, man." His eyes flicked up to the mirror again, met Danny's. "Let me ask you something, man. How come I go to the movies, I can't never see a *black* man be the hero unless they got him with some white guy?" He shook his head. "Shit, they even puttin' 'em with *Chinese* guys now. Black guy tells the jokes while the little Chinese guy does all the fighting."

Danny shrugged. "I don't make movies, but I'd guess they're scared white people won't go see a movie with a black hero."

"Why not? I go watch movies where white guys are the heroes."

"How many white people use your cab company?"

The driver laughed. "Shit, not many. You the first one I seen in a *while,* man."

Danny looked out the window. They were crossing the ditch, heading north into the black section of town. "Most white people aren't out to hurt blacks. There's a few who really believe that stuff, and some others who do it because it's convenient, or they can make a buck. But most white people just don't think about race. They don't *have* to. If they're racist, it's more a matter of not being comfortable with something that they don't know about." He nodded toward the cab's window. "I come up here, and it's like going to a country where I don't speak the language. I'm the outsider here. That scares people, and they don't like being afraid, so they get angry."

"Tell me about it. I been angry all my life."

Danny was silent, then said, "My wife says she didn't know a white person until she got to high school. She was surprised that they didn't all walk around talking about being white all the time."

The driver looked at him in surprise. "Your wife's black?"

"Chicana. She grew up in Phoenix."

The driver shook his head. "Ain't the same thing, man. I spent a couple years out in L.A., and I knew some Mexicans. They got treated bad, but you go ask 'em if they'd trade with a black man, they just laugh in your face."

"That's not what I'm saying," Danny told him. "Look, I'm not claiming I know what your life is like. And I'm not asking you to give me any special credit for helping Etta Jackson. I've got my own reasons."

"You sound like you feelin' guilty about something."

Danny didn't answer, just looked out the window at the rows of tiny houses along Twenty-first Street. The cab turned on the highway, headed out toward Caryl Jackson's farm. He wondered if Randy Brewer had come this way in his pickup the night they'd gone out there to knock over gravestones, at that moment still just a bunch of teenage boys out riding, a case of cold beer at their feet.

At what point do our lives change? he wondered. One minute you're a boy out cruising around on a Saturday night, but when you wake up in the morning, there's blood on your hands and fear in your heart. Danny didn't believe much in free will. It was one of the things he and Mickie argued about. Over the years, he'd come to believe that people stumbled into the events that defined their lives, like a man blindly feeling his way through a dark room.

Looking back, it's all clear. Danny knew the moment in his own life that had led him here. It was the moment when he'd sat at his mother's kitchen table, listening to Jimmy Boudrieux tell him how sorry he was about his father's death, how Roy Chaisson had always been like a brother to him, and now he'd like to fulfill a promise he'd made to him a few years back to make sure that his son got to go to law school, even if it meant paying for it out of his own pocket. Danny had nodded, touched by the gesture, not realizing at the time where it could lead.

The cab turned into the gravel road leading to Etta Jackson's house, and Danny saw that Anna had resumed her excavation around the edges of the burial site. He caught a glimpse of Jabril among the local men helping her.

Danny asked the driver, "You think you could wait for me? I'll only be a couple minutes, then I need to go back to town."

The driver stopped in front of Etta's house, glanced over toward the burial site, where the men were digging. Then he reached over lazily and hit the meter. "Why don't you pay me for this trip now. You're ready to go, we'll start the meter again. I got a break comin' to me, so I'll just go over there, talk to some of my friends."

"Thanks."

The driver shrugged. "Everybody got to do their part."

Danny paid him, got out, and went up the steps to knock on Etta's screen door. He heard footsteps, then she appeared at the back of the kitchen, raising a hand to look out at him against the sunlight. "Who's that?"

"It's Danny Chaisson, Mrs. Jackson."

She came over to the door, took a good look at his face. "Lord, look what they done to you!" She swung the screen door open, stepped back to let him pass. "How's your wife doin'? She ain't gonna lose that baby, huh?"

Danny stepped into the shade of the kitchen, feeling the heat leave his skin as if somebody had yanked a blanket off him. "They're running some tests. It's too soon to know for sure, but she was feeling better when I left."

"So what you doin' out here?" Etta shook her head. "You got a wife in the hospital, that's where you belong, not out here talkin' to me."

Danny smiled. "I'm on my way back there now. I just wanted to stop by here and let you know that I've met with the FBI agent I told you about. He's got a copy of DeWayne's file, and they're going to send a team up here tomorrow to reopen his case."

She nodded, laid a hand on his arm. "You bring him home to me, I'll be grateful." Then her face became angry. "Now, you get on back to the hospital where you belong, you hear?"

DANNY stopped at the nurses' station on the maternity ward, asked if they had any results on Mickie's ultrasound. The nurse on duty dug through some papers on her desk. "Do you know her doctor's name?" she asked.

"Her regular doctor's in New Orleans. We were brought into the emergency room last night, but I think it might have been a different doctor who ordered the test this morning."

She looked through some more papers, then straightened up, shook her head. "I'm sorry. I don't have any results. I could check her file, if you like, find out which doctor's treating her."

Danny shook his head. "She should be back in her room by now. I'll just ask her." He walked up the hall to her room.

Stupid, really, to go asking the nurse when Mickie could tell him everything he needed to know, but it had struck him as he walked into the hospital that he should try to find out the results before he saw her, so he'd have some clue what to say to her if the news wasn't good.

Her bed was empty. The sheets were thrown back, as they had been when they took her away for the ultrasound, and the small tray they'd brought her in the morning, cup of water and some toast, still sat untouched on the table next to the bed.

Okay, Danny thought. *Take it easy. The tests just took longer than you thought.*

But as he turned to go back to the nurses' station, he saw something glitter on Mickie's bed. He paused, then went over to it, picked it up. It was a long, thin piece of metal, broken at one end. Danny looked at it, curious.

And then he knew what it was—a piece of the metal trim that ran along the door on his old Mustang, the part Denton Brewer had ordered for him almost a week before, punching it up on the computer at his body shop.

Danny felt something tighten in his throat. He dropped the piece of metal on the bed, walked quickly out to the nurses' station. The nurse on duty was on the telephone, looking away, smiling slightly as she said something into the receiver. Danny went around behind the desk, put his hand down on the phone's cradle, breaking the connection. The nurse looked up at him, surprised.

"Where's my wife," he demanded.

"Isn't she in her room?"

Danny left her standing there, staring after him. He was running now, down the hallway toward the emergency room.

"Radiology," he yelled to an orderly as he went past. "Where is it?"

The orderly stared at Danny, then silently pointed down a hall to his left. Danny turned, headed that way.

"Danny!"

He stopped, went back to look into the open door of a room he'd just passed. Mickie sat on an examining table, waiting as a nurse prepared to help her into a wheelchair. Behind her, a doctor stood making a note on her medical record.

"Hey there." Mickie smiled at him. "What's your hurry?"

Danny rested a hand against the door, felt his heart slowly return to its place. "Are you okay?"

"I'm fine. I saw the baby's heartbeat."

The nurse took her arm, helped her down off the table, then brought the wheelchair over and got her settled in it.

"Are you just getting finished?" Danny asked.

She winced slightly as she tried to find a comfortable position in the chair. "They ran the ultrasound a couple hours ago, but they thought it would be a good idea to take a close look at my ribs. If they're broken, I'll probably need a C-section."

"But you're done now?"

She looked up at the nurse. "Are we done?"

"For now."

Danny took the handles of the wheelchair and wheeled her out into the hall. He turned left, went up the main corridor, then made a right toward the exit.

Mickie craned her neck back up the hall toward the nurses' station. "My room's that way, Danny."

"I know. We're checking you out."

She looked up at him, and her eyes narrowed. "What's happening?"

"Denton Brewer's been in your room. He left something on your bed."

She was silent for a moment. Her eyes moved over the faces of the people they passed, and he saw her shoulders tighten slightly.

"It'll be fine," he told her. "I'll get you back to New Orleans, and we can go see your doctor."

"I'm not sure I'm up to a long car ride, Danny. My ribs hurt pretty bad."

When they reached the entrance to the emergency room, Danny heard one of the nurses behind the reception desk call out after them, but he didn't answer, just kept going out through the automatic doors to the driveway, where he spotted the cabdriver who'd brought him out there talking on a pay phone. The driver saw them and hung up, walked over to them. "You checkin' out?"

Danny nodded. "Are you free?"

"Sure. You could 'a just told me. I'd wait."

"Didn't know we were leaving." Danny wheeled Mickie over to the cab, opened the door, and helped her into the backseat. He saw her wince as he leaned across her to buckle the shoulder belt. "You okay?"

"I'll make it."

Danny pushed the wheelchair back to the entrance, then walked back, got into the cab beside Mickie. "You want to lean on me?"

"I think I need to sit up straight. Maybe you could put your arm on my shoulder, so I don't move when we turn."

The driver got behind the wheel, glanced back at them. "Where to?"

Danny thought for a moment, then turned to Mickie. "You mind staying with Etta for a day or two until we can figure out how to get you home?"

"You think she'll mind?"

Danny smiled. "She's got half the town out there already, digging up her yard. When I was out there before, she was making them all lunch."

"Damn," the driver said. "Nobody told me Etta was cookin'. That woman can make some food." He started up the cab. "So that's where we goin'?"

"That's where we're goin'. But take it slow, okay?"

"Man, that's askin' a lot, you tell me Etta's cookin' lunch." He put the car in gear. "I know some 'a those boys workin' out there, and you wouldn't *believe* how much they can eat."

ETTA took one look at Mickie's face and shut down her stove. "C'mon and get her in the house," she told Danny. "All that sun can't be doin' her no good."

Danny helped Mickie out of the cab, saw that her face was pale and covered with sweat. But it wasn't the heat. Every time they'd gone around a corner, or even slowed for a stop sign, Mickie had closed her eyes, gritted her teeth, and dug her fingers into Danny's arm. She didn't say a word, but he could see the pain wash over her face, taking her breath away.

"You think giving birth could be worse than this?" she whispered.

"Let's not find out now, okay?"

She gave a weak smile. "Good idea."

He helped her into the house, and they followed Etta down a hallway behind the kitchen to a bedroom in the back.

"This is DeWayne's room when he's with me." She pulled the blanket back off the bed. "I washed the sheets yesterday. Must 'a known you were comin'."

Danny led Mickie over to the bed, and she held his arm while she sat down.

"Go ahead, lie down," Etta told her. "Looks like you better not try to keep your head up." She spread the pillows out so Mickie could lean back on them, and Danny helped her lie down without putting too much weight on her injured ribs.

Etta rested a hand lightly on Mickie's belly for a moment. Then she straightened up, said, "Baby's fine. Feelin' a little restless, maybe. I got somethin' should settle it right down."

She left the room, and Mickie raised her eyebrows at Danny. "You think she can really tell all that just by putting her hand on my stomach?"

"I'd trust her a whole lot more than the people at that hospital." Danny saw something move beyond the window. Etta had stepped out into her back garden, was gathering up some herbs. "Looks like you might be getting herb tea."

Mickie raised her head slightly to look, then winced, let it sink back onto the pillow. "I'll take your word for it."

"Might taste a little nasty."

She smiled. "Can't be worse than the toast they gave me at the hospital this morning."

Danny sat on the edge of the bed. "I have to go see Tournier."

"You think that's a good idea?"

"I don't have a better one."

She studied his face. "Are you going to tell him what you know?"

"Not much point to going down there if I don't." He smiled. "Anyway, what's the worst that could happen? They've already tried to kill me."

"I need to know that you're taking this seriously, Danny."

He leaned over her, spent a minute adjusting her pillows. "You remember the second *Godfather* movie? Michael goes to see that guy Hyman Roth in Florida?"

"Lee Strasberg."

Danny looked at her. "Who?"

"The actor. He did that little click in his throat when he got angry. You can see Pacino getting an acting lesson."

Danny nodded. "He's this little old Jewish guy, lives in a suburban house in Miami, spends his afternoons watching football. Then you find out he's behind half the murders in the movie and he's got a deal running to take over Cuba."

"Yeah, so?"

"I always loved that scene where Michael goes to talk to him. Here's two guys, they both know what's going on, but they talk like they're planning the old guy's retirement." He brushed the hair back off her forehead and suddenly got an image of being a father, sitting on the edge of his little girl's bed, telling her a story before she goes to sleep. "Every time I've been in a room where something bad is about to happen, that's what it's like. Nobody's saying anything, but everybody knows what's getting said."

"This is supposed to make me feel better?"

He smiled. "If Michael Tournier wants me dead, it's not going to happen when I go see him. That's not how a guy like that does things. He's got a problem, he hires lawyers, not killers. The lawyers can't make the problem go away, he calls a friend. Nothing ever happens close to him."

Mickie took his hand. "I'd feel better if somebody went with you."

Danny kissed her on the forehead. "Don't worry, I'll be all right." He stood up. "Anything I can get you before I go?"

"One thing."

"What's that?"

"My gun. Any idea what happened to it after the accident?"

Danny shrugged. "You were wearing it, right? I guess they took it off you in the emergency room. It's probably still at the hospital."

"I'd feel better knowing where it is."

"Okay, I'll take care of it."

"Thanks." She closed her eyes. "I think I have to sleep now."

Danny waited until her breathing became steady, then slipped out of the room. He found Etta in the kitchen, chopping herbs into a large cooking pot.

"She sleepin'?"

"Yeah. That for her?"

Etta nodded. "It's called Bleedin' Tea. My mama used to give it to women when they had too much bleedin' with a baby. Helps 'em get their strength back."

"Your mother was a midwife?"

She gave a laugh. "Midwife, doctor. Wouldn't no white doctor come up here back then. Won't come now, either, but at least they got to look at you, you go down to the hospital." She finished chopping the herbs, scraped the shredded leaves off the wooden cutting board into the pot, then laid her knife in the sink. "You got someplace to be, I'll keep her in bed."

"Thanks. I'm grateful for all your help."

She shrugged. "Everybody does what they know. It ain't just the right-eous that keep the world goin'."

Danny had to laugh. "I'll have to remember that."

"FEEL like taking a ride?"

Jabril looked up from the tiny square of dirt he was carefully scraping away with a trowel, then stood up, reached down to rub at his lower back. "What you have in mind?"

"Thought I'd pay Michael Tournier a visit. But I need somebody to run me down there."

Jabril grinned. "Yeah, I hear you pretty hard on cars lately." He looked over at where Anna was showing one of the other men how to lay out a new section of ground in an archaeological grid with stakes and white string. "Have to check with the boss lady. Make sure she don't need me to go dig up a couple boulders with a toothpick, some evil shit like that."

Danny laughed. "She workin' you hard?"

"*Hard?*" Jabril shook his head wearily. "Man, I had no idea. She point at this little piece of ground, all laid out pretty with white string, says, 'Why don't you go dig there?' I mean, she says *dig,* I'm thinkin' she's gonna give me a shovel, right?" He held up the trowel. "You see this thing she gave me? Hell, my *dentist* uses bigger tools than this."

"So I guess you've got a new respect for archaeology, huh?"

"Just don't be talkin' to me about history no more, okay? This shit's hard work." Jabril dropped the trowel, brushed off his hands. "I'll drive you anywhere you want. Just so there ain't no diggin' involved."

"Let's hope it doesn't go that far."

Jabril walked over, spent a moment talking to Anna. She laughed at something he said, then he touched her arm gently before he came back over to Danny.

"Looks like you're making progress there."

Jabril raised his eyebrows. "You keepin' score?"

Danny raised both hands. "Hey, I just want a ride."

"Uh-huh. And you ain't the only one." Jabril headed to his car, digging his keys out of his pocket. He looked back at Danny. "You comin' or what?"

They drove into New Orleans, and Jabril parked in the alley behind Danny's office. "You gonna stop in," he asked Danny, "say hello to that nice lady works for you?"

"Demitra?" Danny shook his head. "She'd just make me sign things."

"Can't have that." They got out, and Jabril locked the car. "You better hope she don't see you walkin' 'round here, though, or she come down here and whup your sorry ass."

Danny smiled. "Remind me to give her a raise."

"With all you makin' on this case."

"You got it."

They walked up the street to One Shell Square, took the elevator to Tournier's office. Jabril glanced around at the lobby with an approving expression. Then he caught sight of the blond receptionist behind her marble altar, and he broke into a smile. "Ah, man. I do like it here."

"Ain't cheap."

"Just your mortal soul, huh?"

"You're not far off." Danny walked over to the receptionist's desk, put on his most harmless smile. She gave him a cool look as he approached, and Danny felt himself lean into it slightly, as if fighting a strong headwind.

"Can I help you?"

"Danny Chaisson. I'm here to see Mr. Tournier."

She frowned slightly, as if perplexed. "Did you have an appointment?"

Danny gave her an apologetic grin. "Not exactly, but he told me to drop by when I had a moment. I should have called first, but I figured he'd make time to see me."

"Oh, I'm sure he'll want to see you," the receptionist said, in a tone that said she'd be only slightly more surprised to see pigs soaring past her twelfth-floor window. "It's just that he's out of the office today." She gave Danny a small, triumphant smile. "If you'd called ahead, we might have saved you a trip."

Jabril sauntered up to the desk, leaned against it casually. "Your name's Janette, right?"

She looked up at him, startled. "Do I know you?"

He smiled. "I been standing over there this whole time, tryin' to figure out where I know you from. You used to go out with my man Raydell, right?"

Danny saw her swallow hard, then look around quickly to see if anybody had heard. "You must be thinking of somebody else."

"Nah." Jabril winked at her. "I'd never forget a fine woman like you." Then he leaned forward, whispered to her conspiratorially, "Now, how 'bout you tell us where we can find Mr. Tournier this time of day."

"THAT was good," Danny told him when they were back on the elevator. "I should bring you with me more often."

Jabril shrugged. "Couldn't hurt."

Lake Maurepas, the receptionist had told them, her voice low. Tournier had a fishing camp out there where he sometimes took clients.

"Only they don't do much fishing," she whispered, "if you know what I mean."

Jabril grinned. "Uh-huh. I guess we know what you mean."

"You got an address out there?" Danny asked her.

She opened her Rolodex, scribbled an address on a Post-it note, then peeled it off the pad, handed it to Jabril. "Tell Raydell he can call me, he hasn't lost my number."

Jabril tucked the address into his shirt pocket. "What you mean? He ain't been callin' you?"

"Not lately."

Jabril sighed, shook his head. "Boy *must* have lost your number. Or his mind, one." Then he gave her a smile. "Tell you what, how 'bout you give me your number, I'll make sure he gets it."

On the elevator, Jabril slid the Post-it with Tournier's address out of his pocket, passed it to Danny. Then he took out his wallet and tucked the receptionist's phone number into an inner pocket.

"You really gonna give that to Raydell?"

"Do I look stupid?"

They got on I-10 heading up to Baton Rouge, got off at Gonzalez, and took the state highway up into Livingston Parish, watching for a turnoff toward the lake after they crossed the Amite River. The pine forest gave way to bayou stretching out on either side, and when they found the road, it was just a gravel track leading off along a narrow ridge sticking up out of the swamp grass.

Jabril pulled over on the shoulder, looked at it. "You want me to take my car in *there?*"

"You got a better idea?"

"Uh-huh. Go back around to Manchac, rent us a swamp boat."

Danny laughed. "Can you picture some guy handing a swamp boat over to us?"

"You pay 'em enough, they'll hand it over."

"Man, there ain't enough money in the state to make them trust us with a boat."

Jabril looked at him. "This a racial thing, huh?"

"Damn right. Neither one of us is an Aquatic-American."

Jabril sighed, put the car in gear. "All right. But I bust a strut on this road, you payin' for it."

"I'll send the bill to Tournier."

They turned into the gravel road and crept along, with Jabril wincing every time they bounced over a rut. Danny felt the pain in his shoulder start up again, like he'd gotten a stone caught in there, could feel it scraping every time he moved. After a few hundred yards, the road swung abruptly to the right through a small stand of trees. There was a gate hidden beyond the trees, a pair of private security guards sitting in a Ford Explorer, watching them approach. One of the men got out, waved them to a stop, his hand resting on the gun at his hip.

"Looks like somebody knew we was comin'," Jabril said. He brought the car to a stop, hit the button to roll his window down, then put both hands on the wheel where the guard could see them.

The guard came up to the window, bent down to get a good look at Danny. His hand stayed on the gun. "Can I help you gentlemen?"

Danny leaned forward, said, "We're here to see Mr. Tournier."

"He know you're comin'?"

"We don't have an appointment. But if you call up to the house, he'll tell you to let us through. My name's Danny Chaisson. I'm an attorney working for Mr. Tournier on some business matters."

The guard nodded to Jabril. "Who's your friend?"

"He's assisting me."

The guard considered them for a moment, then he straightened up, said, "Wait here." He walked back to the Explorer, got behind the wheel, and took out a cell phone.

Jabril looked over at Danny. "I'm *assisting* you?"

"What was I supposed to say? He's a big, scary black man?"

"Be closer to the truth."

"We're trying to get in, not get shot."

Jabril smiled. "One thing at a time, huh? That's what I like about you, man. You organized."

The guard put down the cell phone, got out of the Explorer, and came back over to the car. Danny saw that he'd let his hand drift away from his gun.

"Okay," he told them. "But he said to tell you he can only give you twenty minutes. He's got some important people coming out this afternoon."

"No problem," Danny told him. "We'll be quick."

The guard walked over to the gate, swung it open, waved them through. Jabril raised a hand to him as they went past. "Look at him. He's all disappointed he didn't get to shoot nobody."

"It's early yet."

They drove on up the road until they came to the house. It had a tin roof and a gallery that ran along three sides, but that was as close as it would ever come to a fishing cabin. Danny looked at the row of plate-glass windows facing out across the marsh grass toward the lake, the satellite dish mounted on the edge of the roof, the row of six chimneys that ran along the back of the house, and guessed that Tournier had over six thousand square feet in there—five bedrooms, probably, plus a living room with its own fireplace big enough to roast a pig on a rainy day, along with a wet bar, big-screen television, and views across the water. Not a place you come to get away from it all, do some quiet fishing. This was the kind of place you built so you could invite other wealthy men out to close a deal. Pour 'em some single-malt whiskey, put the LSU game on the television, and let nature take its course. By the end of the day, the world might be no wiser than it began, but at least there would be a new retail development in Jefferson Parish, with fountains splashing in the atrium and gourmet cookies in the food court.

"Damn," Jabril said. "This guy don't mess around."

Two more security guards sat in a car beside the porch steps, watching as Jabril swung the car around, parked under a cypress tree.

"Tell me that ain't the same two guys," Jabril said. He raised a hand to them. The guards stared at them, expressionless. "See? Same guys."

Danny smiled. "You make new friends so easily."

"Then how come I ain't got a house like that?"

They got out, went up the steps to the front gallery. Danny could smell the smoke from a barbecue pit drifting from around back. It was a smell that he recognized from the years when Jimmy Boudrieux would invite a crowd of state legislators and lobbyists down from Baton Rouge to his big house in the Garden District, serve them beer and ribs while he cut deals that could land them all in prison.

Danny rang the bell, heard somebody moving around inside the house. When the door opened, he looked up into the face of the woman standing there and felt his heart sink slightly.

"Hello, Danny."

"Helen."

Her eyes moved to Jabril, and she held out her hand to him. "I'm Helen Whelan. You must be Jabril Saunders."

Jabril raised his eyebrows. "You know me?"

"Only by reputation, I'm afraid." She smiled. "Danny's never introduced us." She stepped back, held the door for them. "Michael's on the phone, but he told me to ask you what you'd like to drink."

Michael.

"I'm fine," Danny said.

"You sure? It's hot out there."

"Nice and cool in here, though."

She raised her eyebrows, looked at Jabril.

"Got any lemonade?"

"With fresh lemons. I just made it."

"That'd be great."

They followed her back into the kitchen. It was the size of Danny's whole apartment, with a professional-quality Aga stove and an oversized refrigerator with glass doors, like you see in fancy restaurants. Helen opened the refrigerator, took out a glass pitcher full of lemonade, and set it on the counter. Then she went to a cabinet, took down a glass.

"Not too late," she told Danny.

"Thanks. I'm all set."

She went back to the refrigerator, filled the glass with lemonade from the pitcher. Then she handed the glass to Jabril, said, "Let me know if that's too sweet. Michael says I always make it too sweet."

Jabril took a sip, shook his head. "Perfect."

She smiled. "I'll tell him you said so." She glanced toward the kitchen door. "Let me go see if he's free."

She went out, and Jabril looked over at Danny. "That who I think it is?"

Danny nodded. "How's the lemonade?"

"It's too sweet."

Danny gave a smile. "She always made it that way. I just never told her."

"That's 'cause you too sweet." Jabril went over, spilled the lemonade into the sink, and set the glass down. "You know they were together?"

"Last I heard, she was his lawyer."

"This gonna be a problem for you?"

Danny shrugged. "She's a big girl."

"That ain't what I asked you."

Danny hesitated. "It doesn't really surprise me. He's a good-looking guy. Successful. Comes off as real nice."

"And what's a dead black girl between friends?"

Danny shook his head. "She wouldn't know about that."

"She's his lawyer. You don't think he'd tell her?"

"Helen's a corporate lawyer. She handles his business affairs."

Jabril smiled. "Look like she's handlin' more than that." He turned, went over to the window above the sink, looked out at a couple of black men in aprons tending the barbecue pit. "She just got lousy taste in men, huh?"

Danny had to smile. "Well, her luck ain't been too good."

"Wait'll she finds out we got Prince Charming here on a murder rap."

Danny looked away. "We don't have him on anything."

"What you mean? You got that guy to testify, right?"

"Sam Price never made a statement. He shot himself this morning."

The door opened, and Helen stuck her head into the kitchen. "He'll see you now." She looked at Jabril, then over at Danny. "Everything okay?"

"Fine," Danny said. "Lead the way."

They followed her back through the house, along a corridor lined with old wine bottles. Danny glanced back, saw that Jabril was angry, like he'd reached out for something only to see it jerked away.

Michael Tournier sat on a leather sofa in a room with one wall made entirely of glass, so you could look out across the lake and watch the sun rise. Danny wondered how often he'd been out here early enough to see it, but decided the idea of it was probably enough. Tournier had his shoes off, his feet resting on a large slate coffee table. The television was on with the sound turned off, and Danny saw that he was watching preseason football. A bottle of Jack Daniel's and a glass stood on the coffee table within easy reach.

Tournier raised a hand to them lazily. "Hey, glad you could make it." He waved them toward a pair of chairs, then sat forward, picked up the bottle, held it up. "Can I tempt you with a little Tennessee sunlight?"

"Thanks," Danny told him. "We had some of Helen's lemonade in the kitchen."

He grinned. "Then I guess you're all set."

"You want me to stick around?" Helen asked Tournier.

He looked at Danny, raised his eyebrows. "What's the story? We talking business here?"

Danny looked over at Helen. "Thanks, we just need a couple minutes."

"Then I'll leave you boys alone." She glanced at the whiskey bottle, seemed about to say something, then simply tightened her lips and left the room.

Tournier grinned at Danny. "You let a good one go."

"Looks like she's landed on her feet." Danny pulled a chair over. "Watch out, though. She's gonna give you trouble over the whiskey."

Tournier laughed. "Yeah, that's already started. I got some important people coming later, and she wants me to keep a clear head." He poured some more bourbon into his glass. "Can't blame her, really. She's my lawyer. She gets paid to keep me out of trouble."

Danny heard Jabril give a laugh. Tournier glanced over at him, curious. "I don't think I've met your friend."

"Jabril Saunders. He was nice enough to give me a ride out here."

"Something wrong with your car?"

"One of your friends planted a firebomb in it."

Tournier raised his eyebrows. "One of *my* friends?"

"Denton Brewer."

There was a long silence, then Tournier set his glass down on the coffee table. "That's a long time ago, Danny."

"So was Medgar Evers." Danny smiled. "The FBI's got a thing for old civil rights cases right now. I think they're worried about their image."

Tournier picked up the TV remote, switched off the game. "So am I to understand that you came here to warn me?"

"Not exactly. I want you to talk to the FBI, tell them how Denton Brewer killed that girl."

Tournier stared at him. "What are you talking about?"

"Shonya Carter. Sam Price told me about it."

He sat back slowly. "What else did Sam tell you?"

"That it was an accident. You were chasing her, but you didn't mean to kill her. That Denton Brewer and another boy buried her out at the old graveyard, but you two weren't involved in that." Danny spread his hands. "Everything the FBI needs to connect you to that body the sheriff exhumed."

Tournier closed his eyes for a moment, took a deep breath, and let it out slowly. "Sounds like Sam's been doing a lot of talking." He opened his eyes, looked at Danny. "So if he's told the FBI all this, why do they need me?"

"Sam didn't tell the FBI. He told me."

Tournier's eyes narrowed. "So you're saying the FBI doesn't know any of this yet?" He looked off toward the window and the gleaming lake beyond. "Any chance we could convince Sam to keep his mouth shut?"

"Shouldn't be too hard. He shot himself this morning."

Danny expected Tournier to give some response to this, but he kept his eyes on the lake, as if hypnotized by the sun glitter on the motionless water. After a long silence, he sighed, said, "Sam was always the emotional type. Always goin' to confession when we were kids. We'd be out playin', he'd be stuck in church saying forty Hail Marys. Didn't know how to ease his mind."

Jabril picked up the bottle of Jack Daniel's from the table. "But you know, huh?"

Tournier laughed. "Yeah, ole Jack's my therapist. I can trust him. Nothing I say to him ever leaves this room." He picked up his glass, drained it. "Let me see if I've got this straight," he said to Danny. "You're telling me Sam told you about how we killed that black girl . . ."

"Shonya," Jabril said quietly. "Shonya Carter."

Tournier ignored him. "But he never told the FBI, and now he's dead."

"That's right."

"So the FBI doesn't know."

Danny smiled. "They know."

Tournier looked perplexed. "How do they know if Sam never told them?"

"I told them."

"*You* told them?" Tournier frowned. "Danny, you're a lawyer. I've got a right to expect confidentiality from you."

"You didn't hire me as a lawyer," Danny said. "You hired me as a *political consultant* so you could put some distance between your company and the boys who attacked Caryl Jackson. Okay, so I did that. Let's just say I'm throwing in some legal advice, no charge. The FBI knows enough to put you away. You've got about forty-eight hours to cut a deal for your testimony, or you'll find yourself standing next to Denton Brewer in a courtroom." He smiled. "There ain't a political consultant in the world that can help you if that happens."

Tournier looked at him. "I've got a lot to lose here."

"That girl lost her life," Jabril said.

"I can't change that. I wish I could, but I can't."

"So you just gonna let it go?" Jabril asked.

Tournier stood up. "I've heard you out. Now I think it's time for you gentlemen to leave."

Danny looked over at Jabril. "We tried." He stood up, gestured toward the bottle on the table. "I'll let you consult your conscience."

They ran into Helen in the front hall. "Leaving already?"

"Yeah, we don't want to overstay our welcome." Danny nodded at the front door. "That's a lot of security you've got out there. What's going on?"

Helen smiled. "We've got the governor coming out this evening. Michael's taking him out fishing on the lake in the morning. We thought he'd want some privacy."

Jabril grinned. "So nobody hides in the weeds, tries to take his picture, he's guttin' a fish, huh?"

"Something like that." She opened the door for them. "I'm sorry you can't stay."

"No problem," Danny told her. "I've seen fish gutted before. It's not a pretty sight."

In the car, Danny was silent, gazing out at the bayou going past as Jabril drove them back up to Jefferson. When they got off the highway, he said, "Make a left up here at the entrance to the country club."

Jabril looked over at him. "You planning on playin' some golf?"

"I want to go by Sam Price's house, talk to his wife."

Jabril shrugged, made a left into a residential street lined with oak trees. "These people gonna love the sight of me drivin' through their neighborhood. You watch, we'll be crawlin' in deputies in a couple minutes."

"How about if I get in the backseat? Would that help?"

Jabril laughed. "Get me one of those little black caps? Yeah, we might be okay like that."

They followed the road past the golf course and some tennis courts.

Danny watched the street signs until he saw the one he was looking for. "Turn here."

"Which way?"

Danny hesitated. "Right. He'd live back by the river."

The houses got big closer to the water. A couple had stone gates, and Danny caught a glimpse of private tennis courts tucked away behind one house.

Jabril shook his head. "Why would you buy a house in a country club, then build your *own* tennis courts?"

"I guess you don't like sharing."

"You got that kind of money, you could build your own grocery store, too. But nobody does that."

"Maybe they just haven't thought of it." Danny leaned forward, looked at the house number on a mailbox ahead. "That's the one."

Jabril turned into the driveway. It was a large brick colonial, but it looked modest compared to some of the other houses they'd passed. The curtains were drawn, and Danny could see no signs of life.

"Probably went to her mama's," Jabril said.

Danny didn't say anything, but in a way he hoped it was true. *She's lost her son and her husband,* he thought. *And there's nothing you can say that won't make it worse.*

"You mind waiting?" he asked Jabril.

"Nah, man. I'll let you handle this one on your own."

Danny got out of the car, went up the front steps, and rang the bell. Nothing happened, and Danny decided Jabril was probably right, she'd gone away, left this house filled with its endless silence. Then a curtain moved slightly, and he realized that somebody was looking out at him. He clasped his hands behind him, looked down at the ground, doing his best to look like a grieving friend paying a sympathy call. After a few seconds, the curtain dropped back into place, and he heard somebody unlock the door.

The door opened a few inches, and an exhausted-looking woman peered out at him. "Yes? What do you want?"

"Mrs. Price?"

The woman shook her head. "She's sleeping. I'm her sister-in-law."

Behind her, Danny caught a glimpse of a carpeted staircase. A pair of bare feet appeared on the top step, and a woman's voice called out, "Who is it, Janine?"

The woman at the door examined Danny, then answered, "I'd guess insurance, by the look of him."

"Actually, I'm a lawyer," Danny told her.

The woman started to shut the door. Danny quickly stuck his foot between the door and its frame, called out, "I spoke with Sam yesterday."

There was a pause, and then he heard the woman on the stairs say quietly, "Open the door, Janine."

Janine swung the door open, glared at Danny. "My sister-in-law is upset. They only took the body away a few hours ago. There's still blood on the wall in his study. They don't bother cleaning that up before they go. I guess I'll end up doing it." She glanced over at the car, Jabril watching the whole scene from behind the wheel. "I want you to know, I know who you are. I live in this town, too. I had any say about it, you wouldn't get into this house. It wasn't for you, my brother might still be alive. His boy, too."

"That may be," Danny told her quietly. "But I didn't come here to hurt anybody. I'm here because there's still lives that can be saved."

She shook her head angrily. "You mean that nigger boy who killed Bobby. Well, I hope they fry his ass! He gets out, there's people in this town will be looking for a rope and a strong tree. They had any sense, they'd be lookin' for a tree with a couple good branches, get rid of a couple 'a you lawyers while we're at it."

But Danny wasn't listening now. His eyes had moved past Janine to the woman who had appeared at the base of the stairs, her face bloodless and empty, as if she were still sleeping, caught in a dream she couldn't escape. "Mrs. Price?"

She silently laid a hand on her sister-in-law's shoulder, moved her gently aside. "Yes, I'm Emily Price. You're Danny Chaisson?"

"That's right. I spoke with your husband yesterday."

"He told me about you. He said you think that boy they've arrested didn't kill our Bobby."

"It's more than just something I think, Mrs. Price. I've given the evidence to the FBI. They're taking over the case." He looked her squarely in the eye, said, "Your husband believed me, Mrs. Price. He was planning to help them. That's why it's very important that I speak to you. I believe his testimony could make a difference."

She considered him, then stepped back, held the door open for him. "Come in," she said quietly.

The kitchen was neat, as if somebody had spent the morning scrubbing counters, scouring out the sink with soap pads. A fresh pot of coffee sat untouched in the coffeemaker, and Danny wondered if they were expecting company.

"My husband shot himself in his study this morning." Emily Price picked up a sponge, began absently wiping at the counters. "I found the gun lying on the floor next to him."

Her sister-in-law came into the room, took the sponge out of Emily's hands, said, "Sit down. You need to rest."

Emily sat down, but Danny could see by the way her hands immediately began moving along the edges of the table that she was looking for something to do with them.

"Sam seemed so calm last night," she told him. "It was the first time he'd really seemed like himself since Bobby died. I made him a sandwich around nine, and he ate some of it, then went into his study. I thought that was a good sign. You know, he was getting back to work?" She gave a sad smile, shook her head. "Around ten, I called in to him, told him I was going up to bed, and he came to the door to say good night. I could see he had some papers spread out on his desk. Legal forms, insurance papers. Things like that. I told him not to stay up too late, and he just smiled, the way he used to when he was in law school and I'd asked him if he really needed to study that hard. But when I turned to go up the stairs, he caught my hand and kissed me." She took a wadded-up tissue from her pocket and wiped her eyes. "I thought it was because we'd lost Bobby. Like he was trying to comfort me. And as I went upstairs, I remember thinking that maybe we'd find a way to . . ." She paused, looked away. When she spoke again, her voice was barely more than a whisper. "I had trouble sleeping, so I turned on the TV. One of the old movie channels. They were dancing. I left the sound off. I like to watch those old movies that way. It's like a dream. At some point I must have dozed off. When I woke up, it was around five. Sam had come into the room, and he was looking for something in the top drawer of his dresser. I asked him if everything was okay, but he said everything was fine, and I should go back to sleep. I guess I must have, because the next thing I knew was when I heard the gun go off."

Danny braced himself for her tears, but she simply looked past him to the window, as if she'd run out of words. He hesitated, then asked her, "Did he leave a note?"

She looked at him silently, like she was making up her mind about something. He leaned forward, touched her arm gently, said, "I understand that you want to protect him, but he came to see me yesterday because he had something to say. Maybe we should let him say it."

She studied his face, and he knew that there was nothing he could say or do except wait for her to come to her decision. Finally, she sighed, got up, and left the room. Janine went after her, caught her a few steps into the front hall. "Emily, don't. It'll only cause trouble."

But Emily moved Janine's hand gently off her arm. "It's what Sam wanted." Then she walked down the hall to her husband's study.

Janine came back, stood against the counter, glaring at Danny. "This isn't your town," she said, angrily. "Why'd you have to come here and make trouble for us?"

"The trouble started before I got here."

"So let us handle it! We're the ones got to live here."

Danny looked away, said nothing. A moment later, Emily returned. She was carrying a sealed envelope, which she laid on the table in front of Danny. His name was written across the front of the envelope.

Emily Price sat down, looked out the window. Danny picked up the envelope, tore it open. Inside, he found a signed, handwritten affidavit, giving Sam Price's account of the death of Shonya Carter.

Danny slipped the affidavit into his pocket, stood up. "Thank you," he told Emily Price. "I admire your courage."

She didn't answer, just kept her eyes on the window. He turned, walked down the hall to the front door, and let himself out.

SIXTEEN

"So it's over, right? We got 'em."

Danny looked out the window of Jabril's car, watching the houses get smaller as they approached the entrance to the country club. He suddenly felt very tired, and he couldn't shake the image of Emily Price sitting there in her kitchen as the silence that was all that was left of her life settled around her.

"We've got an affidavit," he told Jabril. "From a man who blew his brains out. Won't be hard for a defense lawyer to get that thrown out of court."

Jabril looked over at him, then shook his head in disgust. "So what the hell good is it?"

Danny shrugged. "The FBI should take it seriously. And if nothing else, it breaks the silence. You get one person talking about something like this and it changes the way everybody thinks about it." He gave a weary smile. "Turns out conscience is a virus. You catch it from your neighbors."

"So what you sayin' is a black man can complain all he wants about racism, but it ain't until some *white* guy starts sayin' how bad he feels about it that white folks are gonna take it seriously."

Danny nodded. "You ever read *Uncle Tom's Cabin?*"

"You're kiddin', right?" Jabril looked at him. "What am I gonna go read that shit for?"

"Abraham Lincoln called it the book that started the Civil War. Before that, being an abolitionist was about the same as being a terrorist. That book got white people up north feeling bad, and that's what it took."

Jabril was silent for a moment. "Man, that's just sad."

"Hey, if you're going to the mountaintop, you're gonna have to look over a few cliffs." Danny smiled. "I usually get a good look right before I fall off them."

They followed the highway out to Etta Jackson's house, and as they turned into the long gravel driveway, Danny was surprised to see a crowd of cars parked in the field across from the gravesite. "You got any idea why all these people are here?"

Jabril shook his head. "You think the construction crews came back, tried to start building?"

"Be pretty stupid."

"Uh-huh. That don't mean much, this town." Jabril pulled in at the end of a row of cars, and they got out, walked over to where a large group of people stood around Etta Jackson, listening to something she was saying. Jabril went up to a young woman at the back of the crowd, touched her arm. "What's goin' on?" he asked.

She put her hands on her hips, gave him an appraising look. "You really want to know, or you just want me to know you there?"

He raised his eyebrows. "I want you to know I'm here, won't be by askin' some bullshit question."

"So you really askin'?"

"What did I say?"

"You said, 'What's goin' on?' That could mean all kind 'a ways."

Jabril looked at Danny. "You try."

Danny pointed to the crowd. "What's all this about?"

"The sheriff's cuttin' DeWayne loose. His mama's down at the jail right now, pickin' him up."

Danny stared at her, surprised. "When did this happen?"

"They got the call this morning, come pick him up. Etta says they found something in that white boy's truck after he crashed it, made 'em think those boys done it, not DeWayne." She turned back toward the crowd.

Jabril looked at Danny. "You think it's true?"

He shrugged. "Sheriff knows the FBI's looking at his case files, he probably figures there isn't much point protecting some dead boys, so he's decided to cover his ass."

"I don't guess Etta cares, long as she gets her boy back."

They made their way through the crowd, found Etta talking to a group of women her own age. Some of them were dressed in their work uniforms, having come straight from their jobs in the hospital cafeteria or cleaning rooms out at one of the motels on the highway, but their faces were bright with an emotion that could not be hidden.

"Look at 'em," Jabril said. "Those ladies been waitin' on something to celebrate for a while."

"Well, it looks like they're making up for it now."

Danny managed to work his way up next to Etta, took hold of her arm. "I hear you got some good news."

"There you are! I been wonderin' where you boys wandered off to."

"Is it true they're releasing DeWayne?"

"That's what the sheriff say. We all just waitin' around to see if it's true." She nodded toward the house. "Now, you get on up there, see your wife."

Danny walked up to the house, stopped in the kitchen to find a plastic storage bag, drop Sam Price's affidavit into it, then slip it behind the drawer in Etta's refrigerator. Most people wouldn't think to look for papers there, but it would survive a fire, and if anything happened, the FBI would find it easily. He had watched Seagraves search Jimmy Boudrieux's house after Jimmy's death, turning up a list of political contributors taped to the bottom of a vegetable crisper.

"You always know a guy's hiding something when he won't hire a maid," Seagraves had told Danny, as he carefully peeled the tape off the document, dropped it into an evidence bag. "You wouldn't believe the crud we find in some of these places."

Etta's refrigerator was spotless; she probably scrubbed it down once a week. Danny took a pen, scrawled on the envelope—*Give this to the FBI*—before he slid it behind the drawer.

"What are you doing?"

He straightened up, saw Mickie watching him from the hallway. "Just putting something away."

She looked at him, and her eyes narrowed. "We're keeping secrets now?"

And suddenly, he felt ashamed of himself, as if she'd caught him sneaking out at night. "Sam Price shot himself this morning. His wife gave me an affidavit he drew up, giving the whole story behind Shonya Carter's death."

"And you're keeping it in the refrigerator?"

He smiled. "It's pretty hot stuff."

She gave a sigh, then shook her head. "You bring my gun?"

"Shit, I'm sorry. I forgot."

She started to say something, then suddenly brought her hand up, laid it on her stomach. "The baby just kicked. That's the first time since the crash."

Danny went over, put his hand next to hers. He'd almost never felt it when she told him the baby was kicking. By the time he got his hand there, she'd always smile, say, "Just stopped." Like it was a joke they were both playing on him.

But this time, he felt it, a good strong thump.

"There," she said. "You feel that?"

"Yeah. I can't imagine how that feels inside you."

"I'm not complaining," she said, and he looked up at her face, saw the relief there. "Right now it feels great."

"You drink that tea Etta made you?"

She made a face. "Uh-huh. Nasty. And she wouldn't let me put sugar in it. Sat there and watched me drink it until I finished it."

The baby kicked again.

"There," Danny said. "That felt strong."

She nodded. "I guess the baby didn't like Etta's tea much, either."

"Or else it wants some more."

"Please. Etta already told me she's gonna make me drink some more tonight." She looked at Danny. "You're having some, too. Only seems fair."

"Have to check that with Etta. Might be only for women."

"I already asked her. She said she gives it to Caryl when his back hurts."

"But my back doesn't hurt."

She gave him an ominous look. "Maybe not yet."

Danny smiled, lowered his hand. "You heard the news about DeWayne?"

"I was here when Etta got the call. You think the sheriff had a change of heart?"

"Changed his mind, maybe. I'm not sure the other is possible."

Mickie went over to the window, looked out at the crowd around Etta Jackson. "Well, they seem pretty happy about it."

"Let's hope it lasts."

She turned to him. "You never think you've won, do you?"

"I'll believe that when the FBI gets here." Danny glanced at his watch. "I should call Seagraves, let him know about the affidavit."

"Tell him not to hurry." She smiled, looking at the refrigerator. "I think it'll keep."

She went back into the bedroom while Danny got on the phone, caught Seagraves just as he was getting ready to leave his office, and filled him in on what had happened. Seagraves listened in silence, then said, "Never a dull minute up there, huh?"

"I'm hoping it'll get a little duller when your boys get here."

"Don't count on it. We've had plenty of excitement of our own lately."

Danny laughed. "Listen, I'm sure Etta would let you keep the affidavit in her refrigerator. Won't get lost in there."

"That's funny. Just keep out of trouble, okay? I'm tired of cleaning up after you."

Danny hung up, walked out onto the porch. The crowd was smaller now, and several of the men were sitting on their cars, like they'd decided this was a good place to hang out, wait for the next celebration when DeWayne's mama showed up, bringin' the boy home. Danny sat on the steps, looked out across the fields. The sun was setting, and a faint heat haze clung to the ground.

Danny heard the sirens coming long before the trucks appeared. Two fire trucks, roaring up the highway from town, making the whole crowd turn and watch as they went past. And then, just behind them, a battered Ford pickup with a black man behind the wheel; it hit the brakes hard, swung wide to make the turn into the gravel road leading to Etta's house, then bumped across the field toward the crowd. Danny watched the driver lean out his window, call something out to the men sitting on their cars, then turn his truck around and head back out to the road. The men quickly slid off their cars, got in, and started up their engines with a roar like race day at Daytona. The crowd broke up, and then abruptly the field was empty as the cars streamed down the gravel road, made a left at the highway, and sped away.

"What's going on?" Mickie stood inside the screen door, looking out. "I heard the sirens."

Danny stood up. "Somebody brought some bad news." He went down the steps, walked across the field to where Anna stood, watching the cars vanish in the distance. "What happened?" he asked her.

"There's a fire."

"They say where?"

"Up the road." She looked at him. "At the Baptist church."

They both turned as another siren approached, watched one of the sheriff's department patrol cars race past.

"Etta's church?"

"I guess. She went with them." Anna glanced down at the spade in her hand, dropped it in the dirt. "God, I'm tired."

Danny looked off to the north. He could see black smoke rising above the trees now, drifting on the thick, hot air. He realized that they were alone, standing out close to the road. He laid a hand on Anna's arm. "Come on up to the house. You've been out here all day."

"I'm used to it. It's my job."

"I think it might be a good idea for us to wait up at the house."

She caught the tone in his voice, looked over at him sharply. "You think something's wrong?"

"Church burning's got a long tradition in this part of the country. My guess is somebody wanted to break up the party."

THEY sat in Etta's kitchen as night settled around them. Danny glanced at his watch, saw with surprise that it was almost ten. He glanced out the screen door, saw the last traces of blue light fading in the sky. Then he noticed a red glow above the trees from the direction of the church.

"Looks like we're going to be here a while."

Anna and Mickie came over to look. "Jesus," Mickie whispered. "That's an awful lot of flame to come up so fast. How big was that church?"

"Not that big."

She shook her head. "I was the sheriff, I'd get some arson boys in there, start looking for an accelerant."

"Don't hold your breath."

Anna glanced at her watch. "I'd better get going. I have to go back to Baton Rouge tonight. My cat's probably finished off the couch by now."

Danny walked her out to the car, helped pack up her gear. When she had most of her stuff in the back of the Subaru, she picked up a shovel off the ground, handed it to Danny.

"I borrowed this from Etta. Could you put it up on her porch? We might need it again in the morning if we get more volunteers."

Danny leaned on the shovel, watching as she drove down the gravel drive, made a right at the highway, headed back toward town. Then he walked back up to the house, leaned the shovel against the wall next to the screen door, and went inside. Mickie was sitting at the kitchen table with her eyes closed.

"You okay?" he asked.

"Tired."

He went over to her, took her arm gently. "C'mon, I'll help you get to bed." She stood up, leaned on him. "You feeling weak? Should I get you back to the hospital?"

She shook her head. "I'll be fine. I just need to sleep."

He helped her down the hall to the bedroom, got her stretched out on the bed without too much discomfort in her ribs, then pulled a chair over to sit beside her.

"You planning to tell me a bedtime story?"

"You want one?"

She smiled. "I think you've told me a few already." She rested her hand on her belly. "How do you think I ended up like this?"

"That's the happy ending."

"Let me get this baby out, then we can talk about endings."

"You kidding? That's when we *start* worrying."

She closed her eyes. "Great."

He waited until she fell asleep, then went over to the window, looked out at the red glow above the trees. Like a false sun, rising too soon. What must Etta be feeling, he wondered, standing there in the church's parking lot, watching it burn to the ground? How would her faith survive those flames? He thought about the minister with his mournful eyes, imagined him moving through the crowd watching the church burn, doing his best to keep their spirits up and their rage from turning into violence.

Like holding back the flood.

Danny started to turn away from the window when something caught his eye. A light was moving out among the trees where the graves had been. He saw it clearly for just a moment, then it was gone. At first he thought it might be a reflection in the glass. He went over to the door, switched off the light, then came back to the window, stood there watching. Nothing happened. Then he saw it, a brief flicker in the darkness, as if somebody were shining a flashlight around on the ground, then switching it off quickly, hoping nobody would see.

Danny started out of the room. As he got to the door, Mickie opened her eyes, said, "What's wrong?"

"Nothing," he told her. "Just forgot to do something. Go back to sleep."

She nodded, closed her eyes. Danny went into the kitchen, switched off the light, and stood there in the darkness, looking out through the screen door. A minute passed, then two. And then he saw the light again, closer to the house now, as if the person using it had come right up to the edge of the trees, flicked it on, then just as quickly shut it off.

And suddenly, Danny regretted that he'd never found the time to swing by the hospital and pick up Mickie's gun. *Stupid.* Like she always told him when she saw his Beretta sitting on the top shelf of their closet, *Hey, I'm sure you'll be glad to know it's there when some guy's beating your head against the sidewalk.*

He picked up the phone. No dial tone. His cell phone had been in his Mustang when it burned. Mickie's probably lay in the crumpled wreckage of her Jeep, or else it was with her gun up at the hospital.

"You're really at the top of your game," he said aloud. "Ain't that right, Danny?" He hung up the phone, opened the screen door, stepped out onto the porch. Now he saw that there was a pickup truck parked out by the roadside, a man moving among the trees. The flashlight came on briefly, lit up a single tree standing off by itself, then vanished.

Could be a deputy, he told himself, *checking for evidence.*

At night. In the dark.

Might be one of the guys helping Anna with the excavation, dropped his wallet. Without coming up to the house first, find out if somebody found it?

Danny picked up the shovel leaning against the wall, hefted it like a bat. Then he stepped down off the porch, heard the gravel crunch slightly under his feet. He moved to his left until he reached the grass, then headed for the trees.

"'Bout damn time."

Denton Brewer set the flashlight down on a rock, pointed it off into the trees, and switched it on. Then he crouched down, drew a semiautomatic pistol from the holster on his belt, and made his way down the back slope of the hill, past the edge of the pit the sheriff's backhoe had left when they dug up all those niggers, thinking, *Jesus, and they wanted to come after my boy for kickin' over a couple stones?*

At the bottom of the slope, he straightened up, made his way through the trees to where he could see the house. All the windows were dark now, but he knew that the lawyer's wife was in there, all tucked up in bed. Took some doing to get all them niggers sittin' on their cars out in front of the house to leave, but a couple cans of gasoline and some cherry bombs had done the trick, put some hellfire and brimstone up in that Baptist church, like they always talkin' 'bout. He'd had to walk back through the woods to his truck after the place went up, got his boots all muddy, too. But damn if it wasn't worth it, watchin' 'em all light out like that when the fire trucks went past. Then it was just the lawyer and his two women, sittin' 'round like they was having a tea party, so long he'd started worrying that the church might burn out before he got his business done, he'd have to go find something else to burn.

Just punch a hole in your gas tank and drive up Twenty-first Street, he thought, grinning. *Tossin' cherry bombs out the window.*

But the archaeologist finally came out, packed up her stuff, and left. He'd waited until the lawyer was back in the house, puttin' his wife to bed, then snuck up close to the house, climbed up on the porch rail, and jerked the phone wires right off the edge of the roof. Expecting somebody to open the screen door any moment, find him standin' there like an idiot.

How you doin'? Just come to check the phone lines.

Jesus, imagine the look on their faces, you say that. Then pull out your gun, say, *And we got to have a talk about that long-distance bill!*

Shit, it was tempting, but this was no time to get stupid. Get what you came for, finish the job, and get out. So he climbed down off the porch rail, made his way back through the trees to his truck, got the flashlight out of his toolbox. Then he waited until the lawyer shut off the light in the room where his wife was sleeping, and switched on the flashlight a couple times, waving it around until the guy saw it.

Took him long enough, but when he finally came out on the porch, Brewer could see the guy in the moonlight, saw him pick up a fuckin' *shovel,* for Christ's sake, like that was gonna protect him against a Desert Eagle Mark XIX .50 AE, six-inch barrel, seven shots in the clip. A guy'd have to swing his shovel pretty fast, knock away all that firepower.

Anyway, at least he knew the guy wasn't armed, so it'd be easy to take him down, get the job done. Brewer worked his way around the bottom of the hill, moving carefully in the darkness, picked out the lawyer heading up the slope toward the light. He was trying to move quietly, keeping low and using the trees for cover. Brewer could see that the guy thought he was being pretty sharp, until the moment when he edged up on the flashlight, shovel raised in both hands like he was getting ready to take a swing at a fastball, and saw it was lying on a rock. That gave him a surprise, and he glanced around real quick, like he realized he'd made a mistake, let himself get drawn into the light. He took a quick step back into the shadows, but Brewer knew he had him now. He bent, picked up a rock, tossed it into the bushes off to the lawyer's left. When the lawyer turned to look, Brewer took four quick steps, got the gun right up against the back of his neck, and said, "What you plannin' to do out here, dig for treasure?"

The lawyer froze, and Brewer reached up, lifted the shovel gently out of his hands, tossed it back into the trees.

"My boy's dead," Brewer told him. "Can't nobody change that. We all done here, we gonna have a little talk about that situation. But first, you got something don't belong to you. Little piece of paper you took from Sam Price's wife, got nothin' to do with you. I want it back."

The lawyer's voice was very quiet, like he'd been waiting for this all night, was almost relieved that it was finally happening. "I don't have it anymore."

Brewer grinned. "Yeah? You didn't give it to the sheriff. So where'd you put it?"

"I sent it to the FBI this afternoon."

Brewer grabbed a handful of the lawyer's shirt, pressed the gun into the back of his neck. "That your final answer?"

The lawyer raised his hands. "You can search me, you don't believe me."

Brewer ran his hands through the lawyer's pockets, came up empty. He sighed, shook his head. "Okay, that's how you want it. Now, what do you say we take a walk up to the house, have a little talk with your wife?"

STUPID. Going out there with a shovel, like he was planning to dig up a sewer line. Danny tried not to think about what Mickie would say. His mind flashed briefly to Price's sister, glaring at him as he left the house with the affidavit in his pocket. How long had it taken her to get on the phone, spread the word through town? He pushed the thought away. All that mattered now was keeping Brewer away from the house.

"You can kill me if you want, but you won't find what you're looking for that way."

Brewer smiled, shoved him a few steps closer to the house. "I heard your wife's gonna drop a litter. Thought we might pay her a visit so I can show her my new gun."

"She's got one just like it."

Brewer raised his eyebrows. "My kind of woman." Then he grinned. "Except for the fact she's a Chihuahua." He gave Danny another shove. "Bet you never seen birth control with a six-inch barrel, huh?"

A car's headlights appeared on the highway, then swept through the trees as the car turned into the gravel road.

"What the fuck's this?" Brewer grabbed Danny's shirt, dragged him back into the trees. "Don't you make a sound, now."

The car stopped in front of Etta's house. DeWayne Jackson and his mother got out, stood looking at the dark house like they were surprised to find everybody already asleep.

"Look't him." Brewer gave a laugh. "Boy was expectin' a party when he got home. Thinks everybody forgot about him."

Danny had had the same thought, but now he saw what he had to do. If DeWayne and his mother went into the house, Brewer would simply wait a few minutes until they got settled, then take him down there as he'd planned. What were two extra people once he started shooting? If Danny could warn them while they were still close to their car, they stood a chance. And even if

Brewer shot him, Mickie might wake up when she heard the shot, have enough time to get out of the house before he got down there . . .

"DeWayne!" Danny saw the pair look back at the hill, surprised.

Brewer cursed, slung his arm around Danny's neck, cutting off his air. "Boy, you just don't listen, huh?"

Danny gasped, felt himself start to choke. He saw Brewer bring up the gun, take aim at the two people standing beside the car.

"Now I gotta shoot 'em."

Without thinking, Danny dropped to his knees, threw himself forward. Pain ripped through his shoulder, making him cry out, but the sudden movement caught Brewer by surprise, jerked him off balance.

"Son of a bitch!" Brewer stumbled, caught himself, then raised the gun, brought it down hard on Danny's head.

Danny rolled away, kicking out with both feet. He felt one foot connect, and Brewer stumbled, fell to his knees. Danny's hand found something hard, closed around it. He saw Brewer start to raise the gun. Danny swung, felt the object in his hand slash into Brewer's forehead, and then—suddenly— Brewer was gone. Danny lay there for a moment, stunned. The pain in his head was blinding. He heard DeWayne Jackson call out, "Who's there?" Then a car door slammed, and the engine started up.

Danny forced his eyes open, saw the trees above him lit up by headlights sweeping slowly across the low hill on which he lay. Danny got to his knees, then found he could stand if he rested one hand against a tree. He looked around, but Brewer wasn't there. It was like he'd simply gotten up, walked away into the darkness.

Danny looked down at the object in his hand. It was a chunk of granite, broken off one of the gravestones that Caryl Jackson had put up. As the car's headlights swung over him, he saw something carved in the stone. He ran his fingers across it, then saw it was letters—*ERE LIES*. There was blood on one edge of the stone. He dropped it quickly.

The car's lights moved past him, and Danny saw that he was standing near the edge of the pit made by the sheriff's backhoe when they'd exhumed the bodies. He edged over to it, peered down.

Brewer lay on his back at the bottom of the pit. One leg was twisted beneath him at an awkward angle. He looked up at Danny, said, "I ought to fucking sue you." Then he raised the pistol in one shaky hand, fired. Danny heard the bullet snap a branch off the tree behind him, ducked back away from the edge. The headlights came back, picked him out among the trees. He heard a car door open, and DeWayne shouted up, "That you, Mr. Chaisson?"

"Go get help," he yelled down to DeWayne. "Brewer's up here, and he's got a gun. Everybody's over at the church!"

He heard the car door slam, and then the lights headed back toward the highway. Danny caught a glimpse of the car's taillights as it slowed at the road, then made a left and raced off toward the church. A light came on in the house, and he saw Mickie come out onto the porch, call out—

"Danny?"

"Stay there," Danny shouted to Mickie. "Don't move."

She glanced up in the direction his voice had come from, then he saw her come down the steps, vanish into the darkness.

"Shit!" Danny thought for a moment. "Brewer?"

"What?"

"They're going for help. You sure you want to be here when those folks find out you burned their church?"

Brewer gave a laugh. "You worried them niggers gonna lynch me?"

"You want to take that chance?"

"My leg's all fucked up, son. Where you think I'm goin'?"

"Throw out your gun, and we'll get you out of there. You can wait in the house until the sheriff comes. Etta won't let anybody hurt you."

"Fuck that. Let 'em come get me. First one sticks his head over the edge, I got a nice little surprise for him."

"You better have a lot of bullets."

"I got enough. They can send my ass to hell, but I'm gonna have a whole pack of niggers followin' me when I get there."

Danny heard footsteps, turned. Mickie was struggling up the hill. She paused, leaned against a tree to catch her breath. He slid down to her, took her arm.

"What are you doing?"

"I'm rescuing you. What's it look like?" She rested her head against the tree for a moment, coughed, then shook her head. "That was the plan, anyway."

"You're supposed to stay in bed."

"While you're out here getting killed."

"It's over. Brewer's in the pit. Looks like his leg's broken."

She looked at him, then reached up and touched his forehead. "You're bleeding."

Danny looked up the road, saw a stream of headlights coming toward them from the direction of the church. "We better get moving. This could get messy." He helped her to the top of the hill, found a large rock for her to sit on while she caught her breath. "Stay away from the edge," he warned her. "He's got a gun down there."

"I heard the shot. Was that at you?"

Danny nodded. "Could have some trouble getting him out of there. He's talking like he's got nothing to lose, wants to take some people with him."

Mickie stood up, moved a few steps closer to the pit. "Brewer?"

"Who's that?"

"Special Agent Mickie Vega, ATF. You're making a big mistake here. Toss that gun up and we'll get you some help."

Brewer laughed. "You the wife, huh? Come on over here where I can see you, I'll toss it right up to you."

Danny glanced back at the road. The first cars were turning into the gravel driveway, bouncing across the field toward them. "You're almost out of time," he called to Brewer. "The people from the church are coming."

"Bring it on. I'm ready for 'em."

Mickie looked at Danny. "You couldn't send for the sheriff? You had to raise up an angry mob?"

"Seemed like the thing to do at the time. We haven't had much luck with the sheriff."

"He knows Brewer, right? Might be able to talk him out."

Danny shook his head. "Brewer knows the sheriff's bailed. He saw De-Wayne get out of the car, so he's pretty clear how things are shaking out." He glanced back at the cars pouring into the field. Some of them drove right up to the base of the hill, and the glow from their headlights hung in the trees like sheets of pale silk. A few of the men abandoned their cars, began running toward them. "You got any good ideas how we can keep all these people away?"

"*Good* ideas?" She stood up, took out her ATF identification. "It's a little late for that. Let's just hope we can keep everybody alive."

She held up her I.D., went over toward the men coming up the hill. "This is a crime scene, gentlemen. I'm going to have to ask you to keep your distance."

One of the men took a close look at Mickie's I.D., then glanced around at the darkness beyond the trees. "DeWayne said you got Brewer up here, wavin' a gun around."

There was a crowd gathering now. Danny saw DeWayne Jackson among them, Jabril coming up the slope with some other men. Jabril stumbled over something, bent down, and picked up the shovel Danny had carried up the hill.

"It's under control," Mickie told him. "You folks can go on home."

Brewer gave a laugh. "Under control, my ass!" Then he called out, "Don't listen to her, son. You boys want me, come get me."

The man talking to Mickie looked over at the pit, and his eyes narrowed. He started that way, but Mickie got a hand on his chest, held him back. "I'm asking you to leave, before anybody gets hurt. This man is armed, so—"

But before she could finish, one of the other men brushed past Danny, walked right up to the edge to look.

The shot came more quickly than Danny could have imagined. The man let out a cry, stumbled back. He sat down on the dirt, hard, looked down at his shoulder in surprise. His T-shirt was soaked with blood, and Danny saw that there was a ragged exit wound high on the man's back, close to his neck.

"Damn it!" Mickie started toward him, but Danny caught her arm, stopped her. "Somebody help that man!"

Brewer's high, empty laugh floated up to them from the pit. "Got me one, huh? Plenty more where that come from."

Several men darted forward, keeping low to the ground as they got close to the wounded man, dragged him back out of the way. Mickie went over and knelt beside the man. He cried out in pain as she tore his shirt away from the wound, used it as a compress to slow the bleeding.

"Somebody get an ambulance," she told the men in the crowd. "And for God's sake, stay away from there!"

"Etta's down at the house," one of the men told her. "You want me to go get her?"

Mickie nodded, pressing the T-shirt against the man's shoulder with both hands. Danny saw that the man was trembling. "Tell her to bring a couple blankets," Mickie told the man. "And anything she's got that we can use as bandages."

"Where y'all at?" Brewer called out. "I'm just lyin' here waitin' for you to come get me."

Danny saw several of the men tense up, as if they could barely contain their anger. One of them turned toward the pit, yelled, "Shut up, mother-fucker!"

Brewer laughed. "You gettin' an ambulance for that boy? How 'bout me? My leg's broke bad."

Jabril came over to Danny, leaned on the shovel like he'd just finished cleaning out the barn. "You do this?"

"What?"

"Put that man in the hole, he's still got his gun."

"Hey, at least he's in the hole. That's something."

"You couldn't take his gun away from him first?"

Danny looked at him. "Just like that? Go up to him, take his gun away?"

"Somebody got to do it."

"You want to try?"

"Shit, no problem. You want me to take care of it?"

Danny glanced over at Mickie, talking quietly to the wounded man while she pressed the wadded-up shirt against his shoulder with all her weight. "You serious?"

"Uh-huh. Say the word."

"I'm not gonna regret this, right?"

Jabril grinned. "Man, you regret everything. That's who you are."

Danny hesitated, looked over at the pit. Then, quietly, he said, "Okay, do it."

AMAZING, how many stars you can see, Brewer thought, you lie here in the dark, look up at the sky. Shitload of stars. Big old moon, lookin' like a bowl of oatmeal hanging in the sky. All he had to do was wait for somebody to step between him and that moon, *bang!*

He couldn't feel his leg, no pain at all, which he figured was a bad sign. Not that it fuckin' mattered now. Six shots left in the clip, so five niggers and one for Daddy. His only regret was he'd missed the lawyer, snapping off that shot quick like that. Not much chance he'd get close again. Even a lawyer couldn't be that stupid. Or the ATF bitch. Wouldn't mind getting a shot at her. Plant one in her belly, get two for the price of one. Let that lawyer learn how it feels to lose a child, and go out a hero to the cause.

The first spade full of dirt hit him square in the face. "The *fuck?*" He brushed the dirt out of his eyes, got them open in time to see something black come flying over the edge, and a pile of dirt landed on his chest.

From above him, he heard laughter, and somebody said, "All *right!*"

"Man's got the problem *solved!*"

Brewer saw more dirt come flying toward him, managed to turn his head away and close his eyes just before it hit him on the side of the face. He gripped his gun tightly, looked up at the edge of the pit, but all he saw was another pile of dirt rise up, like a bird flying across that bright moon, then drop toward him. He shut his eyes, threw an arm across his face, felt the dirt land on his good leg. Then a chunk of stone hit the ground next to him, and he heard more laughter, the sound of people scrambling to find rocks, join in the fun.

"C'mon, niggers! That all you got?" He pointed the gun at the moon, squeezed the trigger. More laughter, and a whole shower of rocks came flying toward him. One hit him in the face, and he screamed in pain.

He heard the ATF woman shout, "Stop it!" But more rocks came hurtling toward him. He turned his head, covered his face with his hands, grunted as they struck the ground around him. For a moment, there was silence, then he heard the ATF woman call down to him, "They're getting more rocks. Throw your gun out, and they'll stop."

Brewer opened his eyes. A few inches away, sticking out from the dirt wall, he saw what looked like a white stick, split at one end. It surprised him, something so pale down here in all this dirt. He reached up, touched it with one finger.

Then he realized it was a piece of bone.

He raised the gun, shot himself in the head.

SEVENTEEN

*A*shes. *Dust.*

They held Caryl Jackson's funeral in the field across from his house, buried him up on the hill among the graves he'd fought to protect. During the six weeks that Caryl lay in the hospital, his skin slowly growing thin as paper, Danny had watched from a distance as Tournier & Associates made a series of high-profile public announcements, officially handing title to the land to Salvation Baptist Church, along with a large donation to the church's rebuilding fund. Through his attorney, Helen Whelan, Michael Tournier issued a statement urging the prompt return of all bodies removed from the site during the sheriff's investigation of the death of Shonya Carter. Two weeks later, Danny and Mickie attended a brief ceremony in which the bodies were returned for burial. The stony ground had been restored to its original condition, with two neat rows of graves, into which the coffins containing the bones were lowered, while a choir from the church that included Etta Jackson sang "When I'm Called to That Sweet Hereafter." Danny looked around for Tournier, but he hadn't attended.

And now, barely a month later, it was Caryl Jackson's turn. His grave lay at the end of one of the rows, with a plain stone marker that matched the ones he'd put up two years before. Danny, Mickie, Jabril, and Anna stood a few feet from Etta, watching as the coffin was lowered into the ground. She didn't cry, even smiled a little when the sun broke through the trees, set the ground ablaze with color as it reflected off the bits of broken glass scattered around them.

"Caryl always liked it here," she said. "Used to come up in the mornings, drink his coffee. He liked the way the sun made all these colors." She nodded toward the ground next to Caryl's grave. "They savin' that one for me."

Mickie took her arm. "Be a long time before you need that."

Etta smiled. "I'm in no hurry."

Each of the mourners took a turn with the shovel. When Jabril's turn came, Danny saw several of the men grin at one another. "That's a man knows how to use a shovel," one of them whispered. When the grave was filled, DeWayne moved among the crowd with a small paper bag, shook out bits of colored glass into their cupped hands. They took turns scattering it across the ground around the grave, until the freshly turned soil glittered and burned.

"Every man give off his own light," the minister told them. "Caryl's was just brighter than most." He looked around at the crowd nodding in agreement. "It's up to us now to make sure that light don't go out."

When it was all over, Jabril and Danny sat on the porch steps, drinking coffee from paper cups. "You hear from your FBI guy?"

"Talked to him yesterday. I wanted to let him know Caryl died."

"He say if they goin' after your boy Tournier?"

Danny shrugged. "Seagraves says the U.S. Attorney wants to prosecute, but I can't say I'm confident. It's hard enough getting a conviction on a twenty-year-old homicide, and Tournier's hired some pretty heavy legal talent." He gave a thin smile. "I also heard he's spreading some money around up in Baton Rouge, just in case anybody forgot they're his friends."

Jabril looked out at the crowd of mourners. "I guess it don't really matter. Be nice to get some justice for that girl, but it won't change these folks' lives none."

"You don't think so?"

Jabril leaned back against the steps, shook his head. "You ask 'em, they'll tell you it's enough that somebody paid *any* attention to their dead."

"Be nice if it happened while they're alive."

Jabril laughed. "That's why I like you, man. You never give up."

Mickie came out of the house, taking her time in the dense August heat. She was a week past her due date already, and Danny felt slightly terrified every time he looked at her.

"Don't you two know enough to come in out of the sun?"

Jabril smiled, spread his hands. "We keepin' it cool."

"Yeah, I can see that." She went to sit in the rocking chair beside the screen door, then hesitated. "Danny, I'm gonna sit in this chair. You might have to help me up if I get stuck."

"No problem. I'm sure Etta would lend me a crowbar."

Jabril winced, covered his head with both arms. "Man, you *like* to flirt with death."

But Mickie just smiled, eased back into the chair, taking a moment to find a comfortable position. "Just wait," she told Jabril. "I got Danny one of those baby slings you hang around your neck. His turn's coming."

"Look like you got the tougher deal."

She shrugged. "I'll find some way he can make it up to me."

Jabril looked over at Danny, raised his eyebrows. "You in trouble."

"Tell me about it."

They watched the crowd slowly thin out, people stopping by the kitchen where Etta was bustling around, filling paper plates with jambalaya, making sure there was iced tea in everybody's glass. Nobody could get her to sit down until everyone in the crowd had eaten their fill, raised their hands in surrender when she offered to refill their plates.

Finally, she took her own plate, sat at the kitchen table, pushed the food around with her fork for a few minutes, then stood up, came out onto the porch.

"Here, I'll get out of your chair." Mickie started to get up, but Etta rested a hand on her shoulder, stopped her.

"Nah, you need it more than me. Least for a couple more days."

"The doctor told us it could be as long as a week. Then they'll induce."

Etta looked down at her, smiled. "Won't be no week." She reached down, laid a hand on Mickie's belly, like she was taking a child's temperature. Then she nodded, said, "You come see me in about ten days. I'll give you some tea you can drink while you nursin', it'll take the colic right out of her."

Then she looked over at Danny, winked. "You gonna have your hands full, son. Better hide them guns, 'cause that child, she gonna be just like her mama."

Danny smiled. "Okay with me."

"Better be," Etta said. "'Cause a child don't ask. They just like the weather. Gotta be what they are, and there ain't no stoppin' 'em."

She straightened up, looked out across the field toward the hill where Caryl lay. "You let 'em know where they come from, they'll let you know where you goin'."

For a moment, nobody said anything. They all looked out toward the gravesite, watching as the sun settled among the trees, spreading out across the horizon like wine filling a cup. They watched in silence as the sky slowly turned crimson and then faded, until it looked to Danny like a painful bruise. Finally, Etta gave a sigh, turned back toward the kitchen.

"Well, that's done," she said, and she went back in the house.